Ianthe and the Fighting Foxes

The Fentons Book 4

Alicia Cameron

Copyright © 2020 Alicia Cameron

All rights reserved

The characters and events portrayed in this book are fictitious. Any similarity to real persons, living or dead, is coincidental and not intended by the author.

No part of this book may be reproduced, or stored in a retrieval system, or transmitted in any form or by any means, electronic, mechanical, photocopying, recording, or otherwise, without express written permission of the publisher.

ISBN-13: 9798551488446
ISBN-10: 1477123456

Cover design by: Art Painter
Library of Congress Control Number: 2018675309
Printed in the United States of America

To all of us struggling through the global pandemic, I wish us health and happiness, and offer this tale as a little humorous diversion

A FREE gift for you for joining my newsletter! Angelique and the Pursuit of Destiny https://dl.bookfunnel.com/tsfshs0rs5

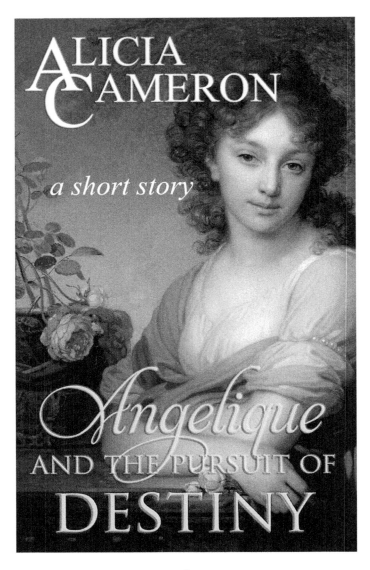

Chapter One

A Hurricane Arrives

'The poor dear,' said Lady Richards, 'I suppose she must be delayed by this wind. To come all the way here,' she gestured to the ancient halls, which her young companion and she knew contained loathing both for them and the prospective guest, 'only to meet the Fighting Foxes. How perfectly dreadful for her.'

'As it was for us!' said her companion wryly. 'If only I had taken in my Season.' She was a handsome girl in her early twenties, looking up at a mother nearly as pretty as herself, with the same brown hair and pale grey eyes and wearing a cap that she seemed too young for, were it not for the addition one could compute knowing the age of her daughter.

'Oh, I thought you would *surely* bring Sir Ralph Eastman to the point! How comfortable we would have been in Cheltenham. And Sir Ralph attends every London Season, I believe.'

'Well, another pleased him more,' said Sally Richards sadly. 'But I minded more for you, Mama. I did not feel a *tendre* for him, although he was very nice.'

Lady Richards sighed, then shook her head. 'You are such a dear girl. If only we were situated as men are, and able to go seek our fortunes in India, or some such place. My second cousin, Gilbert made a fortune, you know, and I never thought him more than moderately intelligent myself. I'm sure we two could be very adventurous if we'd ever had the training for it.'

As usual, Sally enjoyed her mother's flights. The one dimple (that mother and daughter both shared as an enhancement to beauty) showed high on her cheek. 'Instead we have mastered the French Knot!'

Lady Richards giggled, then suddenly remembered the time. 'Miss Ianthe Eames is late, and she will find that, with Lady Fox, it does not do to be late.'

'I *do* hope she leaves it until morning; Her Ladyship is sometimes even *civil* in the mornings, after a hot roll and some chocolate.'

'Oh, my dear Sally, we must hurry!' said Lady Richards, regarding an ormolu clock. 'What if we should fail to be in the drawing room before her?'

The two ladies scuttled out, to achieve the

drawing room in good time.

Two of the Foxes were there before them, the brooding figure of Lord Edward Fox, tall, athletic and dark, saved from handsomeness by the unpleasant look on his face. There had evidently been words before they arrived, for the slight figure of his fair half-brother Curtis was sulking in a chair, his shoulder turned from his sibling. Sally devoutly hoped that he stayed sulky and silent, for the reverse was that he would open his mouth and harp at his brother once again. For money, *always* for money. How Curtis thought this complaining would work, Sally had no idea, since it had never resulted in any more than his brother's wrath, and once caused the peer to throw Curtis from the dining room by the collar. Curtis had recently returned early from London, with his pockets empty again, and would no doubt have started his demands.

Lady Fox arrived, mother of Curtis and stepmother to His Lordship, a woman, who, according to Sally's mama, had been totally changed after birthing her only child. What had once been a plump beauty had become an emaciated wreck of a woman. Those who did not know of her strength believed her still so, but Sally knew that beneath the gaunt face with its iron grey curls arranged in serried ranks upon her head, and the skeleton limbs, lay a woman determined to get her own way in everything, and was not above using her apparent fragility to achieve it. Many arguments with Edward, Lord Fox, ended with the dreadful words *Send for Doctor Tolliver*, with a clutch at her heart. Fox generally left the room at this point, for he could not deal with his stepmother's histrionics with any hint of self-governance. She would win some concession of course, if not all.

There was no Dower House here to banish her to, but Sally thought that if she were Lord Fox, she would build one.

Lady Fox walked in now, tottering a little, and Curtis ran forward to catch at her arm. 'Mama, let me help you!' he said, and led her to her place by the fire.

He was rewarded with a hint of a smile, 'My boy!' Her Ladyship said faintly and patted his arm. She turned to the others. Lord Fox bowed and she inclined her head, but with a frozen look. 'I trust, Edward, that you have dealt with your business with Curtis this afternoon.'

'Yes!' said Lord Fox simply.

'Indeed, he has not, Mama. Not to my satisfaction.' Sally thought the tone a little firmer with the back-up of his mother.

'Entirely to mine,' said Lord Fox grimly.

'Really, do you have no concern for my nerves, Edward? It must and shall be dealt with.'

'I don't think I properly explained, Edward old boy,' began Curtis in a more engaging tone, but still with a whine in his voice.

Mercifully, Jenkins announced dinner.

As they moved to the dining room, Her Ladyship said to Sally's mother, 'Lady Richards, I know you agree with me that Miss Eames has shown a distinct lack of courtesy in her tardiness today.'

'Well,' said Lady Richards faintly, 'it may be that she has met with some accident on the road that has delayed her, my dear Lady Fox. She may need our pity, not our disapproval.'

'Well!' barked Lady Fox, and her elaborate starched cap shook, 'I should not have thought that *you* would have been deficient in respect, my lady, situated as you are! I find you ungrateful.'

Lady Richards recoiled. 'Oh no, I assure your ladyship...'

Lord Fox looked off, his face disgusted, but said nothing.

Sally was, as usual, brought to simmering rage at Lady Fox's daily humiliation of her dear mama, which she tried hard to mask.

'If she arrives this evening,' continued Her Ladyship, 'I may have to repay her disrespect by returning her to London on the first coach tomorrow.'

Sally grasped her mother's hand. After some breach of Lady Fox's imagined etiquette such a fate had been threatened to *them*, and now it brought fear and inclined them to sympathy on the unknown Miss Eames' behalf. Mother and daughter were due to stay with their friends the Houstens in two months' time when that family returned from a trip, but until then their finances would hardly support a respectable lodging in town — or elsewhere for that matter. Sally had sworn to herself last Season that she would marry herself to a cross-eyed man with no more than four hairs to his head, rather than put her mother through another extended visit to Studham, Lord Fox's estate in a dull part of Kent, twenty miles from London. But no one had so far presented himself. She thought of Sir Ralph. She should have tried harder. Perhaps if she had not yawned that time when he was talking to her in Vauxhall Gardens ... but he had been most deadly dull.

'Now, now, Ma,' said Curtis Fox disinterestedly, 'I suppose the woman must have a good excuse.'

'John the Coachman said she was not on the mail. I sent him to collect her,' Lord Fox informed them.

'You sent the coach?' reproved Lady Fox. 'I told you there would be no need for that, Fox. It is barely two miles from the inn, she could have walked easily.' Sally looked at the driving rain and thought this typically cruel. Her mama would not meet her eye lest they gave away their disgust.

'Well, I supposed her to have baggage. She is to make her home here after all.' He frowned at his stepmother. 'And she is a member of my family, hardly a servant.'

'What baggage might she have? If she came from the continent in such a rush, she could hardly have brought much with her. And she must learn her position now.'

'I have no doubt you will teach it to her,' said Fox with some slight acid. Curtis looked like he would like to take issue with his tone, but the second course arrived, and it gave him enough time to reflect on his position as supplicant.

The topics changed to town and country matters, and Sally hardly heard. What had Miss Eames' father done on the continent while the war had raged on? She supposed he must be a soldier, and since she also knew he was widowed, she conceived of an affecting tale where he could not bear to be parted from his motherless daughter, and brought her with him, keeping her safe from the battle's fray, but close to him always. 'Miss Richards, are you quite alright?' Fox asked. Sally had not been aware that a tear had fallen from her eye, and looked up and said vaguely, 'Oh, yes.'

'I had a Great-Aunt Ianthe,' said her mother, also wool-gathering, 'I think it an unusual, but lovely name.'

Lady Fox had nothing to say to that, and returned to the question of Curtis, 'It is beyond my understanding, Edward, that you, who have so much, grudge your own brother any part of it.'

'Madame,' said Fox dangerously, 'I do not need to broach this subject with you again, particularly in front of guests.'

'Guests! If you mean Lady Richards, I count her quite one of the family.' Sally and her mother exchanged incredulous glances at this. Their hostess continued, 'Curtis only asks…'

'Curtis has an allowance, on top of what my father left him, which was a considerable sum. *And* the proceeds of his estate in Wiltshire. He should begin to manage it. If he did not put down all his money on a loose screw of a horse that was bound to lose, he would do so easily.'

'Now Edward…' 'How dare you—' said Curtis and Lady Fox at the same time.

Miss Ianthe Eames was announced. And thus, at first encounter, she saw the Fighting Foxes resemble their name — His Lordship with set jaw, low brows and furious eyes, the sulky Curtis protesting with a pout, Her Ladyship with all the venom showing on her wraith-like face. However, to hear Miss Eames' first words, said before the butler had stepped aside, she seemed oblivious.

'Oh, thank goodness you haven't finished dinner! I am perfectly famished.' A stylish bonnet on the figure in the doorway turned to the butler and the voice continued prettily, 'Jenkins was it? Could you set a place for me? How kind,' she added as he bowed.

The entire company was now aghast. Miss Ianthe Eames seemed to have burst into the room, wearing a violet pelisse and bonnet over a pink silk dress. She was uncovering her head of the most fabulous dark curls, taking from them the bonnet: an enormous poke, a silken profusion of flowers and two ostrich feathers. No one had yet found their voices, so she continued to unbutton her pelisse and revealed the pink silk dress, pleated at one side in a way that could only make it French, thought Sally, embroidered broadly at the hem, and plunging dangerously at the neckline (for she removed a gauze fichu that had been tucked into the bodice when removing her pelisse) — and continued to smile. 'See, I am already dressed for dinner, for I *told* the marquis we should be late.'

A coach sounded outside. Lord Fox, his brows now as high on his forehead as they had been low at her first look at him, finally found his voice. 'The marquis? Do you mean to say *Audley* brought you here?'

'Well, of course!' Ianthe Eames smiled at him. 'When he heard that I was coming here, he remembered he had to visit his estate, which I understand runs next to yours. And when you sent the kind letter, Lady Fox ... that is you is it not?' Here Ianthe Eames ran forward to the end of the table and kissed her appalled stepaunt on the cheek, to her evident mortification. But Miss Eames did not appear to notice. As Jenkins returned with plates and cutlery, and set a seat for her opposite Curtis Fox, she merely said, 'Shall I just curtsy' — doing so — 'to you all *now* and let us make introductions *later*? You will all like to return to your dinner before it quite chills. And I confess I should like to begin mine.' Curtis and Fox fell back into their seats and Jenkins, who Sally thought showed just a hint of a smile, brought her the beef and dumplings. 'How perfectly wonderful, Jenkins,' said that charming voice whose English was slightly inflected by a French cadence, 'Thank the cook. And could you just ask Cherie to bring my lilac shawl? I fear I am a little chilly.' The butler bowed and went, and the matriarch finally found her voice.

'And, who, I pray you, is *Cherie*?' she said with an outrage that made Sally squirm.

It did not appear to touch Miss Eames. 'Why, my French maid to be sure!' she said with a smile at her aunt and continued to eat her meal.

The widow spluttered and could not continue.

Chapter Two

A Night of Shocks

The night was not finished in its shocks.

Sally's mama Lady Richards had continued, glancing at the stunned Lady Fox and venturing to broach the silence that Miss Eames did not seem to notice. 'And how was your journey, Miss Eames?'

'Oh, it was most entertaining, the marquis was telling me about the neighbourhood, you know, for I asked a great many questions.' She smiled again, 'And you are?' The directness of the question was softened by that delectable smile.

'I am Lady Richards.'

'Richards? I know that family meets mine somewhere in the family tree. Were you not once a Miss Fox? Cousins!' her smile encompassed Sally Richards, too. 'But is it twice or thrice removed? Is Mr Richards, or forgive me, is it Lord Richards, not here?'

'Sir Guy Richards, baronet,' said Lady Richards sadly. 'My husband has been deceased for two years now,' said Lady Richards.

'My sincere condolences.' Miss Eames leaned to the side a little to lay her hand on Sally's mother's own. Then she turned to the others. 'I am so sorry never to have met you all. Indeed, on account of my always living on the Continent, I have met none of my family.' She gave her joyous smile once more, beaming around the table.

The widowed Lady Fox, reeling from many blows, picked on the worst and said, 'Do you mean to say that you travelled from London, *alone* with the Marquis of Audley in a *closed carriage?*'

'You forgot the French maid,' said Sally Richards before she could stop herself. She saw Miss Eames, who had appeared to be unknowing of her hostess' dislike, let a hint of mischief into the glance she exchanged with her.

Lord Fox's deep tones interrupted. 'That is as maybe. However, I should inform you, Miss Eames, that the marquis and the Fox family do not visit.'

'Oh, I know!' said Miss Eames blandly, turning her large dark eyes upon him. 'He told me some silliness about a boundary dispute between the old marquis and your papa. That is why he did not come in, but merely delivered me, like a basket of lemons, on your doorstep. *And* all of my baggage. You must see ma'am,' she said, turning to Lady Fox, 'that I could not come by mail, as you suggested, with everything I own.

As it was, the marquis had to hire another coach.'

The company, who had been too interested in Miss Eames to notice more, suddenly became aware of continued movement in the hall beyond. Several persons seemed to be required to move things.

'*Another*—' the widow said.

A slow smile had begun on Fox's face as he looked at his stepmother's outraged expression. But then he, like all the others, returned to Miss Eames' animated face.

'The Marquis of Audley's papa stole that land from mine,' said Curtis hotly, as possessed as his mother by the marquis.

'You must be Curtis Fox, then! Yes, it is very likely that the old marquis stole it,' granted Miss Eames airily. 'The marquis agrees that his father was an old rogue who liked to poke a stick at yours, whom *his* father described as insufferably fusty.'

'I *beg* ...' Curtis spat out as his mother squeaked.

'Oh, I *know*! What a rude old rogue he must have been,' said Miss Eames, casting the rudeness role from herself in one fast move. A maid entered, tall and dark with terrible thick eyebrows that met in the middle of her forehead. She was over forty, wearing a severe dress and even more severe hair style and came in with a shawl, disposing it herself around her mistress's shoulders, then gliding from the room. She had not quite the air of a maid at all, holding herself with a peculiar upright dignity. Sally was sitting next to Miss Eames and only she had seen the gentle squeeze the mistress had delivered to her maid's hand, and the answering squeeze in return. She continued, 'But the present marquis is not to be confused with his son, who is a very lively gentleman and utterly polite, I assure you.'

'You cannot know him, Miss Eames. My père always said the Audleys had bad blood.' Curtis tried adopting the patronising tone he used on the Richards ladies frequently.

'I should not like to argue with you, Mr Fox, but I know the marquis very well. Since I was seven, in fact, and he was seventeen, when he first visited my father in Paris.'

'In Paris?' said Sally's mother, quite unable to resist her curiosity. 'How could that be?'

'Oh, you are thinking of the danger? I cannot quite remember, but I think Papa was pretending to be a *citoyen* lawyer at that time. We were not at that address for long.' The others were agape. 'Did you not know? My father was mostly a spy.' The company gasped. 'You know, for the King.' As they continued to look startled, she added, 'It was secret at the time, of course, but Papa is sadly dead now, so I do not think it matters if I tell you.' She frowned. 'Oh, but perhaps I have exposed the marquis? Thank goodness we are entirely *en famille*.'

'And my father described his cousin as a

wastrel!' exclaimed Lord Fox with a short laugh, loosening his sense of dignity in the face of all this frankness.

'Oh, he *was* of course,' said the beautiful Miss Eames, laughing, 'a sad wastrel.' She clapped her hands. 'Is that a syllabub? I do hope so. We had an English cook — in Frankfurt I think — who used to make them for me.'

'In what way a wastrel?' asked Curtis, with perhaps some fellow feeling. Lady Fox frowned as the horses seemed to be bolting from her.

'Oh, the sort of wastrel who died and left me *not* with the inheritance I had thought of, but with a horrendous pile of gaming debts that meant I had to sell up the Paris house lock, stock and barrel and move back to England. Funny, I say move back, but I have never been here before. However, Father was used to call it home, you know.'

'I have to say—' interjected Her Ladyship with an effort at reasserting her control, 'Miss Eames, that your clothes do not befit your new station in life. You will dress more appropriately for our meeting tomorrow morning.'

'Well, I'll try,' that lady returned cheerfully. 'I mean to be very useful to you, Lady Fox, for your great kindness in inviting me to share your home, but my clothes … well, you see I was most disgustingly well-to-do until only a few months ago, and I do not have either simple garb, or the funds to buy some.'

Lady Richards let out a tiny squeak at this, and Sally nipped her beneath the table.

Lady Fox breathed deeply. Her colour heightened. Her brows lowered dreadfully. 'We will talk of it tomorrow.' She got up with great stateliness, 'I have finished my meal and this shocking conversation. I will go to bed. And I will see you at ten tomorrow in the small salon to discuss *if* your future lies here, Miss Eames.' She moved. 'Curtis!' Her son, still as dazed as the rest of the room's inhabitants, closed his mouth and rose to take his mother's arm, and she went staggeringly from the room.

Miss Eames was the only one still eating.

'Do not fear for your position, Miss Eames,' said His Lordship dryly, 'this is my house.'

'Oh yes, my lord,' Miss Eames favoured him with that dazzling smile, '...and saying that, I have a message from the marquis. He hopes that the whole family come to Audley for dinner on Sunday. I am certain that Lady Richards and her daughter will be included once he knows they are visiting. I shall dash off a note to him this evening.' A choked sound came from His Lordship, preceding, as Sally knew, a roar. But Miss Eames continued, 'And he said to say, quite exactly, *if it means I can visit Miss Eames and we can put all this ancient stupidity behind us, tell Lord Fox that I will happily cede the land in dispute and five years of its rents. He will be welcome in my home.* Is that not perfectly marvellous?'

Lord Fox's dark and brooding face did not appear to be delirious. 'One must assume that the marquis had a romantic interest in you.'

'Oh, I shouldn't think so. It is just that we are such good friends, you know.'

'Is that how he came to know you were in London?'

'Oh, no! I was driving with Mr Fenton and his wife, Lady Aurora, and we came bang up to him in the park! When he heard where I was off to, he naturally offered to accompany me.'

'Naturally. And how did you come to drive with Lady Aurora Fenton?'

'Oh, well, I know Mr Fenton, naturally, and he brought me from the ship to stay with him for a few days before leaving. He was in the same — had business with my papa and travelled often to the continent. He sometimes stayed with us.'

'You are suggesting that Wilbert Fenton, the most well-known of libertines, excuse my language ladies,' with a nod to the Richards, 'was a spy for the King?'

'Now, of course I did not say so.' She smiled again naughtily. 'But don't you think a wastrel — or, or a libertine — could be helpful to the crown in gathering information? There is a general assumption about such men that precludes the guarding of one's tongue around them. And then, I believe Mr Fenton was a dab hand at burglary — so I've heard, of course. And only for sport.' Her eyes were alight with mischief.

'You have lived, as my stepmother would say, quite a different life to us. It may be that this is not quite the place for you. It will be sadly flat, I fear.' His tone was sardonic, but when he looked at her, she had flushed a little. 'Oh, do not fear, Miss Eames, I will, in that case, make provisions for you.'

This seemed, finally, to nettle her. 'Since my father's death many men have offered to *make provisions* for me, my lord, I scorned theirs as I scorn yours.'

This was undoubtedly a challenge. It seemed to Sally that Lord Fox was not quite up to it and it made him (if that were possible) even more resentful. 'Ladies.' He stood up and bowed stiffly. 'You are welcome to the withdrawing room.'

Sally, who was looking forward to some time with the wonderful Miss Eames, was disappointed when she said, seeing her maid awaiting her in the hall, 'Oh, ladies, I long for us to have a quiet talk, but I am so tired. Might we do so tomorrow?'

The ladies curtsied, the maid led Miss Eames to her room and Sally accompanied her mother to Lady Richard's room with becoming dignity at first, but ran the last of the way to achieve it sooner. She was a trifle worried for Miss Eames after the words of Lord Fox, but her mama was in a different mood, jumping onto her bed like a young girl.

'Oh, did you *see* her face?' There was no doubt from her mother's gleeful expression that she referred to Lady Fox.

'When Miss Eames arrived in her Paris finery?' joined in Sally.

'Looking so incredibly beautiful instead of the wet and bedraggled supplicant she hoped to scold. She,' said Mama, obviously referring to Her Ladyship again, 'will be terrified that Curtis may develop a *tendre* for her. She will keep him by her, never fear. And then, when she said she came with the *marquis*,' added Lady Richards, prone on the bed and stamping her silk-clad feet with delight, 'oh, I could have died and gone to heaven!'

'I know, I know,' laughed Sally, joining her mother on the bed, '…and then she was cut off at every turn because Miss Eames did not seem to hear the disapproval in her voice.'

'Or in Lord Fox's when he complained again about the marquis and said that dreadfully cruel thing about sending her away.'

'What did she mean, Mama, about many men offering to make provisions for her? Do you think she has rejected many offers?'

Her mama supposed so, 'Miss Eames no doubt came to her family thinking to get some solace while she grieves, but instead she's ended up with the Foxes. I understood from your poor papa that her father, a second cousin of Fox, left home after a dispute with his own father, whom *he* disowned before being disowned. He made his own way in the world after that, but I always believed it was as a gambler. I'll wager Miss Eames is already thinking she had better have taken one of the offers. How dreadful to have ended up here.'

'But Miss Eames is more spirited than either of us, Mama. I think she will be able to deal with Lady Fox more nimbly than we. I would love to be a fly on the wall in the small salon tomorrow morning at ten.'

'Well...' said her mama, naughtily.

Chapter Three

Ianthe's World

Cherie, the French maid with the troubling eyebrows, was waiting to take off Ianthe's dress after dinner and met the young girl's eyes in the mirror as she undid the buttons.

'It is good to sleep early tonight,' the maid said gruffly in French. 'Let me take the pins from your hair, you will have the headache, *mon petit chat noir*.' Ianthe smiled faintly. The pet name was used for affection and safety, because life with her father had needed many names, and to use the wrong one could be dangerous. Cherie had passed for her mother, her governess and her employer at various of these times, and *'petit chat noir'* had been used universally. Now, Ianthe tried to give her friend a reassuring smile.

'I wonder what can have possessed Lady Fox to invite me?' she asked, a little too brightly, also in French, 'She certainly doesn't want me here.'

Cherie pulled at a pin so hard that Ianthe gave a yelp. 'People with a vicious temper need others to take it out on, or how else can they enjoy themselves?' The maid looked at her hard. 'Can you bear it?'

'Of course.' Ianthe put a hand over Cherie's. 'Am I not my father's daughter?' Tears filled both sets of eyes.

'You are Joseph's daughter indeed.'

'All of those Foxes looked ill-tempered, as I saw.' Cherie pulled at another pin in her anger, and Ianthe yelped, laughing.

'I think Lord Fox's temper is defensive. There is something less ill-intentioned in his eyes.'

'If you say so. I only saw him frown.'

'Where did they put you?' asked Ianthe. 'Is it too ghastly?'

'In the attic. And it is a good place. I think Monsieur Jenkins runs a tight ship, as they say. The servants' rooms are simple, but clean. I only share with three others.'

'Put up a truckle bed here, Cherie, but share my bed as we are used to. Tell the servants I have night terrors or some such.'

'It is better that I get to know the household first.' Ianthe looked at her with troubled eyes and Cherie added with Gallic pragmatism, 'I saw no rats at least. Remember the rooms in Rue Saint-Cécile de Fauberg?'

'And the lice!' Ianthe laughed and shuddered while her nightdress was slid over her head. 'Stay here, please *mon Lou-Lou.*' She moved to the canopied bed, slid beneath the covers and held out her arms. Cherie jumped up beside her on top of the bed cover and pulled Ianthe into an embrace. *'Jusqu'à ce que tu dors, mon chaton.'* The young girl trembled in her arms before quietening down into her chest like the very child she had protected all these years. In the strange household of Joseph Eames, Cherie had been the only other constant. Held by the power of her love for both master and child, she had adventured with them, and though their lives would shock the world perhaps, she had protected the little one's innocence through it all.

As she looked fiercely at the darkened canopy, Cherie knew that now that they lived under the "protection" of the Fox family, there would be little she could do for her own one. She understood Ianthe's spirit, and that she had her own resources, but Cherie had hoped for some comfort and respite for her darling, some recognition of the pain and grief she concealed so well. As soon as the maid had set eyes on Lady Fox, she had known that hope to be dashed.

If nought else, Cherie would watch. She could write to Lady Aurora Fenton if need be. As they left London, Her Ladyship, knowing more of the household they were entering than they did, had instructed Cherie to do just that. 'If Ianthe suffers in her new home, you have only to write to me at once. Indeed, you must do so.' Ianthe would hate it if she did so, but Cherie would brook her wrath if need be. If this were just another move, with her beloved M'sieur Joseph due to arrive soon, they could bear it all and laugh. But there was no master now, and perhaps this place was for the rest of their lives. Should they have stayed in Paris? Ianthe might have married there easily. But to accept an offer at the time of her father's death had been impossible, to live respectably under the aegis of her English family infinitely preferable.

Cherie had already discovered from the staff that the other family guests at Studham, the Richards, were treated little better than servants by Lady Fox and her son Curtis and largely ignored by the master, Baron Fox. It did not seem likely that Her Ladyship would help seek Miss Ianthe's place in the world, or further her interests. This could be a dead end, where all her darling's beauty and brilliance would be hidden from the world and they must continue to exist amongst the Fox's family resentments.

However, as she had seen many times before, whatever situation Ianthe Eames arrived in could become radically changed within a few days of her being there. It was her special talent. No, perhaps it was the Foxes who had better watch out. She would trust her little black cat. Feeling Ianthe asleep, Cherie gently removed her arms and went off to her attic.

**

Nothing much happened in the house before ten the next day. Lord Fox had gone out riding, and by something Jenkins implied, it was in one of his rages, so that meant he would not likely be home before the afternoon. Miss Eames was having a light breakfast in her room and would not be down, the Richards were informed. Since the mistress of the house generally took breakfast in bed, and Curtis never arose before twelve of the clock, Lady Richards and her daughter ate a hearty breakfast in peace. There was ample time to set up their little trick, and they moved their sewing baskets from the green salon to red, where Jenkins was pleased to have a fire lit for them. A door adjoining the small salon was slightly ajar. Jenkins looked at it, and then into Sally Richards' eyes.

'That will be all, Jenkins.'

'Very good, miss,' the butler said, and left.

They heard Lady Fox, sometime later, install herself in the small salon, and Sally looked at her mother, the two silently adjuring silence to the other. For if they could hear, no doubt they could be heard.

Miss Eames arrived on time and they heard her cheerful 'Good morning, Aunt!' and the unmistakable sound of a kiss on the cheek. Her mother stuffed the linen she was working into her mouth so as to trap the laugh trying to escape. Sally's eyes watered in sympathy.

'Sit, Miss Eames,' Lady Fox said, in her coldest tone.

'Thank you,' said Miss Eames. 'What a charming room this is. I do hope you like my dress better today. I have worn the plainest one in my boxes, which I had when Papa and I had to travel as a parson and his daughter, when we were fleeing Spain. The Spanish are mostly Catholic, of course, but are still superstitious when dealing with clergymen and—'

'Allow me to speak!' demanded Her Ladyship. 'I do not wish to hear any more of your dreadful upbringing. It is clear it has left you quite without manners. When I asked you here, it was at the request of your cousin, Fox, who had been informed of your situation — by your father's *majordome*, I believe. I supposed that you might have been of use to me as a sort of companion, as my son is so often in London these days. But I see that you are quite the wrong sort of woman for that. You have shocked me to my core, and your lack of respect is not to be borne. You will leave as soon as you pack a bag. As for the rest of the baggage, if you ever find anywhere to send them on to, I shall do so — if you also send the shillings,' she ended cruelly.

The eavesdroppers gasped.

'In that case, what shall I then do?' said Miss Eames, musingly. Somehow, she did not sound as crushed as Sally and her mother's shocked looks at each other had anticipated.

'That is not my affair,' answered the icicle tones of Lady Fox.

'I suppose I must accept the *carte blanche* offered to me when I was in London by Lord Ransom, then. I thought him a trifle precipitate, having only known me two days, as well as insulting. But it might, at least, be amusing.' There was an audible gasp from Lady Fox, which thankfully masked the one given by Lady Richards. Something shocking had been said, but Sally was not sure what. Lord Ransom was known as a rake, but surely marrying even such a man would be preferable to staying at Studham, thought Sally. But her mama's look said something else.

'You would not!' cried Lady Fox. But there was panic in her voice, thought Sally.

'You would leave me with little choice, my dear aunt. And who is to say that the *ton* would not find out that the latest light o' love of Ransom was a direct relation to the noble house of Fox?'

Now Sally understood what had shocked her mother. Ransom had not offered marriage.

'You are a wicked, *wicked*, woman!'

'Now, how can you know that? You have not yet spent time with me. I too, suspect that you are wicked, but I am willing to give us the time to find out for sure.'

There was a stunned silence. Then a noise

in the hall and Sally heard a door open and the urgent voice of Lord Fox. 'Miss Eames, I cannot permit you to go, whatever my stepmother has had to say to you.'

There was a rustle of fabric. Perhaps Miss Eames arose. 'Thank you, Lord Fox. But your stepmother and I were just discussing how much we wish to pursue our acquaintance.' They heard her move and a door opening.

Without more ado, Sally went over to the open door and shut it silently, then both mother and daughter rushed to follow Miss Eames.

***

Fox had gone off in a rage that morning, it was true. There was no doubt that the arrival of Miss Eames shook him, as it had all of them in their different ways. Seeing his stepmother at a loss was naturally entertaining, but he could not but acknowledge that he, too, had been bested.

When he replayed it in his head, he could not account for it. At first, he had sought to reassure her of the security of the invitation to make her home here, but when she had so confidently relayed the marquis' message, he had been pricked to annoyance. She was rather too self-possessed for his liking. Arriving looking not only like a fashionable young lady but a wealthy leader of fashion, not just young and pretty (like Miss Richards, for example) but ravishingly beautiful. Not to his taste of course, he preferred blonde beauties, but still. This accounted for her confidence, and so he had made the unpleasant and intrusive "romantic interest" remark to her, thinking to set her back on her heels.

This made him angry with himself, but angrier with her — for she had not sat back on her heels at all. She had told him about her connection to Audley and Fenton and it was apparent that she was not without friends, which should have pleased him. The mischief in her eyes when she told him was perfectly friendly and had invited him in to share. That, for some reason, had infuriated him and he had then uttered the unforgivable line about Studham not being the place for her.

This to a girl just come to his home, at *his* invitation. He could not understand himself. It was beyond the bounds of honourable behaviour. However confident and beautiful Miss Eames was, however different her life had been, she was still a woman without income, a young girl whose father had died barely nine months ago. A member of his family that he was bound to protect.

She would be seeing his stepmother now. If he had been roused by Miss Eames' lack of fawning gratitude (the sort he took for granted after housing the Richards) he could hardly imagine what wrath Lady Fox would have stored and simmered in the night, ready to spew all over the girl this morning. He turned his horse around and headed back to the house to save her, thoroughly ashamed of himself.

***

When mother and daughter reached Miss Eames' room, it was to find her removing the plain blue cambric (that had been the dress of the pretend pastor's daughter, Sally supposed) and having a superb riding dress of light blue velvet lowered over her head by the silent French maid.

'It will get covered in mud!' said Sally involuntarily. 'Oh, I beg your pardon!'

'Ladies! Do come in,' said the smiling Miss Eames. 'You are quite right about the riding dress — quite impractical — but it was too delicious to pass up when my Paris dressmaker brought it, and Cherie assures me that it is easily cleaned.'

The grave maid, disposing the folds of the garment about her charge, gave a frosty smile. 'It makes nothing,' she said with a Gallic shrug.

'See?' said Miss Eames.

Lady Richards and her daughter rather thought they did see, having spent an hour trying to get mud from Sally's velvet muff, sadly dropped in the street some months since.

Her Ladyship said. 'We are intruding, my dear Miss Eames. We only wished to become better acquainted and thought perhaps we might all go for a walk this morning.'

'That would have been lovely! But as you can see, I am engaged to ride this morning.'

'Engaged?' said Sally.

'Yes, with Audley. I assured him I would be rested enough to ride this morning, but he insisted it be after breakfast. He doubted my stamina, you see.'

Sally looked at her mother, both wondering how to break the bad news. 'I do not think,' began Lady Richards, 'that Lady Fox will permit you to use any of—' she faltered, and Sally continued.

'We have been forbidden to ride while we are here,' she finished for her mother, looking apologetically at the now magnificent figure of Miss Eames, who laughed. Sally jerked. Who would laugh at such a thing?

'Oh, I assumed some such. My mare Purity is stabled at Audley, and I've already directed Jenkins to bring around a gig to take me there.' She looked at the other women's open mouths and when it seemed like Lady Richards would make a further protest, she added, 'To a side entrance, fear not. I don't wish to argue with Her Ladyship *before* I go to my entertainment.'

'You stabled your mare at—' said Lady Richards.

'You brought her from *France*?' said Sally, and then was prompted into a vulgarity, 'But I thought you had no funds…'

'I really didn't, but the gentleman who secured my passage quite understood that I could not leave my Purity behind.' As there was no reply to this statement, which cast up too many questions to answer, Miss Eames said, 'Do you ride, ladies? Shall I wait until you change so that you can come with me to Audley? I believe it is only four miles hence.'

'I do not ride,' began Lady Richards, 'and besides—'

'Oh,' said Sally, taken over by longing, 'How I wish I could! It is two months since I was on a horse. But Lady Fox would not permit—'

'She need never know about you. Your mama could just say that you are keeping to your room.'

'I could *never*...' objected Lady Richards.

'Oh, falsehoods? I'm afraid as the daughter of a spy I am a little too easy with falsehoods, dear Lady Richards. For the good of the nation, you understand.' She smiled, and even Lady Richards, a little shocked at this, gave a slight answering smile. Miss Eames clapped her hands and turned to Sally. 'Well, I have it! Repeat after me, Miss Richards. *Mama, I believe I will keep to my room this morning.*'

'Mama,' said Sally, as though under a spell, 'I believe I will keep to my room this morning.'

'Now you, my lady, can honestly repeat this to Lady Fox. My daughter has said she will keep to her room this morning. And it will be quite true!' She beamed. 'If she enquires further you may say you are not at all sure, but that it is nothing serious, you believe.' She turned to the bemused Sally, 'Hurry and change, I'll wait for you here.'

'But there is no horse…' protested Sally.

'Audley will no doubt mount you, my dear. Hurry now!'

Sally ran from the room and Lady Richards sat down hard on the bed. Miss Eames joined her, taking her hand, 'Am I a shocking bully, Cousin? Might I call you Cousin?'

Lady Richards squeezed her hand. 'Oh, please do. Call me Cousin Emma if you please. And you are not a bully, only so much braver than we are. You seem to be quite unafraid of your position here.'

'I am not *quite* unafraid,' said Miss Eames, and Lady Richards saw some tears in her eyes. 'Only, I refuse to be squashed by someone so crude as Lady Fox. And you know, though I have no money, I *do* have friends, even here in England. Like the marquis and Mr Fenton. I could have stayed in London with the Fentons, you know. They begged me most sincerely. They had lately had a young lady, a Miss Felicity Oldfield, stay with them for the Season — but she is now married, they told me, and they would welcome my company.'

'Felicity Oldfield!' said Sally, returning. 'Did she reside with the Fentons? I only met her a couple of times, but she really was the loveliest girl. I felt so sorry when I heard there was some scandal around her, and I *knew* it would be false.

And it was, for Viscount Durant married her.'

'So I understand. I was tempted to stay with dear Lady Aurora, but I thought it would be more fitting to come to my family,' said Ianthe.

'Before you met them, you mean,' said Lady Richards, lapsing into the confidentiality this frank young girl seemed to draw from her. 'Sally was so sorry not to get an offer this Season, only to spare me this visit. We have such a tiny income you know, and our friends the Houstens, who have housed us since my husband died, always make a three-month trip at this time of year. We were at Studham last year at the height of our mourning, and I hoped never to return again. I know I am being shamelessly ungrateful, but the family are always at each other's throats and we feel very much in the way. They call them the Fighting Foxes in town.'

'Well, I am glad you are both here, for now we make each other comfortable, whatever Lady Fox chooses.'

'She can be cunningly cruel, my dear Miss Eames,' said Lady Richards, looking into the young woman's eyes. 'I may as well confess that we heard you before. With Lady Fox.' She dropped her voice and said, with frightened sympathy, 'You would not really do such a thing —'

Miss Eames flushed a little, but returned in a laughing tone, 'You are shocked, and I do not wonder. I chose the term *carte blanche* to shock

Her Ladyship, I'm afraid. I have no need to do anything so desperate, I assure you. I've simply had a fevered desire to annoy the woman since the moment I met her. Dreadful, I know!'

'Your instincts were quite right,' said Lady Richards, earnestly. 'She is the most dreadful woman of my acquaintance, Miss Eames.' She sighed. 'How ungrateful that must sound!'

Ianthe laughed and cast her arms around Her Ladyship. 'Oh, dear Cousin Emma, I think I shall love you very much. Please call me Ianthe, for I intend to be your most intimate cousin.'

'Oh, dear Ianthe,' said Lady Richards into her hair. 'Do take care.'

Chapter Four

The First Ride

By dint of squashing themselves into the gig with the groom, the two ladies arrived at the Marquis of Audley's country estate in good time and were taken to the stables directly. Sally Richards had never seen the house up close, but she was able to as they passed. Studham was old and grand, but Audley was more than double the size, and the construction was in some light-coloured stone that seemed to glow white in the sun. It was magnificent, with a multitude of glittering windows, and a dozen white columns on its raised portico.

  The marquis, waiting for them in the stable courtyard, looked equally magnificent. His hair was, well, bronze was the only word she could use for it, burnished bronze. It was swept back from a noble brow, over a chiselled face of perfect symmetry. He was leaning against a wall and languidly moved his limbs to the upright position before coming towards the gig lazily, holding out a hand to Ianthe Eames, whose quick, athletic jump contrasted with his languor. Ianthe looked up at his great height, beaming like a child who had escaped the schoolroom. Only the hooded, laughing eyes looking down into his friend's hinted at something less than godlike, Sally thought. Something Puckish in his look. Sally believed she would have been shaken to receive such a look, but Ianthe, as Miss Eames had been insistent Sally call her, seemed less than shocked. She tried to withdraw her hand, Sally saw, but he seemed to hold it more closely. 'How dare you keep me waiting, Ianthe? Have you no esteem for my consequence?'

'None at all,' Ianthe replied shortly, snatching her hand back. 'You have another guest, Audley. Pray give your hand to her.' She said this pertly, with a smile, and Sally, entranced by their mutual beauty, suddenly realised that those hooded eyes were turning towards her. She jumped from the gig in her haste to avoid them, and fell to adjusting her riding dress, looking down.

'Miss Richards, may I present the Marquis of Audley?' Ianthe's voice was still teasing while Sally turned in Audley's general direction and made a low curtsy. As she looked up, he was bowing perfunctorily, the laugh gone from his eye.

Sally, expecting it, was nevertheless annoyed. She frowned. Ianthe was continuing, 'Audley, you have a mount for my cousin, don't you? I promised her a ride and Lady Fox has ... well, I believe there is nothing suitable at Studham.'

'Of course,' said the marquis. Sally blushed. He must know the stables at Studham were near to full. He turned his regard to her, looking her up and down, and then said to a waiting groom, 'Saddle Missy for Miss Richards please, John.'

'My lord.'

As the marquis mounted a large, shiny, black stallion he called Night, and Ianthe petted a pretty piebald mare, cooing their reunion, the groom at last emerged with a mare of obvious docile disposition, presumably Missy. Sally sighed audibly and encountered a quizzical look from the marquis to whom she attempted a polite smile. 'Thank you, my lord,' she said and mounted the beast.

Ianthe, who had done the same, said, 'Lead on, my lord, I want to blow away the doldrums and you may show me the safest path to do so.'

Sally doubted that *she* would be blowing anything away at this rate, since it was a fine day, and the speed that Missy would reach would not involve creating a wind beneath her. The marquis headed out, Ianthe behind, and she brought up the rear, with an accompanying groom. Eventually they came to a wide expanse, free of trees, where the other two paused and talked a little, waiting for Missy to catch up.

'Go ahead, pray,' Sally said to them as she approached, 'I can see you are itching to get going. I shall enjoy a quiet exercise.' She smiled at them and Ianthe looked torn.

'Yes, go, Ianthe,' said the marquis. 'And John, go with her. I will accompany Miss — eh — Richards is it?'

'Yes,' said Sally at her most colourless, 'it is.' The marquis looked a little stunned at her tone, and fairly arrested. 'You need not accompany me, however,' Sally continued in the same tone. 'Your horse will fidget.'

'Nonsense. He has much better manners,' said the marquis.

'Well, you need not have better manners, my lord,' she said, nettled at this assumption of courtesy from a man who had set her on this horse. She attempted lightness of tone, however, for she *did* have good manners. 'Go with Ianthe, do. I shall be the rear guard.'

Ianthe laughed, looking from Sally's especially bland expression to the marquis' surprised one. 'Now that I see you are becoming well acquainted,' she said with a mischievous grin, 'I shall indeed leave. Yah!' she dug her heels in at this, and the piebald mare took off with even more power than Sally had thought possible. The groom raced to catch her up.

'Oh! I see now why she could not leave her in Paris!' said Sally, with such longing in her voice that the marquis laughed.

'I apologise for mounting you on Missy, Miss Richards,' he said politely. 'You are obviously disappointed.'

Sally was, and his amusement annoyed her. Moreover, she was raw from three weeks of the Foxes. Rubbed and insulted by Lady Fox, patronised by Curtis, ignored by the bad-tempered Lord Fox, she had thought at least she would be granted some bracing exercise today. Her hopes had been lifted by Ianthe's enthusiasm, and were now dashed as she sat upon the most placid nag she had ever thrown her knee over. The marquis, whom she had known about in Town, but who had only a few times been in her orbit, had trampled on all her hopes of an hour's diversion. Moreover, she was so far below him in rank that she was sure he now expected some flattering, perhaps even flirtatious, reply. Another maiden hoping for his attention. She had smiled and smiled at gentlemen in London to gain just such attention and change her fate, but never to someone so above her in rank as he, for she was not such a ninny. And now, the plodding steps of the horse, that his own stallion needed to be held back to match, were simply too depressing for politeness. 'I am only surprised that you house such a slug in your stables.'

He let out a laugh. 'Slug?'

'What else would you call her?'

'My grandmama's favourite mare.'

This was too much. 'Your *grandmama*?'

'Well, how was I to know you had such a seat until I saw it? My other horses are all full of spirit,' he said, still amused. 'You might have been a lady who was easily unseated. I sought to prevent an accident or embarrassment.'

'Just *what* about my appearance made it justifiable to seat me on the …' She held herself back, closed her eyes briefly and put on a polite smile. 'I am sorry, my lord. I am most grateful.'

'No, you are not,' laughed the marquis.

'No, I am not, though it would have been polite of you to pretend to believe me.' The marquis' eyes were more amused than ever as Miss Richards schooled him in manners. She glanced a little resentfully at him. 'Even a lady with limited expectations needs some glimmer of hope in life. Riding today was mine. Blowing away the doldrums, Ianthe called it, and I too thought to do so.'

'I apologise once more, Miss Richards. If you come tomorrow, I will mount you better. But I ask again, how *was* I to know?'

Again, she shot a blank look at him, and again it shook him since he was normally only shown the smiling face of the young ladies he talked to. 'You saw me race,' she said, flatly.

'I beg your pardon?'

'At Housten Hall last summer. Where I have resided since my father's death. There was a ladies' race on the day you came to dine.'

There was a pause. 'Ah, I remember.'

Sally, still depressively plodding on Missy's back, fed him his own sauce, 'No you don't.'

He could not help his laugh of shock at her bluntness. Then, 'Wait! Were you the lady in the red habit who won?'

'I was. We dined together afterwards,' she added, to drive his lack of manners home.

'There were forty people at that table—' He realised he was explaining himself, which the great Marquis of Audley was not given to do.

'I was seated on your left-hand side at the table. *Next* to you.' A decisive blow, she knew, and she enjoyed delivering it.

'I beg your pardon.'

The marquis was, she thought, glancing at him for a moment, looking somewhat ashamed. She decided to let him off her hook. 'Do not. You were very nice indeed to Miss Frampton on your right-hand side. And you did at least greet me.'

He did not attempt to hide the slight frown on his handsome face and Sally liked him better for his honesty. 'Well, at least I had some manners. Miss Frampton was the put-upon young lady with the sandy hair?'

'Yes. And spots. Her mother had been frightful with her the whole time, berating her for not using cucumber water or some such thing. I quite see why you chose to be nice to her and not me.'

'You do?' said the marquis interestedly, not

really quite remembering himself.

'Oh, yes. It is because I am a middling sort of woman.' The marquis raised an inquisitive eyebrow, so she continued, 'At balls you know, it is the best connected or prettiest girls who are fawned on, and the poor little dabs who are protected by the hostesses, making sure they have enough dances.'

'Yes?'

'Yes. I am well enough for at least two or three gentlemen perhaps, to ask me to dance, so there is no need for the hostesses to bother with me. But young ladies like me probably end up more neglected than the poor little dabs. And that night at dinner, you were kind to Miss Frampton, whom no one could expect you to marry, and careful to avoid me, the middling sort of young lady whose hopes might be raised by even such a slight thing as some attention at the dinner table.'

This masterly summation had him stumped. He attempted to lift the conversation with raillery. 'Well, we are talking now, Miss Richards. Am I to suppose your hopes are raised?'

'Of course not,' she said, dismissively. 'It is obvious that to your own guests you have an obligation to be polite, and you have done so very creditably since Ianthe foisted me upon you. And since there is no one here to see you talk to me, we need not fear to give rise to speculation. And then again, as to my own feelings, you may rest assured. I will never forgive your mounting me on a slug.'

He gave an ironic bow from the waist at her, which caused his horse to fidget. 'I am deeply shamed, Miss Richards, and I promise to do better next time — *and* at dinner on Sunday, if Lord Fox can be persuaded to come.'

'Oh, *pray* do not talk to me at dinner,' said his companion with more anxiety than he had seen her show. 'It would encourage my mother in wild speculation, and enrage Lady Fox, with whom we are committed to live for another two months.'

'Shall I disdain you then?' she looked up at him and he gave her a dreadful glare down his nose.

Finally, she laughed. '*Just* like that! Lady Fox will be appeased. But if you do so, watch out for my mother.'

'Will she eat me for my rudeness?'

'No, but it might cause her pain, and break her habitual good humour. She might even frown. You would do better to just ignore me, as you did last time.'

'It will be a much smaller gathering, and harder to achieve.'

'I'm quite sure,' said Sally, looking up at him with a wicked sarcasm, 'that you can manage it.'

When Ianthe finally joined them, she and Audley rode a little ahead of Sally and the groom who had slowed his horse's trot to accompany her.

'Sally is a dear, is she not, Audley? I have only just met her, but I expect that she will become my closest friend in England.'

Audley paused a little. 'Your friend is more unusual than I believed at first.'

'Oh, is your pride hurt? When I looked back at you two, she did not always seem amused by your fatal charm.'

'Do not be vulgar, Ianthe. You are no longer in Paris and must mind your manners.' She laughed up at him and he knew her to be enchanting. 'Don't play those tricks with me. I remember you with missing teeth.'

She grinned and said, 'So you do. Mr Fenton said something similar to me in London. But *you* are only ten years my senior, I believe.'

'It is so. But since I first met you when I was seventeen and a man grown, I shall never be able to think of you without mud on your nose. I believe you were making a pie.' He laughed. 'How does Cherie go on?'

'She is determined on her course at present and will not mind me.'

'I do not doubt it. She cannot go on so, surely?'

'I will think of a way,' Ianthe looked at Audley suspiciously, 'but you are avoiding my question. How is it that Sally is not captivated by your legendary address?'

'I forgot that I had met her before. But worst of all, I mounted her on Missy.'

Ianthe giggled. 'I could see by her enthusiasm that she was a true horsewoman. I should have said something when they brought out the mare.'

'Yes, you *should*, Ianthe,' he drawled. 'Now I think about it, I lay it all at your door.'

'Well, but I was so pleased to see Purity again that I thought only of myself. I am sorry, Audley. But did Sally really scold you?'

'Not precisely. But nearly. It amused me.'

Ianthe was silent for a moment, searching his profile. 'Audley — dearest Rob — do not try to charm my friend simply because she did not fawn at you.'

Audley jerked his body and turned to look directly at Ianthe's serious face. 'I do not behave in that way.'

She smiled sadly. 'I have seen you, my friend. Any hint of reserve in a lady's manner to you has you determined to thaw her.' He looked stunned. 'But do not do so to Sally, I beg. I do not think that the Richards' situation is provident — and I do not wish you to raise—'

He laughed, but still looked a little ashamed at this glance into his own character. 'Expectations? Do not fear, my dear Ianthe. Your friend tells me she could never forgive a man who mounted her on a slug.'

Ianthe laughed too, though not all her

fears were dispersed. 'I am so fortunate to have met with a woman of such spirit at Studham! It would be so dull without her and Lady Richards to watch me tease those Foxes.'

'Is it too dreadful?' asked Audley, concerned. 'If you are become more uncomfortable, send a line to me. Or come here.'

'And then we *would* be in the suds, for you told me you have no female relatives in residence! But I may let you convey me to London to Mr Fenton and Lady Aurora if the need should arise.'

'Will it?'

'Oh, I don't think so,' said Ianthe breezily, 'I am too amused by them at the moment. They all disapprove of me so much, you know, and I shall make them feel their burden before I go.'

'Burden?'

'Oh, they try that all three of us, the Richards and I, shall know our burdensome place.'

'What a household. I'm sorry, my dear.' Ianthe cocked an eyebrow at him. 'Oh, yes. I am very sorry for the Foxes. They are too ignorant to fear you.'

Ianthe laughed.

Chapter Five

Fox Tries and Fails

'Never mind, Sally,' said Ianthe in the gig back to Studham. 'The marquis has promised a better ride for you tomorrow.'

Sally shrugged and shuddered. 'Now I am only hoping we can get back into the house without being seen. The servants might not mention…'

Ianthe looked at her friend's hands, grasped tightly on the side of the gig, and her tense body. How could a girl who disdained the Marquis of Audley be the same one now terrified as they approached the house? 'Do not fear. I have a gift for the clandestine. Lady Fox shall not know.'

Sally relaxed a little. 'How does one acquire a gift for the clandestine?' she asked, more playfully.

'One has a spy for a father!' Ianthe whispered the last in her ear so that the groom who was driving could not overhear.

Sally laughed and the ladies successfully re-entered by a side door and Sally summoned a maid to call for her mother and moved off to her own chamber. As she changed into morning dress (a corded cambric in a warm fawn colour that complemented her hair) her mother joined her.

'Sally dear. Did you enjoy your exercise?'

'You could not call it exercise. It was more like being conveyed in a sedan chair. The marquis gave me his grandmama's mare.'

'Oh dear, and I know how much you longed for a ride!' her mother sympathised and began unpinning and re-pinning some curls to restore Sally's simple hairstyle. She paused, playing with a curl, and her silence let Sally know what was coming. 'And — was the marquis polite?' her mother asked, a trifle too casually.

A small untruth would be better here, judged Sally, uttering a prayer for forgiveness in her head, than to keep her mother hoping for the impossible. 'He rode ahead with Ianthe and I did not much speak with him.'

'I suppose they must be intimate acquaintances. Do you think he has intentions? To wed the marquis would save her from the fate of staying at Studham.'

Sally, who did not like to lie to her mother, only said, 'They looked very well together, I think.' She paused here to consider this. She had not yet caught that middle-aged woman's habit of setting all and every male and female to partners. Could Audley be wooing Ianthe? It was certainly possible — he was handsome and eligible, and she was too fascinating. And they certainly were intimate. Somehow Sally knew already that Ianthe Eames was not a woman who would wed merely for security. Even in this dire situation, she seemed to carry her own security with her, in her extraordinary personality.

***

Passing Ianthe in the hall, Lord Fox nodded her into a small sitting room. Ianthe Eames entered, then raised her eyebrows in enquiry at him. Fox looked slightly conscious, but said, with a serious expression, 'I have something to say.' Ianthe nodded, and he drew a breath. 'If you are bullied by my stepmother, Miss Eames, tell me. I shall know how to deal with it.'

'Shall you?' Miss Eames said below her breath, but Fox caught it and flushed. 'I should say, thank you very much...' Miss Eames' voice tailed off.

'But?' Fox enquired, nettled.

'Well ... I'd as well set your namesake into the hen house to appease the chickens.'

Fox blinked, then his eyes narrowed at the insult. 'Do you mean to set yourself against me, Miss Eames?'

'Oh no, not an enemy. A friend.' She smiled at him. 'Will the weather improve do you think? I shall take a walk in the grounds this afternoon.'

He was continuing to eye her narrowly. 'To survey my estate?'

'Well—' she shrugged.

'Dull country for you, I suppose.' His voice had taken on a sarcastic tone.

'*Well*—' she seemed to be agreeing.

The eyes snapped again, and he said, temper breaking, 'Do you have *any* notion of manners, Miss Eames?'

'I have wonderful company manners. They are frequently remarked upon,' she informed him cheerfully.

'I cannot say I have noted them.'

'But then sir, we are family are we not? No need for company manners.'

He was no match for her brightness, so he tried a more direct tack. 'What did you find to amuse you in my offer of aid with my stepmother?'

She smiled. 'It is simply that I should not ask an inept driver to show me how to use the ribbons. You can barely contain your reaction to each word Her Ladyship issues.' Fox looked slapped. 'If you should wish some aid in dealing with your stepmother,' she added consolingly, 'do not hesitate to ask *me*.'

He shot her a venomous glance. 'Madam! I must suppose that your beauty has forgiven your behaviour in Paris. It will not do so here.'

'You think me beautiful?' asked Miss Eames, enchanted. 'Thank you.'

'That was not my meaning,' he said grimly

'But it *is* your admission. Thank you, my lord!' she declared, clasping her hands together theatrically, 'I shall treasure those words.'

Fox looked at her fluttering eyelids with dislike. 'Can you not be insulted?'

'Certainly. *You* did so on the first occasion of our meeting.'

He searched his memory and alighted on it. 'My offer to make provisions for you? I saw that you took it amiss, but I did not mean to offer an insult.'

'Possibly, but it recalled those who did, and proved that at this time I am more easily insulted than normal. Usually, you know, I do not prick up at every little thing a sour mouth may offer me, like a child.'

'I know how to take that, I suppose.'

She smiled. 'You probably do.' There was a short pause, which seemed a prelude to an explosion from Lord Fox, but Miss Eames cut him off. 'Oh, and about that advice on how to deal with your stepmother. If you do not trust to a mere female, you may watch Lord Audley on Sunday! I'm quite sure he'll be an inspiration to you!'

Lord Fox made a growling sound and stormed from the room.

***

Ianthe thought of Lord Fox's eyes as he had tried to be kind to her. She had seen from the first that a gentle man lived beneath his frustration and rage and had been a little sorry to rebuff him. However, to set him on to attack his dreadful stepmother in her defence would have been to wound him again, for he had no idea how to deal with the woman. Also, it was somehow fun to tease and shake him out of that protective shell he always wore. His face, when she challenged him, had another expression than that brooding, bottled rage look that he displayed to his family. It was angry — but engaged. The tawny eyes lighting up, the face suddenly handsome and alive. She liked that face and meant to prick him often, just to see it again. He was too set in his misery. It was easy to see how it could have happened. What would her own personality be like if she had been brought up not by her roguish, laughing Papa, but by the horrid, unloving Lady Fox?

Not long after she arrived in her room, a package was delivered by an interested footman. It had arrived by carrier, said the servant, and that was all he knew. It was heavy, and it contained a rosewood box with elegant brass boulle work decoration. She did not recognise it, and letting it rest on a table, Ianthe gazed at it for a moment, perplexed. She opened it somewhat fearfully, and the periwinkle blue silk of the interior shocked the eye. Inside were some wrappings of soft cream felt, and Ianthe took each one out and laid them beside the box carefully. The box now contained only one thing — a torn piece of paper on which the words were written in a careless hand: *Tout ce que j'ai pu trouver encore* — All I could find as yet.

'*Antoine!*' breathed Ianthe.

With trembling fingers, she unwrapped one of the bigger parcels. A tear fell when she saw the ruby collar that had been her mother's spill into her hands. The next was a string of pearls, long and beautiful, and unsuitable for an unmarried young lady to wear. Ianthe, now dressed in a rose silk evening dress of a peculiarly stylish cut, wrapped them around her neck three times and admired in the looking glass how they still hung down to nearly her waist. She had done so a hundred times before, even when she was small enough that they reached the floor — had pranced around a room wearing them until her father bade her to return them to the box (another more elegant enamelled one, belonging to her mama) and only be patient until she was older.

She felt very old now. All of the pieces brought back memories to her — her father's cluster of curls and rakish smile. She remembered the places they had hidden these things on their travels, sometimes sewn into garments, sometimes in the shabbiest sacking, under a reeking pile of stolen laundry. The diamond studs for her hair, the pearl droplets for her ears, the silver pendant with the lock of her mama's hair. A miniature on a blue ribbon of Papa's mother, with powdered hair and the pearls about her neck. A tiny plain silver snuffbox caught at her throat. It was Papa's own, carried in nearly all his disguises, and was dented and scratched, reminding her of its many adventures.

Her fingers searched briefly once more. The amber pendant her father had bought her was the only thing missing.

She sank to the ground in a puddle of silk. 'Papa!' she called out and wept the tears she had kept at bay since her arrival. Sally, come to see her toilette for the evening, found her thus and sank down with her, holding her while she cried.

Chapter Six

The Second Ride

Next morning, Sally — still in a holy terror of getting caught — ran downstairs dressed for the ride, following the completely unconcerned figure of Ianthe Eames. Her friend had on yet another enchanting riding dress, in a dark pink colour, with an interesting little hat of the same colour perched high. Sally admired the black French braiding that gave the dress a military air, set off by the veil on her hat.

Lady Richards, in her night attire, clutched a banister and kept watch in the hall for passers-by with the utmost in concentration. Ianthe smiled at Sally as they finally achieved the door. 'All's safe!' intoned Her Ladyship in a whisper as they passed. Sally smiled too. The sight of her mama starting to creep back up the stairs in a stealthy fashion was amusing but affecting too.

Somehow, the lackey who held the door open seemed to be Ianthe's servant, rather than Fox's, for Sally swore he almost gave her a wink as he held the side door open and said, 'The gig's ready, miss! No groom, as you ordered, miss.'

'How does James know you?' enquired Sally as they ran to the gig.

'I spent some time in the kitchens yesterday and he was being fed by Cook.'

As Ianthe got into the vehicle, Sally stood still, looking up at her, 'Do you really think we should?'

'Dispense with the groom? We can talk more freely without him, can we not?' She gave a teasing smile to Sally. 'What did dear Lady Richards think she could do if a servant *had* passed?' laughed Ianthe.

'Oh, she would have feigned a fainting fit or some such. She told me so when I was dressing.'

'So that the servant might thus forget two ladies in riding dress coming down the stairs? That is too amusing.' Sally's slight smile made Ianthe turn to her. 'You are concerned…'

'It is just that I think it is selfish of me to risk so much.'

'Risk?'

'If we displease Lady Fox then we *may* be sent off, you know. I do not have the right to risk Mama in this way.' She sighed. 'Only, I could not resist coming today when I have been promised such a treat as a decent ride. I am a most selfish daughter.'

'Nonsense — did you not see the joy on your mama's face when she saw you so filled with anticipation? You must not concern yourself.' As they came towards Audley, Ianthe continued. 'You know, Lady Fox may say what she wants, but Lord Fox is a different matter. He would never ask you to leave if you did not wish to do so.'

'I do not know that. He hardly speaks to me.'

'He is not like his step-mama at all,' Ianthe assured her.

'He has spoken to you?'

'Not a great deal, but it is quite obvious.'

'It is?'

'Oh, yes,' Ianthe smiled. 'People who have that passionate nature are not cruel to those who have not harmed them.'

'Passion? Lord Fox?' said Sally, astounded. But they had reached the stable yard. Ianthe thrust the reins into the hands of a waiting groom and rushed to greet Purity, while the marquis came forward to give Miss Richards his hand. She took it, but merely nodded to him and looked over his shoulder seeing no other mount than his Night. The marquis nodded to a groom who raised a hand, and another horse was led from the stables. It was a handsome chestnut, half a hand taller than Purity, built on magnificent lines. He shook his great head and kicked out with his back legs in a show of spirit, but if the marquis had expected Miss Richards to be fearful or shocked, he was disappointed.

Ianthe, turning to watch, saw another, smaller horse in the stable door, ready, she was sure, to be brought out if Miss Richards were to falter. But Sally, breathless with joy, moved forward without hesitation and caressed the stallion's head. 'You beauty!' she breathed. And before Ianthe herself had mounted, Sally, without the aid of a block, was on his back, one leg slung around the pommel, adjusting her skirts. How strong she is, thought Ianthe. Sally leaned forward and breathed to the stunned Audley, '*Thank you, my lord.*'

Audley returned to himself at this and moved forward, stroking the neck of the horse. 'This is Sapphire. He's a little strong, so if you desire another mount, then—'

'Oh, how could I? *Thank you* for trusting me with him.' Sally was not looking at the marquis as she said this, but only reaching out and calming the twitching horse, patting his neck and communing with him, even as the groom fought to keep him from moving. As Ianthe mounted Purity, she saw that it worked. The horse was calming with the gentling and whatever Sally Richards was whispering near to his ear. She watched as Audley, hoisted by his own petard, was arrested. Ianthe's eyes narrowed. She had seen that look but once before. She moved Purity forward. 'Mount, sir! We two must return to Studham before breakfast or face the consequences. Delay us not!'

Audley did so and they all moved off, he leading the way. When Sapphire came abreast, they walked on in quietude for a moment, he surprised at the silence from Miss Richards. Eventually he said, 'How do you find him?'

'Oh, he is twitching because we are walking, once we get to shake off his legs in a canter, he'll settle.'

'Ah,' said Audley, wondering at his own lack of address. He glanced over at Miss Richards, and she blushed.

'Thank you so much, my lord.'

He sighed. 'You said so already.'

Instead of the impertinent response, she blushed deeper and looked at the horse's neck. Ianthe, on the other side, said, 'Let us canter.'

They did so, and soon they were both privileged to see Sally Richards' back. She rode forward, and before long he saw that she was kicking in a gallop. He pulled up to watch, and when Ianthe noticed, she rode back to him.

'I can't catch her on that horse,' remarked Ianthe, looking after her. 'Whatever made you give her Sapphire?'

He was still looking in the direction of Sally's gallop. 'I thought she'd refuse him.'

'I saw there was another ready saddled.'

They both gazed ahead. 'She's wonderful, isn't she? On a horse she doesn't know?'

'She's odd today,' said Audley in a distracted tone. 'Doesn't talk.'

Ianthe considered. She looked again, as Audley's eyes were following Sally's. Should she help or not? It may hurt her new friend. But that look in his eye ... She decided to further this just a little, to see where it may lead. If she was concerned afterwards, well then, there was still time to avoid the worst. Sally was a sensible woman. 'That is because she is grateful and embarrassed.' Ianthe explained to him. 'It has restored her to her usual social manner. Keeping her distance from a well-known, and well-distant-in-status, marquis.'

'It is a pity,' he sighed. 'But I suppose you are correct.'

'Don't try to charm her, Audley. She knows enough to avoid a flirtation with you. She has spoken to me on this head when I warned her.'

'Yes?' he looked annoyed. 'You should keep your nose out of my affairs, Ianthe.'

'*Is* this then one of your affairs?' demanded Ianthe with a warning in her voice.

'Do not take me up so. I only meant I liked to hear her real feelings instead of social offerings. I was looking forward to her berating me when I brought out Sapphire.'

'Then you are justly served, my lord.' They both looked as Sapphire, followed by a groom doing his best to keep up, disappeared behind the brow of a hill. 'If you wish to restore her to herself, do not try charm, it will not work.'

'You underestimate my charm.'

'Well,' lied Ianthe, 'it never worked on me.'

His eyes looked like he would call out her lie, but instead he said, 'Very well. What then shall I do?'

In a few minutes, he took her advice.

Once Sally Richards, with hair escaping from her bonnet, a becoming flush on her cheeks and nose, and a deliriously happy smile on her face rode back to them, they all pulled up. 'Are you empty headed?' cried Audley. 'Galloping a horse on roads you did not know?'

Sally's euphoria was not dented. 'But Sapphire knew the road, so I had only to trust him!' She leant forward and caressed the horse's sweaty neck, then looked up a trifle pertly at the marquis. 'I asked the groom if Sapphire knew the road before I galloped.'

'You might have harmed him! Or yourself!'

She looked a trifle guilty. 'I quite understand that it might have worried you. I am sorry! But you see, all is well.' The marquis snorted. 'It is! Why, if you were afraid, did you give him to me then?'

'I had another horse ready saddled. I thought you would refuse him. Instead you mounted a horse so tall without a block, before I could prevent you.'

'Huh!' ejected Sally, 'You were caught in your own net! Serves you right. I'm not sorry at all, now. I suppose that the other horse was Missy's grandmother.'

'A suitable horse for a lady, merely.' He paused. 'And how did you manage that mount? The stirrup was too high for you.'

'I jumped and pulled up! It was easy. My papa had a hunter as tall as Sapphire and I rode him often.'

'Your papa was?'

'Sir Guy Richards. He was not much in town.'

'I knew him!'

'You *did*?' Sally sounded overjoyed.

'Not well, but he was a member of my club. A very affable gentleman.'

Sally's eyes filled. 'He was.'

The marquis was at a loss for a moment but acted by instinct. 'And a good horseman who would not have been amused by his daughter risking her life on a mount too strong for her.'

'Nonsense! He trusted me well!' said Sally fiercely.

Audley was grateful that the tears were gone and added another faggot to the fire. 'When next you come, I shall find a more suitable ride for you.'

'How can you say that when you have just seen me ride without mishap? You *could* not be so cruel, just when I know Sapphire's tricks.'

'Well, if you promise not to gallop without us, perhaps I will permit it. Sapphire does not always take with other riders.'

'And knowing this you gave him to me! You are the most complete hand, my lord. But if you let me ride him again, I will try to be grateful and forgiving.' She smiled at him pertly, and Audley tried to mask his own smile in return.

The marquis pulled behind with Ianthe and the road slowed them both down. 'Thank you for your advice, dear heart. She is now fully restored to insulting me.'

'It seems you enjoy it,' said Ianthe with a laugh. But she was apprehensive. Audley was too engaged, too concerned. This might mean nought. However, if he set out to charm Sally, this might end in pain. Sally, lovely and vivacious, was nevertheless not someone he was likely to marry. She knew that Audley was no saint, his affairs were legendary. If he wanted to play with Sally because she had spirit enough not to worship his looks or position, if he only wanted to win ... but no. Ianthe trusted him, and if he were to pursue something for no good reason, she would pull him up short, before he did any serious damage. He did not trifle with young ladies of quality. His liking for Sally was evident, but probably not ardent. They could both do with a friend, thought Ianthe. And socially, Audley could do much for Sally and her mother. If they ever returned to London, that was. It was part of Ianthe's new ambition to have the Richards less dependent on the unpleasant Foxes and it would be more difficult to negate poor relations who also have powerful friends. Ianthe would, as usual, trust her instincts. They had gotten her out of more fixes than this.

When handing the ladies back into the gig, Audley said, 'I received a reply from Lord Fox last night. You all return tomorrow for dinner here.'

'Well, I wonder what made him give in?' wondered Sally.

'Mmmm,' said Ianthe, and Audley grinned.

'You will find that people around Ianthe Eames frequently behave in a manner out of character.'

'You are right, sir! I am even now being more disobedient than I ever have in my life!'

'You see?' The marquis looked over Ianthe to Sally. 'Just what are my instructions for the party again?' he asked as though about to commit them to memory.

'Do not notice me. Do not ignore me either, because it would pain my mother.'

'It seems impossible, but I will do my level best. Did you not request a sneer?'

'I did. But we thought again.'

'So we did.'

Sally frowned. 'You might have to use it in an emergency.'

'Very well. What emergency might arise?'

'Oh, if my mother becomes enamoured of

you!'

'We wouldn't want that...' said Audley.

'What are you two about?' asked Ianthe, laughing.

'Ah, it is the delicate social balancing of a marquis and a ... a middling sort of woman, I believe.' As Ianthe looked lost, he laughed. 'Ask your friend. Her request might defeat even my notable social address.'

Sally unexpectedly took the gig reins, saying, 'Just be your superior self, my lord.' And led off, leaving him.

Ianthe thought, looking back at her friend the marquis smiling after them, that Sally Richards, when she was not being the terrified satellite of Lady Fox, might be more than even he could handle.

Chapter Seven

Enlisting Lord Fox

'I quite see!' said Ianthe as she and Sally re-entered the side door of Studham. Sally had been instructing her on the "middling sort of woman" social dilemma that the marquis faced, and Ianthe had laughed at her demands of him. She thought that Sally Richards was even more intelligent and delightful than she had guessed, and was looking forward, in a frankly inquisitive way, to the dinner at Audley and her two friends' interaction.

But now her laughter with Sally was halted by encountering Lord Fox, also in riding dress, in the hall.

'I can explain everything!' said Ianthe, holding up an appeasing hand. Lord Fox stood stock still. 'Sally, go and change!' She saw that Sally was frozen into the terrified rabbit again and was distressed to see the figure of Lady Richards above, swaying a little in shock. She nudged Sally roughly. 'Go to your mother!' and Sally stumbled upstairs. Lord Fox wore his habitual frown, but it was tinged today with confusion. 'In the study!' ordered Ianthe, leading the way. He followed her.

In a break from good etiquette, Ianthe moved past him to close the study door firmly behind them. He supposed, as relatives of a sort, it was permissible, and he was too confused to do other than turn to her, as she leaned her back against the door.

'I can explain,' she said.

'You have said so,' he countered. 'What have you to explain?'

'About the ride.'

He was silent, waiting.

'You don't seem shocked,' Ianthe mused, tilting her head a little.

He supposed the head tilt was one of her tricks. He was feeling a little suffocated that his exit was blocked by a lady looking at him with such an open expression. He controlled his breathing. 'I am most shocked that you have come again into my study, a room I have explicitly forbade you to enter.'

'That is all?' Ianthe seemed amused.

'Is that not sufficient?'

'Then you are not shocked by the ride?'

'Why should I be …? *What—?*'

Ianthe straightened herself. 'Ah, so you do not know!' She smiled as though in relief. 'I thought you were too good for that!'

Lord Fox recoiled as though struck. 'I beg your pardon?'

'Lady Fox banned riding,' she explained.

He looked aghast. 'Why would she do so?'

'To be unpleasant,' said Ianthe flatly. He blinked. 'That is not the point. Did you not notice that the Richards have not ridden during their stay here?'

He frowned again, but this time in reflection. 'I did not think of it. I have no idea what they do all day. If I had noticed, I would have assumed that they did not care for it.'

'Not at all. Sally Richards is the most *brilliant* rider I have ever seen.' Ianthe informed him enthusiastically. Then she sighed. 'It is because all horses and carriages are forbidden them.'

'But *why*?' asked Lord Fox, aghast.

'I have already told you why.' Ianthe sat down and Fox watched in amazement. '*Now* what do we do?' she asked him invitingly.

'*We?*' He was taken aback by more than this new information, but further thrown off by her open regard.

'You quite see we have to do *something*.' She looked up at him frankly. His eyes looked down into her dark velvet ones and he gulped, unable to unlock them. It was she who broke the lock, looking off to the side as though her quick brain was creating something. Why it terrified him, he could not fathom. He was still catching up.

'But wait,' he said, 'you are in riding gear.

Does that mean you took the horses against Her Ladyship's prohibition?'

'No! For the head groom is completely in Lady Fox's pocket, you know.'

'My step-mama's? No, I did not know!' He frowned. 'So, how might *you*?'

'Well, Hawkins took *far* too much delight in refusing me a mount when I asked. I could quite see he belongs to Lady Fox. Stephens,' she said, referring to another groom, 'later told me he came with her to Studham.'

'I had not remembered.' Fox frowned again. 'So how come you to be in riding dress, if you did not take any of my horses?'

'Well, I suppose I *have* been stealing the gig. Stephens said he would bring it *as he had not received orders to the contrary*. He's very sweet.' Fox would never have thought to hear of the burly, balding, ugly figure of Stephens as sweet, but he did not question this. 'The best way is for you, over dinner you know, to make a request to the Richards and I to help to exercise your horses.' Fox was too astounded to be angry. Her casual assumption that he was her ally needed rebuking, but he had not yet the words... 'But not yet,' she continued thoughtfully. 'Sally has only just got acquainted with Sapphire and there is nothing to match him in your stables barring your own Thor.'

'Sapphire? Wait — not the chestnut hunter of Audley's?'

'You men do not socialise at all, and yet you know each other's mounts. It is *so* like gentlemen.' Ianthe remarked, amused.

'You mean you have been riding at *Audley*? And he let Miss Richards ride *Sapphire*?'

'Well, he was teasing her because …' Ianthe threw up her hands, 'it is too difficult to explain. He did not expect her to ride him, but she did. And magnificently.'

'But you have been riding at Audley?'

'Well yes, because my mare is there, you know.'

'What?'

'Well, I did not wish to give you yet another burden without at least asking, and Audley agreed to keep her until I got your permission to house her.'

'You brought your mare from *Paris*?' He shook this off. 'And yet you did *not* ask me.'

'Well, I thought you were aware of the riding ban, you know, and I knew Audley would be delighted to house her.'

Fox was beside himself. 'Because of his intimacy with you I presume?' He had made "intimacy" seem like a soiled word, but she did not react.

'Honestly — he is! It is not charity you see, for Purity once saved his life. But that is quite another story.' She stood up, smiling sunnily. 'I must go to see Sally now, for she will be sorely worried, thinking you are about to eject her from

Studham.'

'Why would I eject her…?'

'Oh. Even *I* mistook you for a while. You do not smile, you know, and people think it is because you have no heart. Or at least, a heart as black as your step-mama's.' He shuddered, and her voice softened, consoling. 'It is only because they do not know how kind you are.' He took a step back. She had whisked around to open the study door and put her head out carefully. She turned again, smiling. 'We did it! No one is there. I'll see you at breakfast! Remember, not a peep to Lady Fox yet!' She turned to leave but looked over her shoulder winningly, 'And *do* try a smile at Lady Richards over breakfast, or she will make herself ill worrying that she will be thrown out.' She opened the door and was gone with a conspiratorial wink.

Lord Fox, stunned, sat back in a chair.

***

Lady Fox and Curtis came down to breakfast that morning. Sally Richards, coming into the room with her mama, froze on the threshold before a helpful shove from Lady Richards propelled her in.

'You are late!' said Lady Fox acidly.

'We are at our regular hour, I believe, your ladyship,' ventured Lady Richards faintly.

A look at a clock on the mantelpiece told Lady Fox that it was she who had been mistaken, but said, nevertheless, 'You should be down before the family, I believe. Even Curtis is here this morning and *he* has a delicate constitution.'

The Richards sat down, both trembling and uneasy. Lady Richards shot a look at Ianthe, who smiled at her.

'I am so sorry to hear you are not strong, Mr Fox,' said Ianthe, smiling warmly at Curtis in a way that made him give a reluctant twitch of his lips in exchange. 'What precisely is your malady?'

This was an intrusive question that should not be asked — and Sally Richards understood in it a way to direct Lady Fox's wrath from her mother and her to Ianthe herself. It worked. Lady Fox's breath caught in that precursor to a lengthy tirade, but Lord Edward Fox had entered the room, and he replied dryly, 'No one has yet discovered what that might be, Miss Eames, though many surgeons have been called upon. However, the mystery does seem to be linked to how much of the brandy bottle had been emptied the night before.'

'Damn you, Edward!' Curtis spat.

A servant had brought a plate for His Lordship, and Sally noted that rather than respond to Curtis' venom, as was his wont, Lord Fox merely began to eat. Sally herself, free from attention for the moment, nibbled on a sweet roll and drank some chocolate.

'We dine at Audley tomorrow, remember,

Stepmother.'

'You cannot mean it!' said Lady Fox. 'I will not permit it.'

'You must do as you choose, ma'am, but I shall certainly attend, and invite our guests to do so.' He gave a stiff smile across the table to Sally's mama. 'Lady Richards, you have no objection to dining at Audley?'

Returning his smile with a shy one of her own, Lady Richards replied, 'No objection at all, my lord.'

'What new quirk is this?' said Curtis with rancour. 'You have always avoided Audley before.'

Lord Fox gave a slight shrug. 'As to that, I have no more affection for the marquis than usual. But you must see that to return the land to the estate, as he has just offered, is to the advantage of the family.'

There was a silence broken only by the noise of cutlery and eating for two minutes. Sally gave a nervous glance to Ianthe whose return look was mischievous. Lady Fox broke it. 'Since this concerns the estate, I suppose we must be present, my son.' When Curtis sulkily expostulated, she held up a hand. 'No, my boy, as heir to the estate, this concerns you.' At this, Sally let out a little laugh that became a cough. The ice-cold voice of Lady Fox impaled her. 'Pray, *what* did you find amusing, Miss Richards?'

Sally, putting a napkin to her mouth for a

second, replied quietly, 'Only that I know Curtis *is* the heir, of course, but it sounded so strange.' Sally wished she could stop her own mouth, as Her Ladyship's brows descended below the bridge of her nose.

'Strange? I do not understand you.'

That voice would certainly have effectively shut her mouth with only a few apologetic cries a few days ago, but Lord Fox had smiled, however briefly, at her mama. And Ianthe Eames was here, so Sally ventured the truth. 'Well, it is just that Lord Fox, being a handsome man of fortune, can hardly fail to be expected to have children of his own.'

Lady Fox's rage held her silent, but Curtis said, 'Fox is too unpleasant to attract the ladies. He has no plans to marry at all. Mama has always said so.' He added rather desperately.

'But you have just heard a young lady describe him as *handsome*, you know Curtis,' said Ianthe Eames.

'Is this your plan, my lady?' said Lady Fox with a snarl at Lady Richards. 'To ensnare Lord Fox for your daughter? I did not think you would dare to look so far above yourself. I did not think you *encroaching*.'

A few seconds of stunned silence followed this poison, even Ianthe temporarily bereft of speech. Lady Richards sat up. Instead of denying it, she said with some vigour, 'I do not think the difference so huge between a baron and baronet's daughter, Lady Fox. And let me tell you that the *Duke of Cumberland* once danced with my daughter and said she was *charming*!'

Lord Fox grinned briefly at the lioness defending her cub, and met Lady Richards' eye.

'I suppose the Royal duke considers it his duty to dance with every lady in town,' said Curtis with a sneer.

'Only the pretty ones,' remarked Lord Fox.

'Fox!' His step-mama slapped a hand on the table. 'Are you telling me that you and Miss Sarah Richards are … are…' Words failed Lady Fox at this.

'Oh, no your ladyship,' gasped Sally, hardly knowing how it had come to this, 'I *assure* you…'

'I have not spent more than a minute alone with Miss Richards since her arrival,' mused Lord Edward Fox, 'but she seems a very pleasant person. Perhaps I should pursue the acquaintance.'

Sally heard herself let out a squeak at this, and clutched her napkin to her chest, but His Lordship had finished his meal and rose from the table with a slight bow to Lady Fox. 'I meet with Henderson,' he said, referring to the estate manager, 'You must excuse me.'

Ianthe stood up too, and after bobbing a curtsy, ran after him. She caught him in the hall. 'Lord Fox!' she called.

He stopped and looked around. 'I'm busy,' he said unpleasantly.

'Whoever Henderson is, I'm sure he can

wait a few minutes. I'll follow you into the study.'

'I have already said you are not permitted there. And the Estate Manager is there already.'

'Oh, is that Henderson? You must introduce me before he goes!' She pulled on his sleeve and he looked down at her hand, astounded. 'The green salon then,' she said, and pulled him in that direction.

He jerked his sleeve from her grasp, but followed her anyway, wondering why. 'I am waiting,' he said coldly once they had entered.

'I just wanted to tell you that you did very much better today. You attacked her weaknesses and did not only respond to her attacks. *Very* well done!' she congratulated. Lord Fox clenched his jaw. 'However, your passion led you into the quagmire once more. You are now officially a suitor of Sally Richards,' she added sweetly.

He briefly looked stiffer than ever — and enraged, but at this last he sank in a chair and put his hands over his face, defeated. The enormity of his words, about a woman circumstanced as Miss Sarah Richards was, had hit him harder with every step he had taken from the dining room. What had possessed him? The evil influence of Ianthe Eames, he knew. The attempt to put his stepmother on the retreat had led his unfettered tongue to utter that stupidity. He groaned.

'Of course, you could do a deal worse,' continued Ianthe, as though looking on the bright side. 'She is a delightful girl of good spirit, intelligent and very pretty.'

Each new adjective sounded a death knell in his soul, and he hung his head lower. It was true, he could not hurt such an innocent now that those angry words had left his mouth. "Pursue the acquaintance" he had said. There could be only one meaning to that for an unwed, unprotected female. A louder noise left him, and he rolled his head on the chair back, eyes closed.

After some seconds, he heard a giggle. 'I'm only teasing. Sally wouldn't have you.'

Lord Fox's head shot up and he looked hopefully into the laughing eyes of Ianthe Eames. 'Do you think so?'

'Of course! You have not been pleasant to her at all during her visit.'

'That is true,' he said, remembering with relief. 'It would not be unusual for her to have taken a dislike to me,' he added hopefully.

'Oh, she *has*!' said Ianthe. She smiled as he put his head back once more and uttered a sigh of release.

'Thank goodness!' he said. 'My dashed temper.'

'Yes,' said Ianthe comfortably. 'But there is no saying but that your kind words over breakfast may have given her thoughts a different direction. She might develop a *tendre* after all. She did say you were handsome, remember.'

He shot up again. 'Never say so.' She kept

her mouth prim. Lord Fox grasped at her hands with the air of a drowning man. 'Miss Eames, please help me!'

She laughed down on him then. 'Don't fear, I am playing with you. Sally is not such a zany. She knew why you spoke so.'

He shut his eyes with deliberation and sighed. He still had her hands and squeezed them enough to make her squeal. 'I should be angry with you for deceiving me, but I find I am too relieved. I shall have words with you later on this head, when I can muster my dislike.' He made to stand up.

Ianthe's large dark eyes looked down at his hands and she said, 'Oh, I cannot foist you on Sally, you know. I may have quite other plans for you.'

'What on earth…?' He looked up, but Lord Fox found himself once more alone, only the warmth in his hands saying that Miss Ianthe Eames had ever been there at all.

He did not know why, but as his meeting with Henderson was coming to an end, he called a footman to summon Miss Eames to the study. As she entered, smiling, he said to the interested subordinate, 'Mr Henderson, this is Miss Eames, who wished to make your acquaintance before you left.'

The confused Henderson, a red-headed Scot of middle age and intelligent appearance, bowed and blinked as the most beautiful young lady he had ever seen, in a pink muslin day dress with long gauze sleeves, smiled at him beatifically. 'Can we converse as I walk you out, Mr Henderson? I have lived on the continent all my life and my father did not have an estate. I confess I find your occupation fascinating.'

Henderson, with a bemused look at Lord Fox, saw his nod, and said pleasantly, moving to the door, 'Well if it is not too dull for you, ma'am, I should be pleased to talk of it with you.'

Fox watched them go, wondering what she was about. But as he had been in this state of wondering since she arrived, it made little difference. Did she wish to know the running of Studham in particular, or was that too simple? Perhaps she wished to know more about estate management in preparation for running a great house like Audley. Then again, she was a person of energy who seemed to be interested in everything around her. He would strive not to tease himself about it. But he wondered why he had let her have her head.

Chapter Eight

Lady Aurora Worries

Mr Wilbert Fenton, ever the fashionable gentleman, but with an outré touch around the waistcoat area that suggested the dandy, was lounging on a chair very much at his ease, reading a racing journal. Past forty, he was no longer given to ruinous gambling indulgences, many years of such behaviour had palled, but he was ever the sportsman and occasionally indulged in speculative bets based on knowledge, not luck. He had always been a clever man, handsome and slender of body (though for many years he had feigned corpulence to appease the insecurities of his friend, the Prince Regent) and his indulgences had concealed another life abroad, where he had performed secret services for the crown.

The visit of Ianthe Eames had brought back memories of those times, and he had even been able to divulge aspects of these adventures to his beloved wife, Lady Aurora. She had found it all vastly amusing, but she had not seemed astonished. His wife had intuited things about him that he had never revealed.

He had thought he'd married his wife at this late age as a convenient arrangement for them both. He was to give her an *entrée* in society once more (that had been denied her because she had chosen to run a discreet gaming den instead of starving after her ruinous husband had died); she was to supply the wealth. That freed him from continuing to leech on his kind older brother, Sir Ranalph Fenton. But all this had ceased to be the basis of his marriage to the beautiful Countess Overton as soon as he had touched her. The convenience of the marriage had been, after that, the mere result of their love.

Though he was still reading, Fenton was aware that his wife had twitched twice, and now moved to the window in a distracted fashion, and then back to her chair. He had approved, as he always did, of her exquisite taste today. Her dress was slimmer that the prevailing English fashion. The under dress was caught under her bosom close to her slender figure, with only the sage green muslin overdress fluttering around her now, adding softness.

'Are you going to tell me,' he drawled, not looking up, 'or shall I guess?'

'Oh, it is nothing, my dear.' His wife was not fooled by his careless tone and sought to reassure him.

'I shall tell you, then.' He said, laying down his paper. 'You are worried about Ianthe.'

'If it were not the Foxes, Wil dear, I would not be concerned. But Lord Edward is so miserably forbidding, and Her Ladyship is a cat that I still remember from my young days. She is ten years my senior and still was not married to the widowed Lord Fox yet but had set her eyes on him. She was hideous to me my entire first Season because he once paid me a compliment.'

'As I remember it, Fox did not give out compliments. He must have been moved by your amazing beauty, my dear.'

'Well,' said his wife, 'I suppose he might have been, but his manner of delivery terrified me. Mama later told me that he approached my papa, who would not allow it.'

'He must have been twenty years your senior!' said her husband.

'Oh, Papa would not have scrupled at that. It was that he wished to sell my beauty to a higher bidder.'

At this, Mr Fenton came forward and took his wife in his arms consolingly. She submitted to this for a few seconds before pulling back to look at him and say, 'I just cannot bear the thought that the poor child should be under the same roof as them, Wil. I do not know Lord Fox well, but what if he is like his father? I was crushed by him entirely.'

'Well, Ianthe has lived a different life than you had at that age my dear, she will not be so easily crushed. She has more spirit than any girl I know.'

'Yes, but her father is only months deceased, and to be put into such a household when one's spirits must be at their lowest doesn't bear thinking of.'

'And so?'

She threw herself against his chest again. 'What shall we do, dear Wil?'

He touched her hair affectionately. 'Kent. Now, *who* could we be on our way to?'

'Oh, shall we visit Studham?' Lady Aurora said, delighted, looking up at him again. 'I know it is a bore to go, but it would put my heart at ease. If it is too awful, we shall just take her back with us. We can persuade her, can we not?'

'If need be, I will persuade her, never fear.'

'Sometimes, my darling, you look quite dangerous.'

'Come closer, and I'll remind you how dangerous I can be.'

Lady Aurora, elegant society beauty, lowered herself to giggle at this, as her husband kissed exactly the right spot on her neck.

***

The residents of Studham did not meet again until they were all ready for the evening, dressed for the carriage ride and waiting stiffly in the hall. Curtis had been there first, and Ianthe had complimented his appearance in evening wear. 'You look very handsome,' she said in a friendly fashion.

Curtis rejected the familiarity, answering, 'I suppose that you ladies are handsome too, but as mama suspected, you might be rather overdressed for your *positions*.' At Lady Richards' gasp, he flushed rather. But held his head up, ignoring them further.

'It is admirable, Mr Fox, that a young boy be guided by his mother's opinions and quote them,' said Ianthe in an even voice. Curtis looked at her for half a second, attempting a sneer, before she added, 'But a *man* should take responsibility for his own views and manners, don't you think?'

Fox had joined them, heard Ianthe's words and saw Curtis' inflamed face. His brother was, at least, ashamed. But Curtis face then took on a hard look, and he feigned ignoring Ianthe and the other ladies. Too set on his path, thought Fox, but still… Fox would think about the shame Ianthe had prompted Curtis to display.

Fox opened his mouth to say something now, but Ianthe took him to one side, 'How dreadful to have had only Lady Fox as a mama,' she whispered.

Fox stopped and thought, looking again at his brother. Because Curtis was fawned on, while he himself was ignored, Fox had always thought his brother blessed. But then he remembered the difference between the true warmth of his early life and the poisonous indulgence that marked Curtis'. Ianthe was looking up at him with those deep eyes, seeing his realisation.

It had been decided that two carriages would avoid a dreadful squeeze and presently they arrived before the open doors, one a smart modern travelling coach and another heavier vehicle from a different era, but that was nevertheless a handsome beast, polished for the occasion. Curtis handed his mama into the first of these and joined her, while the Richards and Ianthe Eames moved towards the second. Lord Fox stood undecided for a moment, having been stiffly avoiding the Richards' eyes as he stood in the hall. But he called after Curtis, 'As you protect your mama, I should accompany the ladies...' and moved in the direction of the other carriage.

The baron sat stiffly once in, barely nodding at the other occupants, looking out of the window into the twilight, his classical profile in relief, looking stern.

'Oh, dear Lord Fox,' said Lady Richards leaning forward to touch his knee, 'Do not fear! Ianthe explained everything!'

Fox was startled by the touch, the endearment (which he had not heard before and did not feel he deserved) and her words. He was afraid of just what Ianthe Eames might have said, for much of what she uttered was a complete mystery to him. However, as he looked across at the open, smiling faces of the Richards, and rather reticently to one side to Miss Eames, he relaxed a little. It was hard not to when three ladies were beaming at one. He still was not clear about the reason, but he gave a half smile for a tenth of a second, and was rewarded by Miss Sarah Richards saying, 'Thank you, my lord!' He nodded, still unsure what he was to be thanked for, but too fearful of the explanation to ask questions. He was being drawn into intimacy here, something he avoided at all costs, and he knew who he had to thank for that. He cast a glance of dislike in the direction of his left shoulder, but the woman only laughed. He could not bring himself to frown at the Richards, whose joy seemed to be in part made up of relaxation of a terrible tension. And after all, that Sarah Richards and her mother would put too much meaning on his rash words at breakfast had been his greatest fear. But Miss Richards, if she suspected his words were real, would now be looking at him in either disgust, or coldness, or on the other hand, maidenly modesty. She betrayed none of these but gave him instead the open trust of friendship. This was better than any alternative, he supposed, but he was not quite comfortable.

'Have you been to Audley before, my lord?' enquired Lady Richards comfortably.

'Yes, but not for many years. When I was a child we visited frequently. My own mother was intimate with the late marchioness.'

They talked of this and that for the rest of the journey, Lady Richards directing the conversation onto easy topics, and Fox relented his stiffness just a little, and became nearly polite.

***

Ianthe had been so amused by Fox's demeanour in the carriage that the cold looks from Curtis and Lady Fox earlier were banished. He had sat, looking particularly handsome in evening dress with its dazzling white waistcoat, black coat and fawn knee breeches, trying to look stern but merely looking terrified. Somehow, she had seen from the first time she had spoken to him, the pain in his fox-coloured eyes. He tried to be cold and unapproachable, but she had seen great fires banked down there. His rages had said it: here was a man of passion that had to burst out. No doubt he had other outlets in gentlemen's pursuits, but he tried to keep his emotions in check. Though she had played with him, she had known that he had twice approached her with kindness. He had meant to reassure her and then to close off again, in the same way he treated the Richards. But she had not chosen to let him retreat.

It had taken but a sharp fingernail to scratch at his great wall of protection. She watched as the two Richards ladies, having found the opening in his shell, opened it up further. He was trying not to give way even now, was wary and fearful. But Ianthe was determined that such a splendid man should not live a life so cut off from both others, and even himself.

He looked very handsome tonight, with his brown hair curling against his high collar, his usually serious face softening a little under Lady Richards' warmth and Sally's offer of friendship. Ianthe would continue to drag him from safety whether he liked it or not.

She thought, though, about the incident in the study when he had begged for her help, grasping her hands. Sometimes, when he was physically close to her, Ianthe had to acknowledge that Lord Fox might hold the whip hand. Near to him … well, she was no longer totally in control.

The whole party was looking splendid tonight, Ianthe thought now. Sally was in a charming green silk that enhanced her colouring and Ianthe had been moved to place a simple coronet of ivy and forest flowers in her rich brown hair. Lady Richards was dressed in white and silver, looking very pretty indeed. The girls had prevailed upon her to dispense with her cap and display the thick brown curls to advantage. Ianthe was wearing a claret coloured sarcenet, such a fine silk over a slim satin under dress. It was darker than the preferred English fashion for young ladies, but it suited her pale skin and dark curls admirably.

Ianthe caught a shy look that Lord Fox directed at Lady Richards when she had asked him a personal question and could have sworn that he was just a boy. The passionate, loving boy who had been hidden behind his wall, she thought. He would put up a fuss later, no doubt, would try again and again to push them away, but it was much too late. His fate was sealed.

She knew that her own interest in Fox was particular. She had not quite decided what it was. His eyes looked at her with more annoyance than admiration and that amused her. He offered her rescue, but she felt that it was he who needed it.

Chapter Nine

Dinner at Audley

The opulence of Audley, though less obvious in the twilight, nevertheless made Lady Richards gasp as the carriage bowled towards it. She was, Sally noted, vastly excited at her first social event since their arrival and looking as pretty as a girl in her best silver-trimmed evening gown. Lord Fox handed all three ladies out of the coach himself, and they entered the vast doors of Audley into a brilliantly lit grand hall, chattering their admiration for the marble floor, the vast chandelier, and the number of servants that the marquis had felt necessary to greet his guests. Lord Fox moved behind them, amused at their gaiety, but the presence of Lady Fox and her son in the Hall, newly divested of their outer wear, effectively stopped them. In a more subdued fashion, they handed their garments to the waiting attendants, overseen by a butler who they heard called Forrest, of such majestic corpulence that it was a mystery how he might perform his duties. He had the air, though, of ancient magnificence that went well with the marble hall. Ianthe's eyes danced when she caught Lady Richards' startled gaze.

Lady Fox did not even glance at the others, but Curtis gave them a cold nod, and the whole party was led towards the open door of great salon, decorated in the French style, and quite the prettiest room Sally had ever seen.

There were a number of people present, but the marquis himself came forward to greet them, wearing formal evening wear. His high shirt points grazed his chiselled jaw, the bronze hair was more strictly pomaded to look artfully casual, his hooded eyes lifting in a polite smile, and Sally heard her mother gasp. Or was it she?

Audley made his greetings to Lady Fox, with a nice mix of formality and openness, but was met by a cold response that seemed to affect him very little. He shook Curtis' hand, and when he met with a similar response to that of Her Ladyship, his eyes took on a cool amusement. He greeted Lord Edward next, and Fox was his usual contained self, the marquis more genuinely warm. Sally was beginning to note, however, that Lord Fox's reserved nature held no ire and believed, in observing the continued openness in the marquis' expression, that he knew this too. Audley now bowed to all the other ladies of the party and as one they responded, the marquis giving a particularly kind smile to her mother. His eyes had not met hers, and Sally was congratulating him silently. Perfectly politely ignoring her.

He went onto the introductions, and Sally could judge from his expression what he thought of each of his guests, even though his charming mask did not falter. The Misses Popper (thirty-five and forty respectively) and their papa had obviously been invited for Lady Fox's sake. The sisters, to Sally's amusement, alternated their faces into expressions of superiority (to Studham's poor relations) and obsequiousness (to the rest of the august company). The Poppers visited Studham often, Sally knew, as Her Ladyship enjoyed lording it over them (as vulgar parlance would have it) and as all three seemed to enjoy the same sour view of the world as Lady Fox herself. They were comfortably off, but were sufficiently below Lady Fox in rank as to make her really enjoy her superiority. Tonight, it rather decreased the air of ice that Her Ladyship had sought to bring to the party to have the plain Poppers instantly at her side. Mr Popper, a stout balding man of sixty, was oleaginous in his greeting to Her Ladyship and his daughters similarly deferential. Sally exchanged a quick glance with Ianthe and shared their amusement.

For the rest, there were two younger gentlemen, obviously friends of the marquis, a Mr Markham who had a pleasant open face and easy disposition that Sally liked, and his very handsome friend Lord Jeffries who, with his mass of brown curls and his bright blue eyes, looked more mischievous and daring. Both gentlemen, noted Sally, eyed Ianthe Eames with obvious admiration. The marquis' eyes beamed his appreciation of these two friends, and of a quiet gentleman, in his late thirties perhaps, who came forward quietly and who was introduced as Mr Oscar Steadman. Sally liked his calm face and his serious demeanour. He too was attractive, with brown hair that was swept severely from his long brow. He stepped back as soon as he was able, not a man to impose his personality. Sally thought he looked over to one side of her with a peculiarly arrested expression. No doubt another gentleman entranced by Ianthe.

An elegant blonde lady in silk turned out to be the widowed Lady Sophia Markham, evidently a trifle younger than her stepson's thirty years. It was evident that the marquis admired Lady Sophia's beauty, all large eyes and rosebud lips, with a kind of sophistication Sally knew she would never possess even when she might catch her up in age, perhaps some six or seven years hence. She blinked as the marquis exchanged the briefest of intimate glances with the lady. Sally felt Ianthe's glance upon her but did not meet it.

They sat down, and the appointment of the table was seen to be a masterpiece of planning. Lady Fox was given the honour of the seat to the end of the table, with Mr Popper and Curtis at either side. Then came the Popper ladies, and Her Ladyship's ice had been efficiently sealed off from the rest of the gathering, who were free to enjoy the evening as they pleased. Sally was seated between Mr Markham and Mr Steadman and was very pleased to be so. Ianthe was directly opposite, beside Lord Jeffries and Lord Fox. At the head of the table was the marquis, with Lady Sophia his amusing companion at one side and a Mrs Rosling at the other. Both were handsome women, but Sally could see that he was a friend of one and rather more to the other, who gave him intimate looks. Sally's mother seemed to have made friends with her dinner companions, too, for she was the other side of Steadman and flanked by the young vicar, Mr Bart, on the other, with Miss Bart and the curate opposite. The table was a merry one, even Lord Fox being involved in some sporting conversations, and some laughter about a bet that had gone wrong for the marquis. He told the story against himself with ease, protesting that his horse had strained a fetlock and that his skill as a rider could not be doubted. The gentlemen joshed him — Fox being drawn into it too.

When the ladies left for the withdrawing room, there was a convivial air, and a general decision to pay little but the politest attention to Lady Fox's frost.

When the gentlemen arrived again, the marquis made the round of the guests, Sally noting his change of pace in speaking to each, his smiles changing from social politeness to great good humour depending on the recipient. He stopped at Ianthe and Sally, and said quietly to Ianthe, 'You must ride tomorrow. I brook no opposition.' His eyes were playful, and Ianthe responded in kind.

'I have no objection. But why tomorrow?'

'You will see. And you *must* both breakfast here.'

'I can make some excuses for us tonight,' said Ianthe conspiratorially, after a thought. 'Mmmm. Did Her Ladyship have the turbot?'

'I shall enquire of Grayson,' said the marquis, matching her air.

Ianthe smiled and turned to Lord Jeffries, who had approached, and Audley leaned a little farther towards Sally for the briefest of seconds, not meeting her eye, but looking over her shoulder.

'If you wish me to ignore you, Miss Richards, you should not regard me so all evening.'

Sally gasped, but he had already gone, and a sound like a laugh moved off with him. She was shocked to acknowledge that he was right, her eyes had really sought him all night — but only to observe what Ianthe had called his famous social dexterity. It had fascinated her, and she had been even more fascinated to know that she had been able to see what was beneath each polite or charming expression and descry, as she believed, his true feeling in each case. Now Audley seemed to be teasingly suggesting that she was another of his admirers. She took a teacup from Mr Markham and chatted amiably with him for some minutes but was inwardly seething. Her embarrassment that Audley could really believe what he suggested distracted her and made her even more cross. The thought that he only did so to annoy her was even worse. As she drank her tea her eyes sought his as he flirted with Lady Sophia Markham. He looked over, and she glared at him before turning away to laugh at something Mr Markham had said about the Duchess of Rutland's Ball, which they had both attended, though they had not then been acquainted. She responded merrily to Mr Markham, and then glanced back at the marquis, whose eyes she had felt upon her. This would never do. If her mama saw, she would certainly make a wrong assumption. Sally glanced at her mama in case she had noticed but was relieved that she was being entertained in the group comprising Jeffries, Ianthe and Steadman. Sally was tempted to give Audley back his just deserts for his impudence earlier, but she dare not glare again at him now lest her mama see. She could hardly wait until tomorrow to do so.

As they gained the carriage home, all three ladies sighed in contentment. 'It was a lovely evening!' said Lady Richards, for them all.

'All is set for the ride tomorrow,' Ianthe informed her.

'You ride at Audley again?' asked Lord Edward. 'There is no need. I can have your mare brought to our stables.'

'And poor Sally?'

'I'm sure there is a horse suitable-' said Lord Fox.

'—for a lady? Not you, *too*,' said Sally aggrieved.

'My love—' protested Lady Richards, but Fox looked amused.

'That won't do,' said Ianthe with decision. 'Lady Fox will hear of it and will be displeased that her orders have been disobeyed—'

'It is for me to say—' began Fox.

'Yes, yes,' interrupted Ianthe, 'but there is no sense in provoking Her Ladyship over every little thing, and it is Sally who would have to deal with the unpleasantness, not you.' His Lordship gulped. 'Anyway, Audley wants us to breakfast there tomorrow for some reason, and so I have already begun making excuses, saying to Her Ladyship that Sally and I have stomach cramps — suspecting that the turbot was bad, you know.'

'Oh, so that was why you asked the marquis if she ate the fish?' remarked Sally, impressed.

'Indeed. And fortunately, she had not.' Ianthe looked at Lord Fox. 'Why are you frowning?'

'I shall accompany you tomorrow.'

Ianthe laughed. 'Because of Audley's shocking reputation?'

'Every handsome man has a shocking reputation, I find,' said Lady Richards musingly. 'But I noticed that the marquis flirted with Lady Sophia with great decorum. Never over the line. And the single young ladies,' here she glanced at Sally and Ianthe both, 'he did not mind at all.' She sighed, a little sadly. 'Of course, he does not wish to give rise to speculation. But it *is* a pity.' Ianthe and Sally shared an amused look. 'I was not previously aware of how *excruciatingly* handsome he is.'

'Excruciatingly?' laughed Ianthe.

'A figure such as he was built to cause pain to the weaker sex,' said Lady Richards with certainty.

'I do not find him particularly handsome,' remarked Fox, a trifle sullen. Three sets of eyes regarded him with withering pity and Her Ladyship resumed.

'Such manners! And his handling of your step-mama!' Lady Richards gazed guiltily at Fox. 'Oh, I beg your pardon, my lord.'

'I do not understand. *How* did he deal with her precisely?'

'Why,' said Ianthe, looking at him in amusement, 'he cut her off at the start.'

'He did?'

'Oh, yes,' said Lady Richards. 'Did you not notice?'

'Has he been a soldier?' joined in Sally. 'It was carried out with military precision.'

'*I* saw no precision. Did he even speak to my stepmother beyond the greeting?'

'No, of course not. He foresaw the tactics of the enemy and diverted them from the beginning.'

'I do not see…'

'He invited the Poppers!' said Lady Richards.

A look of dawning enlightenment struck His Lordship. 'He did that on purpose?'

'Why? Did you think them his intimates?' laughed Ianthe. 'Yes, it was quite brilliant! It stopped Lady Fox conversing widely and entertained her, all at once.'

'And whatever unpleasant thing she had to say—' Sally looked conscious, 'Oh excuse me, your lordship-'

'We're past that,' he replied, frankly. 'Let us agree that Lady Fox is a lady of … of uncertain temper. We all live in the same house and you know how we are fixed.' We, he thought. It was strange to be a "we".

Sally sighed in relief. 'Well, whatever unpleasant thing she had to say she could say to the

Poppers and the rest of us did not have to hear any of it.'

'And you think that was his intention?' said Fox, amazed.

'I do. I was quite looking forward to his dealing with Lady Fox's acid remarks — as a tutorial to *you*, you know, who lose your temper too easily,' continued Ianthe breezily. Sally and her mother exchanged looks, and then gazed down at their toes as Fox shot her a glance of dislike. 'But Audley jumped over the fence neatly without the need to engage. Really, it was most accomplished. I would imagine that the Poppers must have been astounded to receive the invitation.'

'Oh, it *was* their first visit to Audley. Mildred Popper told me so,' Sally said.

'You see? It was not likely that he sought their acquaintance. They are not the most convivial of companions.'

'Indeed not.' Fox remarked. 'I leave the vicinity as soon as Jenkins tells me they are visiting.'

This was his first confidence to them, and he blushed slightly as Lady Richards replied. 'Quite right, Lord Fox! *I* should have escaped myself if I had the power.'

Fox seemed struck by this. His manner caused silence, as the ladies waited for him to speak. 'I do not at all see why you are not free to do as you wish in my home. You are my relatives and my guests.'

'Yes, you *do* see,' chided Ianthe, but gently, 'you have just not considered it before.'

He began to see now, it was true. He had been so wrapped up in his own dispute with the other two members of his family that he had used the presence of the Richards as a diversionary tactic. People who stood between him and the other Foxes. He had not considered their feelings in all of this at all. To them he had been scrupulously polite but had left them to cope with whatever his mother dealt out to them in private without a thought. He had kept to himself and expected the servants to make provisions for them, never considering that Lady Fox would make it her business to limit those provisions.

'Do you have fires lit in your rooms?' he said suddenly.

'Eh?' asked Sally Richards, with less than usual erudition. Ianthe was looking amused. 'Well, no. But the weather is—'

'I shall give orders for fires to be lit in the morning and evening. And if you should have need of it, do not hesitate to send for coals at any hour.'

'There is really no need...' began Lady Richards.

'I insist, ma'am. I have been lax in my hospitality and I apologise. It is my cursed temper that prevents me from ... I am sorry, your ladyship, not to have seen what I ought.'

'My dear boy, how kind!'

'Edward,' he instructed her.

'I really could not call you...'

'We have shared the best part of two summers together, ma'am, and known each other years before that. Give me leave to call you Cousin Emma.'

'I should be delighted.'

'Shall you call me by my given name, sir?' asked Sally, amused at Lord Fox's obvious guilt.

'Sarah.' He laughed, embarrassed. 'I shall attempt it if you do not mind it.'

'Call me Sally, sir. All my friends do.'

He blushed again at the word "friends", then looked a little wicked. 'It will terrify Lady Fox.'

Ianthe said with relish, 'Won't it just? I believe Studham is going to begin to be a much happier place to live in. What shall you call *me*, sir?'

'Miss Eames,' he said shortly. 'Our acquaintance is not of long standing,' he added with dislike.

'Oh, *dear* Edward!' His Lordship blanched at Ianthe's dulcet tones. 'We are family after all. You may call me Ianthe.' She batted her eyelids at him sweetly.

'As well call you a vixen!' said Fox shortly.

Ianthe put a hand to her bosom in shock. 'The fox's mate? Really, sir! I believe you are flirting with me.'

Fox looked shocked and astounded both,

but the free laughter of all three of the ladies warmed him a little. 'I do not flirt,' he said with an attempt at his old gruff voice, but his amusement leaked through.

'It is a skill you are still to gain, it is true,' said Ianthe. 'Watch Audley if you wish to see a master at work.'

Fox made a dismissive noise and then said to Ianthe, 'And does he flirt with you?'

'Oh, always! It is his habit, you know, but he does not really mean it. He does it to provoke me.'

'He should not.'

'But because I am his friend, he does. He cannot otherwise practise his skills on young ladies for fear of reprisals.'

'Nevertheless, I shall go with you to Audley in the morning.'

'If you must,' shrugged Ianthe with impolite lack of enthusiasm. She had a thought. 'Actually, it might be better. As we are to return *after* breakfast, you can create a diversion so that we ladies can re-enter the side door without being discovered, should Lady Fox have risen.'

'Don't you notice, Lord F— ... Cousin Edward, that Ianthe seems to turn the littlest things into an adventure?' smiled Lady Richards fondly.

'I hesitate to disagree, Cousin Emma, but I believe that is more likely disaster than adventure,' said Fox, and closed his eyes to lay back on the squabs while the ladies exchanged smiles.

Chapter Ten

The Third Ride and the Secret Breakfast

Fox rode over to Audley before them the next morning, and so both he and the marquis were mounted before Ianthe Eames had handed the groom the gig reins and sprung down. Both Purity and Sapphire were ready-saddled, and Lord Edward had the good fortune to witness Miss Richards mount the tall horse with remarkable ease. It was evident that both ladies were excellent horsewomen, but Sally was soon seen to be exceptional.

His Lordship, here to play the proprieties, he'd thought, somehow got drawn into the ease of the other three. Audley who, although a few years older, he still remembered as a boy, displayed his sardonic humour and charm by turns, and the face he turned to Fox was one of an old companion with whom he had climbed trees and swum as a child. Fox, whose stiff air did not seem to have much starch left in it these last few days, soon relented and enjoyed the ride, still keeping at Ianthe Eames' side in case his first suspicion might be proved correct. Ianthe and the marquis did spar, but Audley seemed perfectly happy to be ousted from Ianthe's side to gallop ahead with Sally Richards. The pair waited for them several times, and strangely Miss Richards seemed to display neither maidenly shyness nor the servile timidity she displayed with Lady Fox.

'Miss R— Sally seems at ease with the marquis. I find it surprising.'

'Oh, that is because on the first day he mounted her on the mare he keeps for his grandmama.'

Fox, having watched Sally ride, with mounting admiration, laughed. 'I can imagine her outrage!'

'Yes, and it had put them at their ease, you know. Audley dislikes the fawning that his rank often excites in others and Sally was too annoyed to fawn.'

'I see,' said Fox. He looked at Ianthe's face as they walked the horses over a particularly pitted path. 'I think, though, that there is something bothering you in all this.'

Ianthe shot him a dimpled smile and raised her brows. 'I should not have suspected you of such acuity of feeling, Edward.'

'Yes,' he said, bored. 'It is new.'

'How was I?' asked the marquis while they awaited the others.

Sally turned to him. 'Last night? You were splendid, my lord! Inviting the Poppers was a move of a general. We were all in admiration in the carriage ride home.'

'You know that is not what I refer to. Did I ignore you with sufficient civility?'

'My mother was suitably sad that you did not pay the unmarried ladies much attention.'

'So, I carried out my mission?'

'Admirably.'

'I am relieved. It was unexpectedly difficult, you know.'

'It was? How so?'

'As I predicted, I was afraid to give you offence, now that we are friends—'

'How silly, when I asked it of you.'

'But asking, and feeling a slight when I carried out your orders, might have been a very different thing.'

'It was not,' lied Sally. When Lady Sophia had laughed or Mrs Rosling had touched his arm, she had felt something that might be described as a slight. She had wanted him to look at her in those moments, to exchange an ironic glance as he did on the rides, to acknowledge her, too. But of course, she could not tell him so.

'Good. But there was another reason that it was difficult.'

'Oh yes?'

'Yes. You looked so charming in that green silk gown that it was hard for my gaze not to seek you out, and my eyes not to tell you.'

Sally's back stiffened. 'Is this the fabled Audley charm, my lord? I fear I do not favour it.' She turned her horse and moved towards the others, a flush on her cheeks.

Audley rode behind them back towards the stables and Ianthe held back to join him.

'*What* did you do to Sally?' she said directly.

Audley's face was cold and unmoving. 'She thinks she has just been the recipient of my "fabled charm" and has taken offence. In fact, I used no charm at all but just the impetuous tongue of a halfling.'

'But why?'

'I have no notion. I have asked myself the same question since she rode off in a pet.' He paused. 'Or perhaps it was that she came to my house for the first time and I was not even allowed to treat her as I ought. It rankled, and I tried to say so, but instead I spewed out words like a dimwit.'

'What words?'

'I told her that she looked charming in green silk and that it was hard for my eyes not to follow her.'

'*Audley!* I told you not to try to move her only because she is not your admirer.'

'Ianthe! If I were really trying to flirt with

her would I have done it so ill?'

'Then I repeat my first question. *Why*?'

'I do not know.'

'Well, until you find out, you had best not talk to her. She looks set to refuse to at any rate. You may have ruined everything.'

He put a hand on Ianthe's arm. 'Help me! I cannot recant it. But you could help her take it lightly so that we can be on the same footing.'

'I will not help you play with her,' Ianthe said warningly. 'I foresaw this and said so. Do you know how delicate is the line the Richards must balance? I have heard that Sally was set to accept a gentleman's offer last Season, all to avoid being at Studham once more.'

'Who was the gentleman?'

'Eastman, I think, one Sir Ralph Eastman.'

'*That* dull dog?' said Audley, disgusted.

'Sally described him as boring, but she was *still* prepared to marry him for her mama's sake. This is their predicament. And now you, Audley, with no serious thought at all, must flirt with her.'

'I did not mean to, I tell you.'

'Well, it is your own fault if she refuses a ride tomorrow.'

'Don't let her, Ianthe. Please.'

'Why do you care whether my friend rides Sapphire?'

'I do not know that either. I wish to be better acquainted with her, but I can hardly pursue that given her family situation. She is too ripe for tittle-tattle.'

'A middling sort of woman?'

'Middling? No. But too good to be made sport of.'

'Then do what you normally do with young ladies — and keep away. It will be safer all round.'

'I know, but cannot we just go on as before? I want her to be angry at me again.'

'It is too dangerous, Audley. It is a trap for her.'

'If I think there is a chance that our friendly rides will become anything to hurt her, I shall retreat at once, I promise.'

Ianthe sighed, dubious. 'I believe you mean well, my friend. But I am not convinced that you know her *or* yourself enough to judge.'

'Then *you* will be the judge, my dear. If we ride tomorrow, you can tell me if I step outside the boundaries of easy friendship. I will abide by your decision.'

'Well,' said Ianthe, 'It may be out of our hands.'

Audley looked ahead at the figure of Sally Richards, already far ahead, and said seriously, 'That would be a pity.' Ianthe, watching him, was taken aback. She saw him shake it off as he added, in his usual sardonic tone, 'When a man of my age makes such a mull of it, it is only what I deserve. We should find breakfast now, and with it your surprise.'

Ianthe rode on with a thoughtful expression. It seemed to her that the marquis was more affected than even he knew. She must, of course, protect Sally from his indecision, but she determined to give them both a little push if she saw further evidence of Audley's feelings. The trouble was, for all his reputation, he avoided destroying the hearts of young ladies at all costs. When she was sure the stupid compliment that he had given her friend was not just a product of his pique because Sally alone did not fall at his feet, Ianthe might act. How, she did not know, but that never concerned her greatly. Ianthe was a young lady schooled in the art of spotting opportunities and acting on them for all her adventurous life.

***

It was a very different Sally Richards that dismounted her horse, thought Fox. Earlier this morning she had been relaxed and happy, and now she was stiff and formal in a way that Fox had not seen before. He, who would normally have ignored such a thing had he even noticed, now felt impelled to say, 'Did Audley say anything to upset you, Miss R— ... Sally?'

'Oh no ... Edward, he merely complimented me on my dress of last evening,' answered Sally, a trifle too brightly.

'I see,' Fox said, sounding perplexed. There

was nothing in this, surely? But he felt the lack of the presence of Ianthe Eames to explain it to him. 'Are you sure you do not want me to say something to Audley?' He asked quietly.

Sally was grateful, but embarrassed. As Audley dismounted, she said to him, to ease Fox's suspicions,'Might I wash my hands before breakfast?'

'Certainly,' replied Audley. 'This way, Miss Richards.' He began to lead her towards the house.

As Ianthe dismounted, Fox whispered, 'Why has Sally become so stiff with Audley when he only complimented her dress?'

'That is because,' Ianthe whispered back, 'she would much rather he insulted her.'

'I do not understand females,' Fox sighed, regarding Sally's back.

'No, Edward dear, that is quite apparent.'

'Stop calling me that!'

'Edward? I thought we had agreed upon it!'

'We did not. But we might as well since the Richards and I ... I meant the other part. I know you do not find me endearing, and it will give others quite the wrong notion.'

'Do not worry, I shall only say so when we are alone, and only because it pleases me so much to annoy you, Edward dear.'

'Someone,' Fox said, with gritted teeth, 'should have schooled you in manners a long time ago.'

Ianthe laughed, and Fox looked down on her shining face with a look of astonishment. How could this little thing have changed his life so much in just a few short days? He was insulting a lady, on intimate terms with the Richards, visiting Audley and tacitly agreeing to deceive his stepmother. He found himself worrying about Sally Richards' feelings, too. It was all most uncomfortable for a man who had cut himself off from all but the most necessary relations with other humans.

Fox moved off and it was some steps before he found that Ianthe was not behind him. He turned back and saw that she had led Sapphire to the mounting block and was pulling herself up, much to the restive horse's annoyance. The groom at Sapphire's head was struggling, but Ianthe managed to seat herself just as Fox arrived. She was demanding the reins when Fox jumped onto the mounting box and grasped her waist.

Ianthe looked at him, astonished and a little breathless. His face was inches from hers. 'Stay still!' he demanded.

Audley and Sally Richards, stopped by the commotion, turned to see the scene. Audley's brows rose as Fox grasped Ianthe to him with one arm, removed her foot from the stirrup with the other, and fairly yanked her off the horse.

'Do you want to kill yourself?' Fox said, putting her down beside him on the block. This was a ridiculous balancing act, and after a second of realisation that he was holding her to him, Fox jumped down.

'He is too strong for you and you know it.' He said it in a quieter tone, waiting for her angry response.

Audley and Sally waited, too, sure that Ianthe would trounce him.

But Ianthe stood, still breathless it seemed. She gazed down at Fox, then leaned a hand on his shoulder to get down from the block. 'Thank you,' was all she said, but it appeared to rob Fox of breath too. The baron turned and went off abruptly.

Sally heard her say to herself, satisfied, 'That silenced him. There's more than one way to deal with a man, I suppose.' But gazing at Ianthe, still stopped for a moment, she believed that her friend was not displaying signs of victory, but confusion.

On the way to the house, Audley attempted anew to win over the stiff figure of Sally Richards.

'How was Sapphire this morning?' he began politely.

'As you saw, my lord,' she answered without turning her head to him.

'And are you still angry with me?' This was said in the tone of a schoolboy hoping for forgiveness from his mama.

'Of course not!' Sally responded brightly. 'What woman would be offended by such a charming compliment from the noble Marquis of Audley?'

'Miss Richards—'

'Shall I return it, sir?' Finally, she looked at him. 'Last night to see the noble marquis in evening wear was to behold my dream,' said Sally clasping her hands to her bosom histrionically.

'Stop it!' he threatened.

'I fear my fluttering heart will never recover.' She continued, one hand over it.

'You have made your point. I was a chuckle-headed nodcock to have opened my mouth. Forgive me.'

'You have spoilt everything,' Sally added, coming down from the boughs and into a mere child's whine.

'I am aware of that,' Audley said seriously, 'and deeply sorry.'

She reverted to the high-handed manner. 'My noble marquis is famous for his dalliances. I should be flattered that you play with me so, of course.'

'Let us call it that. A habit of flirting with young ladies. And from a man who has such vanity that he wished to see, Ianthe informs me, the one lady who did not "fall at my feet" smile at me. It may even be true, and I am sorry for it.'

'Now I can never ride Sapphire again, and for that I wish to *strike* you right now.' Sally was aware that she was the most impolite that she had ever been in her life, but sullen rage possessed her.

'Let us walk into the trees and you can slap me twice if you wish,' he suggested. 'I shall brave it well. And then you can ride Sapphire again.'

'You think I *wouldn't* strike you, my noble marquis?' fired back Sally.

'Stop calling me "my noble marquis" for the sake of my temper. I have already agreed to be slapped, for I deserve it. And I *know* you would dare.' He looked down into her flashing eyes and changed his voice to a coax. 'Just come back tomorrow — because you haven't quite finished insulting me. You will think of even better ripostes during the day and can come afresh at me tomorrow.'

Something like a laugh escaped her. She turned to him and saw a sort of shy hope in his eyes. 'I haven't been insulting you, I have been *complimenting* you.'

'And most uncomfortable I found it. That showed me!'

She smiled then. 'Don't do it again. I am not equipped for such a game.'

'I will only say unpleasant things from now on. Come back to ride tomorrow.'

'If I do, it is for Sapphire alone,' she warned him. She moved off, head held high, and Ianthe caught him up.

'I have decided that I will do my best to

help Sally come back for another ride.'

'No need. Her temper has done the trick and I think we shall fare better. For Sapphire's sake.'

Ianthe giggled. 'You should be grateful that her love of the horse outweighs her dislike of you.'

'Oh I am. She is so-' the amusement in his voice was genuine, but Ianthe cut him short.

'Enough of that, Audley. If she overhears another good word from you, you will never see her again.'

'I know it.' He laughed suddenly. 'How did I get myself into this absurd situation? Oh, I remember, it is the Ianthe effect. Wherever you go, chaos ensues.'

'I did nothing but introduce you, Audley. The rest of this absurdity you managed yourself.'

***

The charming room where breakfast was laid out contained a surprise indeed for Ianthe Eames. An elegant figure of a slender man in his forties and his even more elegant lady in a slender yellow gown embellished with inches of colourful French embroidery, her hair plaited twisted and coiled on her head in the most masterly coiffure Sally Richards had ever seen. The gentleman smiled lazily and the beautiful lady, whom Sally assumed was his wife, beamed as Ianthe ran to her.

'Lady Aurora!' Her Ladyship had caught both of her hands, but Ianthe leaned forward to salute both cheeks with a kiss, in the French familial fashion. She whispered into Her Ladyship's ear. 'Don't be surprised at what I do next!'

They pulled apart and Lady Aurora smiled at her, 'My dear Ianthe!'

Audley was smiling, enjoying the surprise he had set for Ianthe, and Lord Fox was looking stunned. This level of affectionate display was not at all what he was used to. Then, Ianthe Eames turned to the gentleman who was laughing down on her and threw herself into his embrace. 'Dear Mr Fenton!'

With some aplomb, the gentleman returned her embrace, and was not surprised when she whispered at him, as near to his ear as her stature permitted (though she stood on tiptoe) 'I have a problem I need to discuss with you. I am so glad you have come. But not now.' Fenton pulled her back and looked down at her. He saw laughter in her eyes, but concern too, and he gave the tiniest of nods and tried to imbue his smile with reassurance. What he said aloud, for the sake of the frowning Lord Fox, was, 'My dear Ianthe. It seems not so long since I dandled you as a baby.'

Fox said, 'But did you not just see her in town, sir? I thought she had stayed with you some days.'

Mr Wilbert Fenton was unfazed. 'Oh, she

did, my boy. But gentlemen of my age are given to sentimentality.' There seemed, Fox thought, not a hint of sentimentality on that sardonic face. The dandy continued, 'I was a particular friend of Ianthe's father for most of her life.'

'So I understand, sir,' said Lord Fox, with meaning.

Sally was introduced, and the whole party sat down to breakfast. Some pleasantries about the Fentons' journey from London and the morning rides at Audley were discussed, and the marquis was amused to hear Miss Richards enthuse about Sapphire's appearance, disposition and strength, which the Fentons listened to without a blink. 'I am sorry,' she finally ended, 'I am rather fond of horses.'

'An admirable trait in a woman,' said Mr Fenton smoothly. He had seen the marquis' amusement as he had listened to the young girl and his knowing sense was aroused, so he added with devilry, 'Do you not agree, Audley?'

Audley was trapped. He wished to agree with his usual suavity, but he dared not, lest the delicate armistice with Miss Richards was disturbed. He said instead, 'I do not think you have tried the plum jam, sir.'

Mr Fenton's eyes glittered, but he took it, saying merely, 'I shall do so now.'

'I'm afraid that we shall have to leave you sooner than we'd wish today, but please feel free to call on Miss Eames at Studham,' said Lord Fox.

Then he became conscious and said, 'That is—'

Ianthe twinkled at Wilbert Fenton, leaning forward confidentially. 'He means to warn you that this is a *secret* breakfast.'

'It *is*?' asked Lady Aurora, seeming pleased. 'From whom, pray?'

'Everyone but us,' answered Ianthe.

'I can see that you are up to your old tricks again, Ianthe,' sighed Fenton. 'What now?'

Lord Fox looked tense, but Ianthe replied, 'Nothing that need concern you, dear Mr Fenton.'

Fenton addressed Sally. 'You poor girl. Has Ianthe caused many ructions since she arrived at Studham? I am sorry for you.'

'Oh, please do not be, sir,' laughed Sally. 'It has been wonderfully exciting since she arrived. For instance, I have never been to a Secret Breakfast before.'

Fenton laughed. 'And you, Fox? Have you found it all *wonderfully exciting*?'

'Hardly that, sir. My world has been rather upended.'

He looked a little grim when he said this, and Ianthe protested. 'I have done nothing without your permission, Edward.' Audley and Fenton exchanged a look — *Edward*? 'Well most of it, anyway,' Ianthe added honestly.

'I hate to disagree with you Ianthe, but I cannot recall when or how I gave permission for many of the things you have done.'

'The Ianthe effect!' said Audley. 'I'm afraid

to tell you, my friend, that it will only get worse. To a child raised in subterfuge and plotting, the outrageous is mother's milk.'

Fox looked suitably afraid, but said, with a glance at a clock on a side table. 'We must depart for now, I'm afraid.'

As the Studham party took their leave, the Fentons told Ianthe they would drive over to visit again this afternoon. Ianthe looked out of the window, considering. 'It is a fine day. Did you travel by coach, sir?'

'We did,' answered Fenton.

'Well then Audley, you shall have to lend them an open carriage that seats four,' ordered Ianthe briskly.

'I shall,' answered the marquis with servility.

'And remember. We have not had this breakfast,' Ianthe lectured with a definite gesture of both hands.

Lady Aurora put her hand over her heart gamely. 'I shall keep this breakfast secret until my dying day.'

Ianthe smiled brightly while Fox took her elbow and jerked her towards the door, rather as though she were a disobedient child.

'Well!' said Lady Aurora, left with much to chew over in this short time, 'I came because I was afraid that Ianthe was being made miserable by the Fighting Foxes, but I quite see that she is as dangerous as you have told me.'

'She has embroiled Fox in her plans at least, though he does not know his way as yet,' said Audley, cautiously, 'but one look at Lady Fox and her impudent son does not suggest a happy home.'

'I am glad the Richards are there too,' said Lady Aurora. 'I have met Lady Richards once, and she is a most pleasant woman. And Miss Sarah Richards is delightful.'

'But the types to be cowed by the frightful Lady Fox, I fear. I believe they must stay at Studham until they return to their friends the Houstens' place in Surrey. They have lived with them since the death of Sir Guy Richards.'

'I guessed as much. Who would stay with the Foxes if they had the choice?' said Fenton.

'Should we take Ianthe back with us?' wondered Lady Aurora.

'I do not think she would come, until the Richards leave at least. *They* are both too good-natured to deal with Her Ladyship. Judging by today, Ianthe is attached to them now.'

'That is good. She can come to us at any time and so I shall tell her. And I depend on you, Audley, to let us know what she does not *wish* to tell us. You shall have to be with her often to make sure she is not too cast down by it all.'

'I shall do so, never fear. She rides here every morning at present and if that were to cease, trust me to find a way.' He smiled. 'She has already worked a miracle. The two houses of Studham and Audley did not visit for seventeen years, because of some dispute between our fathers. A pity — because I was quite fond of Edward Fox when we were boys. Since Ianthe came, we have had a dinner here at Audley.'

'She is amazing! But she has not long lost her father, and we must support her spirits at all costs.'

'The little whirlwind will more likely support ours,' said Wilbert Fenton with his lazy laugh.

Chapter Eleven

The Fighting Foxes Give Offence

Fox had had something else to think of when they returned to Studham. The upright French maid with the frightening eyebrows had magically appeared in the hall to take Ianthe's hat and whip, and Fox witnessed a hand squeeze that they exchanged. 'The Fentons are come!' he heard Ianthe say in an under voice. The maid's face hardly moved, and she had followed Ianthe upstairs. It reminded him of the other lowered voice exchange he had heard today. Between Wilbert Fenton and Ianthe.

'And Cherie?' that gentleman had said.
Ianthe had replied, 'Well. But determined on her course.'   Fenton had nodded, as though resigned.
Why would Fenton ask after the maid?
Fox had already asked Jenkins about the maid, only because of a look of affection that he

had seen Ianthe give her. She was only a little known below stairs, the butler explained since miss suffered from night terrors the maid lived in a truckle bed in her room. He had coughed as he added, 'Miss gave instructions that the maid, who has been with her since her extreme youth it seems, is in delicate health. She must take exercise for some hours outside, Miss Eames instructed. And miss also asked that she be allowed the gig to complete errands for the young lady.'

This was unusual, but Fox had nodded. 'As our guest requests,' was all he had said to this.

'And miss asked that since her wardrobe is so large another maid might be assigned to help look after it — and do the heavier work, like the laundering.' Jenkins had permitted himself a grim smile. 'I think that the French maid was most upset about that, as it curtailed her proper duties.'

Fox had responded with a trenchant 'Mmm'. He had thought a little. The maid was probably the only connection to Ianthe's past. It mattered not at all to him if she laboured hard or not.

'The expense of the maid,' said Jenkins carefully, 'will not fall on Studham, your lordship.'

'Why on earth should I care for that?'

'Lady Fox did. And when she mentioned it to Miss Eames, the young lady told Her Ladyship that Cherie had already been paid for the year in advance.'

'In advance?' queried Fox.

'The young lady said it was the French custom for old family retainers, your lordship.' Jenkins coughed again. His master raised an eyebrow.

'And?' said Fox, recognising the cough.

'And Miss Eames even offered to pay some shillings for the maid's keep. To relieve Her Ladyship's mind of care, the young lady said.'

'Drat the girl! Must she always set my stepmother at odds?'

The butler's expression, before he had melted away had been clear. *Pot calling kettle black*, it had said.

For the rest, Fox seemed somewhat relieved by the morning's ride. He could not quite like the intimacy between Ianthe and Audley, but it had seemed something other than admiration. Had it been, Fox might have reminded the marquis that Miss Eames was under his protection.

Fox was aware that Ianthe Eames was a beauty. Sometimes, when he saw her turn her head, or when she had shaken him with a dazzling smile, or regarded him warmly with her brown velvet eyes, it had affected him too, just as he had seen it affect the male population of the dinner party at Audley. This was why, as someone now responsible for her, and someone who did not trust in her discretion at all, he had needed to accompany her this morning. It was natural, and his duty as her relative. If Audley were genuinely interested in becoming her suitor, then there was nothing to object to, Fox supposed, except his reputation as a womaniser. This was based on relations of another order, though, and Fox knew many men who changed their behaviours after marriage. No. Audley as a suitor was one thing. Audley as a flirt was another.

But there seemed no need to intervene, since Audley's behaviour seemed friendly rather than seductive. Ianthe was up to something with the Fentons though, Fox had noted that much. How her scheme could affect his peace he could not imagine, but he was nearly sure it would.

It was a constant headache now, wondering what next Ianthe Eames would get him involved in.

***

Later that day, Curtis Fox, closeted with his brother in his study where he had been summoned, looked sulky.

'I heard at the stables that you have ordered the gig to be put to for three o'clock,' said Lord Fox, 'Where are you going?'

'What business is it of yours where I go?' replied Curtis, petulantly.

'None at all, unless you are going to the meet in Milford,' said the elder.

Curtis flushed. 'It is still no affair of yours

if I am!'

Lord Fox strode over to the driving coat that Curtis had thrown over a chair when his brother had yelled at him in the hall to come to the study. The fair head followed his brother's movements as Lord Fox searched two pockets and brought out his brother's leather purse and threw it violently on the desk.

'Do not,' Fox said threateningly, 'gamble more than is in this in that cockpit, or I will peck you to death myself.'

Curtis' grey eyes met his brother's russet ones, and he shook with anger. 'I hate you, Edward.'

'Do so if you wish. I am telling you frankly that if you bet what you do not have once more, I shall not pay the difference.'

'It is just as likely I shall win!' said Curtis. 'Who are you to interfere with a gentleman's pleasure? Just because you are so deuced stuffy yourself.'

'I do not care how you find your pleasure, just know that I will no longer frank it. It is a last warning, Curtis.'

'I shall go, and I shall not lose!' shouted Curtis.

Lord Fox raised his voice back at him. 'Do what you wish, you recalcitrant puppy, but no talk of scandal, no tears from your mama will move me this time. *I will not pay*.'

Curtis gave a great angry laugh. 'I find you

insupportable! Have I asked you to pay anything? Am I here as your supplicant? I am merely going to take in a sporting event five miles away with half the other gentlemen in the area.'

'The most likely result will be that you will lose even what is in your purse and then you will sulk and complain that you cannot find any entertainment and demand more funds. Possibly through your mama, and that will not work anymore.' He glared at Curtis, whose pale face was now tinged with purple, whose red rimmed eyes (from a joust with the brandy bottle last night) were bulging. 'Whatever the pressure, I shall not deprive the estate of one more penny because of your recklessness.'

'This is ridiculous!' shouted Curtis, full of righteous anger. 'I have done nothing. Why do you always undermine me? What is this hatred you have of me? Because I was Papa's favourite? Does that still rankle? Damn it, Edward, it is five years since he passed.'

Lord Fox clenched his jaw and glared at him coldly. 'Not a penny, Curtis.'

'You are already planning to marry and cut me out of the succession. Mama says so,' goaded Curtis. 'Do you really think Sally Richards a match for my mama? How *could you* choose a woman like her? She is practically on the shelf. And Mama says she has no dignity whatsoever.'

Edward Fox lost his temper entirely. 'You will not speak so of Miss Richards. She is my guest!'

Curtis took a step back at the booming voice and watched as Lord Fox came out from behind his desk once more. But having gotten a rise from his opponent, he could not resist another gibe. 'Oh, so you protect that beggar living here for free, while you ignore your own brother?'

Lord Edward grabbed a handful of waistcoat and glared down at Curtis. The young man had been here many times before. Edward threatened him, but he would not take advantage of his superior size and strength to really strike him, so although Curtis now shook, he laughed in his brother's face. 'If you find beggar-girls to your liking, you had best pursue the ravishing one. I'm sure Miss Eames is longing to be mistress of Studham. Or perhaps not. She might do better. She flirted shamelessly with the marquis at Audley!'

Fox hit him.

***

Lady Richards, Sally and Ianthe were in the hall, having divested themselves of bonnets and spencers. It had been a relaxing morning for Ianthe and Sally, who, on account of the fictional spoilt turbot, had been able to chat and read in Ianthe's room and avoid Lady Fox for the entire morning. Eventually Sally had been so worried about her mama, alone with Lady Fox, that Ianthe had sent Cherie. The maid was dispatched to ask for Lady

Richards to come to attend her "ill" daughter.

Lady Richards had arrived in their chamber and said, as she sat herself on Ianthe's bed, 'I wish I had had the foresight to eat the turbot.'

'Was she very horrid?' asked her daughter.

Lady Richards looked peaked and drawn but said, with dramatic inflection, '*Perfectly* horrid!'

'It is her talent I think,' remarked Ianthe. 'Complaints about last night?'

'Hundreds of them. In the last hours she has disparaged Audley's grounds, house, apartments, the colours of the walls, the ostentatious dinner service, the marquis' manners, his person, his clothes.'

'She is never at a loss,' said Ianthe cheerfully. 'One must give her that.'

'*My* manners were shockingly lacking, too. It seems I spoke with gentlemen who did not wish to converse with me and put myself forward unbecomingly.'

'Mama!' cried Sally, distressed and incensed.

'How you are to attend a dinner party and not speak to anyone is beyond me,' laughed Ianthe, 'but *poor* Cousin Emma!'

'Oh, my dear, I did not regard it for myself. I am too used to it, though it does drag one down when one is with a person of such poisonous spirits. It was when she began on Sally and you that I became angry.'

'*You* Cousin? I did not think you capable of anger.'

'I am not in general, but criticising my dearest ones roused me.' Ianthe's eyes widened in glee at the little frown on Emma Richards' pretty face. 'I could not show it of course, but I got my revenge.' Lady Richards tilted her head in pride, her single dimple showing, and Ianthe thought that she looked no more than a girl herself. The young ladies awaited the revelation which Her Ladyship delivered after a dramatic pause. 'When she began on Ianthe, I secretly picked up her silks and tied a *knot* in them. And when she began on you, Sally dear, she was supping at a cup, so I took her work and cut *two stitches* with my scissors!' Her own daring astounded her, and she looked a little nervous. 'She may not find it until tomorrow, and I suppose I must say that I thought it was my own work.'

The girls exchanged glances and Ianthe gave a great guffaw. 'I never thought you full of the spirit of retribution, Cousin Emma, dear. But *do* tell us what she said of us!'

Suddenly, the dire pall of Lady Fox's company became fodder for jocularity. Emma Richards recounted Lady Fox's harsh words on everyone present at last night's dinner, and all three roared with laughter at what now seemed the ludicrousness of her every utterance. It was almost worth the dreadful morning's lowering of spirits for the joy of the hour of retelling. Ianthe sometimes stamped her feet, Sally did impressions of the tone she thought Lady Fox would have adopted, and they laughed long and hard.

Sally regarded her beautiful friend with affection as she laughed at Lady Fox's views on the dinner party. Before Ianthe's arrival, she and her mama were kept from going into a decline only by some shared glances of amusement or some whispered words at the end of the day. They had existed here at Studham in a spirit of endurance, but Ianthe's confident spirit had changed all that. Sally knew that this was not *all* Ianthe felt, for it was not long since that she had held her friend crying in her arms, surrounded by jewels and murmuring grieving words about her papa and some other lost friend. Ianthe was still in her grief, but that winning spirit would always shine through. What a blessing she is! thought Sally.

Later, Sally heard from her mama the most wicked of Her Ladyship's words regarding Ianthe. She had said to Lady Richards that Ianthe had no feeling, for it was not ten months since the death of her father and yet she had not even worn black gloves in company. Sally's mama had said quickly that this was not the custom in France, not at all the custom (though she had no idea if this were so), and that since Ianthe did not know their ways she must be forgiven. She, Lady Richards, knew how keenly Ianthe felt the death of her father. Lady Fox had looked down on this "excessive sensibility" too. Sally's mama was just glad Ianthe had not been there to hear it. 'Such cruelty, Sally. I'm *glad* I cut her stitches.'

It had been decided that after a rest and some food (brought to them from the kitchen by Cherie), they should send word that they were feeling better and that they would take the air before joining Her Ladyship for the afternoon. 'For the Fentons are coming, you know, and I should not like to miss them. I have something particular to discuss with Mr Fenton. Something that only he can advise me on.'

The Richards took this as a call to arms, they would do anything to facilitate Ianthe's need for a private conversation with Mr Fenton. The Secret Breakfast was not, of course, secret to Lady Richards who had avowed herself to keep her countenance surprised by the visit.

They had carried out their plan and had returned from the walk by the side entrance, only to meet the marquis and his friend Mr Steadman in the hall, having just arrived to pay their afternoon visit.

'We rode across,' said the marquis shortly after the greeting. All five prepared to enter the Chinese Room where, Jenkins had informed them, Lady Fox sat — when the commotion in the study held them back. The gentlemen, hearing some dispute coming from behind the heavy study door, quite rightly moved forward as it was no business of theirs. But Ianthe placed a restraining hand on Audley's arm, and he stopped, causing his serious companion to stop too, standing still with his head in the air, feigning deafness. Audley was uncomfortable as the argument continued, but they could not hear the words, just the rumblings of discontent. But when the voices raised suddenly, they could just hear them.

'I shall go out and I shall not lose!' screamed Curtis.

'Do what you wish, you recalcitrant puppy, but no talk of scandal, no tears from your mama will move me this time. I will not pay,' they clearly heard Lord Fox reply.

Lady Richards said, 'Ianthe, dear, I really think—' she touched Ianthe's arm, but Ianthe stood still. Sally, embarrassed, wanted to move again. During this interval they could not make out the words, and Ianthe stirred to move again when the voice of Curtis came clearly through the door.

'You are already planning to marry and cut me out of the succession. Mama says so. Do you really think Sally Richards a match for my mama? How you could choose a woman like her? She is practically on the shelf. And Mama says she has no dignity whatsoever.'

'You will not speak so of Miss Richards. She is my guest!'

'Oh, so you protect that beggar living here for free, while you ignore your own brother?'

Sally looked at the floor, but Ianthe grasped her hand. 'It is only Curtis,' she said softly.

'I know,' answered Sally.

Mr Steadman's head turned at this moment and he looked directly at Lady Richards with her swelling bosom and clasped hands. Had anyone looked his way, they would have seen the look of disgust that had crossed his face at Curtis' last words. They were all stunned, so had not moved on when Curtis continued:

'If you find beggar-girls to your liking, you had best pursue the ravishing one. I'm sure Miss Eames is longing to be mistress of Studham. Although she might do better. She flirted shamelessly with the marquis at Audley!'

Even as they all gasped, they heard the clatter of something falling to the ground. Ianthe moved quickly in the direction of the study but was restrained by Audley's hand on her arm.

'I would have done it sooner,' he said shortly. Ianthe gazed at him. 'Let us to the salon so that you may flirt with me once more under the eager eye of Curtis' mama.' Ianthe gave him a half smile.

The serious Steadman let out a laugh at this, but he moved aside for the group of ladies.

'Ladies, shall we?' he said, his arm gesturing towards the door. Jenkins, his face a mask, opened it and announced the gentlemen to Lady Fox.

'Come, girls!' said Lady Richards, her head held high as she passed Mr Steadman and moved into the salon.

Chapter Twelve

The Fateful Walk

'You are out of breath, Lady Richards. You should exercise more.'

The ladies had become somewhat accustomed, on their half hour walk so far, to the serious Mr Steadman's bald remarks. They had ventured further from the house than usual, with a joint need to be far from Studham's polluted air.

'Once more, ladies,' said Audley resignedly, 'I must apologise for the un-furbished mode of speech of my friend.'

'Did I offend you?' Mr Steadman asked Lady Richards directly.

She smiled at him. 'No indeed! I used to walk a great deal as a girl, and I cannot think how it came to be that I now restrict myself to a daily walk around the gardens. I have become a laggard, I fear. You are correct, Mr Steadman. I am sadly out of condition.'

There was a stile ahead and Mr Steadman ushered her there and indicated that she sat. 'I will keep Lady Richards company while you two walk on,' he informed the others.

'No, no, gentlemen!' protested Sally. '*I* will stay with Mama, and we shall await your return.'

'It would be more convenient that I stay here.' Mr Steadman informed them in a bored tone. 'An old leg injury is plaguing me.'

Sally looked undecided.

'Should you have any objection, ma'am?' asked the marquis to the seated lady.

'No, my lord, for if you mount the hill you will be quite within my sight. But I am so sorry to spoil our walk.'

Sally regarded her mother's wan face closely. It had been a tiring day for her, but at least Sally could detect no burgeoning hope about Audley and herself. The marquis had addressed all his remarks so far to her mother, and had paid her no attention at all. That is perhaps why the distracted Lady Richards, still smarting from Curtis' cruel words, did not seem to think of this as an opportunity to foster a connection. Sally moved off with Audley, therefore, with a relieved heart. Mr Oscar Steadman seemed like a sensible gentleman who would look after Mama well.

Lady Richards looked a trifle embarrassed as Mr Steadman lowered himself to the ground, leaning against the fence close to her stile. 'Perhaps we can catch them up in a moment or two when I have caught my breath, sir,' she said, guiltily.

'No,' said Mr Steadman in that calm tone of command he used. 'The walk back will be sufficient for today. My brother is a physician and holds that exercise should be increased by degrees.' Lady Richards was a little startled by his tone, but nodded agreement. 'You shall have to have some new boots however,' Mr Steadman added in the same resolute tone. He grasped one of Her Ladyship's feet idly and regarded the jean half-boot that poked beneath her dress. Stunned, Lady Richards merely gasped. 'The jean at the top gets damp easily when you walk somewhere other than a cobbled street or a paved path in these. The next ones shall be leather.' He let her foot drop and looked ahead while Lady Richards, startled, gazed at his stern profile. 'I shall ride over in my carriage tomorrow and take you and your daughter to the village to purchase some.'

Ah, thought Her Ladyship. He is interested in Sally and wished to display it by concern for her mother. His manner of doing so was most unusual, but he was obviously a gentleman driven by practicality, as his last odd behaviour suggested. He was a little older than her daughter, by fifteen years at least Lady Richards supposed, but he seemed like a strong and considerate man. There was even a little warmth behind those hazel eyes, she felt, too. And he was handsome, though in a quieter way than Audley or young Lord Jeffries. If Sally could be moved to like him, though, a strong man such as he might be her saviour. She must find out more about his situation, as Sally's mama, but his dress and manner bespoke a gentleman of fortune. As the mother of a marriageable young female, Lady Richard's pretty eye could judge the cost of a gentleman's coat to a guinea. Mr Steadman's, though not of a flashy cut, was made of expensive superfine. However, there was difficulty in responding to his mode of conversation and the best Lady Richards could manage was, 'Well, thank you.'

'We shall walk daily from now on.'

This habit of command rather than request was disconcerting, but Lady Richards did not wish to depress his intentions, and merely said, 'It is kind of you to include me, Mr Steadman, but it is not necessary. I'm sure Miss Eames would join you two. Or if she cannot, a maid may do so.'

'We speak of my plan for the improvement to your own health, not your daughter's.'

Lady Richards could not help smiling at this. 'You are too kind, Mr Steadman. But you need not concern yourself with me. I promise that I shall elongate my morning walks, and so your kind concern will have paid dividends.'

'There is every need to concern myself with you,' Mr Steadman turned his head, holding her gaze. 'I shall accompany you daily.'

Lady Richards blinked. There was something disconcerting in his gaze. 'You are very kind sir. If you wish to pursue the acquaintance of my daughter, I have no objections.' His eyes changed colour from hazel to a stormy green and Lady Richards gulped. 'That is your intention, is it not? I must leave it to my daughter to say—'

He interrupted her. 'Of course, I wish to know Miss Richards better. She seems a charming girl. But it is not Miss Richards who cost me my sleep last night—' Lady Richards blinked again, trying to free herself from that certain gaze, but when her eyes opened, his were still locked on hers. '—but her beautiful mama,' he concluded.

There was a stunned silence with his gaze still locked upon her. At last she managed, 'But I am forty years old.'

'Two years ahead of me only.'

'But women age more quickly. I cannot be a wife again, not to a man of your age. You need someone Sally's age who could bear you children.'

'I find I do not care.'

'This is—' Trembling, she frowned, trying to understand, then looked at him again. 'Do you perhaps seek a wife as a companion and no more, and do not wish to offer such to a young girl?'

He moved then, to kneel directly at her feet. He took one hand and removed her kid glove, looking down at it and playing with it idly. Without raising his head, he took a bare finger and caressed it in the same lazy manner. Lady Richards, unable to move, could not jerk it away, though she knew that this was shocking behaviour that should never be permitted. 'This has happened to me twice in my life.' He continued, still intent on her finger. 'One look and it was decided. On the first occasion, fifteen years ago now, we got engaged the next day. But then she died.' Emma Richards found herself clutching the finger he was playing with around his own fingers briefly, and then released the tension abruptly. 'I thought that this was to be my fate, until I saw you last night at Audley.' He looked up, and his eyes had narrowed. Retaining the small finger in his hand he leaned towards her, raising himself, making her look up at him. 'And to respond to your question about companionship, the answer is *no*,' he moved towards her face another six inches, so that his breath was on her lips. 'I do not want a companion wife.'

Reeling, Lady Richards stayed still, trying to keep her lips from moving the inch towards his, locked in his gaze. She had ignored the wave of something that had overtaken her last night when they had been introduced, ignored the warmth she had felt when she had found his eyes twice upon her that evening, or the smile that had crossed his serious face as they exchanged words. But she was paying attention now. Her heart might stop at any moment, she might fling herself at him right now, but after the longest sixty seconds of her life, he pulled away and sat back on his heels.

'Marriage with me will allow your beloved daughter to marry whom she chooses, rather than some merely eligible anyone.' He gave her a brief smile. 'I wish you to marry only for me, but I know well that in your heart Miss Sarah must be your major concern.' He raised his eyebrows. 'I am not above using that.'

She gave an uncertain laugh at this. 'Mr Steadman, *what* am I to do with you?'

'Lady Richards, you must change your name to mine at your earliest convenience.'

'This is—'

'—madness. But you know it is right.' He said it certainly, but Emma Richards detected the tiniest of questions in his voice.

'The only thing I am committing myself to,' she said with an uncertain smile, 'is purchasing new boots.'

He nodded, sitting further back. 'That will do for today. I can see the others returning, and you have some things to consider.' He sank back against the fence, but took her bare hand in his, resting on the stile, sheltered beneath the skirts of her pelisse. She tried to pull it away, but at this he jerked it firmly and she subsided. 'Let me have this for now,' he breathed, not looking at her, but straight ahead. 'If you knew how I'm struggling to be calm, you would pity me.'

'You seem remarkably calm,' Emma Richards remarked, the hand in his shaking.

'Do not provoke me. I am a second away from doing something that would shock your daughter.' She breathed deeply to steady herself. 'What is your given name, my love?'

'Do not.'

'What is it?'

'Emma,' she said faintly.

'Ah, *Emma*.' He breathed her name like a prayer and closed his eyes. 'How lovely!' After a pause, he added, 'Your head must be exhausted. And I do not wish to leave you in that foul house any longer than I must. You have only one thing to consider, my Emma. *When* will you marry me?'

***

'Are you concerned about your mama, Miss Richards?' said Audley to Sally after they had climbed a little of the way, and Sally Richards had remained oddly silent.

She looked at him for a second and gave the shortest of wry smiles and then her face became grave again, looking at her path.

'There seems little point,' the marquis continued, 'in pretending that I did not hear what the obnoxious young cub Fox said, but I think you too sensible to refine too much upon it.'

'It is not for me, but for Mama. To call us

beggars—' she sighed. 'You must, I suppose, know our situation. We have some income, but without the shelter that our friends the Houstens provide willingly, and that Lady Fox provides reluctantly, we should be in a sorry state, I'm afraid. And Mama, who has been so comfortable all her life, and so good, feels it greatly.'

'It is too common a situation, and I regard the relative who displaced you without providing for you both better a man of no moral worth whatsoever.'

'As do I, though I am not supposed to say so,' said Sally Richards with some acid. 'It would have taken a very little of Papa's fortune to give Mama a cottage at least. And I happen to know that Mama helped that family in many ways before my father's death. It is for her that I am so sorry. I suppose,' she added, dashing away a tear, 'that we *are* beggars, of a sort.'

He was moved, and said quickly, 'Do not be absurd. If it is not right to provide for one's family, what is?'

'Oh, my mama will be so hurt for my sake.'

'She hurts for you, and you for her. You carry each other's burdens.'

Sally let out an angry laugh. 'We had a plan for dinner tonight, you know. Ianthe had stirred us to cheerfulness, as well as a little revenge.'

'Oh yes? Be careful of Ianthe's plans, I tell you.' Audley sought to lighten the atmosphere. 'Once in Cadiz I followed her plan and ended up in a Spanish jail.'

'You must *both* tell me that story one day. I will not hear it from you alone, because I'm sure Ianthe must have had a very good reason to act as she did.'

'You have too much faith in her. She's a termagant. What was your plan for dinner?' He held out his hand since she was struggling to get a footing on the steep path, and she grasped it quite naturally. He dropped it immediately as she was safe.

'Well, we have not all been together since dinner last night, and somehow, through Ianthe's teasing, we have all decided to call each other by name.'

'I noticed. And I am surprised that Fox agreed to any such thing. He has always been somewhat of a stiff-rump.'

'But Ianthe is a genius! After being accused by Lady Fox of showing distinction towards me, a designing female, he was smarting so much from the insult—'

'Surely not *insult*?' laughed Audley.

Sally giggled. 'He did not call it so, it's true. But I'm perfectly sure he felt it so. Would not you, my lord, if someone misjudged the circumstances of our walk today and accused you of singling me out? Would you not be insulted?'

He held her eyes for a moment and answered, jerking his head towards her violently, 'Insulted? No, why should I be?' She smiled a little smile at this, as though grateful. He paused and looked at her candidly. 'Tell me what Ianthe fooled Fox into.'

'Tonight, at dinner, we were all to address each other by name and annoy Lady Fox out of all mind.'

'It sounds like Ianthe,' said Audley, resignedly. 'She is ever one to poke the bear.'

'We should not have dared do so before she arrived of course. Poke the bear, I mean. Mama and I would do anything not to be made even more uncomfortable in this situation. But now, as Ianthe puts it, we have them outnumbered. It is wicked of course, but it might have been fun this evening, if a little heart-racing. But now it is spoilt. It would be to confirm every horrid thing that Curtis said.'

They walked on a little, and the marquis reflected to himself that *this* was why he avoided young single females. He was moved by her situation and felt a real desire to protect this true young girl. He liked her. He liked her face and figure, her seat on a horse, the way she did not fawn upon him, the way sometimes like this that they could speak as friends. He even liked being insulted by her. He could offer for her in a second and be reasonably sure he would never regret it. He had her character already. Who could regret such a mother for their children? But he did not want the restrictions of marriage to such a woman as this. You could not leave her in the country with your children and go back to town to continue your dissipated life. You would pity her too much. Neither could you take her to town with you, and after the birth of your children, let her enjoy the same freedoms you did — with discretion. She could never bear that, and he could never bear to see it. But that was the kind of wife he would have, if ever he married at all. A lady who knew this game. One could not suggest such a union to this bright, fresh girl. She was too good for that. But it was all Audley thought himself able to offer. He looked over at Sally, brushing the windswept curl back beneath her bonnet, her stride trying to match his and failing, but still lithe and strong. She looked — well, it was better not to think about how she looked. But when he thought about the length of time he had known her, less than a week, he was shocked that this internal dialogue about marriage had been going on with him for at least the last three days. No, it was better not to know a young girl's circumstances lest the knight errant in him escape and lead him to disaster. She tilted her head up at him as he had gone ahead and above a pace and held out her hand naturally for his aid. She was so sweet that it made him ache.

'Shall we make it amusing again?' he said suddenly. 'Shall I stay for dinner and make *all* that idiot boy's words correct?' He smiled down at her, taking the outstretched hand at last, and pulled her up. 'I'll flirt with Ianthe wildly, and you can all address each other affectionately, and we will make your mama laugh again today.'

She was too close to him now, but she smiled back and said, 'We should have to warn Mama. She has heard that you are a rake, and she will be worried for Ianthe's reputation.'

'If she did not already think I was a puppy dog, she would not let me walk here alone with her precious daughter.' He paused, looking at the hill and sky. 'I think we should head back now.'

'Ah, I think I know why she permitted it,' Sally said suddenly, after they had turned back. She grasped his shoulder at the steep part of the incline, as they made their descent, he in front.

He looked back at her, his russet hair flying in the wind. 'You do?'

'Did you not see the looks she was giving to Mr Steadman on the walk?' He shook his head.

'I did. I caught her a few times and found it odd. But really, it is not.' She grinned, now walking by his side as the path widened and was less steep. 'She is doing what mamas do. She has summed him up as a suitable single candidate for marriage, and is even now, I suppose, enumerating my virtues to the poor man, who cannot escape at all.'

Audley looked down at the distant figures, oddly close, and had a bad feeling. If this was so, he could not partake of the amusement that Miss Richards wished to share with him. He narrowed his eyes. Something about the minimal distance between them, not touching, but not stiffly avoiding, gave him a worse feeling. If Lady Richards was making an attempt to foster a connection between his friend Oscar and Sally Richards, then, quite remarkably, the hermit Oscar Steadman was not resisting. He was a good man, Audley knew. Just the sort of man that Sally Richards should marry. But Audley's heart sank, nevertheless.

On the ride back home, Audley said to his friend, 'Did you think Miss Richards a pleasant girl?'

'She seems an open and genuine young lady,' said Oscar Steadman dryly. 'But I did not much converse with her.'

'Yet you seemed anxious to visit Studham with me today.'

'I believe it is polite to call upon new acquaintances.'

'You have not before been diligent about the social niceties, Oscar.'

'You are correct. But I had my reasons.' Audley thought back to Steadman's interaction with the lovely Ianthe last evening but could remember nothing special. However, Steadman was not a demonstrative fellow. It may have been a disappointment when the Fentons took Ianthe off with them today. But when he glanced over at Oscar, his friend was looking down with a secretive grin. Audley felt impelled to ask again. 'So, you do not admire Miss Richards?'

'Oh, I did not say that. I admire Miss Richards a great deal.' Audley, with the pall of doom upon him, said nothing. 'But why do you ask, Rob? You are most insistent.'

'Am I? Did Lady Richards soon recover? We did not mean to walk so long. We kept you waiting.'

'No need to apologise at all.'

Audley considered that keeping Lady Richards, however nice she was, entertained for the best part of an hour must have been fatiguing, but he accepted Steadman's good manners. They rode on, Audley feeling strangely rattled. He knew who he had to thank for his present predicament. It was Ianthe Eames. She had drawn Sally Richards into his orbit so that he had no choice but to become friends with her. *Ianthe!* He could strangle her.

Chapter Thirteen

Back at Studham

Sally and her mother parted outside Sally's chamber, Lady Richards apologising for her distraction and pleading fatigue from the walk. Sally was happy to have some time alone. She too needed a rest before dinner. She was full of a warm glow, which must have been from the long walk today. The company had been easy, too. She had still been smarting at Curtis' words, but somehow had found it easy to speak to the marquis, and to have him rail her back into good humour. She knew she should be affected by his rank, and show him more respect, and if it was London, at a party, she would have probably been embarrassed and flattered by any attention he showed her. And wary. She would have been wary. But here he was just the man who had mounted her on Missy, and all honours had thus fallen from his shoulders. Today, for the first time, there had been little dispute and only that warm raillery. She had spent time with a friend today. She would not, remembering his strong hands on hers, be so self-interested as to mistake it for anything else. He said he should not be ashamed to be misunderstood to have singled her out, but he did not single her out today more than any other. It had just transpired thus. And then she had confided in him and felt better. He was a man of the world, of course, and he had a sort of social wisdom in dealing with people. This was not to judge him correctly, however, Sally thought honestly. There was something warm about the marquis. And honest, too.

The walk had assuredly done her good.

***

The walk was not quite as easily gotten over for Emma Richards. She was shaken to the core, and her own behaviour was causing her grief. She should not have let Mr Steadman pull off her glove, or play with her finger. She should have jerked her hand away. It was burning still, and worse than this was that she had let him secretly hold it. When they made their way back to the house, too, their gloved fingers had touched twice, unnoticed by the other two. She had looked deeply into his eyes for much too long. She had told him her name and let him use it without rebuke. What was she thinking?

Since her beloved husband's death, Emma had had no thought but the welfare of Sally. She could not, in her grief, consider anything else. She could only do her best so that Sally could have her time in London. Here she had been helped by their friends the Houstens putting them up in the London house and by a bill that arrived from Lord Fox "to buy such finery as is needed for Miss Richards' Season." She had not applied for this, and it had touched her. Lord Fox was briefly in town that Season and she tried to thank him personally, but he was embarrassed and gruffly refused all thanks. Her own small income had been used to buy the accessories needed to finish any toilette. From ribbons to reticules, gloves to dyed slippers. But Sally, though much admired, had not met anyone prepared to offer for a dower-less female. She had been willing to accept Sir Ralph Eastman had he offered, but Emma had felt that this was only because Sally wished to salve her mother's anxieties and provide for her through marriage. It had not come off, and somehow Emma could not be sorry.

And now today. Could Emma be the one to provide a home for Sally? Was Mr Steadman serious? What was his situation? All of this was a side issue to the singing in Emma's body at the very thought of him. With her dear Sir Guy, it had never been thus. He had been seventeen years her senior and had quietly admired the pretty Miss Fox and had just as quietly asked to marry her. She had accepted and been contentedly happy for all the years that she had been wed, but *this* was something else entirely.

    She knew nothing of Mr Steadman, she should not be thinking of him as she was. When his gloved finger brushed against hers on the way to Studham her legs had lost all strength and she had had to put a hand on a nearby tree trunk to steady herself. She dared not glance at him at all. She was drunk and heady with every word he had said running in her head. Waves of heat swept over her. How was she to meet him tomorrow? Why on earth had this lovely young man settled on her? But when he'd said it was right, she knew it too. She had felt and repressed the frisson of their first meeting. She had lain in bed and thought of him, berated herself, then finally mocked herself. She, a mother, to have such thoughts! Her will was strong and she had slept and had done no more than steal glances at Mr Steadman the next day in Lady Fox's sitting room and calculated his behaviour to her daughter.

    But now there were a great many things to consider. Things she *must* consider, as a mama.

She could not let her urge to run off with him, even if she found out he was a scoundrel, overtake her.

He had not said affectionate words, though he had called her by that name "my love", she still did not know what he meant by any of it. It was ridiculous, wasn't it? Whatever his serious demeanour might suggest, he *must* be of unsteady character. It was only a day ago that they had met.

Her head in a whirl, she was surprised later to find that she had dropped off for an hour and woke up refreshed.

Safe, she thought to herself, could it be that she felt now that she and Sally were finally safe?

***

The butler himself delivered Miss Eames' message to Lord Fox's bedroom at the hour when he was dressing for the evening.

'Miss Eames is in your study, my lord, and wishes a word with you before dinner. She will await you there.'

'No one enters my study without my permission, Jenkins. Why on earth did you permit it?'

'Well, I thought you meant Miss Eames to be an exception, my lord. She has been in your study a number of times now and you even called her there yourself when Mr Henderson…'

'Yes, yes.' Fox looked thunderous. 'Tell her I will arrive when I have dressed.' Jenkins bowed low and turned to leave. 'And Jenkins. I may be ten minutes. Is the fire lit?'

'I shall see to it at once, my lord.' As his back was to his master, Jenkins permitted himself a half-smile.

When Lord Fox came down, rather earlier than ten minutes later, he found Ianthe very much at home there, with her knees raised before her on one of the winged leather chairs. If he cared for such things, he might have thought that her dark ringlets had been arranged perfectly, her French silk gown elegant, and her face and figure perfection, but he just looked annoyed. She seemed to be regarding a ledger and looked up as he came in saying, 'I had no notion how much saddle soap costs a quarter. It seems a prodigious amount.'

Fox strode forward and took the book from her roughly, saying, 'What is it that you want, Ianthe?'

'Practice for this evening? You said my name very naturally. Well done, Edward!'

'If you could stop trying to annoy me and tell me what you wish to say, I would be obliged.' He sat on the edge of his desk, one leg bent, looking under his brows.

'Something occurred that you should know, well two things actually, but I am not sure I should tell you about the second. Mr Fenton will advise me.'

'Mr Wilbert Fenton has not the reputation of a steady and sensible adviser.'

'But he is the master of intrigue, which is what I need advice about.'

'Tell me,' ordered Fox.

'Of *course* — but not today, I think. Another issue has arisen. The Richards overheard your dispute with Curtis.' Fox looked appalled. 'Do not be too concerned. They know Curtis and do not make much of it. But to be called beggars…'

Fox walked around the room, his head bent back as if in supplication to the heavens. 'I do not know what I can say — Lady Richards would be mortified if I were to mention it. I would drag Curtis to his knees before her to apologise if I didn't think it would humiliate her more!' He paced about the room again, and Ianthe looked at him. That repressed, sometimes grim, exterior hid this depth of feeling that she was watching right now. Then he stopped and turned to her, his face full of concern for her. 'And you! You did not hear what he said—?'

'About my designs on Audley?' She smiled down his concern. 'I have no delicate feelings to spare on whatever such a sapskull as Curtis might say. Do not fear.' He came forward to her abruptly, taking her by the shoulders, and she looked up at him, smiling. 'Really!' she said reassuringly. Then, with some mischief, 'Really, Edward dear.'

He threw her from him then and said, 'You are despicable!' but his tone was resigned, not angry. 'But you are my guest and that you have heard this insult is outside of enough. Curtis will, at least, apologise to you.'

'You shall not make him!' She held his arm and he turned to her again, his look dangerous. 'What good is an insincere apology from an empty-headed bone-box that has been fed ill-will from his mother's milk?' He glowered at her. 'I tell you, I do not need it.' She laughed. 'And at least *he* did not call me despicable.'

'You *are* despicable,' Fox said shortly. 'Then how shall we bear dinner? I can excuse myself, but you will have to sit with them.'

'Isn't Curtis at a cock-fight? He won't be back for dinner! And no, you may *not* excuse yourself, my lord, you will offer support to the spirits of your guests.' She reached for his arm again, pinched the fabric of his sleeve and shook it a little, like a child arguing for a treat. 'Yes?'

He looked down at her, his Fox's eyes on hers. 'I say yes to you too often. I am not an obliging man. How is it that you make me do so?'

Their eyes held a little too long before she answered briskly. 'That is because you have realised the wisdom of my designs.'

'It is definitely not that. Merely, on this occasion, that you remind me of a duty to my guests.'

'Let us to the drawing room before the

others come.' She put her arm through his and he looked at it, but made no reproof. 'We shall claim the field before the enemy arrives, as General Napoleon would have it.'

'You do not say you have *seen* him?' said an astonished Fox on his way to the salon.

'I have resided for some years in Paris. It would have been odd if I had not done so.'

Ianthe dropped his arm as they reached the salon threshold, and they entered the room to find Lady Fox in solitary dignity (excepting, of course, her maid, two footmen and the butler in close attendance) on a chair by the fire. She wore a tall turban of violet satin and a purple silk gown, bedecked by a surfeit of black lace. She held onto a silver topped cane, from which purple and violet ribbons fell. Dressed for battle, thought Ianthe, with the cane a token of her fragility. But she said to Fox in an under voice, 'The field has been already claimed.'

'I beg your pardon, Miss Eames?' said Lady Fox.

'She was speaking to me of Napoleon, your ladyship,' Fox informed his step-mama. 'Apparently, Ianthe is acquainted with him.'

'*Really*, dear?' said Lady Richards coming behind them with Sally. 'You have lived the most interesting life. Were you not terrified?'

'We will halt all speech until we achieve the table,' said Lady Fox in stentorian tones. She shot a look of inquiry at the butler.

'Dinner is served, your ladyship.'

In a stately manner, Lady Fox led the way to the dining room, her tall cane before her like the staff of Moses, and affected to be unaware of a stifled laugh (issuing from a sorely-tried Lady Richards) behind her.

'Lady Richards!' she said with a frown as soon as she was seated. 'You were long gone this afternoon. I did not know you would walk so far. I had a fancy to play cards and you were not present.'

Lady Richards flushed and began an apology for this dereliction of duty, but Fox interrupted. 'Was it pleasant exercise, Cousin Emma?'

Lady Fox's fork clattered upon her plate.

'I was sadly out of breath, I'm afraid, Cousin Edward,' answered Lady Richards, only a slight tremor betraying her agitation. The knife fell too. 'But it has firmed my resolve to extend my walks in the afternoons so as to improve my strength.'

'An excellent plan.' Lord Fox turned and added to Ianthe, 'And your drive with your friends, Ianthe? Catching up on the London gossip from Lady Aurora?'

'You forget that my stay in London was but a few days, Edward d—' Ianthe coughed as Fox's eyes *dared* her to call him dear, 'd-ue to my coming here. It would do little good to tell *me* any *on dits* since I know no one.'

The stunned Lady Fox was speechless.

Sally had, as usual, been moved to wrath at the tone that Lady Fox had used to her mama, but this time it was not impotent wrath. Ianthe had given her the weapon and she set about using it. 'Before that, Edward, we had a great many visitors today. The Marquis of Audley came, and Mr Steadman, whom we met at the marquis' house, you know, as well as the Fentons.'

'I do not recall when we have had so many visitors, Sally,' replied Fox conversationally. A gasp from his step-mama made it hard to hold back a smile, but he continued, in a railing tone that was not at all like him. 'I suspect that the local gentry have discovered what a charming trio of ladies I play host to.'

Sally was almost flummoxed by this, as being much further than she had expected him to extend the joke, but Ianthe kicked her, and she managed to reply. 'Flatterer!' with a smile.

Lady Fox gagged.

'It is clear,' said Ianthe brightly, 'that time spent with the marquis is having a beneficial effect on your charm with the ladies, Cousin Edward.'

'What,' uttered Lady Fox, at last catching her breath, 'is the meaning of this?'

All four of the others were stopped for a second by her venom, but it was the quiet voice of Lady Richards who said, 'Oh, you must be referring to our mode of address, Lady Fox. It is just that Lord Fox —' she smiled at him, 'that is, dear Cousin Edward, suggested to us as we rode home from Audley last night, that as we are family who have known each other all our lives, you know, we should be more familiar in our address. I agreed whole-heartedly.'

'And Miss Eames? *She* we have never seen before this week. It is quite beyond the pale to be so familiar on such a short acquaintance.'

'She is family, stepmother, and it would not have done to exclude her,' said Lord Fox in a mock serious tone.

'I know the genesis of this change. I know you well enough, Edward, to know that you value your family's dignity better than a girl who had knocked about Europe doing *who-knows-what*.'

Fox made a sound in his throat that might be the precursor to anger but was interrupted.

'Oh, your ladyship,' said Ianthe enthusiastically, 'do you wish to know what I did in Europe? *Please* do ask me, I would love to tell you of my adventures.'

'I do not wish to know what shocking tales you might tell.'

'Do you not?' Ianthe's eyes glittered, and Sally Richards intuited that her friend was looking for the *most* shocking tale that she could find to tell Her Ladyship. Sally wished to head her off from *actually* sending Lady Fox into an apoplexy, so she asked.

'Napoleon! I cannot believe that you have

breathed the same air as the monster of Europe.'

'Well, Papa was one of his new nobility, you know.' The table gasped — even Lady Fox, whose outrage had no words. 'About two years since,' Ianthe explained, 'Papa wished to move back to Paris and he *acquired*,' Ianthe's eyebrows rose as a parenthesis around the word, 'the papers of one Marcel de Fontaine, who was now deceased. It turned out that M. de Fontaine's brother was a fallen comrade of the general, and he sent out emissaries to seek out his only family, Marcel, to reward him on his brother's behalf. They found us where we were living in Angers in the Loire Valley. It was a close call, but thankfully no one suspected Papa was *not* the real Marcel de Fontaine and he was awarded Chevalier de Fontaine, with a small annual allowance. The prestige allowed Papa to return to Paris and to be able game with the elite once more. It quite restored our fortunes, for Papa was a talented gamester. I saw the general — I do not call him Emperor — briefly on but two occasions. I was too young to be of interest to him, but he stopped and talked to me out of respect for his dead comrade.'

'He *spoke* to you?' asked Sally. 'What did he say?'

'He told me he had beef for breakfast.'

'How disappointing!' said Lady Richards.

'Yes. His manners with men were a trifle abrupt, for one must suppose he had to deal with too many supplicants, but he was always charming to the ladies, in his fashion.'

'So I've heard,' said Fox cynically.

'Shocking,' agreed Ianthe with what Fox had dubbed her dangerous innocent look that preceded something awful, 'but I've heard he could not rival Lord Wellington in that department, who made it his business to … em … *meet* all of Napoleon's mistresses when he first came to town.'

A deathly silence greeted this, and only Ianthe Eames continued with her meal. The word 'mistress' would have been shocking enough to part from the lips of a young lady, but the substance of the insinuation was so far from polite dinner conversation as to have left her audience stunned.

Lady Fox was the first to find her voice. 'England's hero! How dare you speak his name, you dreadful girl? You are beneath my contempt. You do not know, Fox, for I kept it from you, what this creature confessed to me when first she came, threatening the family with scandal when I asked her to leave…'

'You had no right to ask her to leave, your ladyship. She is my guest and a member of this family.'

'So I have no rights in my own home? Is this what you wish to inform me of, now that your poor papa is in his grave?'

'You have rights, and you exercise them frequently. You may invite whom you chose to stay at Studham, it is your home after all. However, you do not have the right to interfere with *my* guests. The Richards and Miss Eames — Ianthe — are welcome guests of mine. I have been remiss in their entertainment. I shall not be so anymore.'

'I,' said Lady Fox in a faint voice, 'must retire. The treatment I have received this evening shall not be forgotten, Fox. Support me, Evans,' she said to her maid who rushed forward to offer her arm. 'Send—' Her Ladyship said, her voice even weaker.

'—for Doctor Tolliver!' finished Lord Fox. His stepmother gave him a look of dislike and got up from the table. Fox stood and bowed as she left the room, a tottering figure of unjust oppression.

There was more silence. Fox sat down again and recommenced eating. 'The duck will get cold,' he advised the others, gesturing with his fork for them to continue. Sally Richards let out a laugh.

'Edward, thank you, my dear,' said Lady Richards, dabbing at her eye with a napkin. Then with a conscious look she added, 'but Ianthe, I do not think you should say such things in public.'

'What things? Oh, about the duke? It is just what I heard. Paris was buzzing with it.'

'The French should not talk so in front of young girls,' remarked Lady Richards.

'I shall mind my tongue, Cousin Emma,

never fear. I only said it to …' she smiled wickedly. 'It is no excuse, I am repentant.'

'What other shocking thing did you say to my stepmother earlier?' asked Fox in a conversational tone.

Lady Richards choked and coughed. '*That* Cousin Edward, I shall tell you later when we are alone.'

'You heard it?'

Lady Richards exchanged a guilty glance with her daughter. 'I did.'

'I only said—' began Ianthe, blithely.

'*Ianthe!*' said Lady Richards in her strictest voice.

'Very well. I'll behave!'

'You girls go ahead to the drawing room,' Fox said once they had finished their dessert. 'Lady Richards will keep me company over the brandy this evening and we will join you in a while.'

Minutes later he laughed uproariously in shock. 'She said *that*? To my step-mama? Oh, that's glorious. She is a frightful girl, with no delicacy at all, but I do wish I had been there.'

'Do not laugh, Edward,' said Lady Richards chidingly. 'We should not encourage her. She is the most delightful child, but she has lived a life without a mother's care, and we cannot allow her to go beyond what is pleasing now that she is in England. Only think what it might do to her marriage prospects.'

'Ianthe Eames does not talk so in company. She knows how to behave, in her fashion. We saw that at Audley, where she was everything that was maidenly at the dinner table. She has not been sheltered from the world, it is true, but she is still an innocent.'

'You are right. And that is why I ask you, Cousin Edward, to look to her comfort when Sally and I are gone from here. She will be alone, with only Her Ladyship as a female companion. It is some time off, but I am already worried about that.' She seemed to have a happy thought. 'But yet, it may be that she will meet someone. Even in this restricted district gentlemen will hear of such a beautiful young lady and seek her out. I know my Sally is lovely, but Ianthe is the sort of beauty to set the town in a spin, so she's bound to cause a stir in the countryside.' She inclined herself towards him. 'You must not allow Lady Fox to deny the visitors.'

Fox's eyes had turned stormy, and Lady Richards feared she had given offence. But he merely said, standing up and holding her chair back, 'Let us join the others, Cousin Emma.'

Chapter Fourteen

The Fourth Ride and a French Comte

'Does Fox not accompany you today?' asked Audley of Ianthe the next morning. Sally Richards had rushed from the gig to greet Sapphire and was making cooing noises.

'No, he has a breakfast appointment, I think,' said Ianthe. Audley's look had her ask, 'You seem disappointed. Are you and Edward so close now?'

'Yes,' he said, to stop her amusement.

'I thought perhaps Mr Fenton might join us.'

'He informs me that I shall not see him before ten, even in the country.'

'Oh, my Purity!' exclaimed Ianthe, petting her. 'Perhaps I should move her to Studham now and then I could visit her in her stall in the evening.'

'Perhaps you should,' answered Audley.

Ianthe looked up, surprised. 'You seem very keen to get rid of us, Audley.'

'I was thinking of you, merely,' he answered, helping her to mount.

'Well, Fox would have no objection, I know, but...' she looked over at Sally, now bent over Sapphire's head, breathing endearments, 'Sally would miss Sapphire so, even if we were to disobey Lady Fox's prohibition. Better stay here if you don't object.'

'No objection at all. I may go to London in a few days. You two can ride here all you would like.'

It was all perfectly polite, but Ianthe felt some restraint from him that she was not used to.

'What are you speaking of?' said Sally as they walked the horses out of the stable yard.

'Audley was telling me he was going to London in a few days.'

'Are you taking Sapphire?' Sally asked anxiously.

'Your favourite will remain at Audley, fear not,' said the marquis a trifle grumpily. Ianthe frowned. What was it about Audley's mood today? But when Sally merely replied *"good"* and rode off, Ianthe caught Audley's rueful expression and had an inkling what was afoot. As they let Sally run free on her own, the others plodded slowly for a while.

'In the suds, my friend?'

'All on account of you, Ianthe Eames.'
'Serious?'
'Nothing I cannot handle.'

'At least she does not know,' said Ianthe. Audley blanched at this. Sally Richards did not know because his feelings were not reciprocated. That allowed him to come out of this encounter without being a cad, but it did not feel good. If he wanted, he could make her—

'Do not even think it,' said Ianthe. 'Get yourself off to London without delay.'

She rode off too, and Audley went forward to catch them up.

Ianthe rode on, deep in thought. It was not only Audley's vanity that was piqued here, she was sure. But he must not be allowed to let Sally get a glimpse of anything more than a sporting comrade. Audley, even without rank or other privileges, was all too attractive. He was a man of the world who could lure a maiden to her doom in short order. That he did not do so showed his integrity, but if Miss Sarah Richards was something the marquis desired, then it must be so tempting for him to make her want him too. They had an affinity, Ianthe was sure, it would be so easy. But if the marquis was denying himself this pleasure (and he did not deny himself many pleasures in life) then it meant he was not about to offer his name. Ianthe was able to intuit why. If Audley ever took a wife (and he had already indicated to her that he had a perfectly fine heir in his beloved cousin Philip, who also had two boys of his own, so the marquis did not feel the need to secure the succession) it would not be to one for whom it was necessary to give up his pleasures. He liked her too much to wish her to experience being the wife of a hedonist. He was selfish, and he knew it, and it was this self-knowledge that made Ianthe like him.

On the ride, she saw that Audley kept her close, and Sally further from him. When the road narrowed, he rode ahead on his own and when Sapphire galloped, out-pacing Purity, Audley, whose horse could certainly keep up, instead slowed down. Ianthe saw that Sally felt the difference, but Audley's good manners and humour made her doubt that it was deliberate.

Mr Wilbert Fenton was in the stable yard when they returned. 'Should you object if a groom brings you back in the gig, Miss Richards?' he said after greetings. 'I will drive Ianthe back in Audley's phaeton. I have something of a private nature I wish to discuss with her.'

'Earlier than ten of the clock?' said Ianthe. 'I am surprised, sir.'

'You should be,' he said urbanely. Then more seriously he added, 'I have some news.'

They rode off together in the phaeton, and Audley handed Sally into the gig. It was perfectly polite, but not strictly necessary, and as Sally took the reins, she looked a little conscious. 'Are you out of sorts today, marquis? You seemed a little occupied by your thoughts.'

Audley looked up at her and wished she would go. 'A little bit of business, merely.'

'Ah,' said Sally. His voice was still friendly, but not teasing or reproving and she was a little at a loss. 'I believe Mr Steadman is calling today, according to my mother.'

'Yes, so I believe. He is to stay with me for a few days. He went this morning to collect some baggage.'

'Ah. And will you come to Studham with him today?'

'I will not, I think.' *I will not watch him pay you court.*

'Ah. Then all being well, I'll see you tomorrow, my lord.'

'At least,' said Audley in his usual manner, 'you have stopped calling me "my noble marquis".'

'Only until I'm angry at you again,' Sally laughed, relieved at his more normal tone. 'Is your stay in London long? When will you return?'

'Ah,' said the marquis, echoing her exclamation, 'it is indeterminate. It may be some time.'

Finally, she looked dismayed, but covered it well. He was glad and unhappy at the same time. Overjoyed because she cared a little, desperately worried in case she may care too much. He knew he was doing the right thing.

She gave him a tremulous smile, an *adieu*,

and she was gone.

***

After breakfast that morning, as the ladies sat down to their stitching with Lady Fox, all three had to be reprimanded by Her Ladyship for lack of attention. It seemed that every one of them had something on their minds, and Her Ladyship had had to ask twice for Sally to pick up her needle, and once for Lady Richards to adjust her shawl. Miss Eames, she asked to ring for refreshments, but Ianthe, after being called to attention, said to Evans, 'Send for refreshments, Evans,' and Her Ladyship's maid disappeared, wearing a surly expression.

'That is not what I requested you to do, Miss Eames,' said Lady Fox. 'Was it too fatiguing for you to stand and ring?'

'Oh no, your ladyship. I was just thinking of the servant. It must be very tiring to stand for so long with nothing to do. She will very likely be pleased with the industry.'

A footman, William, had entered, to clear a table for the refreshments, and had to rely on the severe training of Mr Jenkins not to let a smile cross his lips at this. 'William, is it?' said Ianthe brightly. 'Could you ask Cherie to bring me the fawn shawl?' William was thus free to let his smile out behind the door, safely out of Lady Fox's eye.

In Sally's distracted state, she did not notice this little drama, or even hear the further discussion about whether or not Miss Eames had the right to send off the servants on her trivial assignments. Sally had taken a rough piece of cotton that she used for the purpose and stretched it over a small tambour frame. Then she found a fine linen handkerchief, with the edges already turned, and began to baste one edge with large stitches to the cotton to secure it, with the handkerchief corner exposed, ready to be embroidered. Turning the frame, she cut away a small section of the backing cotton beneath the part of the linen where she would add the design. With diligent stitches, a shade whiter than the natural white of the linen, she embroidered three elegant letters intertwined.

'M-N-M,' read Ianthe after a while. 'Who is it for, dear?'

'A friend, merely,' said Sally, adding mendaciously, 'You do not know them.'

Had Lady Richards not been so distracted herself, she would have later demanded of Sally that she say who it was, for she would not have been able to remember any friend with such initials.

***

That afternoon, Lord Fox surprised a strange scene in his own living room. As well as his stepmother, Curtis and the three ladies, there were no less than three gentlemen. Mr Steadman, with his serious handsome face, was the elder, then came the easy-going Mr James Markham, whose demeanour had obviously been stiffened by contact with the arctic Lady Fox, and who was looking every day of his 32 years. He threw Fox, whom he knew somewhat, a rather desperate look as he entered, and Lord Fox nodded to him in sympathy. Lord Nigel Jeffries, that brown haired imp, did not look quite so daring as usual. He was doing his best to keep up a conversation with Ianthe Eames under the dampening eye of Lady Fox, while being verbally accosted by Curtis Fox, who seemed to be demanding some deeper acquaintance with the young sportsman. It was hardly surprising that Curtis' remarks about horseflesh and sporting events he had not attended granted him little more than the slightest of answers, since Jeffries' eyes were riveted on his prize. Ianthe looked lovely in a pale sprigged muslin of French design that might have been very daring indeed had she not tucked a fichu at the bodice for modesty. Lord Fox was considering whether the scrap of almost transparent muslin was improving the modesty of the gown, or merely drawing the eye, when there was another set of arrivals. Audley and the Fentons were introduced.

The frigid tone of the drawing room took on another aspect with the arrival of the exceptionally glamorous Lady Aurora. She was charm itself to Lady Fox, and when these remarks were greeted with the same ice as before, Lady Aurora gave a return smile of faint deprecation, before turning enthusiastically to the Richards and Miss Eames. Mr Wilbert Fenton threw himself in the chair that had been retrieved by a footman from a corner of the room, a chair that Fox could not remember anyone ever sitting in.

In his memory, Fox had never seen so many people in his drawing room at this hour. He counted. As well as the six residents, there were the six guests, making twelve in all. Audley stood with him and he remarked to the marquis, 'Is not Steadman's place a full ten miles from here? It is a long way for a polite visit, especially when he has already called yesterday.'

'Steadman is to stay at Audley for a few days.'

'To facilitate his visits here?'

'I assumed so.'

'Interesting.' Mr Steadman was at one side of Sally, who looked pretty today in a simple cream muslin gown with fawn ribbons that were a shade lighter than her luxuriant curls. These had been expertly coiffed this morning by Cherie, Ianthe's maid. On her other side was Mr Markham, able to speak to her at last since Lady Fox's spell of formality seemed to have been lifted by Lady Aurora's urbane presence.

'You are to go to London, Ianthe tells me,' Fox said to the marquis.

'Yes.' He seemed to be gazing at a particular spot in the room, the spot where the Richards were speaking to Steadman and Markham. 'I think I must go tomorrow.'

'Something urgent in town?' asked Fox, without much interest.

'No,' said Audley in a strange voice. 'Nothing urgent in town. I'm running away.'

Fox turned towards him and regarded his profile, then followed his eye. Sally Richards was laughing at something John Markham had said and turned to Mr Steadman to share it. Fox's eyes turned back to Audley. Something like pain had crossed the marquis' face.

'I really shouldn't have come today, but the Fentons—'

'Could have come themselves,' said Fox.

Audley met his gaze then, wryly grinning. 'Indeed.'

'Is it impossible?' asked Fox. Somehow, with the ice broken between them, they seemed to have reclaimed their youthful familiarity. Once they had been friends, the older boy being very kind to the younger.

'If she were your sister, Fox, would you wish her to be embroiled with a man like me? I am not fit to be a husband.'

'Then you will never marry?'

'Perhaps. But not to someone so innocent. How could I? My reputation is not exaggerated.'

'Your reputation does not define you, Audley. You have been amusing yourself, but one's amusements may change.'

The allotted time for the first visitors was over, and they were given broad hints to take themselves off. Curtis said he would drive over to Jeffries place with him to see his newest hunter, and Markham left with them. Mr Steadman stayed, and Lady Aurora declared that he had offered to take the Richards to the village where Her Ladyship had an errand to run, and that she would take up Ianthe with her. 'For we leave tomorrow, Lady Fox, and must spend as much time with our dear girl as may be.'

Lady Fox, who had found herself outflanked by the Fentons, with Mr Wilbert Fenton demanding her attention with a constant flow of urbane conversation on the one side while Lady Aurora had changed the tone of the young people's conversation to a more joyful one on the other, was too glad at the news of their departure to object to the outing, and they set off.

'I shall have to go. We took the carriage.'

As the ladies of the house went upstairs in search of pelisses, bonnets and halfboots, the Fentons took a stately leave of Lady Fox, Mr Fenton giving her fulsome compliments that only engraved the sour look on her face, and Lady Aurora thanking her for all the warmth and affection of her welcome these past two days. There could be nothing in this but derision, for Lady Fox had certainly displayed no affection, let alone warmth, but naturally nothing could be said on this point. Her Ladyship merely raised her head higher and made her voice icier when she replied, 'A pleasure.'

'Do let us meet in town,' Lady Aurora said sweetly.

'Do!' said Lady Fox, between clenched teeth.

Audley followed Fox to the study, where he was handed a glass of brandy. The marquis looked at it morosely, and then drank it all swiftly. 'It has begun. What I want for her. Steadman is a good man. Markham too. He is a friendly chap. She would have a happier life, perhaps. Though I'd trust Steadman to be more protective.'

'Are you not being too previous?'

'Steadman's intentions are quite clear. He says he means to visit every day. I do not suppose he did more than glance at Ianthe,' said Audley in a tight voice. 'Only, I don't want to go to the blasted village.'

'I'll come too. We can go off somewhere together,' consoled Fox.

Audley nodded. 'It has been a while, Edward. But you are a good friend.'

With a slap on the shoulder, they went out to the carriages. Ianthe requested that Audley take Mr Steadman's landau as she had something particular to speak to the Fentons about. Fox was debating whether he could fit beside Steadman in a carriage built for four when Ianthe said, 'You come with us, Fox. It is time to tell you of my problem.'

Wilbert Fenton raised an eyebrow at this. Audley grasped Fox's arm and the gaze they exchanged was tinged with desperation on the marquis' part. 'I'll go with Steadman,' said Fox. 'Take Audley up with you.'

'But—' Ianthe looked down on him, Fox reached up and patted the arm that leant on the edge of the landau, giving her a warning look.

'Later.'

She nodded and glanced at Audley, who was standing stiffly beside him, as unlike himself as could be. The Richards were being handed into the other landau, but Sally turned back and crossed the two paces towards Audley. She handed him a scrap of linen.

'I think you dropped this, marquis.'

He took it and glanced at it indifferently, 'I don't think-' he said as he looked up.

She was smiling at him, a little intimate smile. 'It is *definitely* yours,' she said, and turned back to take Mr Steadman's hand, and he aided her to the coach.

On the drive to the village, Audley hardly heard Mr Fenton's talk with Ianthe. It was uttered in a low voice, lest the groom hear it. Audley and Lady Aurora sat opposite them, with their back to the groom, and Her Ladyship said eventually, as he gazed down dazedly at the handkerchief in his hand, 'What is that? Those are not your initials.'

He fingered the three simply but elegantly achieved letters. M-N-M. He had not even asked himself yet what this could signify, was still seeing her smile and wondering how he could last for the next hour watching someone else court her. 'No,' he answered Her Ladyship dully.

'What do they signify, marquis?'

His thumb was touching the third letter as she asked, and suddenly his brain awoke and he gave a crack of laughter. *Marquis*. He thought. *My Noble Marquis*. It was a gift and an insult at the same time. He had had no thought that its purpose was to entice or snare him. He had seen the look in her eyes, that glance a little wicked. It was a parting gift, one that she thought would make him smile. A little jibe at his arrogance. It was, he thought, the perfect souvenir of a woman who had chided him and pricked at his rank and arrogance from the first.

'Is it a jest, then?' asked Lady Aurora, gazing at him with rapt attention.

He turned to face her, the beautiful wife of his friend who had become his friend too, and looked her full in the face. 'It is,' he said simply. 'A lovely, cruel jest.'

She put a gloved hand on his arm. He put the handkerchief away, as though he was freeing himself of it, and looked off to one side, gazing at the hedgerows on the road, bursting with autumn fruits.

The landaus pulled up at the inn, and ostlers came forward to attend, bowing low to the marquis before dealing with the horses. Audley had hardly noticed, but Miss Richards was behind one of these men, revealed by his lowered back. The marquis met her ironic eye.

He frowned and walked over to her casually.

'Am I supposed to thank you for the gift?' he said.

'You understood!' she said delightedly, but with an eye to where her mother was looking. She turned a little away from him, so that they might not seem to be conversing, and began to shake out her pelisse. 'I wanted you to puzzle over it and then have to ask me.'

'Where you would deliver my slap-down personally?' he said. 'And to think I let you ride my Sapphire!'

'You did not mean to do so at all! You meant to terrify me!'

'I did. But why the gift now?'

'Oh, when I heard you were to go to London, I thought you might need something to add to the sweet flattery of society.'

'My noble marquis,' he said. 'Yes, very complimentary and *just* what my rank demands.'

She turned to him then and gave the smallest curtsy she could so as not to draw attention in the inn yard. 'Precisely,' she said and looked up at him to share the joke. He was arrested by her eyes again and then suddenly felt a slap on his shoulder which brought him to his senses.

'Shall we go?' Fox said in a tone loud enough to include the whole party.

'Lady Richards has business at the bootmakers,' announced Steadman. 'I shall take them, never fear.'

Then Sally was gone, walking off from Audley with her mother and Steadman.

'Ianthe has promised to show us the sights,' said Lady Aurora, and Fox laughed.

'That will not take you long, I fear.'

'You underestimate my wife's love of shopping,' said Wilbert Fenton dryly.

'Well, I am only in need of silk pins,' Lady Aurora said lightly, 'but I always find village drapers amusing. There are sometimes bolts of fabric *years* old that are very original if used correctly. One never knows what treasures hide in back rooms.'

'Which you will no doubt search every inch of,' sighed Mr Fenton.

'Audley and I must pay a visit, briefly. We shall see you back at the inn at one o'clock or thereabouts.'

'Yes, make your escape, gentlemen.' Fenton looked at a handsome clock tower and said, 'But you really underestimate my wife. I will do my poor best to return her on time.' He bowed and left them as Audley walked off, in the opposite direction to the bootmakers.

After some minutes in which he hardly noticed the road, the marquis attempted a normal tone. 'I've never asked you, Fox. What will you do about marriage? I have never seen you display much interest in the ladies, though you do your duty at balls.'

Fox kicked a stone on his path. 'I don't know. What should I do? I've always had a vague idea I would be married, and I dance with ladies as you said. I suppose I want a peaceable wife but whenever I've met some gentle soul that attracts me somewhat, I freeze. I imagine bringing her home to Studham and I understand how cruel that would be. Could *you* do that to a wife?'

'Sounds like we are both rather more considerate than I took us for.' Audley looked askance at Fox for a moment. 'But other kinds of female dalliance — you do not indulge? You do not have that reputation.'

'I find it unsavoury,' said Fox, with typical bluntness.

The marquis shrugged at the implied insult. 'You are not wrong, my friend. But old habits die hard.'

***

When Audley and Fox made their way back to the inn an hour later it was to regard the interesting sight of Lady Aurora and Ianthe Eames being accosted by a tall, very broad shouldered individual in a long green coat that swept the ground.

He seemed to be holding out his hands to Ianthe. She, to Fox's horror, took them.

'That,' Audley informed Fox, 'Is the Comte d'Emillion-Orsay.' There was something sober in Audley's voice. 'The other important thing for you to know is, he is in love with Ianthe Eames.'

Chapter Fifteen

Antoine

'Antoine!' Ianthe said, clasping his hands as if in a dream. The memories that she had been ruthlessly suppressing before this, memories of Paris, her papa, and another life entirely, now flooded back and her hands shook in his. Her eyes filled as she gazed up at him, the comte's own eyes nearly black and full of intensity. 'Antoine ... how ... why?'

'To see you,' he answered simply.

The marquis and Fox had arrived, and in a reprise of Fox's move earlier, Audley slapped a hand on the Frenchman's shoulder. 'My dear Comte!'

The spell was broken, and Ianthe's hands were dropped.

***

Re-entering the Hall at Studham, Lord Fox ignored the servants' desire to take the ladies' bonnets and pelisses and jerked his head at Ianthe.

'In here!' he said, heading for the study.

'In a moment,' she answered flatly, untying her bonnet strings.

'Now!' he thundered.

Both of the Richards jerked their heads, not having heard that tone from him in a while. They exchanged worried glances while Ianthe (wearily, thought Lady Richards) followed him. Lady Richards made to go after them, feeling suddenly very protective of the weary Ianthe, but Sally held her back, whispering, 'Edward will not hurt her.'

Ianthe entered the study slowly and looked for a second at Fox's furious back. She sighed. 'I think it will be better, my lord, if—'

He spun on his heel to face her and covered the four paces towards her in a second. He snatched at her bonnet. 'Why are you still wearing this thing?' He plucked it from her head, and she watched, detached, as 600 francs of French millinery flew over the back of a chair. 'Take off that...' his fingers made a gesture of disgust at the military frogging on her bronze pelisse, '... and sit down.'

She did so, but with no answering spark of either amusement or anger, just the same weariness she had had since the encounter with the comte in the village.

None of the things that had come to his lips on the journey home, none of the impudent and intrusive enquiries or demands that he had wished to use to wrest the truth from her could be uttered — they had been raised in his brain on the journey, only to be dismissed. He had no rights here, and he knew it, but he could not abide her pain. So, he said instead, in a low, harsh tone, '*Tell me*!'

She had been sitting with her discarded pelisse beside her and her eyes lowered to her lap, but at this she looked up at him for a second, holding his eye, but then in a quick movement, she had stood and run from the room. Fox, startled, took a step to follow, but instead sunk to the sofa and distractedly began to stroke her pelisse. Broodingly, he remained there for two minutes or more when the quick figure in the fawn striped day dress re-entered the room. She moved past him to the desk and let something spill from her hands. He joined her there, looking down at a dazzling array. A very long pearl necklace, the glint of diamond studs, some collar of large, flawless rubies. She threw down a torn scrap of paper on top. *Tout ce que j'ai pu trouver encore*, he read.

He met her eyes, distant and troubled, but before he could speak, she said. 'My mother's jewels. I knew it must have been him. And now he's here.'

'The comte? I don't understand.'

'Neither do I. There are many things I do not understand about this.'

'This comte held your mother's jewels for you?'

'No, I had to sell them to pay debts before I left Paris.'

'But this is a king's ransom!'

'There were a great many debts. Recent gaming debts. I found a bureau drawer full of them. Debts of honour. Papa did nothing by half.' A rueful laugh shot through her, but he saw her tremble. She had always been so full of spirit, so strong, and it came to him then how much she had concealed. Her papa, whom she still could not mention without deep affection, had died only perhaps ten months ago. She had come to this god-forsaken house only to be met with patronising disdain from the other Foxes and with indifferent avoidance from him, while still in the midst of her grief. His one act of duty, to offer her a home, had included no compassion or care. He knew from her clothes what a fall in position she had taken when she moved here as poor relation, but the riches on his desk now underlined that fall. To her though, he could see them conjure up another, happier life with her papa. Fox frowned. 'But you recognised that the comte had sent these to you even though the note was not signed? How?'

'He … I cannot say how. I knew.' She turned

away, as though shaking something off, and then turned back to him once more. 'I wanted to tell you; I wanted your advice as to what to do about them. They are not mine anymore.'

He picked up the silver locket. 'Could you not even let yourself keep this?'

'I took out the lock of Mama's hair that it used to hold. But the diamond at the centre bought me one less vowel, one less creditor.'

'It must,' he said, deeply ashamed that he had not asked her about any of this before, 'have been very difficult.'

'As to the loss of fortune, I did not mind it. I have never really understood our finances, but in the pretence of being any number of things in many countries, we have not only lived in luxury. I have been a pastor's daughter, or a lawyer's, or a duke's. Latterly we settled into the Paris elite, it was true, but like a soldier I was always ready to move to a worse billet if necessary.'

'It sounds an anxious, difficult life. No security for a young girl.'

'But you are quite wrong. Security does not come from a house like this, or from a settled existence. Papa was my security.' She smiled reminiscently. 'Wherever he was, I was safe, even when *guerrillos* chased us in Portugal, or we escaped with only these jewels in Bordeaux, Papa was with me and I was safe and very happy.'

Her breath caught in a sob and he grasped her hands and drew her to a seat.

'Why did you talk to Mr Fenton about this?'

'Because it is so strange. So many things about this.'

'You mean *why* did he buy them back for you?'

'Oh, I know why he did that. And I feel oppressed by it.'

'Has he offered for you?'

'The situation is much more complicated than that. I cannot speak of it; you would have to understand much of the background…'

'Take as long as you need.'

She looked up and met his eyes piteously. 'Edward, I am very confused and weary about all this. Above all else, Antoine has brought back another…' A tear fell and Fox grasped her hands more firmly. 'That hurts,' she complained, laughing and withdrawing her hands. 'Can we talk later? I *do* want you to know all, but right now I wish to lie down…'

'Go,' he agreed. 'Forget everything and sleep. You need not think of it today.'

'But there is a puzzle that—' Her voice was tense, weak, and it moved him to see her so.

Fox was brisk. 'Whatever it is, you need not solve it today. You've told Fenton. I do not know him well, but I can see that he is not a man to be bested easily.'

'Yes, Mr Fenton will know what is best,' Ianthe said, like a child.

'My dear girl,' Fox said, his voice still harsh

and low. He touched a tear on her cheek. 'Go now and rest.' Her eyes gave him a watery thank you, and she moved from him.

As she left, Fox called for his horse to be saddled, and left the Hall a few minutes later briskly, putting on his curly brimmed beaver.

***

Fox walked into the salon at Audley, where Lady Aurora sat with her husband, very much as though he owned it. He had not waited in the hall to be divested of his coat, and discarded it now, along with gloves, whip and hat on a chair and side table, saying, 'Hello again, sir. I find I have to have words with you and the marquis if I may.'

'I can guess the cause. The mysterious comte. Has Ianthe agreed?'

'She wishes to tell me all, but is too knocked about by this to be strong enough to explain it now. I thought it would be easier if *you* did, sir. I should tell you that I know of your former occupation.'

Wilbert Fenton raised an ironic eyebrow and said lazily, 'I should not, myself, refer to it as an occupation, merely a few breaks in the monotony that was my existence — before the advent of my lady gave me life.' Here he smiled at his lovely wife who returned it warmly. Fenton looked up at Fox and sighed, but seemed to decide to tell all. 'My brother and I have a French grandmother, you know, and consequently a host of French relations and friends.'

'Had you then, visited Paris before the Terror?'

'I had spent some time in Paris and Versailles as a very young buck of seventeen and eighteen. It was very different from the Paris of today, it had seemed eternal then.' He sighed. 'Anyway, I suppose that is why I was approached to deliver a certain package after the Bastille was stormed.' He laughed. 'It turned out that even the nights I'd spent drinking with the riffraff of Europe in Parisian taverns proved helpful. The mode of speech of the great unwashed was something I could ape well if I needed to be part of the mob.' Back to his urbane self he added, 'I was never, I fear, of a heroic disposition.' He laughed at Fox's expression of admiration. 'I assure you, the biggest danger to my person was the day I had to don a lice-ridden shirt in order to escape a damn trap.' He laughed again. 'I still itch when I think of it.'

'Such peril!' laughed his wife, but the look she cast him was not deceived.

'Now,' said Fenton, eyeing Fox with interest, 'you wish to know about the comte?'

'Ianthe says that there is a puzzle at the heart of d'Emillion-Orsay's sending back the jewels. What is his relation to her?'

'As for that, it is for Ianthe to tell you. I can

say that the comte was in the royalist camp all the time I knew him. While outwardly working for Napoleon's Empire, he was able to pass information to us, sometimes through Eames, once to me directly. He had a flair for deception.'

'He was never caught?'

'Now that is something … I heard tell that he was missing for some months. I have sent an express to Paris to see if more is known of it and to investigate his affairs. The central puzzle that Ianthe faces is how the comte, who was rumoured to be in debt, could buy back her treasure.'

'I see. Is not the most central puzzle *why* he should do so?' Lady Aurora laughed and Mr Fenton lifted an ironic eyebrow. Fox felt himself blush. 'Very well,' he said, 'and so *how* could he have done so? Can you think?'

'He may be an agent for another. I do not know. But I do not believe this is to do with French foreign matters any longer, but with Ianthe's heart. He may even have mortgaged his soul to win her heart.'

Surprisingly, Lady Aurora responded to this. 'There is no question that Ianthe was moved by the return of the jewels.' She looked at Fox directly, smiling gently. 'Men believe that women value jewels because they glitter and add to their beauty. But it is not that. Women value the memories that the precious stones contain, the sentiment that a man donates with even his simplest gift.' She looked down, and to Fox's amazement she lifted her silk-ruffled gown to show one delicate ankle. Fox stared. Entwined around was a slender gold chain from which a tiny gold locket hung. 'It was a gift from the young Mr Wilbert Fenton to me, many years ago. It is more precious to me than my diamond collar.' She lowered her skirt. 'Those jewels are Ianthe's past life. She told me the stories she heard about the grandmother who wore the pearls, her mother's rubies, the diamond studs her papa gave her for her hair. All precious memories.'

'I knew Eames to be in the suds many times over the years,' added Fenton, 'but he never sold a stone to ease his problems.'

Fox paced. 'Can you put a value on them, sir?'

Wilbert Fenton laughed. 'What are you about to do?'

'Pay him back.' Fox said.

'Can you afford it?'

'I must. To give her ease.'

'I see. And will she be at ease if her debt is to *you* rather than the comte?'

'I will make her be at ease,' Fox said fiercely.

Wilbert Fenton gave his sardonic laugh. 'Don't sell out the stocks yet. We have some things to discover. I'll get one of Audley's men to stay on the comte discreetly, while he remains in the area.'

'I never thought of that. Damned intrusive

thing to do, but I'll put one of my men on it.'

'You have someone you can trust?'

Fox thought about it. Until recently, he had never seen that his stepmother had spies in his own household. But he had grown up at Studham and had known some of his servants as children. 'Never fear. Anyway, you are to go to town.'

'Perhaps we should all delay until this is settled.'

'No,' said Fox, frowning. 'Audley's case is desperate. He needs to go.' Mr Fenton cocked an eyebrow at his wife at this. 'You can send me word from London when you get the answer to your express.'

'I shall. Audley—?'

Fox met his eye. 'Needs to be somewhere other than here.'

'Ah!'

'I do not understand why but this business with the comte has disturbed Ianthe beyond measure. I won't let it do so for long.' He bowed. 'Farewell, sir. My lady.'

'Do you mean to meet with the comte?' asked Lady Aurora suddenly. 'I should delay until you hear from us. Ianthe may be troubled by it. She may not think it your place.'

Fox's tawny eyes met the beautiful gaze of the older woman. 'I am not concerned with what Ianthe Eames considers "my place". She has overstepped *her* place since the hour I met her.'

Fenton's eyes looked to be in quick

thought. 'Hold, Fox. There may be something else behind all this. Until I know, don't seek out the comte.'

Since this was said in the tone of an order rather than a request, it might be supposed that Fox would take exception, but he only narrowed his eyes. 'I won't. But if he approaches me, or Ianthe, I will not answer for the consequences.' He looked at the clock. 'I must get back for dinner.'

'You are eager to return to Studham these days,' remarked Audley who had come in time to hear his last remark.

Fox gave him a grin. 'Yes,' he said as he reached for his hat and coat, 'Novel, isn't it?'

Chapter Sixteen

The French Connection

Since Lord Fox's precautionary measures were not yet in force, and by dint of the comte's intimate knowledge of Ianthe, it was relatively simple for him to get a message to her. He asked a groom to enter the house in search of her maid.

'Cherie!' he said as that peculiarly upright figure appeared in the small nook of trees where he had summoned her.

The maid was silent, looking at him with cold eyes.

'Are you not pleased to see a friend, my dear?'

Still she was silent.

'I remember many a night in Bordeaux where you were glad to share a meal with me. Why do you look at me so now?'

Cherie did not respond.

He looked down. 'Ah, you suspect my motives.' He looked up again, meeting her eyes with an open expression. 'I just wished to give her what was hers.' He sighed. 'I did not expect thanks, but it is too hard to receive such looks from both of you for only that. Were we not friends, Cherie?'

'Before you were Comte d'Emillion-Orsay, I believed that we were. What is it that you want, comte?'

'Deliver this to "Miss Eames" for me.' He smiled. 'It is strange to call her so. For the last few years, she has been Mademoiselle de Fontaine.' He laughed. 'And before that de Vere, and before that … I do not remember.'

'Did you know us before that? Or are you seeking information?'

He laughed. 'The war is over, Cherie. What information can I sell these days? And I sold *to* Joseph, I didn't sell his secrets, or he should not have lived peacefully as de Fontaine these last years.' Something passed across Cherie's face at this, but she made no comment. 'I wanted Ianthe to have her mother's jewels. What sin have I committed?'

'If that is all you wanted, why are you here? You have delivered them already.'

'There are still some things I could not give her. What about the amber pendant, and her mother's jewellery box?'

'And so?'

But he saw her tremble, and narrowed his

eyes. 'The letter tells her where they may be.'

She held out a hand to receive it. 'I'll give it to her,' she said briefly and turned away.

'Cherie!' he called after her. 'Do not be so cold with a friend. For Joseph's sake.'

She stopped at this, but did not turn around. 'For those precious days, I wish you well comte. But for now, my girl has a new life and her past must stay dead.'

'Don't you want to come home Cherie? Back to Paris? My position there now is secured. I could help you both.'

Cherie turned to him and laughed mirthlessly. 'After all we have seen, my dear comte, the falling of a king's head and an emperor's crown, how can you talk of security?' She walked off, back upright as ever.

Once out of his sight, she ordered a gig at the stables and drove herself to Audley. There was something in all this, something that she needed to discuss. She had never hidden truths from Ianthe, or only one, but just now she felt that the strains of the loss of her father might incline the young girl to need sanctuary of a kind. Cherie was not sure what kind of sanctuary Comte d'Emillion-Orsay might be. He could indeed be a blessing, but Cherie needed advice.

When she reached the stables, she saw a mount she recognised as Lord Fox's being led out and wondered if he had been having the same thoughts. She entered by the servants' quarters, approaching the butler to beg his indulgence in letting her in to see Mr Fenton. She was still clutching the comte's note. 'I must deliver this into his hand,' she said, but her tone was coolly removed.

The corpulent butler, Forrest, approved of her manner. A superior maid indeed. He gave her a respectful gaze from his rheumy eye. 'Certainly.' He led the way, with slow dignity, to the salon where Mr Fenton sat writing another letter. Cherie was surprised that the wheezing butler had made it thus far. 'A maid has brought a letter for you, Mr Fenton.'

Lady Aurora looked up from her sketchbook in mild surprise. Fenton did not look up, but continued writing. When the door closed behind the butler, Cherie said, 'I hope that is not to Sebastian, M'sieur Fenton, for he is already in Geneva.'

Fenton looked up, eyebrows raised, and a slow smile came over his lips. 'Cherie! I told Ianthe to send you, or I would have raided the Servants' Hall to come to you.' He was standing now, and his wife did not blink as he came forward and held out his hands to the maid. The woman grasped them.

'Hello again, Wil-*bert*.' Her pretty accent pronounced it *Weel- berr,* and she smiled at him.

'How do you at Studham? Are there rats in the attic?'

Cherie raised her terrible black brows. 'Do

you care?'

'I cannot bear to think of it. Audley will be sorry to have missed you.'

'I hear Lady Fox is a terrifying mistress,' said Lady Aurora, with concern.

Cherie shrugged. 'Lady Fox does not pay my wages, I work for Ianthe only and so I have made it known. I am housed by Lord Fox, not Her Ladyship, and he has now instructed the butler to keep my duties reserved for my girl.'

'Still, Cherie…' sighed Wilbert Fenton. 'Sit.'

'I won't. Servants. The comte gave me this to give to Ianthe.'

'He met you already?' Mr Fenton's mobile eyebrow rose. 'He is a man of laudable talent. And so? You wish me to read it before she does? That is not like you.'

'Of course not. I will give it to her upon my return, but I cannot like it. I came because I have had a thought.' He nodded for her to continue. 'There was something desperate about Antoine today, *Wil-bert*. I could smell it.'

'Wilbert tells me that your instincts were never wrong, mademoiselle.'

Cherie shrugged at Lady Aurora with a faint smile, but began to pace, displaying her agitation. 'When we were in London, I told you already that everything was wrong after Joseph died. *Tout*. I was not myself, I could not think, not even really care. After the letter from the Foxes arrived, securing my dear one's future, I even stopped considering it, much.' She sighed. 'We were very rich this time in *Paris*. Joseph played hard at the start, but once he had secured enough money, he stopped gaming, I *know* he did. Or only enough for his social obligations. And yet he died, the lawyer said, with many unpaid bills and a drawer full of vowels, some dating back months. *When* did Joseph ever buy time to pay debts of honour?'

Fenton's face was calculating.

She continued. 'And the gentlemen whose names were upon them. I could swear they were not in his circle. He had been going out a good deal in the month previous to his death, but not dressed for society. He talked to me of being tired of the secrets, but it was as though he were once more in the old intrigue. He spoke of taking Ianthe back to England. I think,' Cherie's voice halted and she controlled it, '... that he was hesitant because he knew what *my* life would be here. In Europe, the upset of war and the displacement in peoples made it easier for me to pass as anyone he chose — but here there is only one place for me. I told him he should leave without me.'

'He never could have done so.'

'But his tone was *urgent*, *Wil-bert*. There was some upset coming ... We had almost settled on Cadiz, because he said he wished to avoid "the next change" as he called it. I have no idea what he meant.' She paused. 'I'm not sure if much of this matters. Everyone was shocked when Ianthe sold the jewels, including me. She did so before I knew it. There were those who thought our circumstances made it the perfect time to claim her beauty for themselves. Some who were rich enough to bear the brunt of even Joseph's debts. Some offered marriage, some protection,' Lady Aurora winced, 'but she would not have them, and paid back every penny with those treasures. I was *triste*, for we had carried those baubles the length of Europe, in sacks, hidden in the lining of coats, in many ways. Joseph meant them to be Ianthe's last *securité*. At times they were all he had. But not, I thought, for these last years.' She looked into the distance, remembering, thought her onlookers, a happier time. 'Anyway, the comte was one of those who offered for her.' Cherie paused her pacing, looking at them both. 'As a girl, when we were in Bordeaux, or one earlier time in Paris, I think Ianthe admired Antoine very much. He saw her as a child then, and treated her much as Audley or you did *Wilbert*, but my girl blushed when she saw Antoine d'Arcy. I thought, when Joseph died and she confessed his offer to her, that she would marry him. But all she said was, "Why *now*, Cherie?" Ianthe is no fool. She thought something was wrong. But it broke her heart anew.'

'I see,' said Fenton. 'And now you do, too? Think there is something wrong?'

'*Il y a quelque chose*. *Something*. Someone was in Joseph's study in the Paris house. Things had been moved out of place. Someone was searching.'

'You suspected even then?'

'I saw, but I could not piece together myself or my dear girl, never mind such petty conundrums. I concluded it was perhaps some servant not long in our employ scavenging his dead master's goods.'

'Perhaps the person did not take away, but put in.'

'The vowels? I had that thought today. But it could have been Antoine, the lawyer de Farge, or any of a dozen other visitors. I cannot say.' She laughed. 'At the time, I even asked Antoine to look into it.'

'He may have done so.'

'He is too eager. It is something else, Wil-bert,' she said in that French fashion. 'Something makes him more desperate. Perhaps he is here for Ianthe's heart and perhaps I should trust him as I did in the past.' She shrugged, locking eyes with Fenton. 'Talk to Audley. He knew him, too.'

Mr Wilbert Fenton walked the strange maid to the stables, no doubt to give her further instructions, considered the servants who passed by. As they reached the stable yard, the maid turned to the elegant gentleman.

'There is another thing, *Wil-bert.*' He looked down at her, eyes serious. 'The jewellery box was sold too. You know that there is a compartment in it...'

'Yes. But Joseph was not so dim as to—'

'No, it is something that *I* placed there. But it is a thing I do not wish Ianthe to see.' The look in those large dark eyes, still as beautiful as the first day he had seen them, moved Mr Fenton to take a step towards her as though to offer comfort. A slight gesture with a fluttering hand held him off and he stood, waiting. 'I placed our wedding lines there.' The imperturbable Mr Fenton's jaw dropped a little. 'In truth, Joseph and I were married for many years.' Fenton blinked. 'A year after I came to care for my little one. *He* wanted to tell our close friends, but *I* would not. At first, it was because of the way we lived, adopting different lives. What good would it have been to have Ianthe know I was really her mother now? She would worry if I aped being a maid, or a governess, or whatever. Later, it was because I knew this day would come. We might move back to England, and what will an adventuress such as I lend to Ianthe's reputation in society? I will stay by her until she marries, and then I will disappear. But I do not want the comte to find the box before I do. Will you help me *Wil-bert*? For Ianthe's sake?'

'For your own sake alone, Mrs Eames,' Mr Fenton bowed.

Cherie's eyes filled and her head rose a little. 'Thank you. You are the first, besides my husband, ever to call me so.' She smiled sadly. 'And, I suppose, the last.'

'Leave your worries with me, my dear. We shall see if Antoine is still our friend, and I will find the box and bring you the document. We will solve the puzzle. But this must be a trying time for our girl. You see to her.'

Chapter Seventeen

Times Past

It had made nothing to the servants in the Rue Saint-Jacques in Paris that the lady's maid shared the master's bed. It was a usual situation after all. Gentlemen took their amusement where they may. That even le majordome of the house (the butler) referred decisions to Cherie was unusual, as was the evident affection that the Chevalier de Fontaine's daughter showed to her maid, but then the maid had been a favourite since the girl was a child. Cherie's beauty had obviously held their master, it was true, but everyone knew he visited many of the revels of Paris, and was a gamester. Still, wages were paid, and the household was a joyful one, and the servants accepted the situation unremarked. After the death of their master, some of the more jealous of the maids predicted the comeuppance of the master's mistress, now sure to fall back to her rightful place in the house. But they were wrong. Ianthe insisted that Cherie still sleep in the master's bed, and for the first three days she too had slept there, wrapped in the arms of her maid.

Eventually they had emerged, to face an army of debtors and also mourners. It was Cherie who began to order things, somewhat listlessly, and who behaved in short like the lady of the house. Mademoiselle de Fontaine, catching some slight to Cherie from a jealous maid, rounded on the girl in fury and no other voice lifted against her. When visitors came, Cherie stood in the room as chaperone-maid. When they left, she took her seat beside Mademoiselle as usual, the girl often in her arms.

***

Ianthe told herself to behave like her father's daughter. This weak-kneed behaviour was not to be borne. Antoine was just ... Antoine, an old friend. She could not deceive herself that he alone brought back memories of her father. Actually, so did Audley and Mr Fenton, so it was not merely this.

Antoine's real family name was obscure to her. He had lived, for at least some of the time, as they had — an adventurer with different identities. She had therefore called him by his given name, Antoine, and her father had called him friend. He was handsome, so handsome, and Ianthe's heart had admired him since she was twelve years old and began to feel a tender attachment to his teasing smile. Audley had been handsome, too, but his teasing took the form of cuffing her head, or upending her when she was very little and throwing her onto a haystack. He generally criticised her, in the way of a brother, when they met, and so she had been immune to the marquis' charm. Antoine's teasing had been gentle and playful, and she had fallen for him completely. Later, for fun it seemed, the marquis had taken to paying Ianthe fulsome compliments, often to ape and amplify some kind comment of Antoine's, she'd felt, and Ianthe had merely thrown cushions at him. Ianthe noted that this seemed to rein in Antoine's sweetness to her somewhat, and then it was only at odd moments, when they were one step removed from the company, that Antoine had paid her such compliments.

As time passed, Ianthe could not but know that her beauty had affected others. She became sought after in Paris, and she had received a flattering number of proposals, all of which she had refused in a heartbeat. None were right for her, but when Antoine appeared again, perhaps after some months of absence, her heart skipped a beat. Over the years she had overheard, though she should not have been party to such conversations, of his women. Antoine had a short engagement to a rich Italian contessa, some Parisian mistresses that she knew about, and no doubt many more she had not known of. Why this added to, rather than subtracted from, his attraction Ianthe could not say, but it did. It had fuelled her first jealousy when in her adolescence, and confused her too, since he still found the time to say such sweet words to a mere girl. 'Your hair is as pretty as the night sky,' he said carelessly to her once, and she had slept on these words for a year. His affairs, then, in her earlier years, were none of her business, as she well knew. But when Antoine crossed their paths again after she was fifteen and a woman grown, and once more paid her compliments, she had held back.

'You are the most beautiful woman in Paris, my sweet mademoiselle,' he had said to her once, and she had not smiled.

'Tell it,' she had said, meeting his eyes squarely, 'to *la duchesse.*' She had been referring to his latest flirt. He had raised his eyebrows at this, and bowed formally to her for the first time as she walked off.

After this, Antoine's affairs were not talked about in Paris. She tried hard not to make too much of this, but it had given her hope. He appeared at Ianthe's side from time to time, he took her aside to say pretty things. He implied a great deal. She knew the work he was engaged on, he told her. He could not come to her as yet, but if only she would wait for him... Ianthe had given no promises, but she had waited for him even so. But she noticed he kept his devotion a secret from her father. Only Cherie guessed, Ianthe thought, though she never discussed it. But Cherie could read every mood of hers.

When the comte had proposed after her father's death, Ianthe had finally, in her grief, told Cherie.

'It is what you wanted for so long, ma petite,' said Cherie warmly, but a little guardedly had thought Ianthe. 'When are you to be married?'

'Why *now*, Cherie? Why did he ask only now?'

Cherie nodded, had understood that she had refused him, and had taken Ianthe into her arms as she cried anew.

And now he had followed them to England. Ianthe's heart was wounded once more.

Chapter Eighteen

Jewels at Dinner

Lady Richards looked at the walking boots that they had been able to purchase in the village. This was as far as she had committed herself. They had bought the boots. A groom informed her later that her coin had been refused: the bill had already been settled.

She, who had been avoiding Mr Steadman's eye for the entire day, had sought his gaze then and let hers' express her thanks. The look she had received in return had shaken her. How could Mr Oscar Steadman's quiet, serious eyes turn to fire in just a second?

Sally had been the conduit for her learning more about Mr Steadman's situation in life, as she chatted to him in the carriage.

'Is your home many miles from here, Mr Steadman?'

'I have a small estate five miles the other side of Audley. Ten miles from Studham, then.'

'Ah!' said Sally. 'Yet you are staying at Audley now, you said.'

'Yes. I have some pressing business in the area which requires my attention. It is too far to ride each day, so my friend houses me.'

'The marquis is leaving for town in some days,' said Sally — and there was something in her voice that her mother would consider later, 'I hope that will not upset your plans.'

'Perhaps I shall ask my other old friend to house me instead. Do you think I might add to your party?' Lady Richards dropped her reticule on the floor of the carriage and Mr Steadman retrieved it, handing it to her and saying, 'Should you object, ma'am?'

'St … stay at Studham?' Lady Richards asked faintly. 'I … it is hardly my place …'

Sally was surprised by her mother's lack of address. She had been oddly distracted since the Curtis affair, and Sally had tried hard to restore her to her normal spirits. 'We are guests there too. For my part, another guest at the dinner table would be welcome.' Sally sighed. 'You heard a little of our situation, sir. It is useless to pretend it is a completely happy one.'

'That might change very soon,' said Mr Steadman. 'Sometimes things change in the blink of an eye.'

'Oh yes,' Sally agreed. 'For us it was in the blink of an eye that Miss Eames arrived. Everything changed after that.'

'She seems a remarkable young woman,' Mr Steadman reflected.

Sally looked at him askance. Did Mr Steadman wish to pursue Ianthe? He never seemed to engage her in conversation, but then he was a quiet man. For all the machinations that her mother must have put in while she had walked with Audley, Sally felt no interest more than politeness in her direction. It had relieved her, for she hated to give offence, and Mr Steadman did not have laughing eyes or a teasing smile... but because of his lack of interest in her, she had found herself relaxed in talking to this strangely upright figure. It was a shame, Mr Steadman seemed like the perfect gentleman. The care he took of her mama, for instance, she could only admire. His hand was on her elbow to help her over rough cobbles, he had set the chair for her at the bootmakers' shop, he had enquired whether she needed to rest after their tour of the village and had bought them all refreshments at the inn. He had declared the window draughty and had insisted that her mama exchanged seats with him. He held her chair back like some gentleman of old. If he had had a feathered hat and a cape, Sally thought that he might have laid the cloak over puddles and swept his hat off in a magnificent bow. His manners excelled the more casual modern manners of Fox or even Audley, and Sally admired them.

'Tell us a little about your home, Mr Steadman.'

'It is very old, from old Queen Elizabeth's time, in fact, with the odd wing added rather haphazardly in the centuries after. It has not the opulence of Audley nor the grandeur of Studham, but I think it the prettiest house in the county.' He laughed. 'You must excuse my bias. It is a fine old house to grow up in, and my parents were very happy there.' He smiled. 'I like my house in London too, not as large as Fox House, but it is situated in a good place for all the Seasons' amusements.'

'Do you spend much time there?' asked Sally.

'Not so very much. But I enjoy London and I would happily extend my visits there if my circumstances changed.'

He could only be talking about his marriage! Sally believed that this quiet gentleman was setting out his stall so frankly so that she and her mother would inform Ianthe of his comfortable circumstances. Sally found a second to whisper this to her mother.

Lady Richards was frozen and on fire by turns. The three glances they had exchanged directly during the day had almost made her swoon. As he exchanged chairs with her at the inn, he had looked at her so lovingly that it seemed to melt her insides. He had held her elbow once more and said, 'Are you quite well, my lady?' in a way that had sounded caring but that she knew to be teasing her. How it was possible to feel a searing heat, through the layers of pelisse and dress, she did not know. She had held his sleeve back as they left the inn and hissed, '*Pray* do not look at me! Do not *touch* me.'

He did not turn to her, but she thought his body shook with a chuckle. 'I shall do worse.'

It was no wonder that she was a nervous wreck. The prospect of having to meet Curtis Fox at dinner, which had loomed so large in her mind earlier, now was but the bite of a gnat. Easily squashed.

***

Sally had visited Ianthe's room before dinner and found her much restored in spirits. She was wearing one of the Paris gowns that Sally so envied, this time in striped pink silk with a broad band beneath the bust. The cut was excellent, slimmer than the English style. It was adorned at the low neckline with a starched gauze ruffle that gave it a regal touch. Ianthe wore her hair high and clasped around her neck was a ruby collar, three strands of intricately set fine rubies, that enhanced her long neck to perfection.

'Oh!' sighed Sally. 'How beautiful! But for dinner here at Studham—' Sally gasped as Ianthe took her arm and clasped a diamond bracelet over her wrist. The French maid was at her other side, and had put a diamond hair ornament beside Sally's shining top knot. 'Whatever—?'

'Take these to your mother, and bid her wear them tonight.' Sally's hands were full of the enormously long pearl string and she looked perplexed. 'They may not be so fashionable these days — but ask her to wear them for me. I'll await you both at the top of the stairs.'

Lady Richards, the pearls making a four-tier collar around her neck and falling becomingly over the bosom of her blush satin gown, rushed to meet Ianthe, who was standing back upright, at the top of the stairs. 'I'm wearing them, Ianthe, but why—?'

'Let us to dinner, ladies,' said Ianthe calmly and all of them were shown into the dining room direct, for the family, said Jenkins, awaited them. Ianthe smiled at him as she passed, and then she met the eye of the dragon-lady.

Lady Fox, her mouth ready to castigate her guests for their rude tardiness, gasped, as did her son Curtis, at the ladies' entrance. She could not speak.

The Richards took their seats first, and then Ianthe settled herself opposite Curtis' habitual chair next to his mother's. The gentlemen sat, and Fox took a seat opposite the ladies, next to Curtis. This caused some choreography with place settings being moved from the head of the table, undertaken by Jenkins and two footmen with silent efficiency.

'You are decked with finery this evening, Miss Eames,' sneered Lady Fox. 'No doubt some *gentleman* sent these to you.'

Ianthe blinked, as Fox saw, and her back stiffened and she opened her mouth, but Fox said lazily. 'They were her mother's.'

Lady Fox did not look reassured by this information. Her eyes slid to the Richards and noticed for the first time the fine diamond bracelet on Sally and the pearls which glowed on Lady Richards' breast.

'Where have you these—?' Curtis spluttered. 'They must be worth—'

'Do not be vulgar, Curtis,' reprimanded Fox, bored.

'She has borrowed them from me, Mr Fox,' answered Ianthe.

The baroness' bosom swelled. 'You are all,' intoned Lady Fox at her most disapproving, 'vastly overdressed for a family party.' As she herself was wearing a handsome diamond necklace and a silken gown over-trimmed with lace, as well as a crystal tiara (worn, Ianthe knew, to make her dependants feel her superiority) this was a ridiculous remark.

'Really? It is just that we should not like to appear as *beggars* at your table, your ladyship.'

Sally and Lady Richards gasped, and Fox let out a burst of laughter. Curtis blushed and looked down.

'What ludicrous thing will you next say to cause offence, Miss Eames…?'

'It is not Ianthe who first said it, your ladyship, but Curtis.'

Lady Fox looked at sea, then her eyes went to her son's. 'My son would *never* say such things to a lady.'

'I did not, Mama,' Curtis pleaded. 'If Fox passed on what I said in anger, only because he provoked me, Mama...'

'Did you carry a tale to our guests about my son?' said Her Ladyship, with narrowed eyes on her stepson.

'No. Curtis shouted so loudly that the ladies overheard us.' He looked first at his stepmother and then at his brother. 'The Marquis of Audley heard it too, as did Mr Oscar Steadman. They were,' said Fox with relish, 'quite disgusted.'

'Curtis!' Lady Fox was humiliated.

'He *hit* me, Mama!' Curtis cried.

Ianthe, who had been eating calmly throughout this interchange said, before Lady Fox could turn wrath upon her stepson, 'The Marquis of Audley said that *he* would have hit you much sooner.' She put her fork to her mouth and ate, her eyes blandly regarding Curtis.

'Apologise, Curtis!' said Lady Fox, in a voice Curtis had never heard directed at him.

Ianthe blinked. She had not quite believed this possible.

Curtis quaked, but had the grace to look shame-faced. 'I ... I am deeply sorry, Lady Richards, Miss Richards,' he said, meeting their eye for a tenth of a second each. 'If Fox had not provoked me ... but no, I was wrong and insulting, but I swear I never meant you to hear... That is neither here nor there, I ... I should never have used words—'

'*Desist!*' screamed Lady Fox, 'I did not mean to *them*, but to the marquis and Mr Steadman.'

'So, *this* is where Curtis learns his manners,' remarked Ianthe to Lady Richards at her side. She had not troubled to lower her voice and the baroness frowned awfully, but her cheeks rouged.

Lady Richards gasped and her pearls rattled against a plate, drawing the baroness' eye. 'You have had your apology,' said Lady Fox with heightened colour. 'It was not nice of my son to mention your *circumstances*,' Lady Richards blushed at this verification of Curtis' insult, 'but you well know that his brother makes it his business to goad him, and must not mind it.' This was said in the tone of command, and Sally took exception to it, but her mother nudged her before she could respond.

Ianthe said calmly, 'Why, how could Lady Richards doubt her welcome when her hosts treat her so warmly?' Lady Fox met her ironic eye with pinched lips. 'You must not be concerned, Curtis. It is unlikely that the marquis will tell the district that you behaved so shabbily.' Curtis was now livid, as well as flushed with humiliation. There was a moment's silence, then Ianthe appeared to think again. 'But Mr Steadman, now. I am not sure whether he is so tight-lipped. He did look very conscious, did he not?'

She appealed to the two Richards ladies and Sally said with a courage born of the insult to her mama, 'He clenched his fist.'

'I suppose he said in actions what Audley had already said in words.'

'This topic has worn itself out,' said Lady Fox with finality. 'Let us finish our meal in silence, if you please.'

They did so, and presently the ladies left for the withdrawing room (their hostess sadly deserting them for her bed) while Fox sat opposite the humiliated Curtis, rolling some brandy around his glass. 'Your follies are catching up with you, Curtis.' The young man could not look up, and after a moment Fox relented somewhat. 'You are young yet, there is time to make peace in your life. You are the heir of Studham, it is true. But your mama has led you to the false expectation of inheritance. I have always meant to marry eventually — but even if I did not, there are but six years between us. Unless I die an early death, you will have a short reign as king.'

Curtis gasped.

'Unless you kill me. Is that it, Curtis? You act as though you want me dead.' Curtis rose from the table and went to the fireplace, standing with his back to his brother. 'Father left you with the estate in Wiltshire and an income. Can you really not manage on that?'

'You would love nothing better than that mother and I move there and let you take our home, take what is *ours*.'

Fox sighed heavily. 'It was always mine, Curtis. Was there ever a day of your life when you did not know that?' Curtis said nothing. 'Studham is your home and you may stay as long as you please, of course. But if I have wanted you gone, Curtis, can you blame me? Can you really? Is this hell we live in the happiness you seek?' Fox took a swig of brandy. 'This was once a happy home, you do not know. There was laughter and kindness here. I had almost forgotten it, until lately. I remember Audley chasing me around this very table years ago, along with our friends. There was noise and tumult in this place, it was alive. And then it changed.'

'You blame my mother. *Your* mother was a saint, no doubt. I have heard the servants talk. *"It was very different in Lady Hester's day!"* My mother changed Studham, that's what you all mean.'

'It happened before that,' said Fox quietly.

Curtis turned then, a resentful face giving way to genuine interest. 'How so?'

'My father changed after Mama died. Noise was forbidden, as were smiles. He no longer played with me, talked to me. He did not see me for more than five minutes a day for over three years. No one was allowed into the house. When your mother arrived, at least some of that changed. I was allowed to eat some meals with them. If I behaved correctly, I could converse at the table. I thought eventually she would like me, but she never did, and especially once she was full of child. Any interest she had taken in me halted.'

'She said you were an unruly, ungrateful child,' Curtis said, but it was in a tone that was bemused, rather than resentful.

'I probably was. What I am trying to say is that I do not altogether blame your mother for not liking me. But I *do* blame her for raising you with unreasonable expectations. Otherwise, we might have been friends.' Fox bowed at his brother, somewhat formally. 'Goodnight, Curtis.' He left the room.

Curtis sat with the brandy at his elbow, staring into the fire for some hours. But the butler, clearing up the next morning, noticed that little inroads had been made to the decanter, and that the young gentleman's glass was still half full.

Chapter Nineteen

The Fifth Ride

Before leaving Audley, Mr Fenton had dispatched a number of missives. One was addressed to a Mr Rigby-Blyth, lawyer, of Beltane Buildings, London. It contained another note inside, addressed to one Mr Mosely.

Dear Mr Mosely,

I require you to find some information for me. Discover how long the Comte d'Emillion-Orsay has been in England. I do not believe it could be more than a month. Any information about his route here, or other passengers who arrived at the same time, might be useful too.

I am in Kent at the moment, but leave today, so you may visit me at your earliest convenience at my home. I may have another related job for you, so you should make preparations to visit this county, where the comte is at present to be found.

You have been the champion of two young friends of mine, Delphine, the present Viscountess Gascoigne, was the first you aided, I have discovered. Then my own dear Felicity, now Lady Durant. It is amusing to think that another young beauty needs your assistance, but so it is. A local servant has been put onto it, but I would refine more confidence in your sharply pointed nose, sir.

Until tomorrow then,

Wilbert Fenton Esq.

***

It can be intuited from the story so far that Ianthe Eames liked to tackle her problems head on. And so, it was that after shedding a tear at the affectionate note from Antoine d'Emillion-Orsay, she resolved to evade her protectors (Cherie and Fox) and meet him.

She had thus far never been able to see Antoine with a steady heart, but there was something different about her now. Something that she had seen in Fox's eyes when he was so passionately concerned, something unspoken between them that gave her courage now. Once he knew what she had done he would rage at her. She had seen his passion, his true spirit that he tried to hide beneath the curmudgeonly shell, almost from the first. She had at first decided to set it free in the face of his inept dealings with his stepmother and Curtis. Let him see how he could use it to help himself, rather than treat it like some animal in him he had to cage only in order to live with two of the most unpleasant people in Christendom. They, of course, were only like that because of their own problems, but Ianthe could not spare herself for every battle. She had chosen the hidden man she had seen inside Fox, the one who told her she might stay despite what he would suffer from his step-mama, or when he had offered to protect her from the other Foxes.

Lady Fox's problems might already have petrified whatever heart she once had, and Ianthe had given up the attempt to thoroughly understand her. No, the best she could do was stop the dreadful woman hurting the others under this roof. Whether Curtis might be saved she had not considered very long since his manner had so repulsed her. But at the dinner table this evening he *had* looked ashamed, whether by the social consequences of his words or from real insight, Ianthe could not tell. But she had seen Fox notice, and she had some hopes that, restored in spirit as he had begun to be, he might reach out to young Curtis in a better way, giving the surly youth some chance to become a man.

Antoine had included his direction, the inn in the village where they had all taken tea, and Ianthe thought of how she might get there tomorrow without Fox (or Cherie) finding out. She might enlist a maid, she supposed, but that would prove questionable. A sturdy footman or groom would be better, but even that … she had not been here long enough to accurately divide the servants into Lady or Lord Fox's camps. She thought the former camp was liable to be much smaller, but one might just hit on the wrong person.

Could she drag Sally into this? No, too much risk to her reputation. She was still surveying her options when she fell asleep.

***

Mounting Sapphire, the next morning just after dawn, Sally Richards was told that the Marquis of Audley was already gone, as were his guests, except for Mr Steadman. Sally felt strangely bereft, and she hardly noticed that Ianthe, too, was unusually quiet.

She vaguely saw, when they returned from their ride, that Ianthe seemed to be looking from one groom to another, as though searching for someone in particular. When Mr Steadman appeared in the yard, her friend dismounted quickly and went directly to him, having a quick conversation before she jumped up onto the waiting gig. Sally joined her, and was swift about it, impelled by Ianthe's urgency, and was a little surprised when Mr Steadman's horse followed behind.

Could it be that Ianthe favoured this serious man? He was certainly handsome, in a quieter way than say Audley of course, and very manly, but his personality was so at odds with Ianthe's that Sally looked at her askance. 'Are you quite alright, my dear Ianthe?'

'I have mischief brewing, only. Do not fear for me, my dear.'

Sally had surprised a look of satisfaction on Mr Steadman's face, and was slightly intrigued as to what it could all mean. However, her own slightly flat mood gave way to her reveries. It was wonderful to ride Sapphire still, of course it was, but the atmosphere today had not been so jolly. No doubt the Curtis problem had pulled them both down, and she knew Ianthe had been affected somehow by the appearance of the exotically handsome comte, and none of it had anything to do with the absence of a bronze-haired host at all.

The marquis would be in London now, seeing to the business that prised him away. He seemed to think it would be a long business, too. If they should never visit London again she might, she now realised, never, ever see him again. That would be a pity, that was all, for he made her laugh even when she was cross with him. Even if the Houstens took them to London next Season, they might never speak. It was only on race day at Housten Hall that she had ever previously been by his side. She had had him pointed out at the races and once at a ball, but she had been far from him. On such an occasion now, if he did but see her, he would of course come and make her a bow, but there was no guarantee that he *would* see her — it was not as though his friends would alert him to the presence of a middling sort of woman. Not in the way the crowd might say, "Oh look, it is the Marquis of Audley!" This kind of thinking got her all the way to the side door of Studham and she jumped down with the aid of Mr Steadman. She was surprised when Ianthe remained seated and looked back. 'Are you not coming?' she said.

'I have a headache,' said Ianthe with a smile down at her. Sally frowned a little before she caught on.

'Ah, so now I can honestly say that you said so if Lady Fox should be down for breakfast, by any chance?'

'Yes, it may be that your mother might have the headache too.'

Sally looked a little panicked.

'Don't worry, I think Her Ladyship herself will not be anxious to rise before her time after the events of last evening. She won't appear.'

To Sally's astonishment, her mama, wearing a plain cape and carrying a boulle work box, ran from the house. Mr Steadman wrested the box from her hands, placed it under the seat of the gig, and handed her tenderly into the carriage, then he mounted his horse again.

'Oh Sally—!' said her mother, but Ianthe had whipped the horses, and they were gone.

As the threesome entered the inn some twelve minutes later, Ianthe had the notion that she spotted the bald headed, burly back of Stephens the groom in the taproom, and wondered if Fox might find out about this expedition rather earlier than she had anticipated.

Chapter Twenty

In London

The Marquis of Audley arose from his mistress' bed and began to dress. She still slept soundly beneath the silken coverlet, and he looked back at her red curls on the pillow, at her shapely white limbs, and sighed. He had pretended too much wine last night and had just held her, but the lady had discerned something, nevertheless. 'You will not come again, my lord, will you?' she had said against his chest. He had remained silent. 'It is quite alright, my dear. I do not need a passionless lover. I have my husband for that.'

He'd kissed her head and sighed. 'It has been a beautiful diversion, has it not?'

'Just go to sleep.'

Now he dressed. He saw the little bunch of rosebuds that had decorated the bodice of her dress last night, and he unpinned them and quietly stepped back to the bed and placed them on her pillow.

'Farewell, Jinny,' he said softly, and left. As he walked the almost deserted London streets, he wondered why he felt so dull. Every diversion was before him. He had plunged himself into it with a supper party and then a ball, and then the familiar rooms of Jinny, her husband once more absent. In the arms of another, too. What lives they led. All the freedoms he desired, that he was protecting. Discarding one today just meant more for tomorrow. A two-year liaison ended so easily. He should look about him for another.

Maybe not yet. He needed other diversions. He would box at Jackson's this afternoon, make a bet at White's with anyone who thought they could beat his greys, drink gin this evening and pick up racing tips from the jockeys at *Easy Joe's* and go to bed a free man.

That was the plan. He put his hand in the pocket of his coat and calmed himself by rubbing a finger over the raised letters on the fine linen handkerchief. M-N-M.

***

Barely two hours after the Fentons' arrival in London, a cheery little individual in a moleskin waistcoat, crumpled woollen coat and buckskins arrived in Grosvenor Square and was shown in.

'Mr Mosely!' cried Lady Aurora, looking up

from the latest novel. 'How lovely to see you again.'

'What a welcome, my lady!' said the little man, making a low bow. He winked. 'You look pretty as a peach if I may say so.' This was impertinent from a person whose clothes, plus the pinched face of generations of London poor, declared him far beneath her in class — but Lady Aurora did not seem to mind.

'What can we do for you?' she asked warmly. 'Do you have an investigation on? How thrilling!'

'You husband bade me come on a matter of business, my lady.' He moved around the room a little, at ease, then he remembered something. 'The other week, my lady, when I was walking down the Mall, I saw Miss Oldfield — I should say Viscountess Durant now — and blow me if she didn't stop her carriage and come right up to me! Very grand she looked, too. I was pleased as punch. Other gents in the street couldn't believe the way she was greeting a shady cove like me, taking me hand and all.'

'Felicity would have been so very happy to see you, too, sir. You *are* her saviour after all.'

'And the other young 'un? I forgot to ask the viscountess.'

'Oh, the Black-Hearted Lady?' Lady Aurora laughed. 'Lady Letitia is well, and still firm friends with Felicity.'

'That's alright then.' Mr Mosely smiled.

Mr Fenton entered, and after greetings took the unusual step of shaking Mosely's hand.

'You have something already?' he asked.

'Just a little, Mr Fenton. It looked like it might be somefink urgent. I'll take the mail coach tonight, if you tell me what's what, like.'

After being forty minutes with Mosely in his study, Fenton laid his long limbs on a sofa opposite his wife.

Lady Aurora looked on affectionately. 'Something to think about, Wil dear?'

'Mmmm.'

She continued her book, and Fenton closed his eyes, staying thus for close to an hour. Then: 'Am I a fantasist, Aurora? Do I indulge in flights of fancy on a regular basis?'

'You do not.' His wife's reply was definite.

'I have had several seemingly unconnected pieces of information given me today. They should not fit together, but they do. One piece I should reject, but I cannot. There has been a dreadful fraud perpetrated — that is established, I think. But the other thing … It *cannot* be true. But so many fingers pointing to it in my head …' He sat up. 'It cannot be. It has been almost a year since … Still, whether I look a fool or not, I should alert Edward Nicolls.'

'Who?'

'An officer garrisoned in the South Atlantic Ocean.'

'South Atlantic Ocean?' mused Her Ladyship, frowning prettily. 'Is it something to do with trade, the East India Company, perhaps?'

He did not answer directly, but sought his wife's beautiful eyes. 'What can make a man turn away from his beliefs, risk his all, take an enormous, ridiculous gamble?'

'Money. Love.' His wife answered quickly.

'Yes. If I am right, it is lunacy, plain and simple. And wicked, too.' Fenton sighed. 'But some things I can, at least, do.'

'Does Mr Mosely start for Kent today?' asked the quick Lady Aurora.

'I have delayed him with other matters. We may both go tomorrow.'

'You wish *me* to stay here,' she said sadly.

'I think it best…'

'As you will, my dear!'

Mr Fenton began a letter to Edward Nicolls.

Sir,

It is many years since our paths crossed, perhaps we did not part on the best of terms, but I hope you give this communication your attention, nevertheless.

There is a tale that I am in the midst of unravelling — a tale of innocent maidens, rich jewels and star-crossed lovers, but none of this is your concern. In the process of doing so, however, I came to find some other perplexing thing. The purpose of your stay on Ascension Island is also mine in writing to you. A fantastical plot may be in train, but my facts are slim at best. Here they are:

A Frenchman came to England a short time ago. This man has posed as a friend to our enemy for many years, but was in fact a Royalist, passing information to the British. He now lives under the French King and has been rewarded with a title.

The man suddenly has more money than his position suggests likely. A great deal of money.

Some others came on the ship with him. Two names are known to me as staunch friends of our enemy. Men of great wealth and European influence. Others I must deal with, in regard to the part of the story that is not your concern. However, there was someone else, someone whom my informant's informant says spent a deal of time with the Frenchmen on the voyage — a Chinese scholar.

This last gave me pause. Are there not still hundreds of coolies working in that other place now, since slaves no longer are? Chinese.

Far-fetched, impossible. But perhaps not a direction you might have considered danger could arrive from.

This letter must surely reach you before the plot, if plot there is, advances.

I will pass these wild speculations to someone at the Alien Office, of course — you may not know, but I had a connection to that office since Wickham's time - but I think they are mostly asleep these days, feeling the threat disposed of. Thus, I wrote to you directly.

Until I next beat you at cards,

Wilbert Fenton

PS At our last meeting, you accused me of fuzzing the cards. I cannot well remember after this long time if it was true on that occasion, but it very well might have been. I remember Glenfield was of our company, and I had a score to settle with him. Do not allow my status as a rogue to impair your reading of this letter. I have never been more serious.

There were other letters that Mr Fenton had received that day, and there were more to come no doubt, but he had to leave with Mosely and speak to Fox. Because his friend Antoine was more desperate than Fenton had thought. In their cups on several occasions, Joseph, Cherie, Antoine and he had discussed the general, that revolutionary who now wore a crown.

There was a certain order that the general had established in French affairs, a certain stability to the country that must be admired after the bloodbath of the Terror, had said Antoine. The Englishmen had conceded that much, but all three of them had seen that this man also sought to expand his Empire and that his greed might never be assuaged. Antoine, too, found his *person* objectionable, for there was about him an arrogance that flaunted his power. The spilling of French blood on battlefields might never end as long as Napoleon was Emperor, Antoine had said. Fenton would wager that Antoine's true inclination was against the Empire — so why now? If it was for Ianthe, if it was all to gain Ianthe, what more might he do?

He had to see Audley before he left.

He tracked him down at a gaming hell in Sutton Place, much the worse for wine.

'You started early,' Fenton remarked.

'Fenton! Have a glass.'

'I won't. I'm off to Kent early in the morning.' Fenton stood close to the marquis after sparing just nods for his similarly inebriated table fellows. He talked lazily, but under his breath.

'You are?' said Audley, pouring himself another glass idly, spilling wine. 'Stay at Audley. Give the old place my regards. *I* cannot return for two months at least.'

Fenton raised an eyebrow. 'What will you then do when she arrives in London?'

'How did you—?' the marquis started. Then pulled himself up, but one elbow slid off the table, causing him to have to master his resources to pull up again. 'To whom,' he said with dignity, 'do you refer?'

Mr Fenton sighed. 'I did not come to speak of that. I need you to do something. My wife will open my correspondence tomorrow, but you, Audley, must be ready to go back home with the letters if there is anything important on Ianthe's problem.'

'There is hardly time to have a reply from the letters you sent after Cherie visited.'

'I know, but I had sent earlier requests after Ianthe told me about the jewels. I had an express this afternoon. You know Chaumet's?'

'The jewellers on the Place Vendôme? Of course I do.'

'That is where Ianthe sold her jewels. I thought it an unusual arrangement when I heard. They only sell their own designs.'

'And?' Audley was shaking his head in a bid to focus his scattered wits.

'They accepted the jewels, appraised them fairly and paid her, but I have discovered that the comte had already visited them, arranging the whole thing. For a commission, they simply handed the jewels back to him.'

'So, *he* had them all this time? Why did he not just—?' Audley frowned, then led by Fenton's cynical eyebrow he said, 'Ah, to make it seem difficult. To demonstrate his devotion.' Fenton inclined his head ironically. 'But why,' wondered the marquis, dragging his fingers through his bronze locks, 'do you need me to read the answers to your posts? Have them forwarded by a servant.'

'I cannot entrust the kind of information I may receive to a servant.'

'Sinister goings-on in Paris are not my business, however devoted I am to Ianthe. And she has you and Fox looking out for her. I cannot go back to Audley at present.'

'Think, man. Would I have spoken if the problem were merely fraud?'

Audley stared at him, his eyes finally focused. 'How can there be any more to that old trade? We are at peace.'

'Check any correspondence tomorrow,' Fenton said only, and turned to go. 'Oh, and Audley, these pleasures,' Fenton pointed to the cards and the wine glass while looking at his most sardonic. 'You used to indulge in them with style. They do not sit well on you tonight. From *bon vivant* to a drowning man. If you can no longer carry it off with *élan* best not do it at all, my boy.'

Audley sprawled back in his chair and looked at Fenton's back, watching his leisurely stroll to the door, greeting friends briefly on the way — and muttered curses under his breath.

'I thought Fenton was to join us. What ails him?' said one of the other gamesters.

'He smiles, but I always mistrust those eyes,' said another.

Audley regarded his friends. 'Fenton is leaving London tomorrow to stay at Audley.'

'Without you? That's a strange start. Anyway, deal the cards.'

The marquis got unsteadily to his feet. 'I leave you, gentlemen. I fear I must be up early tomorrow.'

'Audley!'

'Leave him. He's been in a foul mood all

night anyway.'

Chapter Twenty-One

The Visit to the Inn

Ianthe had chosen the longest table at the inn to sit, which accommodated six. This was not a major post road, so the inn was not bustling with people, just a few respectable looking guests eating their breakfasts, stealing looks at the beautiful lady in the cerulean blue riding habit, with the matching hat set high. The lady smiled at anyone whose eyes she crossed, and the spectators seemed to be dazed by her magnificence.

'If only,' remarked Lady Richards sadly, 'you were not wearing that *particular* dress, Ianthe, we might have been less remarked. I should have brought a cape for you, too. But I was in such a rush.'

'I may be remarked, I suppose, but I have you and Mr Steadman here to give me countenance. I thank you both.'

'You wish to speak privately with the gentleman?' asked Mr Steadman with his customary directness.

'I do.'

'Then, ladies, please rise and Lady Richards, will you take off your cloak?'

Doing what Mr Steadman said seemed a given, and he disposed of the cloak on the seat Ianthe had vacated beside Lady Richards. He moved the rosewood and boulle work box onto the seat next to him, saying, 'Let us make ourselves more comfortable.'

Ianthe took the seat next to the cape, leaving only the seat opposite hers for the comte when he came. Ianthe gave a small smile in appreciation to Mr Steadman. He was offering her respectable privacy. A bustling waiter, wearing a moderately clean apron, came up to know of their desire, saying, 'I shall just put the lady's cape on the hook—'

'No, you won't,' said Mr Steadman in a voice of command. Ianthe and Lady Richards shared a grin. The waiter, looking aggrieved, bustled off to collect the hot chocolate, rolls and cheese they had ordered.

A large handsome presence stood in the doorway. D'Emillion-Orsay provided more fodder for the breakfasters' eye, handsome as he was and wearing what must be French clothes. His jacket had enormous padded shoulders, beyond even his own broad build, his linen startlingly white, his silk cravat intricately tied and pinned, his shirt points high against the handsome face, his hair a masterpiece of elaborately careless curls swept forward. His dark-eyed gaze was intense, and landed squarely on Ianthe, over the length of the coffee room. A woman at table nearby audibly sighed.

Interposing the gaze suddenly was the figure of Mr Steadman, with his hand out in a friendly fashion, saying, 'My very dear comte.' The comte looked down at the hand, but was only a fraction of a second before he shook it warmly. This gentleman was claiming friendship with him for Ianthe's sake. This was not how he had imagined meeting her again, but he was ever adaptable, so he moved forward to the table beside Mr Steadman and with a swift glance, greeted the ladies and took the seat opposite Ianthe's.

The waiter went for coffee, and then the comte said quietly, 'What is this?' with a side glance at the box on the adjoining seat.

'Have a roll, comte,' said Lady Richards, stretching her hand with the plate.

The comte accepted one, smiled, and looked again at Ianthe.

'They are no longer mine,' Ianthe answered in an under voice.

Mr Steadman and Lady Richards chatted at the other end of the table, while the comte said, 'Of course they are. And, as I have said, I have recently found the amber pendant your father gave you, and your mother's jewellery box. They will arrive from Paris in a few days.'

Ianthe looked at him. 'They are no longer *mine*, Antoine.' Despite herself, her eyes sparkled with tears, but she looked away from the longing in his gaze. He sat back then, crossing his legs, leaning one long arm over the back of the neighbouring chair in disdain. 'So, what will I do with this, then? Shall I walk to the river and toss in the contents? They were never mine, Ianthe. I did this only for you.'

She stayed silent, and the waiter brought his coffee. Lady Richards, nervous that the meeting remain respectable, said, a little too loudly, 'Do you think it may come on to rain, my dear?'

Ianthe turned and smiled pleasantly. 'I think not. We have ample time to get back before the clouds shift,' she added, glancing out of the window.

'Yes, indeed,' agreed Mr Steadman. 'Comte, how is your stay at the inn?'

'It is very pleasant.'

'Do you plan to stay long?'

'I have some business here that is not quite concluded,' he answered, smoothly.

'Ah yes.' Steadman smiled. 'Well, if I or my friend Lord Fox can be of any help to you during your visit you may apply to us at any time.'

The comte gave him an ironic eyebrow, but inclined his head. He turned back to Ianthe. 'I am not *buying* you,' he said under his breath. Ianthe stilled, but looked wounded. Then she met his eye. 'You know, for I told you often in Paris, how I feel.'

'Yet it was only *then* that you offered me marriage, comte.'

'It brought me to the point sooner, is all. I was already arranging to offer for you, but when Joseph died, I *could* not leave you unprotected.'

'*Arranging?* What can that mean?' she asked. 'I can never understand, if you truly meant it, what was the delay.'

'I needed to secure my life, to have a home for you…'

'To cast off your mistresses?'

'There were no women anymore. There have not been for some time. I thought only of you.'

Ianthe looked down at her saucer. 'Yet you did not tell my father.'

'I could only tell Joseph when everything was in place, else he would have forbidden me the house. There could be no half measures in my ability to protect you, you know that. He would never have let you go else.'

'Your words are sweet as always, comte.' She raised her eyes. 'Who did you have to sell to buy these?' Her eyes flicked to the seat beside him.

For a second his eyes were flint, but all he said was, 'I adore you, Ianthe.'

'Let us end this here.' She stood up and said to her friends, 'Are you quite finished? *En y va.* We should leave before the rain.'

Mr Steadman clapped the shoulder of the comte in a show of fond farewell, Lady Richards curtsied slightly, and they left the room.

The landlord, who had just caught the last of the breakfast visit, said to the waiter, 'Was that Mr Steadman? He and that French gentleman must be friends indeed. Not one to show affection is Mr Steadman.'

'Well, if they is friends, Mr Plodgitt, sir, I don't quite know why Mr Steadman was in such a mood. Fair snapped me 'ead off he did!'

The landlord gave him a slap on the head. 'No doubt you deserved it,' he said and bustled back to his kegs.

***

Sally, eating her breakfast in solitary splendour, wondering what this morning's expedition was about, was interrupted by the entrance of Curtis Fox. He was dressed carefully, his fair hair was tidy, his eyes not ringed with the red of a drunken night. A spoonful of porridge was halfway to her mouth, frozen in mid-air, and Curtis bowed low. 'Miss Richards.' He looked embarrassed and flushed, but determined, and Sally found her voice.

'Mr Fox.'

'Might *I* call you S ... Sally, too?' he stammered.

'I ... Certainly!' Sally croaked and coughed as her porridge went down the wrong way.

'Sally. I hope you will accept once more my apology—'

'No need,' she was saying automatically and with embarrassment, still coughing a little.

'Yes, there is. It was appalling, what I said.' Sally blinked at his grammatical syntax. '*I* am appalling, most of the time. If I grieved you, I truly am—' Curtis' blue eyes were shining with something, and Sally sat upright.

'Mr Fox, Curtis, I can see that you are truly sincere. Pray do not worry over it any longer. You said *that*, perhaps, to goad your brother and I shall not think of it again. Will you not have breakfast? Shall I ring?'

'I told Jenkins not to bother. I just wanted to ... before the others ...' He bowed again. 'Pray tell your mother what I said. I do not think I can bear to. I'm an awful coward.'

'I'm ringing for coffee, Curtis,' she smiled at him openly. 'Please keep me company.'

'Can I? I shall just have some meat then. And some coffee.' He joined her, looking more pleasant in expression than she had ever seen him. There was a schoolboy's hunger for acceptance, and a shy gratitude, in his treatment of her.

'You are very young,' remarked Sally, sometime later, after they had chatted about the food and Curtis' horses.

'I am older than you!' he said, defensively.

'I know, but ladies mature earlier, I believe.'

He looked at her shyly. 'You are right, Sally. But I mean to try to catch up.'

They smiled at each other.

***

An hour later an angry Lord Fox entered the green salon, where Ianthe was reading. 'You met him without me?'

'Look how well I have organised this. I am here on my own precisely so that you can shout at me.' She made a gesture with both hands, palms up, indicating he might start his performance. 'Carry on!'

He advanced into the room, after the pause that had thrown him onto the back foot. 'I don't want you to see him.'

'I won't.'

'I don't trust him.'

'I don't either.'

He was in front of her.

'I'll get your jewels back.'

Her face, which had been in playful mode, turned serious, looking up at him. 'Do not, Edward. They do not matter.'

He took her hand, 'They are yours; I want you to have them.'

'He said so too. But I did not want to be indebted to him. And I do not want to be indebted to you.'

His face turned harsh, almost as she had first seen it, and he dropped her hand. 'I see.'

'You do not,' she said sadly. Then in her old tone she said, 'You are the greatest chump imaginable.' He looked confused, but his expression lightened at the insult. She took his hand and put it to her cheek. 'There,' she said as though to a child. 'There, there.'

'I—'

'I think we have callers. We'll talk later.'

Fox stared at his hand after she left, as usual both completely flummoxed and stirred.

Chapter Twenty-Two

Confidences and Secrets

As expected, Lord Fox was furious again when he sent for Ianthe before dinner. His tawny eyes were stormy, his brows lowered.

'I seem to be regularly admitted to your sanctum, my lord,' Ianthe said, cheerfully entering.

Fox got up from his seat, already raging. 'I am not finished with our conversation. I *told* you not to meet him on your own!'

'But I was not alone. Did not Stephens inform you?' Fox looked surprised at the mention of this name. 'I was *most* respectably accompanied by Lady Richards and Mr Steadman.'

'Why you must drag a mere acquaintance into this, and not me, is another thing—'

'Mr Steadman drove back with me from Audley and I could not well get rid of him. He played his part admirably by the way, claimed a warm friendship with the comte at the inn. I was impressed.'

'So, Steadman encroaches on your acquaintance. There can be little doubt he is pursuing you.'

'*Is* he?' said Ianthe, surprised. 'I am not without vanity, but I never feel it to be so.'

'He visits here every day. If it is not you, it must be Sally.'

Ianthe put her head on one side, as she did when she was in thought. 'I have been so wrapped up in my own concerns that I have not given it much thought. Steadman and Sally.' She was obviously passing some events through her head. 'Well, all three of the gentlemen we met at Audley's dinner have been very polite. Lord Jeffries, Mr Markham and Mr Steadman.' She smiled at Fox's frown. 'Do you know, I have no idea about their intentions, which is quite unlike me. I only was glad that the house was livelier.'

Fox looked stricken. 'It is a horrible, miserable prison for you. Don't think I do not know it!' He looked up, determined. 'But do not worry. You shall have next Season in London. And not alone. Sally can go with you. If my step-mama will not present you, my Aunt Dorothea will. She is not really my aunt, you know, but my mama's dear friend. Anyway, she would gladly do it. It would look better if Lady Fox were to ... but it would be more pleasant if you stayed with ...' He saw her look at him with a fond, pitying smile, and he changed his tack. 'But I meant to rail at you. You should never meet that man on your own. I spoke to Mr Fenton and—'

'You *have* been busy.'

'*Why* will you not listen to me?'

She moved to him then and took his hands again, in that gesture that so much confused him. 'Stop being angry, Edward. I know it is just because you worry for me, but—'

'*Worry*?' he said furiously, 'Who, who had responsibility for such a headstrong piece as you would *not* worry? But for the most part I am just furious because you are the most disobedient, foolhardy little minx that was ever born.' He looked down at her hands and pulled his away. 'You've invaded every part of my life and you upend all my peace and you bewitch every servant and gentleman you meet with that smile of yours that you give away as easily as Curtis disposes of guineas.'

'And do I give that smile to you, Edward?' Ianthe asked, suddenly serious.

'No. You do not like me.'

'*That* is not the reason,' and she was smiling as he looked down at her, his fury still upon him, but her smile was different. It was warm and winning, it was the smile of a doting parent upon an infant. He remembered such a smile from his own childhood, and it warmed him now.

'Ianthe!' he started, but she shook her

head.

'Let us to dinner, Edward. I have some things left to deal with. You are a surprise that I didn't expect, and I don't quite know—' she stopped.

'*I* am a surprise?'

She gave him that smile again. 'Do not be angry. I will not see the comte again without you.' It was as though she were promising a child. 'But I needed to talk to him today, and you would have been too much in my way.' He looked cross again, and a small hand flew to his cheek, the tips of her fingers landing there for a fraction of a second. This was what she did to him to silence him. Surprised him like this. He never knew what she was talking about. He never knew what she would do. Thus, he was like dough in her hands.

He managed a resentful look in response, and she laughed and left the room.

***

The next few days were uneventful. Sally had managed to tell Ianthe about Curtis' apology, and to his mother's confusion, Curtis behaved with shy, apologetic good manners on every occasion of their meeting. Edward exchanged a slight smile with him, and Lady Fox, witnessing it, blanched. Sally felt flat. She still enjoyed the morning rides, and shook off some of her depression on them, but was strangely removed on the gig ride home. They were careless enough one morning to be late, and met Curtis, who had come down for breakfast again. He looked astonished to see the ladies thus attired, but Ianthe said casually, 'We usually ride at Audley before breakfast. My mare is there. You may tell your mother so if you wish.'

Lady Richards, who had also been in the hall, waiting anxiously for the girls' return, had trembled a little at Ianthe's direct attack.

'I will not,' reassured Curtis. 'But why at Audley?'

'Your mother forbids us the horses.'

Curtis flushed. 'I did not know. But surely Fox—?'

'Yes, but Sally likes to ride Sapphire, so we have found no need to disobey Her Ladyship.'

'*Sapphire?*' said Curtis Fox, astounded. 'You never tell me you can ride Audley's Sapphire.'

'She does, and most proficiently,' Ianthe assured him. 'But we must away to change in case your mother comes down.'

'Don't worry, she is taken to bed with a sick headache this morning.' He looked rueful. 'She is not pleased with me, I fear. But just this morning, have breakfast in your dirt! I want to hear about your ride.'

He looked so much like a schoolboy that Sally relented. 'Let us then! We are later than we should be, but we rode a different path and it took us longer to return.'

They headed into breakfast and afterwards, mounting the stairs, Ianthe remarked, 'That was quite the pleasantest time I have ever spent in Curtis' presence.'

'Oh, my dear!' answered Lady Richards. 'For me too, and *our* acquaintance has been much longer. I believe Fox and he have somehow come to understand each other.'

'His brother's heart is opening,' said Ianthe. 'In no small thanks to you, Cousin Emma.'

'It is all you, Ianthe. So many things have happened because of you.'

That afternoon, after their three constant callers had left, Lady Richards put her hand to her stomach.

'Are you unwell *again*, Lady Richards?' said Lady Fox in a complaining tone. 'I wished to play cards this afternoon. The Poppers come for bridge on Friday and I wish to practise some plays.'

'Oh, Mama, do go and rest,' said Sally, worried. 'Lady Fox, I shall defer my drive with Lord Jeffries and play with you.'

'Curtis and I shall make up a four, shall we not Curtis?' offered Ianthe.

Curtis Fox began to look sulky. 'Well, I was going to...' he met Ianthe's eye. 'Oh well then, I suppose I shall.'

'You are ever my good son,' said his mother fondly.

Ianthe arched a brow at him, and he looked

ashamed. 'Yes, Lady Richards. You must rest.'

But while an apologetic message to the stables meant that Lord Jeffries' carriage did not appear, another carriage drew up at a side door, and Lady Richards, dressed in a hare brown pelisse and straw bonnet entered it, accompanied by a maid.

Later, Sally, seeing the little maid Mary with her mother's pelisse in her hand, taking it up the stairs, was somewhat surprised.

'Oh Mary, did my mama go out for some air?'

The maid said, 'Yes miss. She just got back with Annie, miss.'

'Oh, good, she must be feeling better! I'll go to see her now.'

Sally entered her mother's room and found her regarding herself in the looking glass, no doubt repairing her coiffure after the ravages of a bonnet.

'Mama! I see you have been out. I am glad. The card game was *so* dull. The baroness has left me to remember a series of plays for you on Friday. I do not see the point, as different cards will be deployed. But then have little interest in the-' Her eyes alighted on something and she paused. 'Oh, Mama! You forgot to wear your new boots in your walk. And after we went to the village for the purpose of buying them. Did you forget?'

Her mama had turned on her seat at the looking glass and was gazing at her with a strange expression on her face. She rose and said, as she walked to the bed and sat beside Sally on the silken coverlet, 'I did not walk, but went for a drive. I have been gone all afternoon.'

Sally was confused, both by the circumstances and her mother's hand, warmly grasping hers while gazing at her in a particular fashion. 'But who drove you?'

'Mr Steadman.'

'That was kind of him. I did not hear him ask—'

'No. He took me to Stone Manor. His home, you know.' Her mama's voice was trembling, but determined.

Sally was aghast, but remained silent.

'Mr Steadman wishes for it to be my home, too. That is, a home for both of us.' Her mother's face was concerned, anxious. 'I told him I must ask you, I cannot—'

Sally as the words dawned on her, suddenly crushed her mama in her arms, then lay back with her on the bed, convulsed with laughter. 'So, it wasn't me *or* Ianthe Mr Steadman came to visit? I could never decide which of us he came for.' She laughed again. 'How self-interested am I? When my beautiful mama outdid us! Oh, it is *too* wonderful.' She sat up, suddenly more serious. 'But do you like him, Mama? You must not do something only for my security.'

Lady Richards sat too, and grasped Sally's hands. 'Oh Sally, I like him most dreadfully!'

Sally blinked. 'It seems so sudden.'

'He says it was a *coup de foudre* for him.'

Sally was astounded. 'Serious Mr Steadman?' she laughed anew. 'But for you, Mama?'

'I, too, was overwhelmed at our first meeting, but of course I knew I must disregard it. He is too young, and of course, when he called, I believed him interested in either you or Ianthe.'

'Then when did you know other?'

'The walk. He proposed to me when I was sitting on the stile.'

Sally thought back to her descent down the hill with Audley, watching the two oddly close figures with their backs to them. 'I thought you were boring him with my good points as I fear you do with any eligible gentleman.'

'Indeed,' said Lady Richards, 'I meant to do so, but Mr Steadman was so previous in his conversation. He told me his feelings immediately. He is such a determined man.' Sally watched the admiration in her mother's far gaze and smiled. 'I did not know what to do, for it all seemed too ridiculous.' She turned to her daughter, large eyes anxious. 'You do not think him too young for me?' she asked Sally worriedly. 'There are only two years, but—'

'You look much younger than he. Sometimes I forget just how lovely and youthful my mama is. I am so happy for you, *darling* Mama.'

'He wishes us to be married very soon. I agreed that after I spoke to you, he may post the banns.' She looked a little conscious, but Sally smiled, hugging her again. 'We will have our own home in London next Season, can you imagine it, Sally? Mr Steadman says he wishes that you marry to please yourself only, you shall not be dowerless, and that you will not have to consider just *anyone* only because of your worry for me. It is more than I ever dreamed, my dear.'

The ladies were nearly late for dinner, with so much to discuss. After a half-hour Sally ran for Ianthe, who was engaged in choosing an evening gown, and dragged her away from her maid, Ianthe calling back, 'Just anything, Cherie!' and then to Sally, 'Don't pull! Whatever is it?'

'Such news as you will hardly believe. But Mama must tell you. Come along!'

Once appraised of the news, Ianthe hugged Lady Richards with gusto. Then she sat back, smiling. 'So, the mystery of Mr Steadman is revealed. I *knew* there was something.'

'You were probably suffering from the same vanity as me, thinking he must be visiting one of us.'

'I have been too preoccupied to consider it recently. I am truly not myself. He had already chosen the prettiest of us all! Well done, Mr Steadman!'

The three ladies hugged and bounced a little on the bed, but Lady Richards adjured, 'Go and dress, Ianthe, or we shall all be later than Lady Fox — and you know how that puts her in a passion. I want this lovely day to end without discord if you please.'

'But only think how cross she will be at your news!' said Sally.

'We shall not tell her tonight. I could not bear the upset today.'

'May I tell Fox?' said Ianthe, turning at the door.

'Dear Edward. Of course, you may!'

Ianthe was in her gown very quickly, but her hair was not quite so elaborately dressed as usual since she begged Cherie to hurry while giving her the happy news. With a kiss on Cherie's cheek, she ran off to Fox's study before dinner.

She poked her head around the door, and Fox looked up, and frowned. 'Cousin Emma is to wed Mr Steadman!' she hissed in his general direction.

'Wha—?'

'Don't tell Lady Fox at dinner!' She tripped away before he could close his mouth.

Ten minutes later, Fox entered the blue salon to find the household about to dine. Curtis was supporting the frail figure of Lady Fox, and so quite naturally, Fox was able to take Emma's arm which he squeezed warmly. She looked up at him with the dazzling smile that could only come from a woman in love. He returned it, for Her Ladyship had tottered away before them. He patted the hand on his arm and saw Sally quietly happy too.

Edward Fox suddenly wondered, once the Richards left, what life at Studham would hold for Ianthe Eames. He could not imagine the bleak dinners she might have to endure with only the Foxes for company. She would be resilient, he knew, and perhaps win some battles. But she would no longer, as she had phrased it, have them outnumbered.

***

To their amazement, Curtis Fox was waiting in the hall the next morning before breakfast. He was wearing his buckskins and boots, and he begged to accompany them on their ride. They explained about the gig and the side door, but Curtis had already brought his horse around. 'Don't worry. Hawkins doesn't know that I go with you, Stephens saddled my Dash.'

There did not seem to be anything to do but let him come, and so they moved off. Curtis' amazement at Sally's ability was prodigious. He told her thirty times that he could hardly believe it, but it was with such boyish enthusiasm that she could not be annoyed at his incredulity. He even asked her, at a stop, how she managed Sapphire's strong head.

Sally laughed. 'I have just established him as my friend, you see, and so he is gentleman enough to do my bidding!'

Curtis laughed too, but Ianthe thought she saw him consider it, and she was more than pleased with the young man. On the gig ride back, Sally was once again sunk in a rather depressed reverie. Again, Ianthe apostrophised herself internally. She had been too sunk into her own worries recently to really pay attention to Sally. 'Did Curtis plague you, my dear?' she asked, but mendaciously, since she guessed the cause of Sally's low spirits. 'You do not seem yourself these days.'

'Oh, I am sorry, I have bats in my belfry.'

'Worrying about your mama's marriage?'

'Oh, I do not think so, though it is a deal to take in. But there is something so sure and comforting about Mr Steadman, don't you think? I like him.'

'Yes, I do. But as a new stepfather … it must be strange for you.'

'Indeed. How to greet him?' said Sally. 'I won't know how to go on.'

'Yes, especially as we are still not sure when it is to be announced.' Ianthe smiled. 'I do not wonder that you were wool-gathering.'

'Mmm.' But Sally realised that this was not what she had been thinking at all. All her thoughts had been of a man who would not appear before her again this visit. She missed his teasing ways, she wondered who he was smiling at now. She was afraid, she was very afraid, that the charm she had so severely spurned had crept into her bones unbeknown. *Audley,* she thought, I hope *you,* at least, are happy. 'Do you know,

Ianthe, that we might share the next Season in London?'

'Yes,' said Ianthe. 'Edward spoke to me of some such notion. He has an aunt who might present me if Lady Fox will not.'

'Oh, the presentation. You will have to wear hoops and white ostrich feathers! I cannot imagine you in such a rig, so stylish as you are.'

'I hear the Queen still insists. It will be diverting at least.'

'Yes ... I do not know quite how it is, but I am not excited about next Season — though I *shall* be relieved that there is no necessity to bring some poor gentleman to the point.' She smiled sadly. 'Do you think one gets too old for such diversions as balls or assemblies?'

'I do not *quite* think we have achieved such a great age yet,' laughed Ianthe. Then her eyes clouded over, too. 'But I understand you. I am interested to see more of London. And in the Season, too. I am curious, but not excited.'

'You are still grieving, though you hide it well. It must be so strange for you here, with everything different.'

'Not everything. I have Cherie.'

'Your maid? You do seem close to her.'

'I will tell you a secret. Or some of it — all of it is too complicated. Cherie came to me as a governess at first when I was quite little. Her father was in the navy, and she came from a very respectable household to a much less respectable one. My father's. But she became a mother to me, though she has acted in many guises because of our changing identities. These last years in Paris she acted my maid, but really she ran the household.'

Sally blushed. This order of things was of course a shock to her, and she could not ask the many questions that arose. France, during the tumultuous times, must have very different conventions to England's established proprieties. 'But for a governess to act a maid. How Cherie must feel it!' was all she could muster.

Ianthe sighed. 'I have told the household I have night terrors, and Cherie sleeps with me, though a truckle bed is set up in my room for show. We have many a night shared a bed before, especially since my father's death. I am not happy at her position now, but she insisted that we could hardly expect the Foxes to house two guests, and we were determined not to be parted. She has a worry that she will be a detriment to my respectability. I have plans to change things for her soon.'

There was something in this last that Sally did not wish to consider, but she said, 'I am so glad you have her, Ianthe. She must be the source of your confidence.'

'Of course! You have guessed it.'

'Have you heard from the comte?'

'I have not. But Stephens tells me he is still in the village.'

It did not surprise Sally that Ianthe was so intimate with the burly groom. She had charmed all the servants at Studham, except perhaps Evans, Lady Fox's maid, who looked sourly on both of them. 'Fox will get rid of him.'

Ianthe nodded. She had forbidden it, but she was secretly surprised that Fox had *not* acted.

***

In fact, it had taken all Fox's time not to visit the inn, and possibly knock the charming smile from the comte's oh-so-handsome face. Moreover, the Frenchman now had Ianthe's jewels, and Fox wished very much to buy them back, and had striven to release enough funds to do so. Without selling land, it was difficult to accomplish straight away. Funds in bonds were not easy to liberate quickly. Henderson was shaking his head, wondering at his orders to sell and hoping, Fox knew, for a delay. But it was only Fenton's words that had kept Fox from the comte's door. That and the humiliation he would have felt demanding the jewels with only a promissory note to offer in return.

He was brooding over this again when Curtis entered his study, looking a little unsure of his welcome.

'Hello, Curtis. Do you want a glass?'

This was such a difference, since Fox usually berated his drinking habits, that Curtis spluttered. 'I ... I would, thank you.'

Fox handed a glass to his brother, and Curtis sank into the chair opposite him, saying, 'I thought you should know I am leaving for some days.'

'Oh yes?' said Fox easily. 'Back to town?'

'No, I thought I'd visit Broadbank,' Curtis said, referring to his estate in Wiltshire, with an assumption of casualness.

'Very well. It is good that you find the time to do so.'

'I thought I might drive around, you know. See what's what.'

'Richard Gibley is a good agent, but there are many things he cannot do without the master. He will be pleased to see you.'

'I think so. He has written a number of times recently, asking if I might visit, but with one thing and another, I have put it off.' Curtis coughed. 'I asked Mama if she would care to come, but she does not think herself well enough.'

'I shall watch out for her health while you are gone, Curtis, never fear,' said Fox, seriously. He added, 'If need be, I will send—'

'— *for Doctor Tolliver*!' Curtis said with him, and their eyes met in a grin.

They clinked glasses, Fox leaning over the table. 'Enjoy the trip, Curtis!'

'I have noticed … there are some methods that you have adopted here at Studham that I wished to persuade Gibley of. He might be worried since I have been so …'

'You are master there. He must do as you instruct.'

'I know, but I would rather he did not think it merely a boy's fancy. Can I ask him to write to you about it? He respects you.'

'And I have new respect for you, Curtis. I didn't think you noticed anything at all…'

'Well, Mama always took issue with you and Henderson on any changes to the estate, but as I rode about, you know, I *saw* what a difference from Papa's time…'

'And here I thought you had only windmills in your head!'

Instead of pouting, Curtis grinned, and the brothers shared their drinks in comfortable silence.

Chapter Twenty-Three

Lady Fox Plots

Lady Fox, whom no creature on earth called Evadne any longer, was losing her way. Evans put a rosewater cloth to her brow, and another at her wrist to try to diffuse Her Ladyship's "head".'

'Shall I call for the doctor, my lady?' said Evans, worried.

'I fear there is nothing to be done, Evans. I have taken the powders he prescribed, and it does not calm me.'

'You shall have one of my special infusions, my lady. You know they do you good.'

'Yes, Evans. But all my peace is cut up. By that wretched girl. Now Curtis is going to Broadbank, at *this* season, and leaving me here to be agitated every day by that pert young hoyden. She has turned first the Richards into her cohorts, then Fox — by way, no doubt of getting the Richards girl and her mother to dream of attaching themselves to Fox. And Fox, seeing a way to flout me, has joined them. Now my *son* no longer obeys me. It is no wonder than I am abed with a sick headache. And with Curtis gone, there is no one here to protect me from insolence.'

'You are still mistress here, my lady. No one can do what you do not wish.'

'But I cannot send her away, for Fox will forbid it. I am caught in her trap. And if she goes to the Fentons, who by all accounts would have her, the World will talk of *my* lack of welcome! And how she would lord it over me in town. My life in London will never be the same. She will be accredited a beauty, although she has just the sort of empty charm that I cannot abide, and then she will marry. And if it is to someone above me in rank, I shall have to *bow* to her.'

Evans dabbed at her lady's forehead and patted her arm familiarly. 'There, there, my lady, don't let your thoughts run ahead. None of this has happened as yet. When Lady Richards leaves, she will be friendless, and all will be as it was.'

Her Ladyship sat up with a wild look in her eye. 'It may be so. I could send them away, could I not? The Richards. I could send them now.'

Evans shook her head. 'Would there not be talk if you did so, my lady? Of course, you know best.'

Lady Fox subsided, defeated. 'I shall expire of this head,' she moaned. But in truth her thoughts were becoming clearer. It would not do to keep to her room, for example. She would begin by obliging Ianthe Eames to be forever at her side — even though she wished her otherwise. It would be a trial, but she would puncture the girl's pleasures where she could, and take her revenge on the girl. And just before they went to London, Lady Fox knew which of her particular friends she would drop hints to. Hints that she had been saddled with a relative who fell short of respectability. The dratted girl would get vouchers for Almacks even so, she feared, for although Aurora Fenton's gaming parties had made her *persona non grata* for a number of years, she was now fully restored to society, and moreover intimate with at least three of the patronesses of that august establishment that she knew of. If Lady Fox could hint of some real scandal surrounding Ianthe then there would be nothing for Aurora Fenton to do, of course. But suggesting something so big would cast a shadow over the respectability of her *own* name, and this could not happen.

She would insist that Miss Eames come out under the Fenton's aegis then, and watch how her wild spirit would shame her while that louche pair let her run untamed. Then Miss Eames' inevitable fall from grace would be set at the door of the Fentons and not at hers. As for any talk that Ianthe was not welcome under the Fox's roof in town, she could set it about that the Fentons *insisted* on bringing the girl out, owing to their friendship with Miss Eames' deceased papa. Might that work even at the moment? Lady Fox continued to ponder the social consequences.

As they waited that afternoon in the salon for the visitors that the dreadful party at Audley had spurred, the butler announced the Poppers. Lady Fox, looking Ianthe's way, was delighted to see her mouth open. Lady Fox, turning to greet her friends, gave a sour smile.

**

As expressions of affection were being exchanged between Lady Fox and the Poppers, Fox entered, and looked appalled. He moved to escape quickly, but Ianthe held up an admonitory finger, while she leant towards Lady Richards, who was seated on the chair next to the baroness' own. She turned and whispered, 'Audley's tactics!' Lady Richards blinked, then got up from her chair.

'Mr Popper, you must take this seat, please.'

'Yes ladies,' added Ianthe to the Popper sisters, 'and you two must sit near Her Ladyship as *honoured* guests.'

Sally was late catching on, and Fox gave her foot a nudge with his Hessians, whereupon her brain functioned, and she rose with alacrity. 'Miss Mildred, *do* sit here.'

The Poppers, pleased to be so noticed, sat, bodies turned towards Lady Fox, and the conspirators were at liberty to sit far away from Her Ladyship's disapproving eye.

'God bless the Marquis of Audley,' giggled Lady Richards under her breath, and Sally blushed.

'How so?' she asked in confusion.

'Audley's tactics!' whispered Ianthe.

'Ah, yes!' said Sally.

'What do you speak of?' asked Lady Fox acidly. 'It is rude to whisper.'

'The ladies were asking after Curtis, your ladyship,' said Fox mendaciously.

'Oh yes,' said Mr Popper unctuously. 'Where is your dear son this morning?'

'He is gone to his estate in Wiltshire. He has *many* obligations to tend to there, you know.'

'Such *responsibility* in one so young! You must be *very* proud of him, your ladyship,' the elderly sycophant said sweetly.

'I am. He is like his father in his sense of diligence and duty.'

Sally, remembering an evening when she had had to lift Curtis from the floor and summon his valet to take him to bed, giggled, covering it with a cough.

Yet again the Poppers saved them. They began to agree so wholeheartedly with this sentiment that the subject was still not completed five minutes later when the gentlemen were announced, all at once.

'Lord Jeffries, Sir Anthony Lonsdale, Mr

Steadman and Mr Markham.'

Fox stood and bowed at his guests but was unable to stop himself from going forward to shake Mr Steadman's hand. Steadman grinned, an expression that Fox, who had known him for years, had never seen. Mr Markham looked intrigued, but Fox, catching his eye, said, 'Steadman had a recent win.'

'I see,' Markham said. He turned to the enthroned hostess and bowed formally before saying in his open manner, 'I hope your ladyship does not mind me bringing my friend Lonsdale, who is visiting me at the moment. Sir Anthony.' Markham made a gesture of introduction.

Lady Fox was inclining her head regally in welcome, but Sir Anthony had discovered Ianthe. She was dressed today in white muslin, embroidered all over in yellow daisies. It was a modest dress, with long sleeves and a high neck of gauze, but the sleeves were caught in interesting tucks, bunched together with the same yellow ribbon that adorned her dark hair, the cuffs long and sheer with the edges embroidered stiffly so that they lay like a trumpet-shaped flower against her delicate hands. She looked fresh and lovely, Lonsdale thought. *Her dress no doubt from Paris, her face must be from heaven.* 'My word!' The foppish young man said.

'Sir Anthony, Lady Fox!' Markham reminded him, and Lonsdale blushed and made his bow.

'An honour to meet your ladyship,' he said tardily.

Lady Fox shot him a withering look.

Yet another of Ianthe's admirers, thought Lord Fox. She seemed to affect all men this way. Well, Steadman had resisted her — and Audley. He had always thought them sensible fellows. But now Jeffries, with his handsome face and dancing eyes, was sitting beside her, and Markham was at her other side, with Lonsdale making himself ridiculous by leaning across to join the conversation. Markham had the manners to cede his place and sit beside Sally, holding a good-natured conversation with her and making her laugh. He seemed to admire her, too. Perhaps he was another sensible one. Fox saw, though, Markham's eye rest on Ianthe's profile.

From the point of view of those who did not know, it seemed that Mr Steadman might be entertaining the two Richards ladies equally, no doubt for politeness' sake. Sally was able to see the looks that Steadman exchanged with her mama, and one of them, when Mr Steadman affected to wave a fly from Lady Richard's face, made her red all over. This was, thought Sally with a laughing and wondrous heart, indeed a love match. Would she ever find anyone who looked at her in just that way? Some sad place in her heart doubted it, but she was not sure why. She did not remember feeling *quite* so sure that she would never find love before now. Outside of London it seemed unlikely, of course, that she might meet someone. However, there had been the optimism of youth to lift her spirits. Surely one day, coming out of an apothecary's shop (like her friend Mary), or falling from her horse (like Lady Davina Markle, who had married her physician) she would meet her destined one, she had believed. But now, this was an empty belief. Mr Markham called her attention and she smiled at him and admitted she had not heard. She found Fox's eye upon her, a concerned look on his face. She smiled at him brightly, but it did not seem to take, for his gaze remained full of sympathy. She looked away at Mr Markham.

Jeffries, Lonsdale and Markham took their reluctant leave after suggesting a picnic on Friday if the day be fine. The Popper sisters declared their joy at being invited, and only Mr Markham had managed to cover his shock with a smile.

'It is only your presence, Lady Richards,' said Mr Popper with heavy humour, 'that allows me to give my permission. I should not let my girls accompany such young bucks without chaperonage!'

The young gentlemen looked imbued with shock and fear at the suggestion that the Popper sisters were eligible. Their ages excluded this, did it not? But as the men turned their heads as one to the sisters, they were met by the horrible spectacle of blushing, giggling females throwing out flirtatious glances under their batting eyelids. As one, Jeffries, Lonsdale and Markham gave a slight recoil. Ianthe shared a look with the startled Fox.

As they all left the room, Lady Fox to seek her chamber, Ianthe said to the group in the Hall which comprised Studham's residents and Steadman, 'Shall I run after the Poppers' carriage and say two o'clock for the picnic while you tell the gentlemen to come at one, Fox?'

'*Ianthe*,' said Lady Richards, 'you *wouldn't*.'

'I am not *quite* so cruel. But it is a pity.'

'Yes, there is no denying they will put a damper on it.'

Fox was looking strangely pleased. 'It will stop you two flirting at any rate,' he said severely to the younger ladies. 'I never saw such a display. No wonder my stepmother thinks you two *fast*.' He looked at Lady Richards. 'And as for *you,* Cousin Emma, I do not consider you a good example.'

Steadman turned to his beloved at this ordering. 'Up with you now to change your boots! Hurry!'

'Yes, Mr Steadman,' breathed Sally's mother, happily obedient, and Sally shook her head but followed her.

'Sally and I should go with them and provide cover. Are you going to join us, my lord?'

'No. I believe I have had all the company that I desire today.' He glanced at Ianthe and said off-handed, 'I didn't think much of that fellow Lonsdale's waistcoat. So many fobs and seals that he jangled.'

'Oh, it's the fashion you know,' said Ianthe airily. 'You must account him handsome, however.'

'I have never been an admirer of black hair,' said Fox.

'Well, what an unhandsome thing to say!' cried Ianthe, her fingers touching her own dark curls. 'Don't *you* think so, Mr Steadman?'

Fox was blushing. 'I meant on a man—' he began.

'I have to agree with you, Miss Eames,' said Steadman, ever serious. 'Most unhandsome.'

With two bland sets of eyes upon him, Fox looked from one to the other. 'Devil take both of you,' he said, and marched to his study.

Ianthe turned to Mr Steadman. 'It is really too easy.'

'Fox's temper is ever a tinder box.'

'Yes, but he considers himself passionless. It is most diverting.' She smiled again, but more intimately. 'May I just say congratulations, Mr Steadman, on gaining the prettiest and most warm-hearted lady in England.'

'I have never considered myself a fortunate man,' said Mr Steadman looking down on her, 'until that dinner at Audley.'

'So quickly?' blinked Ianthe.

He smiled, turning as he heard the Richards ladies come down the stairs.

Sally linked her arm through Ianthe's. 'We

are to get lost in the shrubbery while they discuss the wedding.'

'Let me just put on my boots,' said Ianthe. 'Go ahead to the South Walk,' she said louder, for the sake of the servants, 'I shall catch up with you there.'

She came back down the stairs having added bonnet, half jean boots and spencer to her ensemble, as it was a fine day.

She put her head around the study door and said, 'I am going now. Are you sure you do not wish for the exercise?'

Fox looked up, still moody. 'No thank you,' he said shortly.

It was a decision he was to rue.

Chapter Twenty-Four

The Dangerous Frenchman

The Comte d'Emillion-Orsay had been silent and still long enough. His meetings with Ianthe had not gone as smoothly as he would have liked, but she had never, even in her extreme youth, been easy.

She had been a lovely child that it had been his amusement to flatter and tease. He had witnessed her first conscious blushes, her blossoming into womanhood. It had been a fascinating display. Their paths crossed, but infrequently. Sometimes it was months until he saw Joseph's family again, once a full year. Each time he blinked when he saw Ianthe. The changes wrought on her were, every time, more lovely. Though an innocent, she became a knowing one. He still remembered how womanly she had looked when she was but fifteen, turning his compliment back with that rebuke 'Tell it to *la duchesse.*' He had been shocked and thrilled at once. He had just then decided to possess her.

But for all Joseph and Cherie ran an unusual household, they nevertheless paid all attention to *les convenances* where their girl was concerned. It was impossible to be alone with Ianthe. He had been extremely discreet in his affairs in the years after Ianthe's rebuke. She would brook no romance if she heard of another woman, he had known it. But the comte's life was as complicated as Joseph's. He did not often adopt other names, his particular serviceability to the royalist cause was to remain in positions of interest where he might be party to useful information. These snippets he could pass perhaps to Joseph or others of his ilk. Sometimes, though, he found himself seeking out the Eames household (though it never bore that name) wherever they were, for no good business reasons. Joseph was a *bon vivant*, an amusing rascal, but not a man to be crossed. Antoine had to tread carefully.

As Joseph took more permanent residence in Paris, under the name de Fontaine, Ianthe had reached the pinnacle of her womanliness. The town was engaged by her beauty. As her father's wealth became more evident, and rumours of a fortune won at play flew around the city, she added fortune hunters to her admirers. Joseph batted them away like flies. But there were those among her suitors some be that gave Antoine d'Arcy pause. De Courcy, for example, was handsome and sincere. M. De Rochefocault was another. The comte still found his moments (easier at public functions where they might dance perhaps, or walk the room) to keep his young love reassured. She was not sophisticated enough to conceal all from him. He saw his effect on her in her blushes, in the tumultuous pulse he felt on her gloved wrist, in the sometimes-trusting eyes she gave him when he said the right words. She *belonged* to him, he told her. She must wait until he settled things and came for her.

The truth had been that his finances and romances had both been tangled. One of his mistresses, the wife of a government official, had been suspicious of his motives and it had necessitated much work on his part to soothe her qualms. Exposure and investigation loomed. It was only after the restoration of the monarchy that he could breathe. *Les Cent Jours,* the hundred days from March 20th of 1815 when Napoleon returned to Paris (after escaping his captivity on the Isle of Elba) and the new monarch had had to flee the city, until the king was able to return on July 18th (after Waterloo), had been terrifying for Antoine d'Arcy. He too, had to flee the country to escape the Emperor's knowledge of those who had betrayed him, moving to Switzerland and living hand-to-mouth among his acquaintances there. He had been in fear of the Emperor dispatching agents to kill his enemies, but it was evident that Napoleon, busy with battle plans, had delayed revenge.

Again, Antoine relied on his looks, living off a widowed *Reichsfreifrau* — Baroness — until it was safe to return to the capital.

Ianthe had greeted him warmly on his return, as had Joseph, but he believed that de Fontaine, with friends everywhere, had heard of his living arrangement in Geneva. Joseph would not judge him, but Ianthe was more difficult to see alone, even for a moment. After being conferred his title as comte, he had nearly approached Joseph formally, so on fire was he for Ianthe. However, his debts were not all discharged, and some attachments still existed in Paris that he must dispose of — one woman with a child she said was his, one married mistress who was now widowed with no need for discretion. It required delicate handling.

He could still summon Ianthe to his side with a look, even when she was among her swains. He wished to marry her, had never wished to marry any other. The tighter the leash around her, the madder he had been for their stolen moments, for the promise of her.

He was casually approached in a *taverne* he went to, was utterly surprised to be so, but his very standing as an enemy of the Emperor was naturally what they needed. His problems, the persistent woman who had his child, and another of a large gaming debt, began to disappear. In truth, he had been afraid of how quickly they disappeared. These people knew everything about him, it seemed. There was, in their leader, a fanatical look of devotion when Napoleon was mentioned. With more riches given him, and other obstacles removed promised him, they began to make a dreadful plan. Antoine's conscience was salved a little by its impossibility. But as the bricks began to be laid meticulously, he feared that it may just be executed. There seemed to be endless resources on hand.

When Joseph had died in the carriage accident, Antoine had been stunned — and even more firmly caught. A mild suggestion that this might pave the way to his happiness showed that his conspirators knew even more than he had believed. He had been wracked with guilt, briefly. But he had known he had to take advantage of the new situation to succeed. He may have unwittingly instigated the death of her father, but at least he could protect Ianthe.

Yet again she had surprised him. She had turned him away, as suspicious as her father had been of him in the last month of his life. Joseph had spotted Antoine talking to the wrong person. What he had done to find out more had sounded his death-knell. The fatal carriage accident had followed. In a quiet country lane just outside the city where the Chevalier de Fontaine had been lured, the collapsing axle accident might not have finished him, but the cudgels of the waiting henchmen had. All this Antoine intuited rather than knew. And all this gripped him with fear of his masters.

It had been necessary to practise his last deception on Ianthe and Cherie. His leader's friend had provided the names he needed. It was for her own good.

So was today. What he did today was for her own good.

***

Ianthe strode off in the direction of the South Walk, smiling as she thought of Fox's temper. Would prodding his humours ever pall? She did not think so. He was so quick to respond, his counter so predictable. He was a man who had repressed his true nature to such an extent that his newest feelings sprung up like so many jack-in-the-boxes, without his volition. It was most entertaining.

As she achieved the turn into the high hedged walk, she saw her friends, the lovers twenty paces ahead of the younger, who was affecting to regard the blooms on the hedges, about halfway along the long avenue. 'Sally!' Ianthe cried, but it was Steadman who was alerted and saw the arm that halted Ianthe's progress and the yank that took her from his view again.

'Fox must have decided to come after all,' he told his beloved, smiling, and Emma Richards looked in the direction of his gaze with mild interest.

'Edward?' she said. 'I do not see him.'

'I think he led Miss Eames away.'

'Sally, come and join us, do!' Emma called to her daughter. 'Ianthe and Edward are nearby.'

***

Why she had not screamed, Ianthe could not afterwards have said. But it was Antoine who stood before her and whatever she had told herself, there was unfinished business between them.

After he had almost dragged her to a spot in a wilderness not far from the formal gardens, he stopped in a little clearing near an open landau whose horses were eating grass in a desultory fashion, their reins tied to a stout tree trunk.

Ianthe looked down at the restraining hand and the comte, who was wearing a silk scarf over his mouth and a wide brimmed hat, let her arm go. Although she shook, Ianthe looked at him derisively. 'What is this? You look like a villain from the play.' She laughed. 'Does it mean you have come to do me mischief?' She raised her brows, regarding him haughtily. 'What? Abduction? Violation? I am interested to know.'

'*Arrête maintenent, Ianthe!*' he said, moving forward to take her in his arms, and throwing off the hat in one move. He grasped her shoulders, but the look in her eyes made him step back. He held her eye and spoke to her in French. 'You loved me once.' Her eyes filled and he took a step forward once more, but she held him off with a gesture. He stopped, but his eyes lingered on the tear that fell from hers. 'I think you do still.'

She dashed away the errant tear. Her eyes glimpsed movement in the shrubbery. A slight figure in a greatcoat appeared from behind a tree and *waved* at her. She blinked, but was silent since the hand that waved also put a finger to his mouth. He held up a pistol sideways, but as it was evidently to display it for her information, she was not afraid. He pointed it in the comte's direction, but dropped it, then saluted her. It was over in a second. The figure disappeared, and Ianthe moved to the landau, mounting it — to the comte's evident surprise. The horses showed a vague interest, then returned to their fodder.

'Let us talk.' She too spoke in French, her native language. He went to unleash the reins, but she said, 'If you please, do not.' She sighed. 'Let us just sit. I will permit you to say what you wish to me.'

He got up on the seat beside her, but she gestured to the one opposite. She sat with her back to a side squab, her knees pointing towards him, her hands pressed into her lap. He adopted the same pose on the seat opposite, as though he feared she would run if he were closer.

'You hired a landau rather than a gig. How resourceful. Were we to raise the roof and ride off together?'

'Yes!' he said harshly. 'We should return to Paris. We could go now. I will send for Cherie, I promise you! She can join us there. We can make her more comfortable than she is here, under Lord Fox's roof.'

'But I do not wish to go, Antoine.' He did not speak. 'Everything in Paris reminds me of Papa.' Something crossed his face. 'I do not want to go there until I am stronger.'

'Then we will stay here. I can rent a house. London, or some country place. Then, when you feel you can, we will return to my land in France.'

'The comte's estate. I forgot.' Ianthe looked down at her hands, still clenched on her lap. 'Won't it be shocking for us to live together?'

'We will be married, and at once. We could go to Scotland, or you could live with Fenton in London while I get a special licence.' His eyes blazed at her. 'I have already told you, Ianthe. You are mine.'

'What I wanted to say to you today Antoine…' she gasped, getting up her courage, 'For years I lived as though I *was* yours, because you told me so. Even after I knew of your other amusements—'

'Ianthe—'

'—I still waited for you. But you did not come.' There was an awful emptiness in her voice, a finality that pierced him.

'I *did* come,' he protested.

'Too late.'

There was silence for a minute. The comte, usually ready of address, wanted to choose his words carefully. 'You talk of other amusements; you think me fickle. That is why you refused me when all I wanted was to protect you at last.'

'Yes, in part that was it.' She met his eye.

'But still you waited, you said.' He reached for her hand, and his thumb rested lightly on her gloved wrist. He kept talking, but low, gentling her. 'Those amusements you spoke of existed in the past. But you forget that when we met you were but a child and I a full-grown man. It was natural that I did as other men did. But as soon as you realised, as soon as you were a woman grown, I stopped all such diversions. My heart was only for you, Ianthe.' He gave a little secretive smile, as he held her wrist, feeling the tumultuous pulse. But when he looked up it was to see that she had raised one eyebrow, dubious.

'You did not come for me,' she said again.

'When Joseph died, I did.'

'It was too late. When you offered for me, even *as* you offered for me, I wanted to claim your arms as my protection against the pain, but I could not.'

'*Why* not? Do you even know yourself?'

'Not clearly, no. Perhaps a heart that yearned as long as mine lost faith. Bit by bit and without knowing it. If Papa had been there, I might have trusted his feelings for you. If his friendship for you had reassured me … but he was gone, Cherie was shattered, and I could only trust myself.'

'You are so lovely, Ianthe...,' and his hand stroked her face. She stayed still. '...the love of my life.'

She closed her eyes at this, as though in pain.

'I'm going to drive off with you and *make* you believe me.'

Chapter Twenty-Five

The Search

Sally, on one arm of Mr Steadman while her mother was on the other, said teasingly, 'I feel very much de trop. Where on earth are Fox and Ianthe?'

'Have you posted the banns *already?*' said her mother worriedly to Mr Steadman. 'I shall have to tell Lady Fox before church on Sunday. Only imagine if she should hear them read before I inform her.'

'I would love to see her face,' imagined Sally, 'but I suppose it *would* be insufferably rude.'

'*I* wish to have you two gone from this house at the earliest opportunity,' said Steadman. 'I have seen enough of Lady Fox to imagine what you might suffer.'

'No, I assure you, since Ianthe came, we are a much merrier household.'

'Do you make a trip after the wedding, sir?' asked Sally. 'I can stay here with Ianthe if you mean to do so.'

'And that also worries me,' Emma Richards said. 'Ianthe shall be all alone when we leave. How dreadful for her.'

'Do you wish her to live with us also?' enquired Steadman.

'Oh, you do not mean it?' said Her Ladyship hopefully.

'Anything to stop you frowning, my love.'

Emma Richards blushed. 'But I do not suppose she will come.'

Sally was amused and a bit embarrassed at her mother being so called. 'Well, I wish she would come now. Any more declarations of affection will make me feel my spinster state.'

Steadman smiled his rare smile at this, but suddenly stopped. 'Yes, why *does* she not come?'

'Well, she is probably off somewhere in the gardens fighting with Edward. They seem to enjoy it,' said Emma comfortably.

'The colour of the coat...' Steadman mused. 'My love, Miss Richards, please continue on. I must just check on something. I will find you again.' To the ladies' amazement, he dropped their arms and began to walk briskly, then run, in the direction of the house.

When he got there, it was to find a carriage being driven off in the direction of the stables. Steadman brushed past Jenkins, saying briefly, 'Is Lord Fox here?'

'Yes sir, he is with a guest in the study, sir.'

'*Dammit* — he's *here*!' said Steadman to himself. Then he looked at the butler. 'In the study?' he said, and surged forward in the direction.

'I will annou—' the butler began, but the study door was already open. The butler sighed.

It was only five minutes past when another gentleman had tossed his hat and coat in the butler's general direction and said 'Fox?' moving forward when the butler pointed to the study door.

Steadman opened the door, saw Fenton perched on Fox's desk, the two men in intimate conversation. They looked up, and Steadman said to Fox without preamble, 'Have you been in the gardens?'

'Why—?'

'You *haven't*. I *thought* I remembered the colour of that—' he stopped. 'Miss Eames hasn't joined us. I think that fellow d'Emillion is with her.'

Fox stood, and Fenton said, 'Damn!'

'How long?' rasped Fox.

'It may be nothing, but his coat is green and … I only saw an arm pull Miss Eames aside. I thought it was you. It was perhaps fifteen minutes ago.'

'You only tell us—' Fox began.

'Let us look for her. Get the servants to make a search of the grounds,' said Fenton.

'That may cause talk,' Steadman warned.

'We will still their mouths later. He may be dangerous,' said Fenton. 'I'll go to the inn.'

'Let me. I know who to ask,' said Steadman.

'Very well.' Fox had been reeling, trying to catch scattered fears and thoughts, but now he focused. 'Go now.'

'It may be better for you to go, Steadman.' But Fenton grasped Steadman's arm as he began to leave. 'But if you find him there, do not tell the comte I am here.'

'*Now*,' Fox urged Steadman, who left instantly. He called in the butler. 'Jenkins, have a group of men search the grounds. Miss Eames is missing.'

Fox ran out of the house, and Fenton followed behind. Fox gestured him to the east, while he took west. '*Ianthe*,' Fenton heard him intone.

As he ran heedlessly through the grounds he tried to think. If it was the comte, if she was with him, he did not know what— "No! Think!" he chided himself, still running and looking around. If the comte had come, he would have had to ride or drive, probably. Fox circled around to the stables, but no groom had seen strange horses, apart for the afternoon visitors and Mr Fenton's. Fox dispatched two grooms to add to the search, telling them they were looking for Miss Eames who was missing. He surprised a look on his head groom's face, and turned to him viciously, gripping a bunch of his malodorous waistcoat. 'If Lady Fox hears of this, Hawkins, I will turn you off and make sure you never work again. Do you understand me?' The man's sharp face recoiled, and he nodded before being thrown back against a stable door.

Fox ran out once more, and as he moved around the corner to the house, he spotted Sally and her mother emerging from the shrubbery.

'Have you seen her?' he said, going towards them.

'What is this, Edward? Is it Ianthe? We saw James searching… I do not understand. Where is Mr Steadman?'

'Gone to the village,' said Fox shortly. 'Ianthe is missing.'

A light step, running towards them alerted him, 'Oh, Edward, are you to join us on our walk?' Ianthe's voice said.

He turned, halted for a second, then bridged the gap in two strides. 'Where were you, you wretched, *wretched* girl,' he said, grasping her shoulders and shaking her soundly. 'The whole house is looking for—'

'Edward dear,' Lady Richards pulled gently at one arm, 'You are hurting her.'

He looked down then and stopped shaking her. She was dry-eyed, looking up at him openly, but he could see that she had been crying lately. The thought disgusted him, and he threw her from him, so that she had to take two paces to regain her balance.

'Edward!' reproved Lady Richards, shocked.

'You deal with her. I cannot!' he said and strode off. James the footman was standing near and Fox ordered, 'Look for Mr Fenton in that direction. Then call off the search. Miss Eames is found.'

Lady Richards and Sally were at Ianthe's side as all three watched his back. 'Whatever—?' began Lady Richards.

'Cousin Emma,' sighed Ianthe brightly, but her voice was trembling, 'I fear I am in a scrape this time.'

***

Mr Steadman made short work of the ride to the village. He asked for the comte at the inn, but was not surprised that the man was not there. When he afterwards asked at the stables, a groom thought he had been out this way, but had returned from a drive then gone out for a walk.

The landlord appeared and slapped the groom's head. Gossiping about guests was not allowed. Steadman was just about to remount his horse when a small figure appeared before him.

'Nancy!' Steadman said to the tiny woman. 'How do you and Bill fare in the village?'

'Oh, very good sir, all thanks to you, Mr Steadman. We live right in the village now. In the last house sir.'

'Isn't that Granny Chester's house?'

'Oh yes sir, but she is abed the whole time now sir, and she has me to help her and we have the lodging to boot.'

'That is good news, Nancy.'

'Yes sir. Only, you was asking about the Frenchman, sir?' The girl looked around.

'Yes,' said Steadman, 'but I hear he is gone for a walk.'

'That's as may be, sir. But I don't think he meant to come back earlier.'

'What do you mean?' Seeing a groom give them an enquiring look he pulled her into a more sheltered spot.

'Well sir. When I straightened up this morning, the room was empty. Neither his bag nor the box was there.'

'You mean the rosewood box?'

'Yes sir. There were a few things discarded sir, as though…'

'He made room in the bag for a rosewood box,' said Steadman.

'Yes sir,' said the intelligent Nancy who was once a maid in his house, until she had married a farrier and come to work at the inn. 'I checked if he paid his shot sir, there being so many who try not to do so—'

'Yes, and—'

'He had sir, but paid for one more night.'

'Just in case,' reflected Steadman.

'The bag is back in the room, sir. He left word not to unpack it.'

'Thank you, Nancy!' said Steadman. 'I must go—'

A small detaining hand came to his arm. 'Then there was the carriage, sir.'

He looked down at her intelligent eyes. 'Carriage?'

'This not being a post road the landlord just has the two gigs for rent sir. The Frenchman had to go to Faversham to rent a landau. It is in the stables now, sir.'

'Is that everything, Nancy?'

'No sir. It has all been bothering me sir. I had to pack some items in a smaller bag. A toothbrush, a ladies comb and pins, some night things and a plain woollen cape.' Steadman's blood ran cold. 'It seemed to me, sir, that even a lady eloping with a gentleman could bring that much sir, so when he drove off this morning I was concerned. It is not my business to enquire into what a gentleman might do—'

'It is very natural that you think of it. You were ever a perceptive girl.'

'Does that mean noticing? My Bill says I'm much too noticing. But the gentleman came back. So, no harm done.'

'Yes,' said Steadman distractedly.

'That's alright then. Only—'

Finally, he was amused. 'There is more?'

'He ordered the small bag to remain in the carriage, sir.'

Steadman placed a hand on the girl's

shoulder and reached for his purse. But the girl waved a hand. 'No, no, sir!' she said. 'Bill and me know what you done for us already sir.'

'Then I shall send a basket from my hothouse to you both, Nancy.'

'I'd accept that with pleasure, sir.'

Steadman rode back to Studham. So, Ianthe was not with the comte. Had they found her yet? And if they had, was she still in danger?

***

Ianthe had run into the house, ignoring the questions of her friends, and only just registering the unhurried walk of Mr Wilbert Fenton coming towards her. She touched his arm in passing, but said. 'So happy! But Fox—' She ran into the house and straight to the study, but Jenkins stood before the door. 'Just let me—'

'I was given orders miss,' Jenkins said, stepping in her way as she tried to get around him.

'No one to be admitted, I know, but *I*—' said Ianthe, stepping quickly to the other side.

'Not *no one* ma'am.'

Ianthe stopped and paused, looking at Jenkins in the eye for the first time. 'Just me?'

'Miss.' The butler was short.

Ianthe sighed. 'Edward!' she called. '*Fox!*'

There was no reply, but a penetrating voice rent the hall. '*Miss Eames!* What is the meaning of this?'

'Oh,' said Ianthe in a voice that carried further than she intended, '*Not now!*'

Steadman, Lady Richards and Sally bustled into the hall, with Mr Fenton at a leisurely pace bringing up the rear. 'Oh dearest, what has occurred?' began Lady Richards, moving to Ianthe's side.

'Why is Edward so angry, Ianthe?' asked Sally, more interested than concerned.

But Ianthe was looking upward, over Lady Richards' shoulder, and Emma Richards shuddered her understanding. *Lady Fox was behind her.* Emma sunk to the floor, holding a hand to her head affectingly. Sally knelt beside her in a trice, Ianthe was stunned. Lady Richards opened one eye, however, and Ianthe giggled before the swooning lady managed to say, 'Sally, Ianthe, could you aid me to get to my room?' The girls lifted her arms tenderly, waving off a hovering footman. The afflicted lady got to her feet and held on to both girls, her demeanour rivalling the tottering of Lady Fox when she was being supported by her beloved son.

Lady Fox had come to the bottom of the stairs. Fenton stood to one side of the staircase, where Lady Fox had arrived, frowning terribly. 'Miss Eames, I demand an explanation!'

'You may not have noticed, but your guest is ill,' said Mr Fenton helpfully.

Lady Fox looked at him with dislike as the girls approached, supporting Lady Richards in their arms.

'What *is* this?' said Lady Fox.

'Mama is ill,' said Sally, knowing it was not she whom Her Ladyship was addressing.

Lady Fox was focused on Ianthe. '*You* will remain—'

Sally intervened. 'If Mr Steadman arrives, your ladyship, do tell him to come up.'

Lady Fox took her fulminating eye from Ianthe. 'Come up?'

'I can see you are disapproving,' smiled Sally apologetically. 'But it is quite alright — he is to wed Mama, you know.'

Lady Richards turned her head in her daughter's direction with surprising vigour for an invalid, but Sally and Ianthe nudged her on.

The resulting shock caused Lady Fox to lean her back on the banister, but it allowed the escape of the Richards and Ianthe. Sally turned back to look, and encountered Mr Fenton's eye. He nodded up at her and his ironic smile said, *"Well done!"*

Evans appeared magically and bore her mistress to the salon, and Fenton moved past Jenkins into the study.

'I think Ianthe is about to tell us what occurred this afternoon.'

'I do not wish to hear it.'

Fox's cold voice might have daunted another, but Fenton merely nodded. 'I thought that was *all* you wanted to know but fifteen minutes ago,' he remarked, serving himself a glass of port.

'Well, now I do not.' Fox now sounded merely sulky.

Fenton sat and drank before he continued, 'Lady Richards has just fainted.'

Fox stood. 'Cousin Emma! Where is she now?'

'In her room,' said Fenton unconcernedly.

Fox, already high on anger, moved at lightning speed to the bottom of the stairs and mounted them two at a time while Fenton followed at his own pace.

Lady Richards' chamber door was ajar, and Fox was just about to open the door when he heard Ianthe say, 'Do you always jump on the bed when you are so happy, cousin?'

Fox paused, perplexed. He heard the surprisingly strong voice of Cousin Emma say, 'Oh, but it was so clever of Sally to rescue Ianthe. Now all I have to do is be fevered all day and have you both accompany me. We won't have to see Her Ladyship until dinner.'

'On top of that, Lady Fox will be getting over the shock of knowing about your marriage. She will be almost used to the notion by dinner. And *you* did not have to tell her at all, Cousin Emma.'

Lady Richards sighed happily. 'She may hardly be rude to me at all.'

'You underestimate her,' said Sally's voice.

'I wonder where Mr Steadman went?'

sighed Lady Richards.

'Yes, I do hope he will come back for dinner,' said Ianthe. 'Lady Fox could hardly be foul to us if he were here.'

'Do you think so?' asked Sally.

'Well, we shall have Mr Fenton and Edward to defend us too,' said Her Ladyship comfortably.

'I do not think,' said Ianthe, 'that Fox is likely to defend me in his present humour.'

'You know his temper dear,' Lady Richards soothed. 'You will be friends again soon.'

'Mmm,' Ianthe mouthed, uncommitted.

'But Ianthe,' said Sally's voice. 'You still have not told us what happened.'

'I wish to tell Fox first,' said Ianthe in a small voice that froze her auditor in the corridor. *Guilty*, he thought wrathfully. She added, 'He has that right.'

'He was *frantic* with worry,' Lady Richards offered in appeasement.

'I know. My shoulders will bear the bruises of his worry tomorrow.'

Fox, in the corridor, looked down at his hands.

'He did not mean to hurt you, I'm sure—' said Sally. 'What did happen, Ianthe?'

'Please,' sighed Ianthe. 'Let me talk to him … and then—'

'He seems determined *not* to speak to you,' sighed Lady Richards sadly.

'He must be there at least, before I speak.'

Fox stepped back and realised Fenton was behind him. The older man gestured to the door with his head, but Fox shook his. He turned and walked back down the stairs, Fenton following once more.

'It was amusing histrionics earlier,' the elder remarked.

'You knew that the faint was false?'

'So would you, if you had seen the display. Lady Richards should *never* tread the boards.'

A side smile crossed Fox's face. 'Why did you worry me then?'

'I thought you needed to speak to Ianthe.'

'The last person I want to talk to today is Ianthe Eames,' said Fox, venomously.

Chapter Twenty-Six

The Aftermath

The servants of Studham had been warned, via the conduit of the butler, that anyone who mentioned that day's search to Her Ladyship or her maid would be dismissed instantly, and so Lady Fox was still in the dark about Ianthe's behaviour of this afternoon and determined to get to the bottom of it.

Fox did not come to dinner, and Ianthe had therefore requested that Fenton keep him company.

'What about the dragon?' asked Fenton. 'Don't you ladies require my protection?'

'We have decided to brave her fire this evening.' Fenton raised an eyebrow at Ianthe. 'The poor woman will probably expire if she does not get to vent her spleen today. It is best she breathes fire, and then we can go on with our lives.'

'Even Lady Richards? She does not seem at home with conflict.'

'She is too happy to feel much else.'

'Steadman and she — a real love match?'

'Indubitably.'

'But you do not seem in the spirits to deal with any more unpleasantness, whatever it was that occurred today.'

'It is not what occurred today. And do *not* try to tease me to tell you sir.'

'Then it is Fox who has laid your spirits so low?'

'He is *too* exhausting. I do not know if I can bear his temper.'

'For a lifetime?' Fenton asked ironically. 'I can see it is a difficult decision.'

This did bring some spark to Ianthe's eye. 'My decision? I think that it is not mine.' She looked a little more like herself as she added, 'It has never been necessary before, but I *may* have to learn how to bring a gentleman to the point.'

'He has no notion, you know,' offered Fenton. 'About how he feels.'

'Yes. And I am not sure it is for me to tell him. Only—'

'Yes?'

'These are more things I should say to Fox before I tell you. From the moment we met—'

'Ah, *coup de foudre?*' Fenton teased.

'Not at all,' said Ianthe. She looked down. 'Do you remember what Papa always said was necessary for us, with the life we led, to survive?'

'Trust your instincts.'

'Always. And I always *trusted* Edward Fox. Even when he tried to hide himself behind his anger.' She smiled at him. 'And I realised that I had never trusted another in *just* that way. On sight, you know.' She looked suddenly angry. 'But it is not my duty to show him everything. *He* must come towards me on his own.'

Fenton strolled off to join Fox in the study for an easy supper. He had, earlier this afternoon, managed to intercept Steadman before he found the baron.

Hearing Steadman's findings, Fenton frowned. 'It is as I thought. Fox does not need to know all this until Ianthe tells us exactly what occurred. He might murder someone.'

'She has not done so?'

'No, she wants to tell Fox first, but he will not speak to her.'

'*Why* on earth—?'

'We are spectators on a difficult relationship.'

'Relationship?' Steadman frowned. 'Fox and Miss Eames?' Fenton inclined his head. 'Well, why does he not tell her his feelings?'

'I admire your clarity of vision, Steadman. Not all of us understand ourselves as well as you.'

'Surely—'

'I myself had no notion I was in love—'

'I'll take your word for it, sir. But even

so. The comte still has that carriage. Fox should know Ianthe may not be safe.'

'Don't worry. I know just what to do. Come back tomorrow afternoon. I'll sow some seeds in Fox's temper tonight. He'll talk to her tomorrow. Perhaps with a little more insight.'

***

Dinner might have been completely horrible, so determined was Her Ladyship to make the guests feel their sins. However, it was saved by just how *very* horrible Lady Fox tried to be, for overreacting can present itself as farce.

When Lady Fox, in arctic accents, supposed that Lady Richards wished to be congratulated, Emma Richards found that she was buoyed up by two things. One was how extraordinarily happy the mere mention of her prospective marriage made her, however acidly it was referenced, and the other by the lessons she had learnt from watching Ianthe. Instead of withering under the icicle stare, Lady Richards smiled instead. She could not quite pull off Ianthe's nonchalant tone, but she did her best with her shaken but happy voice. 'Oh, *thank* you, Lady Fox.'

'Am I to understand that you have known the gentleman only since the evening at Audley?'

'I have,' said Emma, faltering somewhat.

'Such a decision, even coming from a woman in *your* desperate position, should never be taken so precipitately.'

'Have you heard ill of Mr Steadman, then?' asked Ianthe, interested.

'I have heard no good of him.'

Emma Richards sat to attention, but Sally grasped her hand and smiled, mouthing, *"Dragon fire!"* to her and it made her smile.

'And I need to know, Miss Eames, why *you* made such a spectacle of yourself before the servants today. Why did you have the temerity to call the baron in that familiar and impudent manner?'

'It is very kind of you to protect the baron's dignity. I am very sure he will be moved when he hears,' remarked Ianthe.

'Every word from your mouth is *bile!*' said Lady Fox. 'Civility seems beyond you.'

'I am sorry you find it so.'

'What business had you with Fox that made you scream in that hoydenish way? You sounded like a London fishwife.'

'*Your ladyship!* protested Emma Richards.

'Oh, *quarrelsome* business, of course,' said Ianthe, but Sally thought she could hear some strain in her friend's voice. 'The baron and I fight a good deal, you know.'

'I did *not* know. You will please me by telling me what this dispute was about.'

'I cannot quite recall,' said Ianthe musingly.

'Dissembler! You have no shame.'

'You are quite right to say I dissemble. I do remember, but I do not wish to tell you.'

'You are insufferably rude, a woman of no conscience or integrity at all. I am pleased that Fox has apparently seen through your shallow charm. You think yourself a beauty, but neither of the Fox brothers were taken in by you.' She gave a harsh laugh. 'A new experience for you, I might imagine.'

'Lady Fox, I *must* protest!' said Emma Richards.

'*You?* When you *too* have deceived me? Have you no gratitude, no feelings of …'

'Indeed, I *am* grateful,' replied Lady Richards. 'And I had no wish to deceive you—'

'Really? Conducting a *clandestine* relationship…'

There was much more of the same, and the ladies went to bed early, the worse for wear.

'The storm will blow over, I am sure, dear one,' said Lady Richards to Ianthe as they left the dining room.

'Oh, it is not *she* who gives me the headache.' Ianthe turned an evil eye to the study door. 'I shall punish him, trust me.' She moved off.

Mother and daughter reviewed the evening, safe in Sally's chamber.

'Oh *dear*. Why ever will he not talk to her? His passions are too ridiculous. Ianthe is well and safe — what *more* does he want?' wondered Her Ladyship.

'It is what he *doesn't* want,' considered Sally. 'He doesn't want to know what happened while she was gone.'

'But why *not*?' asked her mother.

'I'm beginning to get an inkling…' said Sally, gazing into the distance. 'But *surely* not?'

They sat on Sally's bed and held hands, this new thought riveting both their gazes on each other. A myriad of images ran between them, memories of the tiniest of interactions between their two friends, and their hands grasped tighter, so that Sally yelped.

'Goodness!' was all she could think to say.

***

Cherie brought word that Ianthe would forgo the ride today, and Sally sent to delay the gig until after breakfast, when she would ride instead.

Her mama was not equal to the possibility of starting the day with Lady Fox's tirade, so Sally ended by having a solitary breakfast, Fox, Fenton and Her Ladyship still abed.

She set off in the gig afterwards, accompanied by Stephens, the burly groom. He was of a loquacious disposition and, receiving no rebuff from the young lady, revealed his opinion on all the servants of Studham in a frank and funny manner, so the short distance to Audley was quickly passed. When they entered the stable yard, it was to see a handsome travelling carriage there, being unhitched. Sally jumped down, wondering if Mr Steadman had sent for his carriage from home, the better to drive her mama on inclement days. She was instructing a groom to saddle Sapphire when she saw a tall figure emerge from the stables, whip still in hand, and move off in the direction of the house.

It was he! Sally ran forward to intercept him, just as he was about to turn the corner.

She stood before him, halting him in his tracks, looking up at him with a face so joyous and open. '*Audley!*' she cried, delighted. 'You have returned so quickly.'

He stopped, dropping the whip, and seemed stunned. 'Why are you here?' he said harshly, no trace of a smile on his face. No teasing look to dilute his meaning. 'I made sure you would be gone by now.'

Sally stepped back, her beatific smile wiped suddenly from her face, the colour draining.

'I ... thought I was permitted ... you said I could continue to ride Sapphire.'

'Of course!' he said, but stiffly.

'I ... I beg your pardon,' she said, and ran away to a gig which he had not noticed being parked behind his carriage. She jumped up and took the reins from a groom who was about to lead it away, and began to turn the horses, jumping up and driving swiftly out of the gates.

'*Miss!*' cried a burly groom, running after it belatedly. Audley had found his mobility too, and had run over to watch the gig disappear. 'She forgot me, your lordship,' the groom, Stephens, informed him.

'Alone!' Audley exclaimed distractedly. 'I need a horse.'

Sapphire was being led out and Audley said 'He will do…'

His head groom informed him, 'Side saddle, sir.'

Audley pulled himself up nevertheless, and tried to throw a knee over the pommel. 'Drat!' he said. 'How on earth do they—' Several grinning grooms were regarding him. 'It is no use,' he said furiously, sliding to the ground, 'I cannot. *Somebody get me a horse!*'

The Head Groom had already signalled for this, and it was not many minutes before his black stallion arrived.

He rode off precipitately, grooms murmuring to themselves in the yard behind him as they watched.

He only managed to catch up with the gig a mile from Studham, but he rode his horse past nevertheless, and obliged Sally to pull on the reins and slow the carriage to a halt. Audley jumped off his horse, casting reins over a handy bush.

'Miss Richards!' he began on reaching the gig, and then he noticed something. Her face, her lovely face, was wet with tears. He jumped on to the box beside her. 'I'm deeply sorry!'

'*Please!*' Sally Richards was shaking now, because his cruelty had broken through her denial, and she recognised the utter joy she had felt in seeing him again. Saw what that meant. Saw that he was disgusted. And now she could not stop the tears, the terrible, terrible revealing tears. Bad enough that she felt this way. How awful that he was witnessing it. He had taken the reins and tied them, then possessed himself of her shaking hands.

'Do not!' he cried to her. 'Please, my dear sweet girl, do not.' He was holding her gloved hands tightly, grasping them and changing the position in a frantic manner as though he too were wringing them, to stop himself from something more.

Sally was trying to master herself, and his words were going over her head for the present, in the search for something to say to him — some words she could conceal herself beneath. 'You have no manners,' she finally said, feigning anger.

'What?' Audley, regarding her, was confused.

'It is only that you were so rude when *I* thought we were friends. Pray do not refine any more upon it.' She hiccupped, then took back her hands from his frantic ones, clasping them together and regarding them.

'Yes,' he agreed flatly. 'That was it. It was my insufferable rudeness.'

'Yes,' and then, 'Why did you follow me?'

'You left your groom behind. You should not drive alone.'

'You could have sent *him*.'

'But I realised that I had been insufferably rude,' he said carefully. 'And I thought I needed to apologise.'

'Oh!' She took a glance at his troubled face and said, 'You can get down now. Follow me to Studham on Night if you must.'

'I must,' he said — but did not move.

Sally ventured, in a very small voice, 'I was not so *very* glad to see you.'

'No.'

'You mistake if you think so.'

'Yes.'

Another hiccup and a sob escaped her, and he took back her twisting little fingers into his. 'Do not. *Please,*' he said, looking down at them in despair. 'It would not do. I have thought and thought these past days and it would not do.'

'What … you have thought *what*?' A new idea was occurring to her. The words he used earlier. My dear sweet girl. *His.*

'I am not a good man, my dear. I have never coveted a wife. It would interfere with my pleasures too much you see,' he added, but the sardonic note rang false, and his voice was broken.

The dawning was flushing over her. Not just *she*, but *he…*

'You thought of me in London.' It was not

a question, but a realisation. 'You *thought and thought*.'

'I could think of little else. But—'

'Your pleasures?' she said reflectively, as though no longer listening to him. 'What are they? *Female* pleasures?' She flushed, thought of Lady Sophia Markham at that dinner, and began to understand.

'There are other things,' he said curtly. 'I am nothing if not diverse in my pleasures.'

'You are, perhaps, a gamester?' she ventured, not looking at him, but gazing into the distance as though calculating something.

'Yes.' He did not want this to continue, but hardly knew how to stop it.

'You wager huge sums, I imagine?'

'I do, but that is not the—'

'And you could lose your whole fortune on the turn of a die?' she supposed lightly.

'I said I'm a gamester, not a fool,' Audley said dryly. 'I'm good at it. I play the odds.'

'You ... I suppose you also *drink* then? Some gentlemen do, more than others.'

'I drink a great deal. But Miss Richards—' Somehow though, her honest eyes held his.

'Mr Housten, our family friend you know, told me of his misspent youth,' she recalled. 'He drank a great deal, he told us, and sometimes even awoke in strange places. It was not quite polite for him to tell us that of course, but we are such close friends.' Audley looked at her, even though she did not meet his eye as she talked, not understanding what she was about, but hardly able to move since he was so close to her. Sally continued in a conversational tone. 'He was once robbed and beaten in a tavern he frequented.' She turned her clear eyes on him. 'You too?'

'Again,' Audley said, still dry, 'not a fool.'

'And there are *women*.' Her voice shook a little on the last word, but she met his eye again and asked brightly, 'How many?'

He held her gaze. 'Too many,' he said darkly. Then he tried for insouciance. 'Are we papists? Are you taking confession?'

'Because like *gaming* or *drinking*,' she replied, not attending to the latter interjection, 'you stop before you are a *fool*.'

He looked down at her. *'Sally!'* he breathed.

She looked up at him, managing a half smile as she said, 'Do something to *excess*, Audley. Be a *fool* — for me.' Her voice caught and she looked down once more, not daring to look into his lost eyes longer. 'I love you so very much, you see. Though I have only known it for ten minutes.'

He touched her face, lifting her chin to him and tears poured down his own cheeks now. 'It is not fair to you, my lovely, lovely … I *cannot* —' but his eyes were searching hers, his body was moving ever closer, of its own volition.

She had somehow got the reins in a quicksilver move. *'Get down!'* she ordered in a bark he had never heard from her. A second's pause, and he obeyed. She waited, eyes staring straight ahead, as he mounted his horse. She manoeuvred the gig past him and drove away, not regarding him at all.

Chapter Twenty-Seven

Miss Richards is Enraged

J enkins was astounded. First, Miss Richards had entered from one of her supposedly secret rides (which of course he had known of from the first day) by the front door, not the side, and second, because she stood in the Hall in a towering rage, taking off her kid gloves as though she were strangling each fingertip as she did so.

'Where is everyone, Jenkins?' she asked, not the retiring young lady of his acquaintance, but a Valkyrie in full battle armour. She was removing pins from her bonnet with remarkable ferocity and yanked it from her head, dislodging some curls from her coiffure.

'The ladies are in the green salon, ma'am, and the gentlemen are, I think, in Lord Fox's study.'

'*Still* not talking? *Men!*' said the young

woman fiercely. She marched to the study, flinging open the door.

'Sally!' said Fox, standing up from a chair by the fire in surprise.

'Audley is coming in shortly. He is seeing to his horse now. It is injured because the fool rode him ill.' Mr Fenton, sitting on a chair opposite the one that Fox had just vacated, raised his eyebrows and sat back, as though to enjoy the spectacle.

'I—' began Fox, but the gentle maiden interrupted him.

'When he comes, *don't* let him appear before *me.* I warn you.'

'What—?' asked Fox, but she was gone. He looked at Fenton for explanation.

'It seems the dam has broken,' remarked that gentleman, crossing his legs. 'We shall have to see where the water floods.'

***

Jenkins witnessed Miss Richards leaving the study, slamming the oak door behind her with gusto, only a minute after she had entered, and now she marched purposefully towards the green salon. He was too late to open the door for her, which he regretted. A light straightening of the room might assuredly have been necessary and would have allowed him to see what next occurred — but his curiosity would be salved soon enough. William was in there, (along with James, of course), but William had a keen eye and a gift of relating all the details he saw for Mr Jenkins to hear later. He was also a gifted mimic, so the butler looked forward to the show.

Sally's entrance into the room was purposeful enough to cause three heads to look up from their tambour frames swiftly.

'Ianthe,' Sally said briefly in a terrible commanding tone, 'Come! I need you.'

'*Miss Richards*,' said the outraged voice of Lady Fox. 'No greeting?'

'Good morning.' Sally did not spare her a glance but looked at the other two ladies, whose arms were frozen in mid-air over their work, mouths slightly agape. '*Ianthe!*' prodded the urgent tone.

Ianthe began to rise, her eyes fully opened with intrigue and dancing a little, as Lady Richards managed, 'Sally dear, whatever—'

'And you have *ridden,*' interrupted Lady Fox, finally taking in Miss Richards' red velvet habit.

'Yes,' said Sally, looking at her coldly for half a second.

'Against my *direct*—' began Her Ladyship, but Sally interrupted the tirade.

'At Audley,' she said tersely, then she swept from the room, Ianthe following, hardly able to keep a grin from her face as she curtsied briefly to Lady Fox.

Ianthe caught her up in the hall, capturing

her arm to halt Sally's passage to the stairs.

'What *is* the matter, Sally dear?'

The great front doors had opened again, and Audley walked in, handing his hat and crop to a footman.

'*He* is!' Sally hissed at her, finger pointing across the ten-foot gap to the marquis. Ianthe blinked, met Audley's haunted eye briefly, then realised that Sally was marching once more, and turned to follow her up the stairs.

***

Ianthe watched as Sally Richards threw herself seated on the bed of her chamber, her wrath seeming to dissipate somewhat with a large expulsion of air.

'What did he do?' enquired Ianthe, amused and concerned at once, sitting beside her.

'It is what he *will not* do!' said Sally, closing her eyes to control the once more mounting rage. 'How can one find out that one loves someone and that one wants to *kill* him — all in the same day.'

Ianthe conjured up another face in her head and nodded in agreement. 'It is quite possible,' she concluded.

Sally looked at her, understanding her. 'Edward still will not hear you?'

'No. I'm hoping Mr Fenton might persuade him. But do tell what happened with Audley. Why has he returned from London?'

'To *torture* me!' Sally said wrathfully. 'And why should I tell *you* — you have refused to say what happened to you yesterday.'

'That is because I want to tell you all at once or not at all. And Edward—' she sighed. 'Never mind. My story is not as interesting as yours, I'll wager. Tell me what stupid thing Audley did.'

'I thought you told me he had address?' said Sally sulkily. 'He has no finesse at all. He neither says what he ought, nor holds back what he ought not. I *hate* him.' During the latter sentence her rage had built again, and Ianthe put an arm around her shoulder to calm her.

'Tell me,' she said again.

'He called me,' sobbed Sally, '… he called me his *lovely, lovely* …'

'His lovely, lovely *what?*' asked Ianthe.

'That is *all!*' cried Sally, aggrieved.

'That complete idiot!' cried Ianthe, but smiling a little.

'I *know!*' her friend said, beginning to hiccup.

Sally burst into tears of both fury and despair, casting herself into her friend's arms. Ianthe held her and let her go her distance, waiting until she could do more than utter half sentences and cry. But Ianthe's spirits were broken also, and it was not long before she, too, burst into relieving tears, saying, as Sally had in the hall, '*Men!*'

***

Lady Richards' spell in Purgatory was interrupted by her love's arrival.

After making his formal greeting to Lady Fox, who eyed him with dislike and disapprobation, he said, in that oddly bald way he had, 'I am come to take Lady Richards on her walk.'

'We are at our work, sir, as you see,' answered Lady Fox.

'Then I must disturb you, I fear,' said Steadman, insistent.

Lady Fox found that the grey eyes of the polite Mr Steadman were not as yeilding as she had first thought, so she nodded her head permissively, then turned back to her work in disdain.

'Come, Emma!' Steadman said, opening the door and Emma Richards escaped the room like a young girl escaping the confines of the schoolroom.

'I shall run and get my things.'

'I have sent for them already.' A small maid came down the stairs bearing bonnet, pelisse and leather boots.

Once outside, Her Ladyship caught her love's arm, saying, 'I do not think I want a very long walk today, Mr Steadman, we have had the most upsetting time.' She looked up at him shyly. 'Though I do want to stay with you, of course.'

'It is not a long walk,' he said briefly. She

wondered that his serious face was not a mystery but a promise to her now, and moved along on his arm, her peace restoring.

He took her to a spot just outside the formal gardens. Emma Richards saw at once that he had chosen well if rather worryingly. The tiny clearing was surrounded by trees. There was no possibility of being overlooked, of being unable to hear another approach. There was a simple wooden bench placed there, and Emma Richards assumed that other owners of the great house had had trysts there, for it was evidently made for the purpose. She tried to imagine Lady Fox and her husband sitting on the bench, but somehow, she could not. But perhaps old Lord Fox, with Edward's mama …? Once, Edward had told her, Studham had been a happy house.

Steadman led her to the seat and sat close, an arm about her shoulder. She should not, perhaps, but she sank against his shoulder, sighing, 'My dearest dear. My dearest Mr Steadman.'

'Oscar,' he instructed. 'My Emma.'

'I jumped when you called me so before Lady Fox.'

'She is a woman who needs the obvious underlined.'

'How can you be so wise when you know her so little?'

'Her reputation in the neighbourhood tells me a great deal.'

'I suppose she must have upset half her

neighbours,' Emma giggled.

'The fraction is higher.' He looked down at her. 'Will you take off your bonnet, love?'

She sat up and did so, with trembling fingers, and Steadman helped. 'Do not worry,' he said in that serious tone, his eyes directly on hers as he loosened the ribbons. 'I shall not kiss your lips.' She blinked. 'I dare not.'

He removed the bonnet, placed it carefully, then smoothed her hair with one caressing hand. He smiled as he looked at her difficulty in breathing, at her parted lips. *'Darling!'* he murmured, catching her to him, *'My darling!'*

He pulled away ten minutes later, and her face was ablaze with every inch that he had kissed (excepting only her lips), with every promise he had whispered. Both of them were shaken, and Steadman took a great breath, still holding her shoulders. She gazed up at him, her face open with love, too hypnotised to stop. 'Don't, love, or I shall have to start all over again.'

'Oscar!' she breathed.

He stood up abruptly.

'Let us leave this place,' he said, not turning back. His voice was harsh, but Emma Richards laughed to herself, putting on her bonnet.

She stood and slid her hand through his arm.

'Only six weeks now,' he told her, and they moved off together.

They walked the grounds and she began to

tell him of Sally's discovery of Ianthe's feelings for Fox, and her new worry about her. She looked a trifle embarrassed. 'Sally was in such a rage as I have never seen her earlier. I would have gone to her immediately, but she somehow wanted to talk to Ianthe.' She looked a little conscious. 'We are so very close that I thought we told each other everything,' she added sadly.

'However close you are, she will not want to tell you what might make you worry. As you do not her.'

'That makes it worse, Oscar dear,' Emma said. 'It means it is some serious consideration, and I'm more worried than ever.'

'She will share the cause of her anger with Ianthe, calm down a little, and then discuss it rationally with you later, I'm sure.'

'You are right, of course,' said Emma, relieved. 'That is *just* what is happening. I can go to them now and she will tell me.' She smiled at him. 'Are you going back to Audley?'

'No. I have some business to discuss with Fenton, and possibly Fox. And it may be that Audley is here too. His carriage is in the stables, Lady Aurora came with the marquis from London, she said, but Audley did not come into his house. I thought he might be here.'

'Perhaps. I have been setting stitches with Lady Fox, so I do not know.'

It is only that her heart was so full of her love that caused Lady Richards' motherly instincts to sleep for a moment. Had she considered the three facts she knew — one, that her daughter had ridden, *on her own,* at Audley this morning; two, that her daughter was unnaturally enraged; and three, that the Marquis of Audley was no longer in London — she might have suspected much more than she did. But, as she ordered refreshments to be sent to her daughter's room, where a maid had told her she was to find the young ladies, she walked up in complete ignorance of the facts at issue.

Chapter Twenty-Eight

Curtis At Home

Nancy Badger had already been asked by Mr Plodgitt, the landlord of the Crown and Sceptre Inn, about her conversation with Mr Steadman. Li'l Davie the groom, who was but five-foot tall, had a grudge against her, having once tried to kiss her after church when she was still a scullery maid and she had pushed him off. Li'l Davie had, that day after church, taken his violent dismissal without rancour, but when he'd next month seen Bill Badger, the farrier's apprentice, being granted the boon he was denied, he'd taken against her. Working at the inn gave him numerous opportunities to make her life difficult, all of which she dealt with dexterously.

'Whyn't ye jist tell Bill?' said Mrs Higgins the cook, after witnessing the girl being tripped up by a dirty straw-and-mud stained boot, Nancy dropping several plates which were afterwards taken out of her wages by the furious Mr Plodgitt.

'And have me visit him in county gaol? He wouldn't mean to, but I fink a blow from Bill would snap the li'l one in two.'

'Evil li'l imp. I hope the faeries take him back soon!' Nancy had laughed. 'Want me to 'ave a word with ol' Plodgitt?'

''E don't care. They is two of a kind.'

It was true that the landlord's genial, sugared demeanour to the guests seemed to curdle his own stomach and made him full of bile to his staff. But Nancy knew she couldn't work in no big house no more, being married, and that she was lucky to find work at the inn, so nearly situated to her husband.

So, it was not without fear that she kept an eye on the Frenchie. The landlord had warned her, if Li'l Davie proved right and she *was* talking about the guests, he would dismiss her on the spot. Nancy had told him that Davie's tongue was forked and that she were just talking to Mr Steadman, because, as Mr Plodgitt knew, he was her kind former master. Plodgitt had known it, and also that Davie was a sneak besides, so he let it go with the dire warning. Nancy and Bill needed the shillings she worked for, so she had to be careful what she was about. She knew what Bill would say about this without asking. Anything for Mr Steadman, who had encouraged the smith to let Badger, just back from his years of being a journeyman, and now a master farrier, work out of his shop. The smith had shod horses himself and was not sure he needed the help, but Mr Steadman persuaded him, pointing out the number of people he had had to send away to Farnham and further, when he could have all the local business to themselves. On top of that, Mr Steadman had given the couple a handsome wedding gift. No, Bill would know her risk, but agree with her.

The Frenchie had taken out a gig today, and when she heard this, Nancy had been disappointed, for except for being able to know the direction he had set off in, there was no way of knowing what he was up to. Granny Chester, Bill and she had discussed the landau and the lady's accoutrements therein, and all had agreed that it was a case of planned abduction. Mr Steadman had visited the Frenchie once, said the bald-headed waiter, along with Lady Richards and the new and beautiful young lady who had not long arrived from France herself, it seemed. So, it wasn't hard to conclude who he might be after. Mr Steadman would be aware, she was sure, and would warn Lord Fox to keep an eye on her. Granny Chester, infirm in body but not in mind, had relished the tale, saying with glee, 'I'd love to set me only good eye on that fog-swindling, snail-gobbing snatcher. I'd feed 'im 'is guts for gaiters.'

But the Frenchie made mistakes, for he took a groom with him that day, and moreover he'd thought that half a sovereign would stop Dickory's mouth. Dickory was likely to tell you about his trips to the outhouse if you'd let him, so something as interesting as a foreign comte driving country lanes and asking, after a time, which of them might lead back to the main post road to Dover was too good to pass on. Dickory had told the comte not to look so hard, since it was only two miles direct to the Dover road, but the comte had not been interested. 'I would like to see more of the scenery, and drive through your amusing English farms. They are much different from *les fermes en France*, quite different.' Dickory thought all foreigners odd, so he hadn't been fazed by this. They ate frogs, so maybe the farms in France raised monkeys instead of cows for all he knew. He could think of some less than amusing English farmers who might not be pleased at an excursionist blocking his lanes with a landau coach. The comte might be Quality but being Frenchie Quality didn't much count. Finally, he'd given the groom the half-sovereign to shut up, which caused Dickory to mouth off even more.

'What route did he favour, in the end?' asked Nancy.

'Funny that,' said Dickory, 'he said he might take Cowper Hill road.'

'Barely passable for a big rig in places, that,' remarked Mrs Higgins, who was feeding Dickory some bread and dripping.

'Yes, but he said he was keen on it, said it would work for him. Seemed mighty taken wif the bit of the road we drove. Liked the views apparently.'

'And the whiff of muck, no doubt. Well, there's no saying what them Frenchies might do.'

'No, had said Nancy, thinking. 'But did you drive Calderbeck Farm too, Dicks?'

'We did, Nance. He didn't seem much interested.'

'Mmmm,' said Nancy, going upstairs to clean.

She had tidied the gentleman's room earlier, safe in the knowledge that he was out. Nancy, an honourable girl, nevertheless only hesitated for a moment. Having decided to pry, it was necessary to do it thoroughly. After she had marvelled at the fineness of his linen, the invisible stitching on his coat and the incredible contents of the wooden box (hidden beneath the bed and behind his portmanteau) she searched in pockets, examined his silver hair brush, smelt the preparation he used on his hair (which reeked like a woman's). She had only the small sack that had been delivered a few hours ago to deal with. Inside was something wrapped in linen. Another box, but prettier than the rosewood one, in coloured enamels. It looked like it belonged to a lady, but there were semi-naked people painted on it, dancing. But Nancy had worked in a great house before. Shocking pictures on the walls were permitted when they depicted the ancient past, it seemed. 'Something Greek!' she told herself, looking at the enamels. She carefully replaced the pretty box and was disappointed that she had not much to tell Mr Steadman.

Her opinion on that changed after Dickory had spoken that late afternoon, and something else was still nagging at her when she had gone home, exhausted, to Granny Chester's cottage, where Bill was taking off his boots at the door.

'You're late this evening,' she said lovingly, picking up the leather apron he had laid aside and feeling an unusual weight.

'A carriage stopped, a fine one, there was a beautiful lady inside too,' he teased her. 'One of the horses threw a shoe.'

'A lady?' Bill looked and saw that his Nancy's brain was working. 'She went to the inn, didn't she? I saw her just as I left.'

'I think she knows Mr Steadman. She was with that party of folks from Studham who were walking around the village the other week. The marquis was with them too.'

It didn't surprise Nancy that Bill knew this; the entire village had gawped at such a collection of swells walking around all in the same day. Friends of the local gentry. London folks.

'She might not have gone yet! She was just having some supper sent in.' Nancy kissed her seated husband's head and said, 'I have to go back, Bill. I'll shouldn't be more 'n a 'alf 'our.'

'Don't get caught by Splodgitt!' he called after her, and she laughed at the nickname.

Five minutes later, Lady Aurora Fenton, in the finest bonnet ever seen in the village, approached the carriage in the inn yard. She was surprised to see a young girl beside it, but even more so when the pretty young damsel whispered, looking over her shoulder, 'Excuse me my lady, but might I come inside? I have something particular to say to you and I cannot do so here.' Lady Aurora, looking at that pretty, open face, made a decision. She was ever attracted by the unusual, so she waved off her maid and gestured the girl inside the carriage.

'Could we drive on a-ways, my lady? I hear you are going to Studham, and that Mr Steadman is there now. And I got a comp-li-cated message for him, begging your pardon, my lady.'

'Steadman? Is he?' said Lady Aurora. She gave the sign to drive on, telling her maid to wait in the inn, she would send the carriage back, and then gave the sign to stop a little while outside the village.

'Who are you?' said Lady Aurora, but since her smile was warm and her expression avid, Nancy did not fear. 'Is this message concerning the comte?'

'However did you know, my lady?'

'It is Lady Aurora Fenton. I think that Mr Steadman, indeed a great many others, are concerned about the presence of the comte in the area.'

'So they should be, in my opinion, your ladyship,' said the girl with some ferocity.

Lady Aurora's eyes danced. 'Tell me.'

'Well, I told Mr Steadman earlier about the landau and the small cloak bag.'

'Tell *me* now!'

Nancy did. 'So, it made me worry, my lady. And I was sure it might concern the young lady just come back from France herself. The one who is at Studham now.'

'Very intelligent,' approved Lady Aurora. 'And you have more to say to Mr Steadman?'

'The trouble is, none of it is very clear. The Frenchie, sorry my lady, the com-mont drove about in a gig today with a groom. He paid the groom to say nuffing, but he paid the wrong man.'

'Lax of mouth, I take it?'

'Yes, my lady. He was looking, we finks, for a road that joins the Dover road. But not direct. He wants one that takes a cross-country path for six or seven miles.'

'Very suspicious,' said Lady Aurora enjoying herself.

'Yes, my lady. And he ses to the groom that he'll likely take the Cowper Hill road. He said it twice.'

'But you don't think so.'

'The wider roads are on Calderbeck Farm, my lady,' Nancy said, glad she had such a quick-witted auditor. 'I searched his room, my lady. I'm not proud of doing so, but—'

'Needs must at war, my dear!' approved Her Ladyship.

'Yes, my lady. But there was nothing very interesting, except the contents of a rosewood box—'

'We knew about that.'

'And a sack that was delivered today, with another box with naked Greek people on it.'

'Dancing, I expect,' said Lady Aurora, knowingly.

'The Greeks do seem to do a deal of dancing,' frowned Nancy, whom Lady Aurora was beginning to love. 'And that was all — until I went home, my lady.'

'At home?'

'My Bill is a farrier, miss. He shod your horse.' She smiled proudly. 'But when I lifted his apron this evening — he never remembers to leave it at the smith's, my lady — he'd left a nail clincher in the pocket.'

Lady Aurora had no idea what a nail clincher was, but she forewent interruption, nodding sagely.

'And I remember the other day I was moving a coat of the Frenchie's, sorry the—' but Lady

Aurora waved her onto the point, '—that had a similar weight in it.' As Lady Aurora looked stumped Nancy forgave her, since she herself had missed it at the time. She helped her along. 'Something metal must have been in the pocket, my lady, something—'

'A pistol!' said Lady Aurora. 'It is something that many travelling gentlemen carry, I suppose. But in this case, it really is chilling.'

'I can't be sure, my lady.'

'But it *is* likely,' nodded Lady Aurora. 'You wish me to relay all this to Mr Steadman?' The young woman nodded. 'Well, he will be very grateful, as am I. Thank you so much for your help, Nancy.'

'I'll get down, my lady,' said Nancy, before the lady finished opening her reticule. 'Thank you for listening, my lady.' Then, like a flash, she was gone.

***

Curtis Fox entered his brother's study, in the late afternoon, but Jenkins informed him that His Lordship was in the green salon. 'He is?' Curtis was surprised.

'Your mother,' added Jenkins, 'is abed.'

'Has she sent for the doctor?' Curtis enquired, with only a slight interest.

'No sir. She's merely resting.'

'Good then, I'll go and find Fox.'

He entered the green salon, and seeing Fox

standing by the fire he said laughingly, 'They tell me in the stables that a search was mounted for Miss Eames yesterday but that they will all be sent off without a character if I am to mention it to Mama.' Belatedly Curtis noticed the presence of another three gentlemen, sitting on two chairs and a sofa on the other side of the room, a table between them with cards on it. He bowed slightly. 'Oh, hello Audley, Steadman, Mr Fenton, sir. Here to visit the ladies?'

All three gentlemen were surprised at the most human face of Curtis Fox they had ever seen. His usually pale face was lightly tanned, perhaps from riding his estate in Wiltshire, but it was more than that. The friendly tone he used on Fox, the lack of the pout that had so disfigured a young and handsome face, the relaxed demeanour, made him look like a new man.

'I must suppose everyone here knows what happened,' the young man continued easily. 'Where did she go missing? Did she fall in the lake or some such thing? You really should see to the blue bridge, Edward, it's damnedly old,' he added as an afterthought.

'I'll keep it in mind,' said Fox, dully.

'So, what transpired?'

'We do not know.' Audley informed him.

'Still?' said Curtis confused.

'We *would* know,' continued Steadman, 'If Fox would talk to Miss Eames.'

Fox's brows were down, his foot tapping

on the metal bars at the hearth, in a posture Curtis knew well. 'What, in the sullens, Edward? I thought you liked the girl.'

'He does,' purred Fenton. 'That is why he will not talk to her.'

If looks could kill, Fenton would be slain, but it only caused the three guests to exchange grins. Curtis, happy not to be the target of Fox's rage this time, said, 'Well, I don't suppose it matters if she is now safe.' He looked at his brother, and threw a faggot in the fire for old time's sake. '*Unless*,' he said significantly, 'Mama finds out.'

Fox's head shot up as he hissed, 'Curtis!' but met his brother's grin instead of a threatening smirk. He expelled air.

'The ladies are in the red salon, including my newly arrived wife.' Fenton sighed, as though tasked with a great burden. '*I* shall go and ask Ianthe once more.'

Mr Fenton did not actually go into the red salon, but instead took a footman's seat against the wall in the Hall, and under the interested eye of Jenkins, three footmen and a maid on her way to deliver tea to the ladies, he buffed his nails on his jacket sleeves with great attention then leant back against the wall, endangering the delicate legs of the chair, and whistled. After five minutes of this, he stood unhurriedly and re-entered the green salon.

'Yesterday Ianthe met the comte, agreed to marry him and is leaving for France tomorrow,' he announced.

There was a stunned silence before Fox moved, '*Where* is she?'

The servants were newly entertained as a furious Fox, followed by a tail of gentlemen, marched across the Hall and into the red salon.

Chapter Twenty-Nine

Secrets Unleashed

Two of the ladies in the red room were a trifle wan, having spent an hour of the day in concentrated tears, and, in the case of Sally, many other moments in spontaneous spurts of them. Lady Aurora and Lady Richards were serving tea to the afflicted ones (though both young ladies were now wearing plucky little smiles), with Cherie hovering in the vicinity of her mistress, and two footmen at the doors.

'*Out!*' ordered Fox to the servants, who departed, all except the French maid, who did not move from behind Ianthe's chair. 'You,' he said, marching forward and pointing threateningly at Ianthe, 'are *not* going to France.'

Ianthe stood, a game bantam ready for the fray.

'Oh yes?' she said derisively. 'And *who*, pray,

will prevent me?

'But Ianthe is not *intending* to go—' began Lady Richards, appeasing, before her swain, who had arrived at her side, nudged her. Lady Aurora gave Steadman an approving smile.

'*I* will! You shall not leave this house.'

'Oh *no*?' said Ianthe, reverting to the negative. He was looming over her now, and she looked up at him belligerently. Sally was close to the energy coming from the two bodies, and it shook her.

'You will not marry that French fop,' Fox snarled.

'Oh yes?' said Ianthe.

Fenton, who had found himself a seat beside Steadman said, 'Wonderful performance! But the dialogue lacks finesse.'

Steadman's serious face broke.

'Fenton and Audley brought word this afternoon. There is much you do not know about that comte of yours.'

'And *I*,' said Lady Aurora. 'I brought word, too.'

'So you did, my dear,' soothed her husband. Her Ladyship smiled at him.

'What word?' demanded Ianthe. 'What have you kept from me?'

'I did not tell you,' spat Fox, 'because you hadn't told *me* anything.'

'Because you would not listen!' she hit back.

'Why would I want to listen to what I already knew. You had been crying. And it was probably over *him*!'

'You are right as always, my lord. Lord Fox, always known for his sensibility and empathy!' Curtis laughed at this and was frowned down by Sally. As Sally turned her head, she noticed Audley's presence.

'What is *he* still doing here?' she said venomously.

'*Sally!*' cried her mother, shocked. But at the same moment the marquis had cried the same thing. Her mother's instinct snapped awake again, and Emma Richards jerked upright. *What* had the marquis just called her daughter? And in *what* tone?

'This reminds me of a similar performance,' Fenton leaned over Steadman to say to his wife. 'All we need is Mr Mosely to make it complete.'

'He's here somewhere,' said Her Ladyship. 'I saw him.'

'You did? How perfect. Perhaps we should send for him.' Fenton looked around. 'Oh. No footmen. Shh!'

'If I *want* to forgive Antoine and m… marry him, it is quite my affair. How is it yours? You,' she informed him, 'don't even *like* me.'

'*Antoine!*' mocked Fox, '*Antoine!* Your precious Antoine has robbed you blind and you didn't even know it.'

(An aside took place between Mr Fenton and Mr Steadman. 'Steadman, this might be a good time to send for Mr Mosely, if you'd find a footman.'

Steadman nodded and left.)

'Fox!' reproved Audley, moving forward, 'That is hardly the way.' He moved past the dead eye of Sally Richards and past the looming figure of Fox and reached out for Ianthe's hands, which he held as he said, 'It is true, Ianthe.' He looked over her head at the Frenchwoman and said, 'You guessed some of it aright, Cherie. The vowels were all false, put in the bureau drawer by Antoine himself, as I believe.'

Cherie came forward putting an arm about her charge's shoulders, and Ianthe looked at her piteously for a moment before recovering herself. Fox, ousted by the marquis, was now standing next to Curtis. 'The maid!' said his brother, confused.

'Sshh!' said Fox, concentrating on Ianthe's face. Suddenly, he desperately wanted to know what he had spent the day avoiding knowing.

'What benefit could there be to Antoine in my paying those vowels to other people?'

Cherie spoke. 'The names, *Wil-bert*? Was it the names?'

Curtis, Steadman and the Richards were shocked by the use of Fenton's first name in the mouth of a servant, but all were too enthralled by the tale to interrupt.

Fenton spoke, not rising from his comfortable seat. 'That is it, Cherie. Joseph did not play with those people, just as you thought. But I recognised a name on the list you gave me. A Bonapartist.'

'Ah!'

'Audley brought more word from France today. *All* were Bonapartists.'

'So, Antoine — *Antoine* — used my inheritance to support the *general's* cause? But why? What good could come of that now? Even if Antoine had changed—' Ianthe shook her dark curls. 'No, it is not possible.'

Fox gave an expulsion of air. *Still* she defended him!

'The money from your jewels was given back to Antoine. They were just names to be used to gain the funds.'

'He wanted you to have nothing, to *need* him ... *je comprends bien!*' muttered Cherie, and Ianthe cast her a glance.

'I think he *was* ensuring that you would take him, it is true,' said Audley.

'Not so sure of himself, the so-charming comte,' laughed Fenton derisively.

'He mistook me.' Fox looked back at her, admiring the tilt of her head as she stood there unsupported once more.

Audley had dropped her hands, Cherie had taken a step back, as though considering things on her own. 'I should have known...' she said.

'But the other things, the debts…'

'The gaming debts did not exist. There may have been other debts, Ianthe, but Joseph left a fortune. They were nothing.' Fenton's hand gestured lazily.

'*What?*'

'De Farge the lawyer is at the root of it.'

'He avoided seeing us as much as possible,' remembered Cherie.

'Yes. He was being threatened to keep something from you. It was not possible to steal your fortune from the Parisian bank where it was lodged. All De Farge had to do was deny the existence of the account.' Fenton smiled. 'You are quite a wealthy young lady, as I understand it.'

Ianthe sat down on a chair; Cherie put a hand on her shoulder. 'Papa did not fail us—' Cherie squeezed the shoulder. Ianthe looked up to Audley and Fenton. 'And if I had married Antoine …'

'De Farge would have discovered the account,' said Fenton.

The butler had entered with Mr Mosely, and now the servant edged to Fox, saying at a whisper, 'I was in the process of denying Lord Jeffries and Mr Markham, your lordship, thinking this was not the time—'

'Yes, very good,' said Fox distractedly.

'— but as I was doing so, Lady Fox came downstairs.'

Fox looked the butler full in the face. 'You

don't mean to tell me—?'

'In the green salon now, sir. Her Ladyship sent me to find the ladies, sir.'

'Don't let them in here.'

Jenkins, receiving no further instructions, left.

'Mama is *entertaining*?' said Curtis, amused.

'I might have to send you to—'

'Not a hope. This is much too interesting.'

'I never liked you,' remarked Fox. The tone lacked rancour though, and Curtis grinned.

'You've obviously heard all of this, Steadman,' whispered Curtis to that man. 'Who is Antoine? And why does Ianthe hold her maid's hand?'

'Antoine is a French comte in love with Ianthe. And the maid — I am not sure about the maid.'

'Audley, what made de Farge talk?' asked Cherie.

It was Fenton who answered shortly, with a sinister laugh. 'Sebastian. He returned from Geneva.'

'It was all for the *money*?' said Ianthe.

'The comte did not want to keep the money, I think,' said Audley. 'He just wanted you to need him.'

'What about those jewels?' asked Lady Richards.

Ianthe lifted a hand as though to swat a fly.

It was a gesture of dismissal, but the little man by the doorway said, in his oddly carrying and cheerful voice, 'Don't be worrying about that, miss. I picked them up myself today, after I had a little word with the gentleman.' Everyone had turned to him and he walked forward with a confident air. Ianthe recognised the man from the clearing who had secretly guarded her. 'That and another jewellery box in pretty colours.' Cherie stepped forward.

'Empty?' she said, rather desperately.

'All except...' The sharp-nosed fellow had walked forward and now reached into a capacious pocket and drew out a piece of paper with a flourish. '*This*.'

Cherie came towards him, but the little man held the paper back. 'I just have to establish that this here document belongs to you, miss,' he said, in the tones of an official.

'Yes, it does,' Cherie said, reaching for it. Ianthe stood regarding Cherie, frowning. '*S'il vous plâit*, monsieur.' Cherie's hand was shaking. Fox noted that the man shared a glance with Fenton.

'Then you were the *former,*' he intoned with emphasis, 'Ma'amoiselle Charlotte Dubois?'

'Yes, *please...*' Cherie was reaching but the paper seemed always to be just beyond her.

'*Parents,*' Mosely said, reading the paper, then looking up affably. 'It's the same word as in English, thankfully. *Monsoor Pierre Dubois.*' He held out the paper to Mr Fenton. 'What are the Frenchie words after Capitaine?' He grinned to the company. 'I guessed that one,' he confided.

'*Capitaine de corvette*,' said Fenton, entertained. 'It means lieutenant commander in the French navy.'

'A maid's father?' Curtis said, aghast.

'*Mother*, I think that is the word...' took up the little man, '*Lady Margaret Price.* That's nice and English in any event.'

Ianthe came forward. 'What is this document?'

'It is also yours, I suppose miss,' said Mr Mosely. 'If you is the daughter of a Mr Joseph Eames?'

Ianthe's hand was swifter than Cherie's, or perhaps Mr Mosely helped, for she had twitched the document from his hand and was reading it avidly.

'Wil-*bert!*' said Cherie wrathfully, knowing the true culprit.

'My dear,' said Mrs Fenton soothingly. 'It is time she knows.'

'*Married*!' said Ianthe turning to her maid. 'Since 1804! She threw her hands around Cherie, and after half a second was wrapped in a warm embrace. '*Why* did you not tell me you were my true step-mama? *Why* did you make me worry for you and be annoyed with Papa?'

'Good job you sent the servants out, Fox,' approved Curtis Fox cheerily. 'These are rum old goings on. We've had a peer's granddaughter living in our servants' attic?'

'It was because of how we lived at first,' Cherie was answering into Ianthe's hair. 'I came to you as a governess who could speak my mother's tongue, but we had to live so perilously, changing ourselves so frequently. And then, it was because I knew the day might come when we had to live in England.'

'But your mama was *Lady* Margaret. You cannot think that this would bring me dishonour.'

'It could not add to your respectability. The Price family cast off my mother when she married a Frenchman.'

'What about the Bonapartists?' asked Steadman practically, as this affecting display was occurring.

'It seems the comte accepted money to aid a plan to free the general from St Helena,' said Audley.

'Impossible!' said Curtis. 'It is in the middle of the South Atlantic Ocean. They took very good care he cannot escape again.'

'*Antoine* conspired? No!' said Ianthe at this, pulling away from her mama slightly. 'Mr Fenton — *you* know how Antoine despised the Emperor.'

'He did not think it would succeed miss,' joined in the voice of Mr Mosely. 'That is why he was involved. He was desperate for the money, even with his new allowance. And he wanted to marry you, he told me, and he said he knew your father would not permit it with his accounts in such disorder.' The little man rubbed at his nose. 'But your father saw the comte with someone he shouldn't be talking to — not now the King is back in France. And so, he began to look into it.'

'*That* was the intrigue he was drawn back into,' said Cherie.

'And the conspirators found out,' said Ianthe.

'The accident to the carriage!' said Cherie.

'Arranged, Ianthe,' said Mr Fenton, quite sadly.

'*Oh!*'

Fox was beside her even before Cherie, who was looking stunned herself. He led Ianthe back to the chair, and she looked up at him. 'Are you better?' he asked.

Sally went helpfully to fetch some ratafia from a side table, poured a draught, and put it into her friend's hands.

Ianthe sipped.

'The whole scheme was preposterous,' remarked Steadman. How could they think it would succeed?'

'A bit less preposterous than we thought, as Mr Fenton discovered,' said Audley.

'The Chinese,' Fenton said briefly. 'But success or not, they were about to make the attempt.'

'So, Audley came merely to deliver your

mail, Mr Fenton?' asked Sally Richards suddenly.

'I did,' answered the marquis, although he had not been addressed.

'I see,' said Sally icily, and her mother wondered at her tone of gloom. She looked at Audley's face, too. He was unnaturally still, his own gaze on her daughter's. It *could* not be. *When?* On the rides of course! And the walk. Perhaps the same day that she and Mr Steadman…? But she thought back to Sally on the way home. She had no consciousness, though she had seemed enlivened by the exercise. But now —? Audley's eyes. Haunted. Would Sally not have him? Had he done something to disgust her? Or was he the person who was rejecting her daughter, his haunted eyes the guilt of giving too much hope? Sally had been crying today — Emma had suspected, but not known it. Her daughter had flown into a passion, so very unlike her, and had then relieved her feelings with tears.

Emma had hoped that, before the entrance of the gentlemen, both Sally and Ianthe would unburden themselves, but there had been too little time. Lady Aurora had been there, but she had not felt restraint, as slight an acquaintance as she was. Somehow her warmth, the silly conspiracies, and her evident love for Ianthe had made that delicate bridge to intimacy. No, given more time, Emma might have gotten her daughter to talk about the source of her rage and more, even in the presence of Lady Aurora.

'Where is Antoine now, sir?'

'Name's Mosely, miss. An old acquaintance of Mr Fenton's miss. He put me in the way of one of my beauties. And now he's had me following the third one.'

'Beauties?' Curtis diverted him.

'Mentioning no names, but my previous two young beauties are famous, and both of them very well married — though it might have come a cropper in either case. And I met Lady Aurora, too. You cannot say,' he said smiling at that lady, 'that she is not another.' He turned back to Ianthe. 'And now you miss. I never thought to meet anyone else as pretty as the others, but you are all enough to made statues for the museum miss. Can't imagine meeting another such a three in me life. And a fourth and fifth!' he turned to Sally and her mother. 'Two shining ones, there!' he twinkled at them impertinently.

'I've remarked before on what a dreadful flirt you are, Mr Mosely. Not but what you are right. I shall commission the statues, depicting the muses, perhaps.' He counted them off, Delphine, Felicity, you, my dear, now Ianthe, Miss Richards and her mama. It would make a charming group. But sadly, short three figures.'

'We could add the Black-Hearted Lady!' said Lady Aurora, having fun.

'Lady Letitia!' recalled Fenton. 'So we could. We now have but two muses to find. But somehow, Mr Mosely, I think our paths might cross again.'

'I believe they might sir, but I doubt we'll find beauties to match this four.'

'I do not know you Mr Mosely,' smiled Lady Richards, 'but Mr Fenton is undoubtedly right. You are a shocking flirt.'

'A perspicacious man, merely,' said Mr Steadman.

'But Antoine?' asked Ianthe again. Fox frowned.

'There are gentlemen from the government speaking to him at the inn, miss. That is why he told me so much. I brought them with me, being as how the list Mrs Eames gave us was so damning, miss.'

'Will he go to prison?' Ianthe asked in a faint voice.

'It is for the French government to deal with their citizens, I should think.'

'I want to see him!' Ianthe said, determinedly.

'Of *course* you do,' said Fox with disgust. She looked at him squarely in the eye. He sighed. 'I'll take you.'

'Now!' urged Ianthe. 'They may move him to London.'

Lady Fox came into the room, followed by a smiling Mr Markham and Lord Jeffries.

'Why I should have to come and look for you, ladies,' Her Ladyships complaining voice began, 'when gentlemen have called to meet the family— What—?' she looked at the room full of people. '*Curtis!*' she finally said.

Curtis moved towards her saying, 'Mama!'

'Why did you not inform me?'

'*Not* a subject for that there statue collection,' remarked Mr Mosely to Mr Fenton in a lowered tone. The gentleman let out a short laugh.

Footmen reappeared to set chairs and soon everyone was re-seated — Ianthe a trifle restive on her chair, Cherie merging into the background, and Fox next to Ianthe, ready to depart. Steadman sat beside Sally on one of the large sofas that bracketed the fire, and Mr Markham took the seat on the other side of her. Lady Aurora sat beside her husband on the other sofa, Ianthe at the other end. Jeffries headed towards Ianthe, but Fox blocked his view from the seat. A throne like chair had been set for Her Ladyship just opposite the fire, making a circular arrangement of visitors and residents. Curtis took a chair equidistant from his mama and Jeffries. Mr Mosely stepped back to the door. The butler nodded him out, but the little man caught Fenton's eye, and withdrew to a seat up against the wall of the room, away from the visitors and guests.

'Curtis! You did not tell us that you had returned,' said Lady Fox, once seated.

'I had only just arrived Mama,' said Curtis defensively. 'Tell her, Fox!'

His mama was not impressed with the call for support her son made to Fox, suggesting, as it did, a level of new intimacy she was not pleased with. 'My son,' she informed Lord Jeffries, 'has returned from Broadbank. His own estate, in Wiltshire.'

'Ah,' returned Jeffries, attempting to sound impressed. 'All well there, I hope, Fox?'

'There are a few things I need to see to, but I have to say,' said Curtis proudly, 'that it is fine country.'

'I am afraid, gentlemen,' said Ianthe, 'that I have been called away into the village.'

'I would be happy to take you, Miss Eames,' said Jeffries. 'As it happens, I have brought my rig today.'

'There is no need, sir. I will take Miss Eames,' said Fox coldly.

'I see no need for you to go, Fox. None at all,' said his stepmother.

'Got to see a French fellow,' said Curtis to his mama. 'Better have Fox.'

Sally, who once disliked Curtis thoroughly, was beginning to take to him — just as his mother, having lost her one support, frowned terribly. The departure permitted, Fox and Ianthe left.

'What bulls do you keep, Jeffries?' asked Curtis.

'Eh? That is, I have no clue. My papa sees to the estate. Or Finch does, the steward, you know.'

'Oh,' said Curtis proudly, 'I mean to be much more involved. A steward is all very well, but an estate needs a master's touch, don't you think, Audley?'

Audley, Curtis' enthusiasm finally rousing him, said indulgently, 'I do.'

'And not a *visiting* master, either. I mean to make my home there.'

'Curtis!' cried his mama.

'I meant to talk to you about it earlier, Mama,' said Curtis, eagerly. 'You'll love it there. And you can order the place as you like it, until I take a wife, you know.'

Curtis looked a little dreamy and Jeffries said, in an under voice, 'Met someone, Curtis?'

'As a matter of fact, I was invited to dinner by the family of the neighbouring estate. A Mr Pearson.'

'He has a daughter, I take it?' said Jeffries with a humorous look.

'*Well…*' said Curtis, but smiling shyly.

Curtis' mama, straining to hear, was distressed. '*Curtis,*' she mewed.

Mr Markham, on the other side of the room, made a joke that amused Miss Richards. Curtis spoke to Audley again, trying to recall his attention from the pair. 'Thought you'd gone to London, marquis?'

'I did, and then I came back,' said the marquis distractedly.

'Ah, something about delivering Fenton's

mail? Won't discuss it now but that was a dashed interesting tale.' He followed the direction of the marquis' blank gaze. 'Looks like Miss Richards has made some progress with the gentlemen. She's looking very pretty these days. Can't say I really noticed before.' He glanced at Audley who did not reply. 'I wondered if they have visited *every* day since I have been gone. Who do you bet on, Steadman or Markham? Markham has it by a nose at the moment, but my instinct tells me that Steadman could gallop up from the rear.'

'That is why you should never wager, Curtis,' said Audley dryly. 'Steadman is to marry Lady Richards.'

'Lady Richards?' said Curtis in a louder tone.

All eyes were on him as Emma Richards looked up and said mildly, 'Yes Curtis?'

'I … I understand congratulations are in order, cousin.'

'Oh,' blushed Emma Richards, turning to her swain. 'Yes, my dear.'

'Congratulations?' asked Jeffries.

'Lady Richards is betrothed to Mr Steadman,' said Lady Fox's stony voice.

Markham and Jeffries gasped audibly. Lady Aurora said, 'Oh I did not know! How splendid.' She turned to her husband, 'Did you know dear?'

'I guessed.'

'Of *course* you did!'

Hands were shaken, and Jeffries and Markham were astounded and cheered at once.

'And it all happened at Studham! You must be so pleased that the happy couple have been able to pursue their acquaintance here, Lady Fox,' said Lady Aurora.

'Certainly,' lied Her Ladyship. 'I did think it a trifle precipitate, however, but I believe there is to be an early wedding.'

'I am hoping that Miss Richards will visit Stone Manor tomorrow to see her new home,' Steadman said.

'How kind!' said Sally.

'We could make a party of it,' enthused Curtis. 'I want to see what beasts you keep, Steadman.'

Mr Steadman agreed, if a trifle wryly.

'*I* shall not travel so far!' announced Lady Fox. 'Do not look for me.'

Regrets were expressed, though no one had feared missing her. 'Will you come, marquis?' asked Markham.

'I am not sure. I may have to return to London.'

'We should not wish you to forgo your pleasures,' said Sally politely. But she added, 'We will not look for you. Do not come.'

'Sally!' breathed her mother, alarmed less at her words than her tone.

'I believe I *will* come, Steadman, if you do not object,' said Audley suavely. His eyes crossed Sally's, looking down his nose.

A conversation developed about which carriages should be ordered to accommodate the company, and they all assumed that the absent Fox and Ianthe would make two of their number.

The gentlemen took their leave, and Sally left the room. The Marquis of Audley lingered in the Hall.

'Sapphire awaits you in the morning, don't let him down.'

'I will let him down. I shall not ride tomorrow.'

'Then when?'

Lady Richards, in the hall bidding farewell to her betrothed, could not quite hear the conversation, but saw its intensity.

'Perhaps never. I was an imposition today. I apologise for it.'

'If you will not come tomorrow, then I will come to dinner tonight.'

'Why?'

'Because, like Sapphire, I need to take a better goodbye of you.'

'I have had quite enough of your goodbyes. And I do not find them comforting.'

'That is because my tongue has stopped working around you. I say things that I do not mean to, I hurt you when I did not wish to.'

'And tonight, you will do more of the same. You should never have come back. You should never have let me realise that I … let me know that…' her voice became suspended. She glanced across at her mama.

'I will con a more fitting goodbye. I will make you understand that it is better, better by far for you...'

'Go!' said Sally, and it was loud enough to raise her mother's head.

Audley bowed and left, and Emma said to Steadman, 'I must go after Sally. Whatever—'

'I understand that Audley is a complicated man. Like Fox,' her betrothed added, arcanely.

Chapter Thirty

The Past Dealt With

'You said,' Fox stated, as he was negotiating the road ahead in his phaeton, 'that he had mistaken you.'

Ianthe was silent. He took a quick glance at her profile. The tears that she had shed were not visible any longer. 'I keep forgetting,' Fox remarked in a gentler tone, 'that your father is not long dead. I have been too concerned for myself to comfort you today. Too concerned at what you might say to me to be of help to you. It was selfish and I am sorry, Ianthe.'

She looked up at him. 'Stop it! I need to be angry at *you* at least so that I can preserve my face right now.' They rode on for another minute before she asked, 'What did you fear I might say?'

'That you would leave.'

'You have wanted me to leave since I have arrived,' she reminded him.

He gave her a look from the side of his eyes.

'You have known that not to be true — even before I did.'

'Edward Fox. Is that insight I hear from your lips?'

'I did not know myself before you came here. You understand that. I flailed around in a temper most of the time, unable to escape my situation. I gave no thought to how anyone else felt. You changed all that, Ianthe.'

'If you were not a good man, Edward,' said Ianthe softly, 'I could not have done so.'

He breathed deeply. 'You have told me so before. *You are good, you are kind.* I had never heard those words since Lady Fox entered this house. I was stuck in the dispirited resentment of an eight-year-old. It infected every friendship I ever made, or could have made. It stopped me being able to help poor Curtis.' He looked across at her, his Fox eyes soft and gentle. 'You made me see myself.'

'And so, you did not want me to leave?' said Ianthe, ironically, not meeting his gaze. 'Well, Edward, my task here is done. I think you will live a happier life. Will do more of what you desire, will make new friends.' Then her tone turned a little colder. 'You can do so without me.'

Fox pulled up the team. He turned to her. 'Does that mean you *will* leave here?'

'Fox, start the carriage. I need to see Antoine.'

He did so, the frown once more on his face.

'What happened today? He did not offer you insult?'

'*Now* you ask me,' she remarked. 'You did not trust me before.'

'Did he hurt you?' he asked through his teeth.

'No. Perhaps he meant to force me to leave with him, I am not sure. He brought a carriage with him, talked of a wedding at the Scottish Border, or a flight to France.'

'But he did not succeed in forcing you.'

'He thought better of it.' She glanced at him for a second. 'I know Antoine. I was not really in danger. He loves me, in his way.'

'Stealing and…'

'It is difficult for you to understand, but all of that only shocked me for a moment.' She shuddered.

Fox said, 'Longer than a moment.'

'Yes,' she laughed. 'Perhaps.' She shook her head, and looked like she was calculating her next words. 'But our lives have been so full of extreme measures, desperate steps to achieve an end. I think I understand him better than you can imagine.'

'And you excuse him to me?' demanded Fox.

'No.' She smiled at Fox. 'But you must understand, if he had called me to him a year ago, if he had approached my papa as a gentleman…'

'You would have gone to him?'

'I may have — even though for at least three years I have known it would never be easy with Antoine. That it was not *right*.' She looked up at Fox's face, full of attention and concentration, but having to stare ahead at his horses. 'It still gave me pain, even on the journey to England. I questioned whether I should have refused him.'

Fox grunted, and she saw his decision not to interrupt. She smiled.

'But as soon as I came here, the confusion lifted.'

Fox dropped his reins to his knee. He turned to her. 'When you came *here*? Why?'

Ianthe looked at him with a reprise of her old pertness as well as some disgust. 'I find your question intrusive,' she said, with lifted eyebrows. Fox paid attention to his horses, since he needed to turn into the inn, but his hands shook.

***

Ianthe was granted, by both Fox and the gentlemen from London sent to bring the comte back to the capitol, the right to speak to the Comte d'Emillion-Orsay on her own.

Antoine stood by the window, and in that light, it was hard to read his expression.

'I know it all,' said Ianthe at once. 'My fortune. Why, Antoine?' Her voice was gentle, not bitter, but the comte laughed harshly.

'Because I was mad for you, Ianthe. Because you are not an easy woman.'

'On top of my father's death, to give Cherie and me so much more care…'

'I was there,' he defended himself. 'I told you not to worry. If you had just agreed to come to me …'

'I wanted to … but there was something about you, Antoine. Something I always knew. A weakness that was not in my father, whatever his supposed vices.'

'I failed to live up to the gaming, unreliable Joseph Eames. Cherie complained that he was never where he should be, that he drank and wagered—'

'Yes,' said Ianthe, 'but you know she said it with a smile. You said unreliable. But Papa was there when one needed him. You, too, have reason to know t*hat*, Antoine.'

He hung his head at this. 'This is how I end. They send me back to King Louis to be sentenced.'

'I have no doubt, Antoine, that your clever mind is already arranging the facts to suit you.' He laughed, and had come forward so that she saw a more sardonic expression on his handsome face. 'But Bonapartists, Antoine?'

'I believed it to be a scheme impossible to succeed. And so, for the money, I helped them.' For the first time he looked ashamed. 'But I am almost glad to be uncovered. It began to look like they might achieve a miracle. And more war would occur.'

Ianthe's eyes were on him, but her hands were clasped together, betraying an agitation he had not before seen in her. He tried for a casual tone. 'How was that discovered, by the way?'

'Mr Fenton. Cherie had kept the list of creditors, and Mr Fenton recognised a few names on the list. It was soon apparent that it was a list of Bonapartists. That, and something I did not understand about someone Chinese.'

'Wilbert Fenton was always a clever one. Chinese now work on St Helena since slavery ended. The Bonapartists had already infiltrated a Chinese worker who was offering his countrymen return to China with wealth, if only they were ready to help on the island if their ship could get in. A Chinese army, in effect, though badly armed. But it would have ensured attack from two places, the rescuers on the ship and the Chinese on the island. That was what made me fear for the success of the undertaking. I could hardly believe it possible, but each day it became more real.' He sighed. 'I suppose, too, that it was clumsy of me to use the Bonapartists as the gaming debtors, but where else could I find that number of conspirators, none of whom needed to be paid for the use of their names?'

'I still have not heard it, Antoine,' Ianthe said. 'What I came for.'

'I am sorry I loved you too much,' He said, looking deep into her eyes.

She took a step back, raising her head. '*That* will not do.'

'I am sorry, Ianthe,' his voice was broken, but still the deep thrilling voice that had troubled her young dreams. 'Sorry that I deceived and hurt you. I meant to make it all up to you — and to Cherie, if only you had married me.'

'Thank you, Antoine. Thank you for loving me, even if it was in a way that I cannot respect.' She looked at him, her eyes filling, but her voice sardonic. 'I hope you do not lose your handsome head over this.'

He shrugged, with his old raffish air. Then he said, more seriously, 'Goodbye, Ianthe.'

She had gone to the chamber door, but turned to him. 'Papa and Cherie. They were always married.'

Antoine, whose eyes had filled once she'd turned from him, gave a crack of laughter at this. 'Mrs Eames! Send her my ... send her my apologies, and my wish for her good health.'

'Goodbye, Antoine.'

'Take this,' he held out his hand and from it dropped the amber pendant.

'Papa's gift to me.' Ianthe reached for it. 'You kept it back because—'

He shrugged in that French manner. 'Another excuse to see you.' Their eyes caught, and despite herself Ianthe's filled. 'Will you be with him? The man who came in with you and looked like he would have liked to kill me?'

'If he ever understands ...' She smiled at the comte a little. '... he is new to understanding things.'

They exchanged a warm look. 'I'll ask Mr Fenton, Antoine. Ask him to arrange things.'

'If I could escape—' Antoine was suddenly energised.

'Then we can trust in your wits.' She searched her reticule, pulling out a purse. 'Conceal this. It is not much.'

He took it, kissing her gloved hand with fervour, and she pulled away, laughing. 'Farewell, my old friend,' she said, and left.

***

The journey back in the gig tasked Ianthe's patience. She was imagining telling Fox what she had just done for Antoine, about what she hoped Fenton would do for him, knowing that the baron could never understand it. He had never lived as she had, running from discovery all her life, taking outrageous risks to achieve one's aim. She believed Fenton understood her and would help see that Antoine never reached Paris and his judgement. Fox's voice interrupted her reverie.

'What did you mean that your confusion about the comte lifted when you came to Studham?'

'Never mind that now ... I am sad. Everything Antoine did with the Bonapartists he did thinking that it could never succeed. That he was simply relieving mad men of their money. And taking my money was never meant to be serious. That is why he gave the jewels back. He just wanted—'

'To have you need him.' Fox paused. 'As Fenton said, he must never have been secure of you.'

'No, I suppose not. And I thought it was *I* who was never secure about him.'

'Is it finished, the remnants of that first love?'

'If you do not listen to what I have already told you,' Ianthe said, annoyed, 'I shall simply stop speaking.' She closed her eyes. 'I have the headache. Tell me when we reach home.'

***

Curtis had been summoned to his mother's room, where Her Ladyship lay prone on a chaise longue; Evans hovered nearby with her vinaigrette. He mentally balked at the door, but entered like a man, attempting cheerfulness.

'Laid up, Mama?' he asked hopefully. 'No need to talk now, I'll let you rest.'

'*Curtis!* You will come here.'

'Yes, Mama.'

'What did you say about removing to Broadbank? I was never more dumbfounded. Only a few days away and then to come back ready to leave your only home. And *me*? You would abandon your mama so easily?'

'I told you already that I wish to take you with me, Mama,' Curtis said. 'You must remember that.'

'But you are the heir to Studham! *This* is your home.'

'That is where we both went wrong, Mama. It was always Edward's.'

'I have never been deficient in my respect for Fox as master here,' sniffed his mother, head held high, 'but he will never marry, he—'

'I think he *will* marry one day, Mama. I mean, why ever should he not?' said Curtis reasonably. 'He's got a temper, but I think the ladies find him handsome,' considered Curtis, surprised. 'But as Fox said to me, even if he did *not* marry, I will likely be a very old man before Studham became mine.'

'So, this is Fox's doing? Making you feel unwanted in your own—'

'*No,* Mama!' exclaimed her son quietly, and with a new maturity she had not seen in him previously. 'He just wanted me to consider if I would rather be master on my own place, and he was quite right. I was too young to appreciate it before, Mama, but a man needs to be independent. Papa left me the means to do so, and I intend to make better use of it. Gibley and I were talking, you know, and it is very likely that I can increase the estate profits in a very few years. Enough for both of us, Mama, to live extremely comfortably. And there is a neighbouring estate that might …'

Curtis smiled, '… but it is too soon to talk of that. Think of it, Mama. I would be settled. I know you worried about my excesses, though you have always defended me like a champion, saying that a young man must be free to have some. And you were right, Mama. I have been too idle, that is it. Just a short time at Broadbank and I understand what it is to have a rewarding occupation. It is very exciting. You will like the house, Mama. You can help me arrange things. It is very invigorating to be the man whom the staff look to please, you know. You will like to see it, rather than me being someone who is always second in line. Whose orders must be checked with the master, even though Jenkins does not say so.'

It was a long speech, and Her Ladyship had tried to interrupt a number of times by making a sound, but Curtis had sat on the edge of the bed, and looked at her with concerned eyes, alternating with boyish enthusiasm. He held her hand and his mother said, eventually, 'Have you been so very unhappy here, Curtis?'

'Not unhappy. But I think I can be much happier at Broadbank.'

Lady Fox sighed in defeat. 'I will consider it, my son. Because you wish it. And because all my felicity in life has been stolen since that girl arrived. I cannot understand it. The house is constantly full of people. Audley comes and goes as he wants. Fox entertains her friends the Fentons as though he had known them forever. The

Richards have both become *ungovernable* and Fox unrecognisable. She is a wicked, wicked girl.'

'Miss Eames?' Curtis asked. 'I think she's just a little French, you know.'

He patted his mother's hand, soothingly.

She removed hers from his, reaching blindly for the vinaigrette. It was as near to a complaint as she could muster.

Chaptr Thirty-One

Dinner and Wooing

Ianthe entered Sally's chamber when she returned. 'Fox is as stupid as Audley,' she announced.

'I thought you went to see the wicked comte?'

'I did. And he's stupid, too.' Ianthe sighed. 'He is not really wicked, though. I must see Mr Fenton before dinner to imagine what might be done for Antoine.'

'Surely nothing can be if he acted against the King.'

'It will appear so, but actually …' Ianthe looked worried. 'But Mr Fenton will know what to do.'

'You seem to have a great deal of faith in Mr Fenton.'

'I do. Do you know that when Antoine took me to the clearing where he had hidden his carriage, that I was not alone? That little man from today, Mr Mosely, was there, behind the shrubbery. He showed himself to me, and the pistol in his hands.'

'Were you not even more afraid?' said Sally, comfortably shocked.

'No. He winked at me!'

'I'm sure that would have made me shudder.'

'Somehow it did not. Antoine did not coerce me, but I was safe in the knowledge that he *could* not.'

'And you believed that the little man was from Mr Fenton?'

'He or Fox. But I thought afterwards that if he were Fox's man, he would more likely be a servant that I would recognise.'

'True. How swift you are in thinking.' Sally regarded her friend whose beautiful dark eyes looked even darker. 'But how is Fox stupid?' She giggled. 'I agree of course, but what has he done to convince you of it on this occasion?'

'You heard us in the drawing room. I told him he did not like me.'

'You *did*.'

'And he did not *deny* it!'

'Yes, an idiot,' agreed Sally.

'*And* I told him I might marry Antoine—'

'Well,' said Sally, as though to be fair, 'he did forbid you that — most forcibly.' Sally lowered her voice and took on a terrible frown. *'You shall not marry that French fop!'* she quoted.

'But he did not say *why* I could not marry him,' said Ianthe resentfully. 'And then, when we were alone on the way to the inn, I even told him that as soon as I had come to Studham, all my confusion about Antoine disappeared.'

'And he *still* did not say anything to the point?' said Sally, aggrieved. 'You are quite right — men are ridiculously stupid. They only call you their *lovely, lovely* and then do not finish at all.'

'We shall defeat them, Sally! We shall crush them beneath our satin slippers and make them pay!' Ianthe vowed.

***

Mr Wilbert Fenton was the only resident in the salon when Audley was announced.

'You here?' asked Fenton redundantly.

'For dinner.'

'So early?'

'I hoped I might get a chance for a word with…' He sighed, admitting defeat. 'I made another mull of it. I do not know what comes over me when I am with her, I cannot string sensible words together. I need to apologise. Again.'

'Oh yes? Still determined on your life as a hellion?'

'It is not that, precisely. You know, Fenton. Once a libertine always … I could decide on a different life, but what if I failed? What if I were to hurt her?'

'It seems you have done so already. She looked like someone who had spent the day crying.'

'Better a day than a lifetime.'

'So, you come to bother her again?' Fenton laughed.

'I will be gone tomorrow. I just wanted to say...'

'Don't lie to yourself, Rob. You cannot keep away. Even if you go tomorrow, you will find her again. Bother her again.'

'I cannot. I *will* not.' Said Audley, desperately.

Fenton crossed his legs and looked at his friend, amused. 'So, you return to your days as a libertine once more. I saw you go to the dogs with a greater will than ever this time in London. Did you enjoy it, Audley? Any of it?'

'It is who I am accustomed to be. Even if now...'

'Do not be mistaken, my friend. Your vices? It is not that you must decide to leave your vices behind. *They* have already left *you.*' Audley stood regarding him, shaken. Fenton sipped his wine and then looked down at the glass, long fingers playing with the stem. 'Once you get a taste of the real thing, Audley, nothing else will ever taste as sweet.'

Fox came in and threw himself into a chair. 'What are you doing here?' he asked the marquis with not much interest.

'For dinner,' said Audley, who had helped himself to some sherry, and now sat on a sofa.

'Jenkins knows?'

'I suppose so.'

There was a depressed silence.

'Young persons of today!' remarked Fenton. 'Have neither of you a store of pleasant conversation?'

'No,' the two young men said together.

Others began to drift into the salon. Lady Aurora and Lady Fox, the Richards and Curtis, and finally, Mr Steadman.

'Did you invite him?' whispered Curtis.

'No,' sighed Fox. 'But he practically lives here.'

Jenkins dispatched a footman to set another extra place at the table and to inform the hard-pressed cook that he must find another chop.

'What afflicts our two peers?' asked Steadman.

'They cannot see the wood for the trees,' answered Fenton confidingly.

The gentlemen had formed a pack, rather separate from the ladies, and were speaking apart. 'Were you previously acquainted with Lady Richards, Steadman?' asked Curtis Fox.

'No. I met her at the marquis' dinner.'

'Really? It was rather sudden that you proposed.' Curtis looked a little shy. 'It is sometimes a little difficult to speak, even when…'

'I saw her that night and spoke the next day,' said Steadman with his uninflected tone. 'It was quite simple.'

'And she said yes?'

Steadman looked as though he would not answer what was becoming a more intimate set of questions. But something in the young man's face indicated more than prurient interest. 'Not that day. But I believed she would.'

'But you knew nothing about her.'

'It did not seem so. It seemed I knew all about her.'

'Yes,' said Curtis, a little dreamily. 'It can be just like that. So, a man must speak, then?'

'Is it not, then, simple?' asked Steadman.

Fox and Audley shot him looks of dislike, and Fenton laughed, placing a comradely arm on Steadman's shoulders. 'Indeed, it is,' said Fenton. 'It is only fools who make trouble for themselves by thinking too much.' He gazed at the marquis. 'Or not thinking at all.' Here he looked at Fox.

Dinner was announced.

'Mrs Eames does not join us?' asked Fox. 'I did send word to her to make one of the table.'

'She does not choose to today,' said Ianthe briefly. 'I shall insist for tomorrow breakfast.'

'*Mrs* Eames?' said Lady Fox, confused.

'I forgot to tell you, Mama!' said Curtis cheerily. 'The French maid is really Ianthe's stepmama.'

'A *maid?*' began Her Ladyship.

'She was just pretending to be a maid, your ladyship,' said Lady Richards, helpfully. 'She is really the daughter of a French lieutenant commander of the navy and one of Lord Price's aunts. I asked her about it today. The mother ran off to Paris to be with the Frenchman and the family disowned her. Then she died when poor Cherie was only twenty. Her father had perished at sea, and Cherie took the job as a governess to the widower, Mr Eames. They fell in love and married, but on account of the life that led them into danger, she had to appear as a maid, or governess, or sometimes as a wife. Ianthe was never clear what her role was. Only that her father and she loved her dearly. Is that not an affecting story?'

'I do not understand!' complained Lady Fox, but her voice was less forceful.

'We have lived very differently — as you and your family have remarked, Lady Fox. How should you understand?' Ianthe smiled a genuine smile. 'I thank you for making the attempt.'

'The maid with the disfiguring eyebrows is really your stepmother?'

'She is and ... no! You will see tomorrow.'

'The servants ... the talk!' intoned Her Ladyship.

'Leave the servants to me,' said Fox shortly. 'And Ianthe, I did not say about you living differently meaning an insult. You *know*—'

'Yes, you did,' said Ianthe coldly. 'You said that you would make *provisions* for me since I would not be suited to living the life at Studham.'

'That was on the first day. I explained myself already.'

'You still *said* it.' Ianthe turned to Lady Aurora. 'Wouldn't *you* be insulted if a man said that to you?'

Her Ladyship looked amused. '*Well—*' she began judiciously.

Sally interrupted. '*I* would,' she said to Ianthe. 'I *certainly* would.'

'Sally!' said her mama. 'Not at the dinner table.'

'We are all family here,' said Ianthe, defending her friend. 'Mr Steadman will be part of the family very soon, after all.'

'Less than five weeks,' agreed Steadman, taking his betrothed's hand and looking at her meaningfully.

'All family, except for *him!*' added Sally wrathfully, looking at the marquis. The impolite use of the pronoun raised eyebrows around the table.

'Yes,' said Ianthe supportively. 'I cannot think what has brought him here.'

'This is beyond the bounds of good manners,' said Lady Fox. 'I might not have welcomed the marquis here before, but that was a matter of a familial dispute. Since Fox welcomes him now, it is not for you young ladies to be so—' she turned to Lady Richards. 'What is happening? Why has every hint of good breeding been wrenched from this conversation?'

'You are quite right, Lady Fox,' said Lady Richards. 'Girls! I do not know where your manners have gone, but pray apologise to the marquis.'

'Oh, there is no need, Lady Richards,' Audley said, with a wry smile. 'I invited myself to a family dinner and Miss Richards has only spoken the truth.'

'The truth,' said Lady Fox, 'is seldom required at dinner.'

'What have you done, Audley, to put the girls out so?' asked Curtis interestedly.

Audley closed his mouth firmly, casting Curtis a warning look.

'I look on Audley as an old family friend,' said Fox dismissively. 'He is welcome at any time.'

'That is because you two are *just* the same,' said Ianthe. And it was apparent it was not a compliment.

'Yes. Why cannot all men be like Mr Steadman?' said Sally. 'Upright and straightforward.'

Steadman's serious face let a sardonic smile pass over. He did not think these remarks addressed to himself.

'Yes,' said Ianthe. 'Precisely.' The girls looked at each other and nodded decisively.

Lady Richards was caught between pleasure at the compliment to her love and the need to stop the implied rudeness. 'Perhaps dear, but there is no need to—'

'Here, what about me?' said Curtis.

Sally gave him a withering look.

'No, I suppose *upright* is—' he grinned.

'And my husband is ... well perhaps *upright* might not *best* describe him,' Lady Aurora giggled, 'and definitely not *straightforward*.'

'I thought you were coming to my defence?' said her husband, wounded.

'Yes dear. But such *commonplace* words could not be used for you. One would have to describe you as...' he raised an eyebrow at her, '*magnificent.*'

'You are never wrong, my dear,' he remarked. 'But it is evident that Fox and Audley fall short of Steadman's standards. We arrived at that point.'

'Yes indeed.'

'Ladies,' intoned Lady Fox, rising. 'We shall not have dessert. I could not digest it. We shall leave the gentlemen to their port and retire.'

Ianthe, regretting the blancmange, rose with the other ladies.

In the withdrawing room, Emma Richards had sought her daughter's confidence at once, drawing her aside from their hostess. 'Sally my dear, what has the Marquis of Audley done to displease you? Can it be— is there any insult?'

'Do not worry about insult, Mama,' said Sally in high colour. 'He does not give me *insult.*' This was said as though the lack of insult was insult itself, and Lady Richards remained confused.

Seeing her daughter's rage mount once more, Sally's mama was thrown back. 'Well, if not insult, then does he … can it be that the marquis has *intentions?*'

'Oh, he has intentions. He intends to return to London where all his *pleasures-*' The venom that dripped from her daughter's voice informed the mama that Sally was not referring to driving in the park.

'Sally!' said Her Ladyship, shocked, 'What do you know of gentlemen's pleasures?'

'What do you speak of? I insist on knowing!' called Lady Fox.

'Gentlemen's pleasures,' said Sally, her rage cold.

'But *why?*'

'It is a pity, Sally was saying earlier, that ladies are not allowed to race,' Ianthe informed Lady Fox, blandly.

'Race? Horses? What a ridiculous notion! Quite ungenteel.'

'Oh, there was a ladies' race at Housten Hall. Sally won it, you know,' Ianthe informed the baroness.

'There will be no such event at Studham. I will not model my conduct on such as a mere Mrs Housten.'

'No, my lady,' said Lady Richards in a depressed voice. The gentlemen entered.

'Sally, Ianthe, you must behave!' hissed Emma.

'It is *they* who must behave!' said Ianthe, with determination.

'I think, Lady Richards,' laughed Lady Aurora quietly to that lady, 'that we must leave the girls to their endeavours.

***

The gentlemen, at their port earlier, fell into two camps. The marquis and Fox in the depressed and confused camp, Fenton, Curtis and Steadman into the amused and interested camp.

'Why is Ianthe mad with you, Fox?' asked Curtis.

'She does not say,' said Fox, lost. 'Do you know, sir?' he asked Fenton.

'Yes, approximately.' Fox looked hopeful. 'It is because you are an ass.'

'I thought,' said Fox resentfully, 'that you might help me.'

'I already attempted to help Audley,' said Fenton, passing a hand over his brow, 'and my resources are depleted. Work it out for yourself. I am sure that Ianthe, a fair girl, would not leave you without any information on your wrongdoing.'

'You were no help to *me*,' remarked Audley.

'What did he tell you?' asked Curtis, interested.

'He said not to worry about leaving my

vices, that my vices have left me.' He looked at Fox. 'Do you see Edward? No help at all.'

'Ah, so *that* was the problem,' sighed Steadman. 'I understand now.'

'You do?' Curtis was confused.

'Of course. If that is the impediment, Audley, you are being ridiculous.'

'You know?'

'My eyes can see. It is hardly difficult.'

'What isn't?' asked Curtis.

'You are a simple man, Steadman,' said Fenton. 'I like you.'

Steadman did not look overawed at the compliment, but inclined his head.

'The impediment to what?' asked Curtis. 'And what impediment?' As no one replied, he looked to Fox. 'And how can Mr Fenton help with Ianthe being angry at you?'

'He could explain the reason, perhaps,' answered Steadman when Curtis' brother remained silent.

'Did Ianthe tell you what it was, sir?'

'No. I just know the root cause. Fox is an ass,' Fenton repeated.

'I have always thought so,' said Curtis. 'He needs to ask Ianthe.'

'That will produce no results,' said Fenton wisely. 'He needs to work it out for himself this time.'

'Oh,' had said Fox, discarding his port glass. 'Let us go to them. It does no good sitting here.'

Chapter Thirty-Two

After Dinner Endings

The first to enter were Audley and his host, and they paused on the threshold as two sets of irate eyes bored into them.

'*Bon courage*, gentlemen!' remarked Mr Fenton, behind them.

The gentlemen moved forward. The ladies sat silent, the young girls cold, Lady Aurora amused, Lady Richards confused. Lady Fox was waiting to be addressed in good form. Curtis opened his mouth, but Steadman frowned him down. Tea was served by a nervous Lady Richards, who tried once or twice to speak. But then she noticed that Lady Aurora, catching a mood, put a finger to her lips, so she remained silent. As she passed the tea to the marquis, she saw that his eye was riveted on the form of her daughter, seated on the sofa, a little back from the chairs by the fire. Could it be? thought Lady Richards. Sally's rage denoted something so *intimate*…

Audley moved to sit on one side of Sally, saying in an under breath, 'I am sorry for today, Miss Richards. I spoke too…'

'Yes, you spoke, but made no sense at all. I see no reason for us to continue to speak now. You have made me understand. Do not think I shall go into a decline, for I shall not.' His mouth worked, but as usual recently, the master of social dexterity was thrown into confusion.

'I did not think it,' he said. 'We cannot talk here.' He looked over at Lady Fox who had an eye on him, briefly, then at Lady Richards, who Fenton's wife was doing her best to keep occupied. 'I came tonight—'

'Yes, why *did* you come tonight?' she said, with heightened colour.

'I was just about to tell you,' said Audley, with an attempt at raillery. 'Be quiet and listen.'

'I see no reason to—' she was preparing to rise, but Audley grasped the back of her gown at the bodice, unseen by the others. Dignity required that she keep her seat.

'Listen, you horrible girl,' he said, remembering Ianthe's lesson to him a little late. 'We need to talk. I must apologise for being what Fenton would describe as an ass. I know it. I just came to urge you to ride Sapphire tomorrow and then you can shout at me all you like and relieve your feelings.'

Sally's eyes filled at this, and she looked down at her teacup. Audley was shaken. 'So easily? I have only to shout at you for half an hour and everything will be well?'

A tear splashed onto her cup. Lady Aurora, observing it, was glad that she had called Lady Richards' attention to herself, and that that lady did not see. A quick look around the room and it was obvious that no other person had seen. Though her husband, there was no telling what Wilbert saw or did not just by his expression.

'Come tomorrow and let us talk. I cannot bear to see you…'

'Do not dare to be kind to me Audley. I will not have it!'

'No,' he said, knowing that her rage was hiding her pain and that she would soon be unable to stop the tears. What on earth had he been thinking? What had he thought he could do at a dinner party? But he had believed that she would have refused herself to him had he visited tomorrow before he left. Fenton was right. He could not keep away. His excuse tonight was that he wished to talk to her more, to let her know that this would *really* be better for her, to end things with her knowing at least that he meant no insult to her, quite the contrary. It was *because* he loved her … He heard himself think it, and realised he was a full-blown lunatic. How could it help her to tell her he loved her? He should not be here.

Another tear fell. First, he had to help her regain herself. He searched his brain for an insult. 'That dress does not become you.'

'I beg your pardon?' said Sally, looking first at him and then at the offending evening dress of orange sarcanet.

'It is too thin. You look like you might freeze to death.'

She narrowed her eyes. 'You comment too freely on female apparel. Tell someone who is interested.'

On the other side of the room, Fox had made his delicate approach to Ianthe. 'I keep wondering,' he said beneath the hearing of their neighbours, 'what you meant when you said that Studham gave you clarity about the comte? I did not know that you liked Studham so well—'

She looked at him. He felt himself dwindle in size. Her disdain was enormous. 'I did not say that *Studham* had—' She closed her eyes and shook her head. 'Do not concern yourself with the topic, Lord Fox. We shall not speak of it again.'

'Why are you angry with me? I never understand you—'

'You do not need to understand *me*,' she replied trenchantly. 'Understand yourself first, my lord.'

'Ianthe—' He wanted to be angry with her. She looked very beautiful with her eyes sparkling as much as the spangles on her shawl. The dress, of fine red silk, was perhaps not the English fashion for an unmarried lady, but it set off her dark curls to perfection. It was of a superior cut, full of intricate, but subtle detail from the seed pearl encrusting the band below her breast, to the pintucks at the bodice. But however beautiful she looked, he had always been able to be angry with her. Tonight, though, was different. She did not usually respond to his ill humour with anger of her own. No, he had disappointed her, and instead of anger he felt a quiet desperation to understand. She was hurt — somehow, he had been part of the cause of her hurt. But why? She never gave his starts much attention. She had always been able to laugh at him, understand him better than he understood himself. But this time she seemed to require him to know things all on his own. He felt unequal to the challenge. He needed her to tell him how he was to go on. He always needed Ianthe to explain things.

'So, my dear Ianthe, your fortunes have been restored,' Mr Fenton suddenly interrupted.

'What is this? Miss Eames is once again wealthy?' asked Lady Fox.

'Oh yes, Mama, I forgot to tell you that too. The comte stole Miss Eames' fortune, but now it is all come back to her. He was part of a Bonapartist scheme, you know, and he is now on his way back to France to be punished.'

'*What* comte? Who—? Did you say *Bonapartists?*' Lady Fox looked like she would faint, and Sally helpfully handed her the vinaigrette from a side table between them.

'You,' continued Fenton, 'with your beauty and your wealth, will take the town by storm next Season, my dear Ianthe.'

Fox blanched. He had not thought of this.

'Oh,' said Curtis laughing. 'I think old Jeffries might have something to say about that. He'll snatch you up before you reach town, Miss Eames, never fear.'

'The tone of this conversation, Curtis, is vulgar in the extreme.'

'Sorry, Mama.'

Fenton appeared not to have heard Her Ladyship's request to turn the subject, for he added, 'Markham, too. Both gentlemen have been in close attendance to the young ladies.'

'Oh, I think that Mr Markham showed more interest in Miss Richards,' said Lady Aurora, an eye on Audley. The marquis put down his cup on a table forcibly.

He got up suddenly and crossed to Sally's mama. 'Lady Richards,' he said, as though a new decision had been made, 'might I ask for your permission—'

Lady Richards grasped her lover's hand until his lost all feeling, but with her eyes riveted on the perfect form of the Marquis of Audley, she interrupted him in her nervousness. 'Yes?' she asked, almost holding her breath.

Ianthe, in a carrying voice, interrupted, too. Moving to the sofa where Sally was sitting, she said, 'I shall not go to town now that my fortune has returned, I do not wish a Season. Sally and I have decided. We shall stay here until the wedding — then we shall both remove to Bath and set up home together.'

'Bath?' said Audley and Fox in unison.

'Sally!' said Sally's mama.

'Yes, Mama. You and Mr Steadman must stay with us regularly of course, but Ianthe and I shall live a life of retirement in Bath.'

'Retirement?' said Curtis. 'You two? I don't think so, ladies. I don't know why I didn't notice it overmuch, but you are really too pretty to live alone in *Bath,*' said Curtis with feeling, having developed a dislike of the place where he had had to accompany his ailing mama. 'Rum customers in Bath.'

'Cherie, my *maman*, will chaperone us, and we will live quietly.'

'But why, Sally?' shrieked Lady Richards. 'When we might visit London all together? You love the balls and the play and everything. I know they have the same in Bath, but...'

'We do not intend to attend balls,' said Ianthe.

'No,' said Sally, holding her friend's hand even more firmly. 'We have developed a disgust of such things.'

'You mean,' said Lady Aurora, enjoying herself, 'a disgust of the male sex in particular.'

'That,' said Ianthe, 'is quite correct.'

'Sally!' wailed her mother.

'Which *particular* characteristic of gentlemen do you object to most?' asked Lady Aurora, in the spirit of helping the thing along.

'Gentlemen who are determined to flirt and flirt all their lives and never love at all,' said Sally.

'Quite right!' said Fenton. 'Those gentlemen are to be despised.'

'What else?' enquired Lady Aurora, eyebrows raised, regarding Ianthe.

'Gentlemen who do not know their own feelings but expect a woman to tell them everything.'

'The worst kind,' agreed Lady Aurora, looking askance at Fox.

The baron stood, concentrating on Ianthe's face. There was show in all this, he knew well, but still it terrified him. Jeffries. First, he had been disturbed by the notion of Ianthe's foreseen success in town. Then there had been the thought of Jeffries, whom he suddenly felt a huge repulsion for. Now there was the fear of her going away. Of not needing him for anything anymore, not even her shelter. And there was no way that two women so pretty would not have a string of ... As his stomach churned, the scales fell from his eyes.

'I love her,' he said wonderingly, for himself alone. It had the effect of halting all the others nearby him.

Lady Richards, too distracted to hear him,

too panicked by the plans for her daughter's future, focussed on the figure still before her. The marquis had turned his shoulder to look at the sofa, but was still in position.

'Marquis!' said Lady Richards desperately. 'What was it you wanted my permission for?'

Audley, as though shaken from shock, turned back abruptly. 'To pay court to your daughter,' he replied, swift and desperate.

'You have it,' said Emma Richards, determined.

'Whatever—' moaned the baroness, 'Curtis, I am not hearing aright, what is *happening* this evening?'

'I do not know, Mama … but let's hear more.'

'Whoever said that the country is dull?' asked Fenton.

'Miss Richards,' said the Marquis of Audley in clear and carrying accents, 'Will you be my wife?'

He reached his hands for her, and she took them, rising. 'Really? *Really* Audley?' She heard herself sound overawed, and was trifle annoyed with herself, but too hapy to care. She fought for her teasing tone, however. 'What about your *pleasures,* my noble marquis?' she said, but smiling in a way that made his heart ache with happiness.

'You shall be, from this day forth, my one amusement.'

She smiled deliriously, and he took a step closer to her.

'*Audley!*' said the outraged voice of Lady Fox.

He halted, turning to Her Ladyship, but drawing his beloved's hand through his arm.

'Yes,' said Curtis, before the marquis could say anything. 'Stop it, do, Audley. Edward just made an interesting remark.'

The newly betrothed, holding his hand tightly over Sally's, turned in Fox's direction and discovered that the baron was looking at Ianthe Eames in a fascinated and amazed way.

'Yes,' said Mr Fenton. 'What *was* that you said, Fox?'

'I love you,' Fox said, but not in reply to Fenton. He was looking across the three-foot divide, to the beautiful young girl sitting still on the sofa, gazing back at him with fierce intensity. 'Why did you not tell me so, Ianthe? You know me so well.'

'An ass,' said Mr Fenton to his wife. 'I told you he was an ass.' She took his arm and gave it an admonitory tug.

'I could tell you everything but that, Edward. You could not expect that I should tell you *that*.'

'Can you ... do you love *me*, Ianthe?'

'I have already *told* you,' she said, with some of her former temper.

He was struggling to keep up. 'About

d'Emillion-Orsay? You were no longer confused about him — not when you came *here* precisely, but ... but—'

'When I met you,' Ianthe finished for him.

'But *why*?'

Steadman looked at Emma Richards and shrugged. 'An ass,' he whispered. 'Fenton got it right.'

'Just because,' Ianthe was answering. 'Because it was *you.*'

Fox knelt before her, putting his arms around her waist, *'Ianthe!'* he breathed.

'Fox!' fairly screamed the soon-to-be Dowager Baroness.

Curtis helped her up. 'Let us go up to your room, Mama,' he said cheerfully. 'That is quite enough upset for tonight. We can tell them our news tomorrow at breakfast.'

Lady Fox, her tottering genuine this time, leant on her son's arm as he walked her to the door, held open by a stone-faced footman. Curtis turned on the threshold. 'Wish you very happy, all of you!'

There was a silence for a second, before Lady Aurora announced, 'I think, don't you, Lady Richards, that some exercise could do the younger people some good. Audley, take Miss Richards for a walk around the house. Borrow my shawl, Miss Richards,' she said, removing a gorgeous Paisley-patterned shawl that she had worn against the chill.

Audley took it from her and placed it tenderly around the shoulders of his love, and they left the room at a run.

'And Fox?'

'I have had a fire lit in the study, your lordship,' said Jenkins in a removed tone.

'Yes, that's it!' said Fox and pulled Ianthe laughing from the room.

'Oh, how did that all happen, Oscar?' said Emma Richards. 'Is Sally really to be the marquis' wife?'

'I think that she replied to his sudden proposal more clearly than you did to mine, my love.'

'Oh, she looked happy, did she not? She is not making a mistake?'

'If there was ever a smitten individual, it is Audley. He was trying not to marry her because he was not good enough for her.'

'I do not understand. But it seems he loves her.'

'We shall leave Sally to tell you all about it when she visits your room later,' said Lady Aurora, knowingly.

'Oh, should I have left her alone with him?'

'They are affianced now. I think it quite permissible, do not you?'

'You should go, my love,' said Emma Richards to her betrothed. 'It is late to travel, even so far as Audley.'

'I will stay the night,' said Steadman decidedly. 'I will want to interview Audley at breakfast time in my new role as Papa.'

'Oh yes, dear, so you should. Although I think it impossible to stop them now, do not you?' said Emma Richards.

'I must say, both you and Audley are making free with bed and board at the baron's expense,' Fenton remarked.

'And *you*, sir,' countered Steadman. 'Did you receive a formal invitation to stay?'

'I shall take my wife to her chamber now,' said Fenton, ignoring him. 'While you await the lovers. You should order more tea. I foresee a long wait.'

'Ianthe and Fox—' said Lady Richards, once more worried about the proprieties.

'Don't worry about Ianthe. I *never* worry about Ianthe. She always comes about.' Leading out his wife, he left the room.

'Jenkins,' he ordered that individual when in the hall, 'have another two rooms made up this evening. Lord Fox is too occupied to mention it, but I believe that Mr Steadman and the Marquis of Audley will stay the night.'

'Yes sir, I had already foreseen the possibility, sir, and have arranged the matter.'

'Of course you have,' approved Mr Fenton, nodding his head in passing.

***

It was a little chilly on the terrace and Sally drew the shawl tight around her as they walked, her head resting on Audley's upper arm where he had drawn it to him, her hand threaded through his arm.

'Is my gown really unbecoming?'

'In this light, it is tolerable,' replied Audley, in a rollicking mood.

'It was very expensive. In fact, Lord Fox bought it for me.'

'What?'

'He sent Mama funds for my come out.'

'Damn his hide. I will buy you a dozen prettier ones.'

'Will you? But I like this one.'

He pulled her closer. 'And I like it too. I like everything about you since you have agreed to be my wife.'

'Did I? I wonder why I did that?' said Sally, in a rollicking mood herself.

'So that you may ride Sapphire on a daily basis, I expect.'

'I expect that was it,' agreed Sally seriously. Then her voice became low and husky. 'Audley, *why* did you change your mind?'

'Your little performance with Ianthe must have worked,' he said with one raised eyebrow.

'It was not a performance, but a resolution,' Sally sniffed.

'Which you changed with alarming promptness when somebody made you an offer,' remarked the marquis, to see her light up again. He had his arms firmly around her waist, however, and was laughing down at her.

'Not someone — *you!*' said Sally fiercely. 'Ianthe and I resolved never to marry since the two idiots whom we loved would never propose.'

Audley stopped and pulled her closer. 'Love. I needed to hear that word from your lips.' He kissed her and she closed her eyes and melted further into his arms. Her lips were soft and warm, she was a little shy, but as his mouth moved on hers, she raised her hands to his shoulders as if to stop herself from swooning.

'Oh, so that is how you kiss women,' she said as she pulled away. 'How many of them?'

'I told you before. Too many.'

'Five?' she asked. 'Ten?' She looked aghast. 'Not *more*?'

'Remember that I have ten years start on you,' he said, playing with a curl and looking deep into her eyes.

Sally said, 'Oh well, if you have had ten years start, I had better catch up quickly. Where can I find ten men to kiss? Mr Markham might oblige. But that is only one.'

He shook her by the waist. 'That's enough. I found lately that jealousy, an emotion I thought for schoolboys, was near to eating me alive.'

'You were jealous? Of me?' Sally jumped up and down in delight. 'Oh, how wonderful! I wanted to poke Lady Sophia's eye out with my fork, only for smiling at you.' He blinked and grinned at this new side to his love. 'And I was even a little jealous of Ianthe on our rides, though I was very ashamed of myself.'

'My jealousy was *not* wonderful. It was beneath me. But though I had decided *I* could not offer for you, I had to leave for London in case I killed my old friend Markham stone dead when he smiled at you.'

'You made me suffer so much. I thought you just a friend, but when you were gone I felt as though a limb had been torn from me,' he touched a soothing hand to her hair, but it was evident he was delighted. 'And even when Mr Markham smiled at me, I just wanted you to be horrid instead.'

'You may now be horrid to me every day for a lifetime,' he said encouragingly.

'I will!' she assured him. Then her tone changed to being a little uncertain. 'Do you think you will miss them, those dreadful pleasures?' she asked, touching his cheek.

'No.' He was smiling and smiling at her.

Her eyebrows shot up. 'Then you will no longer wager?'

'Well,' he tempered, 'at my club of course, like any man.'

'Or drink?'

'Well every man must savour wine in his life,' he said reasonably.

'Not to excess then?' She inquired.

'There *may* be occasions when it is needful to keep my good friends company. Sometimes one *may* be excessive—'

'Audley!' Sally reprimanded. 'You are not intending to deny a single *one* of your pleasures so far.' She held on to his lapels and looked up at him piteously. 'And the *female* amusements?'

The marquis was not deceived by her look but reassured her anyway. He gazed down into her lovely pale eyes. 'I shall need no other female amusement than you, my lovely, lovely—' he broke off to kiss her, and inside, Sally laughed and laughed.

***

Fox dragged Ianthe into his study and locked the door, which she regarded with an approving eye. He moved towards her hesitating just a second, took her shoulders and bent to brush his lips gently on hers. As she stepped forward and lifted her fingers to his face, all hesitation flew and he took her to a winged chair near to the fire and sat, pulling her on to his knee.

He kissed her thoroughly, violently holding her curls, then pulled back, taking a breath and looked at her. '*Why* did you not tell me I adored you?' he asked her again.

'I was not always confident that you did,' she said surprisingly shyly, pulling at his cravat in a distracted manner.

'*You?* Not confident?'

'Is anyone confident in love?' she fingered the damage she had done to his cravat, still not looking at him. 'I could not really be sure. Especially as you did not know yourself. I only knew it had happened to me.'

He hugged her to him, and his chin rested on the top of her curls, and her arms snaked around his neck.

'When?' he asked her.

'I think from the first, but I did not really know what it was. You are very handsome of course—'

'*Am* I?' he asked, amazed.

'I am so glad you did not realise that. Well done for not becoming Audley. Do not the young ladies in town pursue you?'

'No.'

'I expect they do,' she said wisely, 'but you have not noticed. Has a young lady ever fallen at your feet?'

'Miss Young tripped once, and Lady ... never mind,' he said, seeing the martial light in Ianthe's eye. 'Well, she slid on a stair at the opera.'

'They were both trying to entrap you, in all probability, but you were too foolish to notice. I am so glad you are Mr Fenton's ass.' She played with his hair. 'Was there really no one that you felt that *coup de foudre* for? No one at all?'

'There was.' Ianthe sat up straight and pulled back. 'A maid who put cream in my porridge when I was in school. She smiled at me a lot and I loved her madly. I was eight.'

'I hate her,' said Ianthe, but laid back on

him again. 'At first, or perhaps second, glance, I *trusted* you, Edward. It was new to me to trust a man of your age. Audley did not count, and I never quite trusted Antoine. But I trusted you immediately even when you were offering to make those dreadful *provisions* for me.'

'I was awful to you and spent most of my time being angry — why on earth would you bestow your trust on someone like me?' he wondered, searching her face.

'You were saying ridiculous things, of course, because you have no facility to express how you feel, but your eyes were kind.' She looked into his fox eyes now, those warm and deep eyes, a little dreamily. 'And though I often have seen you angry, and so mired in your own misery that you could not consider those around you properly, still you never were first to do the hurtful thing.' She raised her brows. '*I* am much worse than you, there.

'I agree. I cannot count the designing things you have come up with to torture Lady Fox. I could not have thought of the half of them.'

'That is because you are much kinder than I,' she said, taking his face in both of her hands.

'No. We are all changed by your kindness, Ianthe, though it might have come in a strange form.' He kissed her again. 'Ah, I cannot believe you will agree to marry me and live all your life with the Fighting Foxes.' He sighed. 'I will try to make it up to you.'

'Do not fear.' She looked so like her old naughty self that he raised an eyebrow. 'Curtis will move to Broadbank and take his mama with him. Sally thinks he has fallen in love on his last visit there and means to marry a young lady from a neighbouring estate. We shall be just us three. You and I and *maman*, of course. My Cherie.'

'I could always tell that she was special to you. The servants will talk, I suppose, but we will keep the secret within the walls.'

'Oh, don't worry about that.' Ianthe grinned. 'Wait until you see her tomorrow. She has had little to do with anyone but Jenkins, at my request. She has slept and eaten in my room for the most part, and when the other servants see her tomorrow, they will not recognise her.'

'You think so?'

'Audley will take her out in the carriage and bring her back later. I shall instruct him to do so. She will come as my *maman*, newly arrived from France.' Ianthe twinkled. 'Freeing my maid to return to her family in France.'

'Still,' said Fox, as though loath to mention it, 'there is a rather identifying mark.'

'Ah!' laughed Ianthe wickedly. 'The eyebrows are not real, you know, but drawn on. *Wait* until you see how lovely she is! I insisted on the disguise you know, because whatever she thought, I knew I would claim her to stand beside me, even when I did not know she was my real *maman*. You will love her, Edward. It is impossible not to, Papa always said. She is as kind as you. And she has a temper too, but only when someone tries to harm me.'

'I shall do my level best not to incur her displeasure.'

'You had better not. She carries a pistol, you know.'

'*What?*'

She laughed. 'Oh, Edward!' She moved her mouth to him again, and he claimed it.

'Ianthe, I know I have come to this realisation of love so late, but from the first day I was shaken by you. Not just because you are lovely—'

'You think so? You have never seemed swept away by beauty. I have not seen your eyes linger on me as some others have.'

'But they did. I must have been rather better than them at not getting caught. But I did not *want* to admire you, to fall for a pretty face. Only, you kept upending my life. You invited me in to play — first with you and then with the Richards. And suddenly I had a real family, as I remembered from childhood. One where people laughed and teased each other, where they trusted and backed each other up in adversity. I began to love you all then. I felt alive again.'

'And you shall not lose that family, with Cousin Emma at Stone Manor and Sally at Audley.' He smiled, and Fox's genuine smile was enough to make Ianthe's knees turn to water. 'It is not surprising that you locked that big heart away, for it had been badly treated. But your mother's love must have made you the man I trusted from the beginning.'

'When did you know that the trust was more than that? That it was love?'

'Trust is always love, I think. The very best kind of love.' He gazed at her, his strong fingers tracing her face, his breath coming deep. 'But when you were near me, my heart fluttered a little. No, a lot.'

'Mmm. I frequently lost my ability to breathe, but I thought it was just the usual male reaction to the nearness to a beauty such as you. I had never before experienced that, you know.' He kissed her neck. 'You have always *touched* me. I was so affected by that, since it is practically unknown in my adult life. I believe you have touched me more since I have known you than in my life previously.'

'I suppose I *did* touch you somewhat.' She laughed at him. 'But *you* did so more.' He looked stunned. 'It seemed natural to me to have you do so, but it shook me, too.'

Edward Fox's face became dreamy. 'It *was* me,' he said, thinking back. 'I grasped your hands, your shoulders. I never have done so before, but somehow...'

'Yes. *Somehow...*' she said, dotingly, watching him understand.

'But you, too, touched me. Your hand on

my arm, or on my cheek. I thought it perhaps a French custom. But I began to long for it.'

'A *Frenchman,* given such encouragement, would have taken full advantage. And *still* you did not know you loved me?' she teased.

'There is no denying it,' Fox laughed at himself. 'Fenton is right. I am a complete ass.'

'Yes, my dear, dear idiot. You were.'

He kissed her again long, deeply and lovingly. 'I seem to be becoming proficient at this,' he remarked. 'Today, I'm afraid to tell you, was my first kiss.'

Ianthe curled her legs up and squirmed around to face him, still on his knees.

'Ouch,' he complained.

'Never mind that. Your first kiss? But you are so *oooollllld*.'

'Yes,' he said, kissing her again. 'I have a lot of time to make up for.'

'You did not manage to kiss the maid?'

'I was not tall enough to reach her, alas.'

'And in London? Not even with ladies, with ladies from *those* places?'

'No. *Those* places, which young ladies should not know of,' he reproved her, tapping her nose, 'never interested me.'

'You are as different from Antoine as it is possible to be,' she sighed. 'I am so glad.'

He narrowed his eyes. 'I must suppose you to have been kissed many times, racketing around Europe as you did.'

'I did racket around Europe. But I did it with Mr Joseph Eames and Cherie. Let us just say that certain behaviours would not be tolerated.'

'Not even…' he paused.

'Not even Antoine. He did kiss me on the hand a number of times. Passionately too. It was thrilling.'

Fox growled like the animal he was. He took her hands in his and showered every inch of them with kisses. 'He shall not do so again,' he said.

'No, my love, my dearest, dearest love.' She was laughing at him.

'You are a vixen!' he cried and kissed her again. He laid back, hugging her closer. 'How did I come to be this happy, Ianthe? It has been creeping up on me in steps since you arrived, and I cannot find the words to tell you.'

'Finally, I am a vixen! The proper Fox's mate. Let us sit like this for a while, Edward.' He moved his head. 'No, do not kiss me, for if we do so, we may never stop. As beginners, we are too proficient, I find.' He laughed and pulled her to him again, but she did not permit it. 'Lady Richards will be waiting. And Sally.' She laid her head on his chest. 'Let us just stay like this for a while before I go to them.'

'Tomorrow and tomorrow and tomorrow,' he quoted, 'you will still be mine.' He hugged her close, and they stayed that way for some time.

Chapter Thirty-Three

Epilogue

When Mrs Eames arrived, the mother of the future Lady Fox, Jenkins the butler blinked for half a second, met her eye, then bowed, very low.

Mrs Eames was found to have a copious amount of natural black curls, only a few silver strands to reflect her age, and her beautiful black, luminous eyes, rimmed with long dark lashes and framed by delicately shaped brows, rivalled those of her step daughter. She was dressed in a claret coloured moiré pelisse that Ianthe remembered from London as Lady Aurora's. That lady had obviously decided that Cherie's true clothes, hidden so long among Ianthe's, while lovely, needed an extra punch from herself. A large velvet muff covered her hands, a reticule hung from her wrist, an extraordinary bonnet, soon discarded, had been atop her head and framed the dark curls beneath. Her hands and feet were clad in the finest kid. The maids, with not a hint of recognition from one of them, curtsied low, and Cherie swept in to meet the others. She was greeted by Ianthe, who naturally enough, ran into her mother's arms.

Wilbert Fenton smiled as the others were stunned by the transformation. Mrs Eames bowed to the baroness with just the right degree of discernment while that lady was goggle-eyed.

'My word,' said Curtis. 'What a beauty!'

It was said so innocently that the company laughed. Edward led her to a chair and seated her with great attention. Mrs Eames sat with the grace of a true lady.

Fenton bowed at her ironically.

'My dear friend Wil-*bert*,' Cherie said pleasantly. 'It is an age since we met.'

It had been but a few hours ago that he had seen her in his wife's chamber. Fenton smiled at her, a twinkle in his eye, then looked at first at Curtis' smiling face, then Lady Fox's expression, reluctantly accepting, and even relieved that this woman would not disgrace them. And Fox beamed. It was disconcerting, admitted Fenton to himself, that Fox beamed. That stone cold, or alternately angry face seemed gone for ever. He exchanged a humorous glance with Audley, who was standing nearby with his betrothed.

'It could only be done by Ianthe. So many happy endings, it seems, are due to her persuading Fox to your dinner that night.'

'Ianthe's process is a difficult one for all involved,' said Audley dryly, as the elder ladies exchanged polite chatter, 'but she produces the right results in the end.'

'Yes,' agreed Fenton, humorously. 'But I confess one thing has surprised me. Who could have predicted the end of hostilities and the Treaty of the Fighting Foxes?'

Some chapters of another series to tempt you:

Georgette and the Unrequited Love

Alicia Cameron

Prologue

If you were to see all the Fortune sisters together in a line, you would be living in a fairy tale, for the girls, first because their mama was a trifle frail, and later because she was no longer with them, were too unruly ever to have been held in line for more than a second without some of them escaping to another room in the cavernous Castle Fortune, or into the rivers and wilderness beyond.

For the benefit of this presentation, we will imagine them all kept in place to shake your hand. We shall capture them all in this day of 1812, and make it a sunny day. First will be Miss Fortune as was, the lovely and gentle Violetta, twenty-three, who must now disappear into the mist of Scotland to be with her husband. Loud and vibrant Cassie, twenty-two, is next, but her equally loud swain, Mr Hudson, has swept them off to Somerset, where the whole neighbourhood may hear their business from a mile away. Next there is Georgette, twenty-one, who is the principal subject of this tale. She has particularly large eyes, and has now become Miss Fortune in her turn, being the eldest unwed sister. Mary, twenty, her romantic and wilful sister, ran off with a Mr Fredericks, a music master, and they made their poor home in Bath. If Mr Fredericks hoped that marriage to the daughter of a Castle might increase his wealth, he was disabused of this notion after he met his father-in-law, Baron Fortune. Susan, eighteen, the plainest of the girls (which is to say not plain at all), married sober Mr Steeplethorpe, and seemed quietly content at her bargain.

So, our reception line now has only the unmarried Fortune ladies. Georgette now lives with the shame (her neighbours said) of having two younger siblings marry before her. Next is the sprite Jocasta, at seventeen not too like a fairy of the tales in behaviour, but who nevertheless entranced London this season with her wispy gaiety. The final four girls are not out yet and have seen little beyond the castle grounds and their few friends in the district. Red-haired Katerina, at sixteen, still thinks boys are boorish and stupid, an opinion no doubt suggested by her closest male acquaintance, her brother George (at twenty-five the only male sibling and proud heir to his father's dignities and debt). Portia, at 15, was rather more romantic, with hair a shade between the blond of Jocasta's and the brunette of Georgette's. She is taller than her sisters. The little twins, at 14, were probably the prettiest of the bunch (which is to say very pretty indeed), with still-white blond curls and big blue eyes. They would arrest the eye together in a ballroom in another three or four years.

Georgette, the median age of all her married sisters, was now on the shelf, doomed to haunt the shades of Fortune Castle till her death, unless her brother George were to eject her on the day of his inheritance. If George remembered the days of her childhood when Georgette had still seen the point of poking a bully in the eyes, perhaps he would do so, and swiftly, too. But most probably, he would let her stay to keep up the numbers of people he could ignore, insult and command.

Chapter 1

She was invisible, Georgette discovered. Quite invisible. She had suspected as much in the glazed-over glances the other guests to this house party had cast over her during the introductions, but this longed-for but entirely unexpected meeting with the Marquis of Onslow had completely underscored the matter. He had even reached past her to shake her father's hand and had touched her arm in passing, raising her heartbeat until it seemed the organ would leave her chest, without any seeming awareness of having done so.

One could blame Papa perhaps, but with ten daughters and one son (heaven be praised) to provide for, and no wife living to aid Lord Fortune with understanding the subtleties of female feelings, she did not really think that she could. She had quite understood that she, the third daughter of the impoverished baron, had to surrender her place in the London season to allow her younger sisters their turn at society. Their eldest sister, twenty-three-year-old Violetta (named for their dead mother) was already wed to her Scottish gentleman before Georgette had come out. Georgette had enjoyed two seasons already, one with elder sister Cassie, who had married the eligible, if very loud, Mr Hudson. This slight defect that Georgette had discerned in his otherwise excellent, convivial character was shared by Cassie herself, who talked as though addressing a congregation even at breakfast, and who had been used to clattering downstairs in satin slippers as though the blacksmith had shod her. After Cassie's baby was born last year, Georgette had visited her home in distant Somerset and had informed her father afterwards that the child's lungs seemed to have double the capacity of each parent, making him audible ten miles hence. Her father had remarked that he would write to his daughter, kindly understanding that such a journey as the three days it would take to reach Castle Fortune should on no account be undertaken with an infant, and that they could henceforth meet during the London season for his beloved daughter's convenience. How thoughtful.

Georgette's second season had been with her younger sister Mary, who married (much to her father's wrath) a mere Mr Fredericks, who had been employed to teach them the pianoforte. Both sisters could play, but not exceptionally, and their father had conceived the notion that it was young ladies of musical talent who snared the richest, that is the most eligible, of gentlemen — an opinion he came to rue. Mrs Fredericks now lived in genteel poverty with her swain in Bath and seemed happy enough, thought Georgette, but where they might dispose of future children in two rooms was beyond her. Perhaps they might be suspended in tiny hammocks on the ceiling, she'd considered as she'd regarded the linen slung on the washing pulley in their tiny kitchen, but what to do with them on laundry day exceeded her imagination.

Susan, 18, had wed a quiet country gentleman much in her own style. This had occurred in the previous season, when Georgette remained at home to make way for Jocasta Fortune, her pretty blond seventeen-year-old sister, who had already shown herself popular in town, so she had heard.

With three of her sisters wed already after Georgette's second season, her father's looks toward her had suggested that she had rather let him down. The cost of each season was a prodigious run on the estate every year, and some decent settlements from an eligible parti might have eased a situation which, with six daughters still to provide for, seemed never-ending. After her last season, two years ago now, when they had returned to the crumbling Castle Fortune, he had looked at her from beneath his bushy eyebrows. 'You are not bad looking,' he barked, as though contemplating inwardly, 'even if your bosom suggests you might run to fat at a later date.' Georgette had swallowed with difficulty. 'But young men don't think of that. You don't have much conversation of course, but your birth is good and you have a small portion from your mama, which makes you at least respectable. All those gowns and bonnets,' he lamented, 'and no one could be persuaded to take you!' He shook his head and tutted.

When Susan got married the next year, he could not look at Georgette for a week without audibly betraying his great disappointment. 'Still here, miss? Eating my meat when even your younger sisters—' he shook his giant head with the shaggy mane of hair and muttered into his soup, 'Females! What use are females at all — especially unwed females? A leech for life, I suppose.'

There had been two people prepared to take her, who had indeed offered for her, had her papa but known, and others whose interest Georgette had, with difficulty, discouraged. The first offer was from a deliciously conceited, round-bodied clergyman, bound for a bishopric, he told her confidentially during only the first dance. It was in the family, it transpired, that all the second sons became bishops (though his granduncle had disappointed his family by rising no further than Dean). Georgette had accepted his offers to dance as was polite, but Cassie had been unable to understand why she allowed the fusty cleric to walk her to the supper room, or take her apart to sit and talk a dance away. The sad truth was that Georgette, though listening with a grave air to the Reverend Mr Fullerton's conversation, had been inwardly bursting with delight. He was so utterly ridiculous that she found herself fuelling his climb to the precipice of bumptious absurdity. The dreadful propensity of hers to judge the ridiculous was understood by none in her family since the death of her mother. They looked upon Georgette's placid exterior as her substance, never guessing the bubbling cauldron of devilry beneath. 'I hold,' said the reverend gentleman, 'that the exercise of dancing may become injurious to the health and, to the morals of the nation.' Georgette was sipping a negus cup in the throng around the supper table, and she answered, as his bulging eyes looked at her expectantly, 'Indeed sir, you think dancing dangerous to the body?'

'I see you are surprised, my dear Miss Fortune! I do not wonder at it. It is so common to think of dancing these days as beneficial. Indeed, parents employ dancing popinjays to teach their daughters. Then those same young ladies are encouraged to dance every dance and quite wear their feet away.'

'It is the feet, then, which you seek to protect?' said Georgette, still sipping the negus.

'Worse than the feet, I fear, are the temperate humours that keep the passions in check. These are vital to our health, yet let a man (or worse, a lady, I suggest) caper about a room for even an half-hour, and these have been so agitated that the very rules of civilisation may be ignored because such excitations have been allowed. Why, the English temperament becomes ever closer to the Latin.' Georgette's eyes widened in faux shock over her cup. 'We know how they conduct themselves. It is, in my idea, the product of the heat and being ill-bred.'

'I expect you warn your parishioners of the dangers,' remarked Georgette, enjoying herself shamefully, still sipping at her cup.

'I do. It may be that the upper classes might just possess the discipline of spirit to control themselves in a ballroom, but all country dances for the working man are to be discouraged. A young gentleman, but ten years ago, was taken ill after much dancing and when the surgeons opened him up there was seen to be putrefaction of the organs. Ah! I have shocked you, I fear. I might have spared your delicate ears such sad truths. But a warning I must give to those I regard.' Georgette gave a jolt to be included in this company, but stilled as he continued. 'I myself have felt the ill effects. It is not natural for a man to jump and shake his innards so! It was not thus decreed by the Almighty. You have observed that persons beyond the age of thirty restrict such posturing. With age comes wisdom, perhaps.'

Or exhaustion, thought Georgette. 'But I have met you at three balls already this season, Reverend Fullerton, and I do not believe you would seek to injure yourself.'

'You are very wise, my dear Miss Fortune, very wise. I dance, it is true. But here is the secret, my dear.' He bent forward, as though imparting one, but his voice was still booming. 'I do not dance to excess, never to excess.'

'It is true, Mr Fullerton,' said Georgette as though much struck. 'You danced perhaps three dances all evening, I have observed. When you did me the honour to dance with me this evening you did so with the most economy of movement. I remarked upon it. It was almost as though you were not dancing at all …'

Then came the moment that changed her life. For over the shoulder of the vicar, and over the shoulder of a gentleman with his back to him, Georgette met the humorous eye of a tall, blond gentleman who seemed to have been listening for some time, perhaps. In that look, which caused the lines around sky-blue eyes to deepen, she saw his shared joy of the absurdity, and his knowledge of her own role in encouraging the display. The six feet between them seemed to retract as the look held, and she felt as though his whole being was closer to her than any gentleman had ever been, excepting her father and brother. But it was a simple illusion, neither of them had moved. She dimpled and blushed — then his attention was taken once more by his male companion. It was the work of but two seconds.

The Reverend Mr Fullerton continued to praise her for her observation and she hardly heard him. She had turned her face towards him once more and saw the fleshly lips move and bulging eyes search her face, but was only vaguely aware.

Someone had seen her, really seen her — and she was shaken to the core.

She was so aware of the tall gentleman that her peripheral vision grew larger. He moved away with his friend in the direction of the ballroom and she was able to notice a thatch of blond hair whose curls disobeyed pomade, whose tall frame was elegantly covered in a black coat and buff knee breeches, and whose large form carried away with it her heart.

This was the Lord Onslow that now, two years later, had not even recognised her.

Chapter 2

Two seasons had come and gone since Georgette Fortune had espied Lord Onslow that day. She had re-entered the ballroom, escorted by an enraged Reverend Fullerton, who had been aghast at her refusal of his offer, once her attention had been called back to him.

'Is your father present, my dearest Miss Fortune? I shall spare no time in making an appointment to call upon him,' she'd become aware of him saying.

'Concerning what, sir?' she replied with a slight frown.

He'd looked affronted, 'Why, concerning our betrothal.'

'You wish to be betrothed to me?' Georgette was too shocked to find this even vaguely amusing.

'Of course. Have not my actions said more than mere words? I have danced with you on three occasions! For a man in my position, this behaviour would be quite shocking if my intentions were not honourable.'

'Three dances over four balls, Mr Fullerton. I cannot say I marked the frequency.' '

At Lady Rider's ball I held myself back. I was not yet sure of your affection, or my own feelings. And I knew the world would mark my behaviour. Tonight, when you smiled at me upon my entrance to the ballroom, I knew our destiny.'

Georgette's brow furrowed, recalling the moment. 'I believe I was smiling at my sister, who was standing behind you. I am very sorry if I gave you the wrong impression, sir.'

He blew up to his full balloon shape. 'Am I to understand that you are refusing me, Miss Fortune?'

'I am very sorry sir, but we would not suit.'

'But you danced with me three times.'

Her hilarity returned at this absurdity and threatened to seep on to her face, but she repressed it nobly. 'If this be a sign of engagement sir, I fear there are at least eight gentlemen here tonight to whom I am already promised.'

'I see that I have misunderstood your character, madam. I shall leave you.' She was a little sorry for his wounded pride, but he had so much of it, he was bound to trip over it frequently. How she wished her mama was still alive to recount this ridiculousness to. But she was not. So Georgette curtsied. And turned to the dancers.

Georgette's eyes had raked the ballroom,

and had easily seen the tall gentleman, half a head taller than any other around him, dancing with the entrancing Julia White. Georgette, having been presented at court with Miss White in equally ridiculous hooped dresses upon the same occasion, was acquainted with that young lady, whose vivaciousness reminded her a little of her sister Mary, but whose captivating wiles excited Georgette's inner love of absurdity. She had watched the season through as Miss White had smiled and turned her shoulder at will, glancing back with a shy yet warm look to some gentleman who might be losing heart as a suitor, causing him to remain hopeful and attentive, if confused. Mary (who had not yet decided on the dancing teacher) had opined that Julia, though a pleasant girl, had best leave some gentlemen for the other young ladies of the ton, but Georgette had been too entertained to agree. The ease with which the belle called and dismissed her court had given Georgette a low opinion of male intelligence, or subtlety of feeling. Not to see that Miss White was toying with them all, rather as the Pied Piper had caused children (and rats) to dance to his tune, was to be deeply and absurdly stupid. It seemed that gentlemen's self-esteem would not permit them to see the coquette in her. Each one believed that in their case it was genuine affection. Georgette had watched and been silently amused.

As she looked that evening at the ball, Julia's

eyes met her tall gentleman's, and all Georgette's amusement had departed. His hand was at Miss White's waist, he looked down at his partner with an intense expression. Julia White looked up at him, and Georgette believed her more vulnerable and true than she had ever seen her. But perhaps, she had afterwards reflected, it was her own vulnerability that made her think so. Their blond heads and charming forms had looked delightful together as they traversed the floor, though Georgette had felt no delight. Restored to her chaperon, she stood watching helplessly as Julia White and Lord Onslow (for so she had heard the people remarking the handsome partners call him) fall in love.

She had never cared to find out if that was their first dance. All she knew was that some half-laid plans of her own to see that look on his face again, the one which made Georgette know that he alone understood her, had shattered. She felt alone again — for she had always moved, in the vast rout of her family, completely unknown.

In the weeks that followed, as she saw the Marquis of Onslow everywhere it seemed, she noted that he gifted the look that she craved for herself a great deal. It seemed that though he could be reserved, he offered this intimate regard to friends, his aunt, his cousins, and most especially to Miss White. Georgette, who had grudged Julia all but one of her admirers, could hardly bear it. And there was worse to come.

She looked on in the next weeks as Lord Onslow, although doing nothing so unmanly as sit in Miss White's pocket, wooed her. He danced twice with her at every assembly, he frequently escorted her to the supper room, a boon that many gentlemen craved as it was the occasion at a ball where ladies and gentlemen might have time to extend their conversation. If Julia played her tricks, Georgette noticed, Onslow did not respond quite as her other suitors did. If Miss White could not quite remember if she had a dance to spare, rather than press her, Lord Onslow did not reappear at her side again that night. Some other would be favoured to take her to the supper room, and no one who was not looking as closely as Georgette would know what that cost him. His eye might follow Miss White for a brief second, and she saw a dark gravity that she knew to be pain cross his face. At any time that Julia might see him, however, he never looked her way. Georgette applauded this manly dignity inwardly, but she began to see her own inexperience.

On one such evening, she, Cassie and Julia had been standing at the edge of the ballroom talking to a number of young bucks who were primarily of Miss White's court, when Georgette, impaled by a blade of hot awareness behind her shoulder, turned to see Lord Onslow approach, moving elegantly through the throng. The entire party, drawn by Georgette's eyes, turned their attention towards him, and Julia gasped. Georgette was not surprised. Even in his beautifully cut evening coat, with the high starched shirt points touching his cheeks, there was a predatory elegance to his walk to claim Miss White. Finally, he arrived. He bowed briefly. 'May I have this dance?' Georgette, who had not taken her eyes from him, now realised he was facing her. Was Julia behind her? But no, the trembling figure of Julia White was at her side, having held her breath waiting for him to arrive. 'I—?' Georgette remembered herself. Her mouth could not be trusted, but she placed her gloved hand on his outstretched arm and flowed to the floor on his arm.

She peeped up at him shyly as she did so, and was relieved to see him looking ahead, at the sets just making up. It was a country dance, thankfully, and she had time to arrange herself and to breathe away her blushes as she stood opposite him in the set. She looked up from her feet, ready to smile, but found Lord Onslow looking somewhere over her head — not so difficult, as, though she was of average height, with at least one inch beyond five foot, he could give her a foot or more. Yet it was not quite normal for a partner to be so removed in himself. It was better, she thought. This way she would not make a fool of herself. If he did not mind her — well, she could better mind her steps. The figures of the dance took her skipping towards him, he looked at her indifferently for a second, and they reversed.

Miss White and Lord Newcombe had joined the same set she discovered, as she performed her steps side by side His Lordship towards them. Lord Onslow gave Miss White even less acknowledgement than his partner.

Above their heads, Georgette's fingers met his as they turned, and his eyes dropped a little. It was the custom that partners looked at each other during this step, but his eyes were only looking at her brown hair, evidently less absorbing than the golden locks of Miss White, whom she had seen him regard in fascination, even when their owner was unaware. As when Miss White's back was turned to him by the steps, and he allowed his eyes to look at her dancing curls. When Onslow and Miss White were brought together by the dance, His Lordship deliberately ignored Julia. Ignoring his partner, however, was completely without intention. She hardly existed to him. Her body trembled when their gloved hands met, when a light hand touched her waist in guidance. He looked at her exactly three times, and Georgette remembered each one. The glance at the start, a slightly annoyed frown as she fumbled a step, and then the final faint smile as he thanked her for the dance. A swift bow, and he was gone. Julia White had left the floor quickly too, and in a haze, Georgette saw her depart for an anteroom set aside for the comfort of ladies. Georgette followed as in a dream, trembling and needing to feel no eyes upon her until she had herself better in hand.

She found Julia White sitting on an elegant gold covered sofa, whose legs were so delicately wrought that they looked like they might break even under her slight weight. An attendant was fanning her, but Georgette saw tears in her eyes, and gestured the maid away, braving the settle. 'Are you quite well, Miss White?'

'Oh, Miss Georgette Fortune.' It seemed to her that Miss White stiffened at her sight, and it took that stiffness for Georgette to be reminded that she was the object of Miss White's mortification. Or was it more than that? Could Julia really be wounded? 'I am quite well. Such a lovely ball, do you not th—'

Her voice was too polite, and Georgette interrupted. Perhaps it was not hers to help this young girl's machinations, but she saw clearly what Miss White did not. 'Lord Onslow hardly spoke to me and his eyes followed you.' Miss White's gaze turned to her. 'He is telling you, I think, that such games as you play with others will not do for him.'

'He plays with me, you believe?'

'He makes you feel the other side of your game.' Georgette did not stay to see what effect her words had upon the other, but stood up and adjusted her dress. Julia White stood too, and for a moment, Georgette saw them both reflected in the tall, gilded mirror on one wall. She was some two inches shorter than Julia, her light brown hair so much duller than Julia's glinting blond. Her eyes were larger than Julia's — but brown, not enchanting blue. Georgette's yellow muslin, which had pleased her well at the beginning of the ball, could not be compared to the willowy figure in figured white gauze over a silver petticoat. Though Julia was the taller, that form was almost fairy-like and made Georgette's plump bosom and broader shoulders seem squat. One should avoid standing next to Miss White if one wished to be seen to advantage. Why would Lord Onslow see her when his eye might be distracted by such a bright star? She was only so much background.

She felt her eyes fill, and was afraid that Miss White had noticed. But she was quite wrong, Julia was pinching her cheeks, preparing to re-enter the ballroom. Georgette left her. She tried hard to laugh at herself, and at him. Two lovers whose eyes searched in different directions. He would win his love, how could he not? But Georgette could never win him.

For three seconds, perhaps less, Georgette had seen a sliver of hope. He remembered her, she'd thought, he remembered that he understood her, and had asked her to dance to further their acquaintance. By the time they had taken their place in the set, that had been shown as foolish, ludicrous even. A stronger adjective had occurred at every step, sending little knife blades into her heart.

Chapter 3

Georgette's life since she had returned to the castle over a year since had been full of activity, but a trifle dull. Georgette was not, by temperament, a busy bee. But after the death of her mother, two years before her first season, she had looked up from a book one day and noticed that the house had become tarnished and gloomy. It could not then be ignored. Without a mistress to oversee them, servants consigned dust to the corners, it seemed. The number of the household had not diminished since Lady Fortune's day, but old chests and mantles bore layers of dust, the table and bed linens overused without being refreshed, and in naval parlance, it was not ship shape. Since then, she had served as a reluctant mistress of Fortune

Castle, her papa and sisters still living in the wonderful state of obliviousness that she had so reluctantly left herself.

Dickson, who ran the household, and still bore the ancient title of steward of the castle, was not pleasto have a young lady, whom as a child he'd been called upon to reprimand, question his oversight. But he did acknowledge the problem. He offered, with some relish, to send Mrs Firestone to her to discuss the matter. Mrs Firestone being the housekeeper.

Mrs Firestone, whose tenure had only one year under her mother's oversight before being left to her own devices, had taken this interference badly too, and Georgette, barely eighteen, had hardly known how to behave. She had been most apologetic at first, but then Mrs Firestone in a mob cap and a stuff dress bursting at the seams had made the mistake of being impertinent. 'There are a great many rooms in this place, you know.' Ridiculous creature, thought Georgette, almost tempted to encourage to let her innumerate them to one who had lived here all her life. 'Lord Fortune is not as pernickety as my lady was, always checking on my work. I believe he is happy enough, for he has never mentioned it.'

'My father is a gentleman, and gentlemen do not concern themselves in housekeeping matters, Mrs Firestone. He has assigned this task,' she added mendaciously, for she had not troubled him with the business, 'to me. You will cause the rooms to be swept every day—'

'Impossible!' said Mrs Firestone in a righteous tone, 'I have not the staff to do so!'

'You will cause those rooms in use to be swept daily — and well—' Mrs Firestone blushed in humiliation and Georgette foresaw a dreadful time for the maid staff below, 'and you will inspect them yourself. Dinners must be cleaned away the same evening, it should not be necessary to mention this to you.' Mrs Firestone's bosom heaved, but she held her tongue. 'And,' added Georgette, quite pleased with this tiny victory, 'dinners themselves are falling off rather. We had stew for the fifth time this week.'

'I'll send Mrs Scroggins to you directly.' By her tone, Georgette deduced that she was delighted for the same humiliating fate to befall the cook.

'And flowers,' added Georgette, pushing her wins forward, before Mrs Firestone could take her leave, '— there are no flowers. There used to be flowers on the dinner table each evening.'

Mrs Firestone looked triumphant. 'It was Her Ladyship herself that saw to the flowers, miss. We haven't time to be fetching no flowers.' Georgette blushed, seeing a vision of her mother with her shallow basket over her arm going out to pick some blooms. 'Of course it was. I'll see to it.'

Mrs Firestone left, some of her dignity restored.

All of this endeavour, and the endeavours of

the following year, had hardly been noticed by the family. Jocasta had sat down at dinner that evening and said, 'Where is the stew? I like stew.' And not a single person remarked on her flower arrangements, which had caused her pricked fingers and a worse temper. But she liked to see them there herself, so she continued to make them, but every three days only. The blooms may droop, but her commitment to her invisible labours had some limits.

With Violetta and Cassie gone, she was now the eldest except her brother George, whom they seldom saw. He had some rooms in London, since Fortune House, the family's London residence, had long been sold. Thus it was that she could go to town for a third or fourth season. Papa had to rent an establishment in a genteel part of town, but he could not afford one large enough, he said, to accommodate all of his spinster daughters. But in the two seasons where Jocasta (more fairy-like than even Miss White, though not quite so pretty) and Susan (the plainest of the sisters, and the most unconcerned about it) had gone to London, they had not disappointed. Susan had received an offer first, from a comfortably-off country squire Sir John Steeplethorpe, quite as plain as she. The small settlement made by the groom to Lord Fortune had been a disappointment though, which was the kind of thing the young ladies of the house should not know, but did — given Papa's propensity to think aloud, without knowing he did so. Susan had put off the wedding for some months, and Papa had set Georgette to find out if she were about to recant. Susan had answered her bluntly, 'I'm not sure. I have discovered a thing about him I dislike.' And while Georgette was wondering if she had discovered some iniquity of character, Susan had added, 'He snorts.' This was the kind of thing that set Georgette into silent whoops, though she'd trained her face not to give offence. Evidently, Susan had reconciled herself to this defect and had wed two months ago.

'Never thought I'd see her fired off at all with that nose,' had said her father to himself in the church, quite audibly. Only a titter had suggested anyone had been aware, and the service had continued with only a darkling look from the vicar at the Fortunes' pew.

She missed Susan's bluntness, and its unknowing effect on others. 'I hope,' she'd said to her husband of one hour, as they entered the packed carriage destined to take them to his estate, 'that you do not expect to act the bull to my Daisy. There will be none of that.' Sir John's shock and dismay were evident as the carriage door closed. Georgette had walked away, berating herself for finding all this funny, while comforting herself that Sir John was a sensible fellow who might be trusted to explain things to Susan in a gentle way. Any woman who could get over snorting might be depended on to bear children with equanimity.

The things he had to explain were largely a mystery to Georgette herself, but country living gave her an inkling.

It transpired that Jocasta had, at the last month of this season (her second), been shown a marked degree of attention from Lord Paxton, a poetical young man, who had taken a shine to Miss Jocasta's delicate form. Lord Paxton was, moreover, the heir to an Earldom, and by far the richest suitor any Fortune girl had attracted. Georgette could not recall having met the gentleman, but Jocasta had shown her a small volume of his verse, handsomely inscribed by the author. She had sat down to read, and had found a piece of paper marking a poem about Titania. She supposed it to have been meant to relate (in the baron's view) to Jocasta herself, but Georgette had got no further than the lines,

'When fair Titania trips through wooded dells,
'Neath her dainty foot blooms grow, where 'ere they fell. '

It was not at all to her poetic taste.

Georgette shut the volume, wondering whether Jocasta would find the poem where she was compared to Titania and be flattered. Her sister was not fond of reading, so she doubted it.

'It was all,' said Papa, 'looking promising.' But there had been no time to secure the match.

Thus, the baron had arrived at home with a grand scheme in mind. Hardly had he shaken the dust off from the drive than he said to Georgette, 'We are to have a house party in three weeks.'

Georgette laughed, then stopped. Her father was not in jest. 'You see to it, Georgette. I was just going to invite Paxton and a friend, and your aunt as chaperon perhaps. Let Jocasta and His Lordship renew their acquaintance. But a party with more guests is better, I feel.'

'You cannot, Papa! This place is hardly in a state for a house party,' she gestured to tattered sofa, which the baron's favourite hound chewed when he was allowed into the house. 'And only think how embarrassing for Jocasta and His Lordship to be sitting at dinner together, with everyone looking to see how they do. I doubt that he would care to place himself in that position.'

'Well, in the first case, I trust to you to make it ready.' He looked around the cavernous room with a careless eye. 'Don't see what's needed in here but a bit of dusting, or some such. But in the second place, you're wrong. Paxton and his friend Carswell have already accepted.'

Georgette's mouth opened.

'You will catch flies if you're not careful, daughter. Anyway, when I conceived the notion, I thought of the same problem. We cannot drive a man into a corner, even such a nodcock as Lord Paxton.' This last was not really addressed to her, but were his voluble thoughts. 'So I came up with a better notion. Invite a larger party, a few friends from town, you know, so that the intention gets lost in the throng. And the good thing is, we might even be able to fire off Katerina and Portia into the bargain, at a much smaller cost, for I have invited several single gentlemen. I daresay you have a few gowns that might fit Portia,' who was three inches taller, 'and Jocasta has her season's clothes, you know. It will be but a fortnight.' Four sisters included at the party, for two weeks. Even morning gowns would be a problem. They could not make do with two or three as they did usually, it may be the country, but it was still society. They could probably repeat twice, but that was still seven morning dresses, multiplied by four. Riding and walking gear that was a little shabby might be expected of easy country living, but they would also be obliged to wear half dress in the evening, in the same quantities. Jocasta had just had a season, so she had sufficient ensembles, but her own London wardrobe had shrunk since her last season, some gowns being made over for one or other of the girls for an assembly, or just to furbish up their Sunday best. She remembered drooling over Violetta's London finery, so she could not resent their wish to share hers. And in their cramped social circle, she didn't really want to draw attention anymore.

'Portia is barely fifteen,' Georgette began, but then her sharp brain fixed on the worst of this list of calamities. 'How large a throng?'

'Oh,' said His Lordship with an insouciance that did not fool her, 'we shall be not above thirty.' Given that her father would not consider her youngest of all sisters in that computation, that meant that he had invited, to this crumbling, draughty castle, twenty-six people. He sat down on his customary chair and picked up an old journal, stretching out his legs. Hades, his favourite wolfhound, entered, and after a greeting, set about chewing the damask on his master's chair.

Georgette, her hands metaphorically thrown in the air, left the room.

Now, as she walked from the withdrawing room and into the Grand Hall, Georgette was taking in every fault in her surroundings, and was suddenly lost in the absurdity. Twenty-six guests! And Lord Paxton's friends were bound to be of the very first circles. All the world lived differently in the country, with more relaxed standards. But there were limits. What had Papa asked her to do? Dust a little and see to the food, she supposed. Her head ached at finding the necessary sustenance to dress a dining table fourteen times for thirty people. It was like the story of the visit of Good Queen Bess to their house three hundred years ago. She and her court arrived, causing the emptying of the Fortunes' winter storehouses of game and produce as well as that of much of the surrounding gentry, and departed to do the same elsewhere. There were many tales of the baron's family existing solely on oats and rabbit for some weeks afterwards. But supposing she could find provisions and dust a little. What might the party find? Draughty accommodations with rent linen, mouse nibbled mattresses, and broken casements. The gentlemen would hunt, no doubt, but it was summer now and not the right season for many sports. And what might the ladies, if ladies there be, do? She knew to her own cost that it did not do to sit still anywhere indoors further away than three feet from the fire in the Great Hall. Thank goodness it was summer, otherwise the entire party would depart after the first morning, when they found that ice had formed on their coverlets.

The Castle was ancient and venerable, no doubt. The muniments room attested to the importance of it and the Fortune family since medieval times. However, there was no doubt it was draughty. Their family and servants were numerous, but Georgette was convinced that a bustling medieval castle would have had far more people and that it would have been heated mostly by bodies. Modern fashions for ladies, with thin muslins and only one petticoat, were not suitable for castle life. She had found a lustring sack dress of her grandmama's in a chest upstairs and the acres of heavy silk and the multiple petticoats that went under it seemed to

Georgette the minimum necessary for comfort on these windy halls, needing only three cashmere shawls and woollen hose extra. Even better, the ancient lords had known how to brave the cold, as she had discovered as an inquisitive child. In a chest in one of the attics there was a very ancient, floor-length, fur-lined robe, with the remnants of intricate embroidery still visible, that had no doubt been everyday castle wear centuries ago. She had longed to put it on, but it had begun to rot even as she touched it.

Nowadays, Georgette took refuge in a tiny room off the Great Hall, that her mama had used as a sitting room, where she could think a little. The window seat allowed one to bask in the sunshine in summer, and in the winter one could pull the curtains over the embrasure, arrange a bolster at the window panes to keep out the worst of the draughts, wrap one's self in several shawls, and read. There were ways, in other words, to make living here tolerable, but it took a lifetime of knowing to adopt them. How could one say to Lady Hoity-toity, 'If you keep some slippers near you by the bed to throw when you hear the chomping, the mice are quite harmless. And if you stick some folded paper and two shawls over the shaky casement, you might not be awakened in the night by the wind plucking at the bed curtains.' This last had caused a childhood friend of hers to scream that the castle was haunted.

Today, her seventeen-year-old sister Jocasta

tripped in excitedly, and Georgette thought of Titania indeed. She was a fair creature, rivalling Miss White's fairy-like features. Her hair was not so blond though, and occasionally her pretty face betrayed her self-satisfaction, whereas Miss White showed an innocent face to the world. Jocasta was dressed today in a charming sprigged muslin gown, bought for the season she had just enjoyed — but no doubt she had added a flannel petticoat beneath. 'Have you heard of the party? Isn't it exciting? I don't suppose we have ever had a house party so large here before.'

Georgette looked at her. 'And there is a reason for that Jocasta. Can't you see? The place is hardly fit for visitors.'

'Papa says that very few gentlemen can boast such an ancient home and so old a lineage,' said Jocasta pertly.

'Yes, but who in their right minds would come to this veritable sty for entertainment?'

She watched as Jocasta, never the quickest spark, arrived at the truth 'Oh my goodness! The bed chambers!'

'And much more!' sighed Georgette. You had best bring the girls here, we have some work to do.' The younger girls arrived eventually, and Georgette began the task list she had frantically concocted in her head since her father had broken the news. 'Leonora and Marguerite,' she said to the fourteen-year-old blond twins, who showed fair to be the prettiest of the Fortune girls, 'Find some chalk and search the chambers on the first and second floors for the least damaged mattresses. Any that can be patched, let us know by marking the door with a circle and a tick if the mattress is good, a cross if it is useless. We need at least as many sound ones as we can find. You will have to open the shutters to do it, but shut them up again when you are finished. There are some broken casements and we do not mean birds to enter if we can avoid it.' She would set the servants to move the best to the floor above, on the same level as their own chambers, where the centuries of dust had at least been disturbed recently.

'May not the servants do that?' asked Jocasta with a whine.

'Trust me, the servants will not be idle. Oh, and girls,' she said as the twins tripped away, obviously treating their task as an adventure, Leonora in the lead, as ever, 'any chipped jug and ewers, lay outside the doors for the servants to find. Katerina,' she said to a young lady of sixteen with red hair and a mulish look on her face, 'you may lay out everyone's best gowns in your room, so that we may plan our ensembles.'

'What ensembles? I do not have any ensembles,' replied Katerina.

'Well you are to have some. Papa wishes you to - to enjoy your first party and be presented to the ladies and gentlemen.'

'I do not wish to be presented. I am too young

to be presented. Then I shall become silly, like Jocasta.'

Jocasta pulled her hair, reverting to schoolroom ways.

'Stop that, girls,' sighed Georgette, 'we shall all do what Papa wishes. Katerina, get the dresses, the rest of us shall arrive in a half hour to begin to sort. Leave Jocasta's. She has quite enough after her season.'

And to Portia she said, 'You may check the casements in the rooms. Use your judgement. Make a list of the most broken, and take a look at the curtains and coverlets. If there are any that are too moth eaten, we must change them out for something better, if it can be found.'

'My coverlet is completely full of moth holes, but it is so heavy that I cannot give it up,' said Portia. At fifteen, she was Katerina's junior by a year, but much the more mature. She had Cassie's self-assurance and vivacity, but was taller, with red lights in her copious brown hair, and was moreover a trifle more intelligent.

'Since I do not suppose many guests will enter our chambers,' instructed Georgette, 'we might all have the damaged ewers and the moth-holed coverlets, I suppose. Just so long as our guests do not.'

'I do not suppose that Papa would have thought of any of this, Georgette,' Jocasta said. 'We do not notice the state of the place generally, but whenever any of the Baileys come over, I perceive a pained look, though they try to suppress it. It was some time after Mama died that I noticed the state the place was in. And then it got rather better afterwards,' she added vaguely.

Well, at least she'd noticed the effort, if not who'd made it, thought Georgette. The girls were dispatched on their errands, and she sighed contentedly. She was going to enjoy her next task. She summoned Dickson the steward, Mrs Firestone the housekeeper, and Mrs Scroggins the cook to meet her in her mother's sitting room. Her father, who had come in to look for her, saw their backs, and left precipitately.

'Lord Fortune is giving a house party the weekend after next. There will be twenty-six guests.' Mrs Firestone gasped, and Georgette said lightly, 'Or perhaps more. These occasions are not at all formal as to arrangements, you know. Someone may bring a friend or two at the last moment.'

'Twenty-six rooms to prepare?'

'Indeed, you had probably better make it thirty.' She explained what she had already set her sisters to do to Mrs Firestone. 'They will need to be thoroughly cleaned, of course,' she added as Mrs Firestone looked as though her blood would boil. 'You may hire another four girls from the villages or farms, if you wish. And perhaps some extra staff for the stable. And then, you know,' she turned to the steward, 'the garden needs some attention… The trees on the carriage drive need to be cut back, the courtyard tidied. You may give the orders, Dickson.' The steward regarded her with a baleful eye, but did not speak.

'And where are we to find food to feed all those folk?' Mrs Scroggins said rudely, in her rage. Georgette's eyebrows rose. 'The ladies and gentlemen,' amended Mrs Scroggins with bad grace.

'Where indeed?' said Georgette lightly, but thinking it high time someone else made a contribution. 'I am sure Mr Dickson is full of ideas. You have related tales of the parties in my grandmama's days, have you not, Dickson? How fine those days were?'

'Those were different times, Miss Georgette. Very different,' the steward answered repressively, annoyed that he had been moved to comment.

Georgette smiled upon him sweetly. 'But I have faith in you Dickson, I'm sure you can rise to the occasion.' His eyes glittered, but he remained silent. 'That is all. I thank you.'

The hard-pressed ladies left muttering, and only Dickson remained. 'I shall attend you with a list of my needs tomorrow morning, ma'am,' he said, with relish.

Georgette, feeling a sudden energy of panic, put on a cloak and bonnet and took off along the woodland path, to Great-Aunt Hester's abode. Lady Hester never visited the castle, since she had for many years declared that she never wanted to see her idiot nephew's face again. 'I could bear it for your mother's sake, dear, but not a one of you will be cross with me for saving myself from killing a man.' As a child, she had fancied that this cottage, set in a wooded clearing, was very like that of the grandmother in M. Perrault's tale of Red Riding Hood, the original French version one of her favourites from her mother's library. Her cloak today was red, and so she laughed at herself, but surreptitiously kept a lookout for the wolf.

The old lady, dressed in an old-fashioned mob cap and still in her peignoir, greeted her warmly, and Georgette quickly told her the reason for their visit.

'So — what do ladies do on such a visit, great-aunt? Can you remember?'

'Of course I can. I am not yet senile.' Georgette looked suitably reproved, and her aunt continued. 'Well … there was hunting of course. Ladies rode to hounds—'

'Not quite the season—'

'Well, we embroidered and read, oh and there was archery! We would practice a little each day and have a tournament at the end.'

'Archery! I wonder if we can find the equipment?'

'I doubt your father would give himself the trouble to dispose of it, so I imagine you may … and there was often a treasure hunt on good days, this was a really good opportunity to get lost in the woods with a beau!'

'They were, I fear, less God-fearing days,' said Georgette primly, forestalling one of her great-aunt's shocking tales. Old King George's early reign seemed rather full of young ladies taking snuff from gentlemen's wrists, arranging secret assignations by the deft use of a fan, being led astray for a kiss in Vauxhall Gardens, and thinking that a masked ball permitted all sorts of scandalous behaviour to be indulged in because one may not be recognised. No such liberties would be permitted in the modern world of today. 'What might we hide for the hunt?'

'Oh, a trinket, like a trumpery piece of jewellery, perhaps, or even a lady's ribbon, in those romantic times, was quite sufficient. It was all for the fun of the hunt. And then there are the walks you know, or the lady's bathing pool.'

'We could not take our guests there!'

'Why not? The cove is not overlooked, if you set a servant to guard the path. And if the weather is good, it is such a sheltered spot.' Georgette frowned, 'I do not know how such a generation as mine spawned such prissy grandchildren. I suppose George has foisted it all upon you?'

'Well,' said Georgette honestly, 'Papa had only to foist the knowledge that he was not about to lift a finger himself upon me, aunt. I could not bear the humiliation of a house party arriving and nothing done. I doubt he even knows that I am doing anything at all.'

'Depend upon it, my nephew knows what he

is about. He sees a deal more than his lazy eyes would have you believe.' She sipped her tea with narrowed eyes.

Thus, for the next week, the castle was in an uproar. The nursery, where the girls by habit occasionally congregated, was permitted a small fire, and Georgette had made the mistake of volunteering all of them to help with the task of patching linen. It was evident that Mrs Firestone took this as carte blanche to avoid the task at all, and a mountain of sheets and pillows cases was delivered to that chamber, and with many groans, the work began. Some of the sheets had avoided the moth, and Georgette took delight in delivering these back to Mrs Firestone for laundering. Soon, every bush and tree around the grounds was decked with linen, rugs were hung and beaten, and dust banished from one room, only to find its way into the next. The kitchen garden and hothouse yields were computed by Georgette, accompanied by a snorting Mrs Scroggins, there to tell her how far she was off in her computation. Another sack of flour and some sides of beef were ordered to accompany their own meat and game supplies and meeting with Lady Ludlow in the village while doing so had been fortuitous, for she offered the fruits of her own garden and hot houses, and therefore Georgette extended an invitation for one of the evenings of the party to the Ludlow family. Papa would not be best pleased, since this included two very pretty daughters of Lady Ludlow's own. Mrs Scroggins, too, would no doubt be delighted at the four extra guests. This knowledge warmed Georgette's heart, for since reluctantly taking up some of Mama's duties, the cook and housekeeper had set out to make their young mistress feel her youth and inexperience.

Georgette made Papa banish Hades for a week from anywhere but his own chamber or the stables, and she was able to trim the chewed damask in Papa's chair with some scissors, slide a piece of similar coloured fabric (from Grandpapa's waistcoat) beneath one slit, stick it down with flour paste and some stitches, and hope it might be ignored. Mama would have been appalled and amused in equal measure, but Georgette must move along to the next task. Hades' favourite sofa was beyond redemption and in need of being completely upholstered, so they exchanged it for a very heavy, possibly even medieval, carved wooden structure, for which Jocasta discovered some dusty hassocks to make it tolerable to sit on. The ancient wainscoting and tables were waxed and polished, candlesticks found for nearly every bedchamber, and flowers arranged — though not with the artistry of the late baroness, Georgette feared.

Their wardrobes were a little more difficult. Georgette sacrificed all but four of her London morning dresses to the other girls, and there had been much taking in and out and letting up and down, and ribbons or silk flower garlands disguising the alterations. No one would be looking at her, after all, and the twins were very young, so their wardrobe need not be so extensive. Evening dress had tried them to the utmost, and each of the elder girls had a bare five dresses each, by dint of jiggling Georgette and Jocasta's stock to fit three. Twins Leonora and Marguerite would not need evening dress, of course, being excluded from dinner in favour of supper in the nursery. Simple muslin would be sufficient for the twins.

The chambers had swept floors, jugs and ewers largely un-chipped, clean linen that no one might put a toe through, spotted mirrors ferreted out from corners of old rooms, and a candlestick each with wax candles, not tallow, though Papa would scream at the expense.

The family (all but Papa, who had spent a great deal of time at Ludlow Hall or at the Baileys', recently) and the servants were all exhausted. And this was before the party began.

Her brother George arrived a day before the guests, and Georgette heard him give a satisfying gasp at the state of the Grand Hall, denuded of chewed furniture and dog hair, and gleaming with wax upon the huge dining table. The area close to the fire had been bracketed by chairs and sofas from various other rooms while draught screens (some worked by ancestors whose dusty portraits hung on the staiase wall) were arranged nearby in case of inclement winds. Georgette was perfectly sure that even when all was still without, the Great Hall of the castle was plagued by inclement winds. 'Well done Dickson,' George said to that functionary as he dropped his driving coat into Dickson's arms negligently. 'I never thought the old place could look so handsome.'

'Thank you, sir,' said Dickson, one eye meeting Georgette's with an evil gleam.

'You are not wearing that tomorrow, Georgette, are you?' asked George looking at her faded cambric gown.

'No, it's my gardening—'

'Good!' he said and threw himself into a settle. George Fortune was a rather handsomer version of his papa. He was taller than the usual, and had what her father referred to as the Fortune build: broad and athletic. The height was certainly reflected in the rather over-sized suits of armour that were dotted about the castle corridors, so Georgette was sure it was hereditary. He had a copious shock of black hair, similar to the grey of his father in its tendency to stand up from the head, though George kept it from being a mane by dint of a scented pomade. He was modish, in a careless fashion, and supremely confident of his own worth. 'Where are the dogs?' George asked, idly looking around.

'Outside, where they will stay until after our guests have left,' said Georgette with rather more force than she usually used to him.

George looked at her interestedly. 'Nonsense,' he said with all his father's command. 'People expect dogs around in the country.'

Dickson entered and exchanged a look with Georgette, who was composing a suitable answer, without recourse to tearing her brother's pomaded locks. 'They do, sir. But the dogs of Fortune Castle are a little unregulated, sir. They have a propensity to chew furniture, and perhaps the odd boot, sir.'

George laughed. 'Yes, Papa has not trained his brutes well, I suppose. Very well, no dogs for the time being,' he added with the air of one conferring a boon. 'Lord Paxton is rather too fond of his boots as it is.'

Georgette gave the wan smile that she always gave in George's presence, and asked casually (for George abhorred any hint of being compelled), 'Do you have any clear idea of the persons who are coming?'

'No,' said George disobligingly, and picked up a racing journal as a sign of being finished with her. Georgette glided away silently, too frazzled by work exhaustion to find her brother in any way ridiculous today.

To read on: getbook.at/Georgette

Author's Note

Dear Lovely Readers,

This is the next in the Fentons series, and I do hope you liked it! You'll find information about the others in the series and my previous books further on.

A little historical note:
As Ianthe was newly arrived from France, I had an interesting time imagining what was occurring there in 1816 when our story is set.
The monarchy had been restored, although when Napoleon had escaped from Elba he had to flee until the Emperor was again defeated at Waterloo. This period was known as The Hundred Days, and the king then returned to Paris with Napoleon being sent to St Helena, an island much more isolated.
Researching this, I found that there had indeed been a plot to release him even from there, although it was never implimented. I thus made

up my own plot, where the coincidental presence of 600 Chinese working on the island might help an escape plan from the inside. On Ascension Island, the nearest island to St Helena, Mr Fenton's correspondant Edward Nicolls was truly the officer stationed, ready to prevent any attempt at rescuing Napoleon from St Helena.

The Alien Office did exist and organised a spy network during the Napoleonic Wars. This was unknown to the public, but as Fenton did some work for them he would have known of it.

Some time blips might have occurred to facilitate the story, and I apologise to historians for my blend of fact and fiction.

I hope you will follow me on Facebook and on Twitter and visit me on my website aliciacameron.co.uk for your FREE short (and a favorite story of mine) **Angelique and the Pursuit of Destiny** .

Please feel free to contact me at **alicia@aliciacameron.co.uk**. My Number One joy is hearing from my readers.

All of my books are available at Audible.com for those of you who like to listen, all are read by truly wonderful narrators.

Keep safe and laugh a lot in these troubled times,

Alicia

After I write and edit the book, after professional editors do their thing, it is sent volunteer beta readers for their thoughts before publication. I want to acknowledge two of the most dedicated beta readers that a writer has ever known, both of whom have worked on several of my books before publicatiion: Corinne Lehmann and Vivian Burns. Their meticulous brains, copious notes and enlightened thoughts keep a space cadet writer like me in check. All mistakes are my own. (E.g. Corinne sent her notes first, and in making changes, I made mistakes again that Vivian had to correct! Should I now send it back to Corinne then back to Vivian? *ad infinitum*...) Ladies, thanks always. It is difficult to say how much I appreciate it.

Books By This Author

Angelique And The Pursuit Of Destiny

Beth And The Mistaken Identity

Clarissa And The Poor Relations

Delphine And The Dangerous Arrangement

Euphemia And The Unexpected Enchantment: The Fentons 3

Felicity And The Damaged Reputation: The Fentons 2

Georgette And The Unrequited

Love: Sisters Of Castle Fortune 1

Honoria And The Family Obligation: The Fentons 1

Francine And The Art Of Transformation: Francine Book 1

Francine And The Winter's Gift: Francine Book 2

Printed in Great Britain
by Amazon